Percy Hetherington Fitzgerald

Life of James Boswell

With an Account of His Sayings, Doings, and Writings

Percy Hetherington Fitzgerald

Life of James Boswell
With an Account of His Sayings, Doings, and Writings

ISBN/EAN: 9783337167677

Printed in Europe, USA, Canada, Australia, Japan

Cover: Foto ©Raphael Reischuk / pixelio.de

More available books at **www.hansebooks.com**

LIFE OF
JAMES BOSWELL
(OF AUCHINLECK)

WITH AN ACCOUNT OF

HIS SAYINGS, DOINGS, AND WRITINGS

BY

PERCY FITZGERALD, M.A., F.S.A.

AUTHOR OF

"THE LIFE OF GARRICK," "FATAL ZERO," ETC.

WITH FOUR PORTRAITS

IN TWO VOLUMES.—VOL. II.

NEW YORK

D. APPLETON & COMPANY

1891

ABSTRACT OF CONTENTS OF VOL. II.

ERRATA.

Page 131, note, *for* " Poland " *read* " Great Portland."
 „   132, note †, *for* " the following year " *read* " some months later."

LIFE OF JAMES BOSWELL.

CHAPTER XXII.

DEATH OF JOHNSON.

1784.

ON May 5, 1784, after all this excitement, Boswell arrived. He found Johnson somewhat recovered. After a month's stay, during which he reports only a few meagre conversations—a proof of his relaxing attention to the invalid,—they set off together, on June 3rd, on a jaunt to Oxford, where they remained till the 19th. This proved to be the last of their many pleasant expeditions, and the faithful companion had the satisfaction of thinking that he contributed not a little to make it agreeable. He even took the trouble of going down with Johnson, although he had to return almost as soon as he arrived, to keep an engagement in town ; setting off again at once for Oxford, to stay with his friend. There are some very touching passages in this episode, described with true feeling by Boswell, for Johnson was then virtually under sentence of death.

It was when they returned to town, that a serious plan for the comfort of his friend occurred to the faithful "Bozzy," and which he set himself to carry out, with much earnestness and ingenuity. This, one of the most creditable passages in his life, was the securing an addition to Johnson's pension from Government, that he might set off for Italy, and thus prolong his valuable life. The idea had occurred to some others, but nothing was done until Boswell addressed a letter to the chancellor, Lord Thurlow, and laid the case before him. In this step he took counsel only with Sir Joshua Reynolds, who perfectly agreed with him as to its propriety. It was kept secret from Johnson. Boswell soon received a sympathizing letter from the chancellor, promising to "adopt and press" the suggestion, as far as he could, and he even held out hopes that it was likely to succeed.

Boswell tells, in his own amiable unaffected manner, what followed : " I intended to set out for Scotland next morning ; but Sir Joshua cordially insisted that I should stay another day, that Johnson and I might dine with him, that we three might talk of his Italian Tour, and, as Sir Joshua expressed himself, 'have it all out.' I hastened to Johnson, and was told by him that he was rather better to-day. BOSWELL. 'I am very anxious about you, Sir, and particularly that you should go to Italy for the winter, which I believe is your own wish.' JOHNSON. 'It is, Sir.' BOSWELL. 'You have no objection, I presume, but the money it would require.' JOHNSON. 'Why, no, Sir.'—Upon which I gave him a particular account of what had been done, and read to him the Lord Chancellor's letter.—He listened with much attention ; then warmly said, 'This is taking prodigious pains about a man.'—' O, Sir, (said I, with most sincere affection), your friends would do every thing for you.' He paused,—grew more and more agitated, —till tears started into his eyes, and he exclaimed with fervent emotion, 'GOD bless you all.' I was so affected that I also shed tears.—After a short silence, he renewed and extended his grateful benediction, 'GOD bless you all, for JESUS CHRIST'S sake.' We both remained for some time unable to speak.—He rose suddenly and quitted the room, quite melted in tenderness. He staid but a short time, till he had recovered his firmness ; soon after he returned I left him, having first engaged him to dine at Sir Joshua Reynolds's next day.—*I never was again under that roof which I had so long reverenced.*

"On Wednesday, June 30, the friendly confidential dinner with Sir Joshua Reynolds took place, no other company being present. Had I known that this was the last time that I should enjoy, in this world, the conversation of a friend whom I so much respected, and from whom I derived so much instruction and entertainment, I should have been deeply affected. When I now look back to it, I am vexed that a single word should have been forgotten.

"Both Sir Joshua and I were so sanguine in our expectations, that we expatiated with confidence on the liberal provision which we were sure would be made for him, conjecturing whether munificence would be displayed in one large donation, or in an ample increase of his pension. He himself catched so much of our enthusiasm, as to allow himself to suppose it not impossible that our hopes might in one way or other be realised. He said that he would rather have his pension doubled than a grant of a thousand pounds ; 'for, (said he,) though probably I may not live to receive as much as a thousand pounds, a man would have the consciousness that he should pass the remainder of his life in splendour, how long soever it might be.' "

Unhappily, however, these well-meant exertions were destined to fail. The application was unsuccessful, but the generous Thurlow himself offered to advance five or six hundred pounds to Johnson on a mortgage of his pension; explaining that this form was merely adopted to satisfy his sense of independence. There is nothing more pleasing or touching than this, in the records of official life. But Johnson, mortified and disappointed, refused the aid. The reason of the rejection of the petition was, as Mr. Elwin has written to me, "that Pitt never granted any favour or pension to a literary man, during all the time he was in power." But a more substantial one might be that there was no reason for such an indulgence; for it turned out that Johnson had a large sum of money saved, £2,300, as is shown by his will! Not long before, Thrale had left him a legacy, all which makes the matter rather perplexing. In any case his friends might easily have helped him with the moderate sum for the expenses of the journey. Two hundred pounds would certainly have covered the actual charges of travel: and the cost of living in Italy would have been no more, or little more, than that of living in London.

Thurlow, a few months later, was much annoyed, when he found that his generous offer had been made public, and was talked about. It was, indeed, given out that the king had refused his sanction to the pension being mortgaged, which was untrue. Again the chancellor renewed his kind offer, which Johnson was too ill to avail himself of.*

* In another work I undertook the task of exposing some of the very amusing "mare's nests" which Mr. Croker, carried away by his Boswellian speculations, absolutely revelled in. One of the most ludicrous is connected with this incident. Narrowly scrutinizing this letter of Thurlow's to Sir Joshua, he discovered, or

With one matter during this last visit it is, however, impossible not to be struck, viz. that, towards the close of their intimacy, Boswell seemed to tire a little of his servitude, and perhaps to resent the many " tossings " and " rebuffs " he had to endure from his monitor. The connection had now lasted over twenty years. His own gloom and consciousness of increasing indulgence in dissipation made him shrink from the society of his friend, even when he was in town : and he relaxed a great deal in his important task of note-taking. We later find that he allowed long intervals to elapse without writing, which fretted and annoyed Johnson a good deal. In April, 1781, we find him noting down that, "for some time after this day I did not see him very often, and, of the conversation, I am sorry to find I have preserved but little." He was much engaged in a variety of other matters. In May there was a dinner at Thrale's, after which there " was a pretty long interval, during which I and Dr. Johnson did not meet." They did, however, meet ; but " of his conversation on that and other occasions, during this period, I neglected to keep any regular record." From May 1st till May 15th, he says, he had no minutes of any inter-

fancied that he discovered, an erasure in the sentence, "It would have suited the purpose better, if nobody had heard of it except Dr. Johnson, *you and I.*" The "I" he makes out to have stood originally, "J. Boswell," which he calls "an uncandid trick, to defraud Boswell of his merit in the matter." From this he also reasons that Thurlow had never applied to the king for the pension at all. This speculation can be disposed of at once. Mr. Croker was confounding the application for the pension with the later mortgage proposal, to which this letter (dated four months after the pension had been refused) only can refer. Boswell had left town long before, and knew nothing of the matter ; so that the chancellor's statement, that it was "only Johnson, you and I," that were in the secret, was strictly correct. Finally, Thurlow would never have named him so familiarly as " J. Boswell," who was scarcely known to him ; but as " Mr. Boswell."

views, and he had now got the habit of putting together
any little scraps or observations of the doctor's which
belonged to different periods and interviews. He
mentions a dinner at Dr. Brocklesby's, but says : " Of
these days and *others* on which I saw him *I have
no memorials*, except the general recollection of his
being able and animated in conversation." Again he
writes : " I find only three small particulars." On the
17th, at another house, he says Johnson was " quiescent."
" Perhaps, too, I was indolent. I find nothing more of
him in my notes, but a remark about the ' imitation.' "

Of their visit to Oxford, Boswell's notes are very full,
as he had no distractions ; and, after Johnson's return to
town in June, Boswell saw him frequently, " but still
had few memorandums." He therefore fell back upon
what may be called his " omnium gatherum." On June
24th, there was another dinner at Dilly's, where he again
neglected to preserve the conversation. It is plain from
all this, that Boswell, either from his intemperate habits,
or longings for pleasure, was suffering from the languor
or torpor that usually follows excess.

The energy and vigour of Johnson's mind was shown
in his gallant struggle with the diseases which were
hurrying him to his death. This is shown by Boswell's
record of dinners and discussions. Their last pleasant
meeting was at Sir Joshua's, on June 30th, 1784, the day
before Mr. Boswell left town, and Johnson's last word to
his old friend and admirer was, " Nay, sir, be as perfect
as you can." " I accompanied him," says Boswell, " in
Sir Joshua Reynolds's coach "—which the good host must
have had ordered out—" to the entry of Bolt Court. He
asked me whether I would not go with him to his house.
I declined, from an apprehension that my spirits would
sink. We bade adieu to each other affectionately on

the carriage. When he had got down upon the pave-ment he called out, ' Fare you well,' and, without looking back, sprung away with a kind of pathetic briskness, if I may use that expression, which seemed to indicate a struggle to conceal uneasiness, and impressed me with a foreboding of our long long separation." A pleasingly natural, and artless description, full of feeling.*

Nearly five months went by, and Boswell continued at his castle. As Johnson's last sickness came on, it is curious to find how diligent he was as a correspondent. Boswell furnishes a number of letters written at this time of trial, to Dr. Brocklesby, Windham, Burney, Hoole, Langton, Perkins, Gerard Hamilton, Paradise, Nichols, Davies, Sir Joshua Reynolds, and others. It seems strange that there should be so few addressed to Boswell. Johnson wrote sadly to him of his state of desolation: " I have no company;" and, in reply, Boswell inflicted on the sick man a letter filled with his own dejection and fretfulness. Johnson then reproached him, naturally, " with affecting discontent and indulging in the vanity of complaint ;" yet adding, most kindly, " My dear friend, life is very short and uncertain ; let us spend it as well as we can . . . *write to me often and write like a man.*" Considering that Johnson was dying at the moment, this request was an affecting and reason-able one. Nay, two days later, he wrote another letter, apologizing for his roughness. Boswell, himself a prey to his morbid disease, and sunk in dejection, now took refuge in what his friend would call " sullenness," or sulk. " I unfortunately," he acknowledges, " was so much indisposed during a considerable part of the year,

* Boswell, however, remained one more day in town, in the hope of seeing the chancellor, but did not again call upon his friend.

that it was not, or at least I thought it was not, in my power to write to my illustrious friend as formerly, or without expressing such complaints as offended him. Having conjured him not to do me the injustice of charging me with affectation, I was with much regret long silent. His last letter to me then came, and affected me very tenderly."

The admirable Johnson was now approaching the term of his long and honourable life, and at the end of November, 1784, lay on his death-bed. Among those who so affectionately ministered to him at this trying crisis, we miss the figure of the faithful Boswell, who certainly ought to have been by his side. This has always seemed most unaccountable. He must have surely known of the danger, as Langton and other friends on the spot would have informed him. Four days would have brought him to town, and Johnson did not die until December 13th. Boswell gives no excuse for his absence. But he certainly should have been present, and, as his old friend used to say, "there's an end on't." The truth we believe to be is, that Boswell was in one of his dejected querulous states, or probably did not believe that the end was so near. It may be that to the thorough convivialist the sick or the dying are disagreeable and odious reminders. "Yet it was not a little painful to me," goes on this strange being, excusing himself, "to find that in a paragraph of this letter, which I have omitted, he still persevered in arraigning me as before, which was strange in him who had so much experience of what I suffered. I, however, wrote to him two as kind letters as I could, the last of which came too late to be read by him, for his illness increased more rapidly upon him than I had apprehended; but I had the consolation of being informed that he spoke of me on his death-bed with affection, and I look forward with humble hope of renewing our friendship in a better world."

"I now," goes on this chronicler, faithful as Griffith, "relieve the readers of this work from any further personal notice of its author; who, if he should be thought to have obtruded himself too much on their attention, requests them to consider the peculiar plan of his biographical undertaking."

As he wrote this curious passage, Boswell may have felt the necessity of some vindication of his behaviour. Being sensitive, he no doubt experienced some self-reproach; but his explanation really amounts to no more than laying the blame on Johnson, who did not deserve it.

At the last solemn scene, Boswell could not refrain from intruding himself, as it were, from a distance, in a rather indelicate fashion, bringing out at this moment confidences which should have been held sacred, and almost injuring the memory and character of his friend. The passage is one of the most characteristic in his book —amusingly characteristic, we had almost said, but for the solemnity of the occasion. "His great fear of death, and the *strange dark manner in which Sir John Haw-kins imparts the uneasiness* which he expressed, on account of offences with which he charged himself, may give occasion to injurious suspicions, as if there had been something of more than ordinary criminality weighing upon his conscience. On that account, therefore, as well as from the regard for truth which he inculcated, I am to mention (*with all possible respect and delicacy, how-ever*) that his conduct, after he came to London, and had associated with Savage and others, was not so strictly virtuous in one respect, as when he was a younger man.

It was well known that his inclinations were uncommonly strong and impetuous.

"In short, it must not be concealed, that, like many other good and pious men, among whom we might place the Apostle Paul, upon his own authority, Johnson was not free from propensities which were ever warring against the law of his mind, and that in his combats with them he was, sometimes overcome. Here let the profane and licentious pause, and let them not thoughtlessly say Johnson was a hypocrite, or that his principles were not firm because his practice was not uniformly conformable to what he professed."

As we said, this is one of the most "characteristical" passages in the whole. And the object would seem to be to put forward a plea for himself, as his loose practice had now unhappily become a habit. This was well known to all his friends, and he could preach morality on the text of Johnson's weakness. He therefore put forward his favourite theory of "good impressions," and of a general moral feeling being compatible with bad practice. He seizes the opportunity to dwell unctuously on, and to enforce this fatal doctrine, which in the end was unhappily to shipwreck himself. But it is difficult to speak too severely of this exposure of Johnson's supposed failings, which he so gratuitously chose to imagine were disturbing Johnson's last moments.

In a letter to Lord Brougham, Mr. Croker disposes in a very satisfactory way of these morbid insinuations against Johnson, and very acutely shows that it was instinctively, if not intentionally, a veiling of Boswell's own weaknesses. "His acquaintance with Savage I have shown to have been much shorter and in every way more insignificant than was before supposed. When I began my Johnsonian enquiries I knew several persons

who had known Bozzy, and those that I consulted upon
this very point (wondering why he should at the close
of his book trump up these old and apocryphal stories)
explained it as one of Bozzy's crazy tricks, introduced
to sanction his own practices." Then he adds these
sagacious remarks, convincing to any one who has deeply
studied human character. "Boswell's book is a most
curious picture of the human mind in a vast variety of
aspects; but there was one view of it which I was
unwilling to open more largely, namely, the numberless
little touches by which he exhibited, sometimes unconsciously and apologetically, his own follies and frailties,
and, in fact, his own mental disorder. I have just hinted
this, but I abstained from dilating on it out of regard
to his family, but it is a clue very essential to the right
appreciation of his most extraordinary book."

Another motive, however, was to discredit Hawkins,
who, he contended, had imputed to Johnson these very
early excesses! Nothing could be more unwarrantable
than the insinuation of the "strange dark manner in
which Sir John Hawkins imparts the uneasiness which
he expressed," which might give rise to "injurious suspicions, as if there had been something of more than
ordinary criminality weighing on his conscience." If
the knight threw out such a suspicion, Boswell, as we
have seen, made it a certainty by his indecorous revelations. Sir John did nothing of the kind, behaving with
propriety all through the trying scene. He merely says
that he found him in great dejection, and, "with a look
that cut me to the heart, told me that he had the prospect of death before him, and that he dreaded to meet
his Saviour." Being then encouraged to reflect on his
long, good life and writings, he replied that he had
written as a philosopher, but had not lived like one.

"Every man knows his own sins, *and what grace he has resisted*, and he is to look on himself as the greatest sinner he knows of." In other conversations he dwelt on the same topic, and the knight wondered, he said, not merely at the freedom with which he opened his mind, and the compunction he seemed to feel for the errors of his past life, but at his—"making choice of me for his confessor."

Boswell's dislike of Sir John also betrayed him into another equally libellous perversion of what the knight stated. Johnson, who always fancied he knew a good deal of medicine and surgery, after being scarified and punctured, so as to open the swellings in his legs, reproached the doctors with not cutting deep enough; he then tried to do the work himself, and made incisions with a pair of scissors in the calf of his leg. The feeling Langton rushed to Hawkins "in an agony," to tell him "that our friend had wounded himself in several parts of his body." But, on examination, he found it was as we have described. Langton, who was excited at the news, evidently thought it was an attempt on his life, but Sir John found that he had made these incisions in his legs. "That this," he says, "*was not done to hasten his end*, but to discharge the water he conceived to be in him, *I have not the least doubt.*" Could anything be plainer than this statement? Yet Boswell could twist it thus: "This bold experiment, Sir John Hawkins has related in such a manner, as to suggest a charge against Johnson of hastening his end. A charge so very inconsistent with his character in every respect, that it is injurious even to refute it." *

* Dr. Johnson's death was announced in the principal country papers of December 16 to 23, 1784, by a paragraph in the summary of London news which used then to be supplied to them weekly:

That Boswell felt the loss of his friend and mentor deeply, was to be expected; and his letter to Bishop Percy expresses a natural and poignant grief. He wrote to him on March 20, 1785: "I certainly need not enlarge on the shock it gave my mind. *I do not expect to recover from it;* I mean, I do not expect that I can ever in this world have so weighty a loss supplied. *I gaze after him with an eager eye; and I hope again to be with him.*" This is happily and affectionately expressed.

A subscription was set on foot by the members of a literary club for the erection of a monument to Dr. Johnson in St. Paul's Cathedral, and the details were settled by a committee of members, of which Boswell was one, and who were rather pedantically styled "curators." The curators invited Dr. Parr to furnish a Latin inscription, which, however, did not give much satisfaction. Boswell particularly did not relish his production, as will be seen from this letter.

Boswell to Malone.

"DEAR SIR,—Whatever respect you and I and all who take a concern in erecting a monument to Dr. Johnson may have for the learning and abilities of

" *Dec. 14.*—Yesterday afternoon, about ten minutes before seven of the clock, there departed this life, at his house in Bolt Court, Fleet Street, in his seventy-sixth year, to the inexpressible grief of his friends, and to the infinite loss of his Majesty's subjects, that eminent ornament of literature, and firm friend of virtue and religion, Dr. Samuel Johnson. His venerated remains will be interred in Westminster Abbey. Sir Joshua Reynolds, Sir John Hawkins, and the learned Dr. Scott of the Commons are appointed his executors. Dr. Johnson settled his worldly affairs five days before his death. He was entirely resigned to the will of God, and rarely spoke during his last days, except upon religious subjects. He passed away without a struggle, and so quietly, that the persons in his chamber were not aware of his dissolution."

Dr. Parr, I am clear that we could not be justified in adopting implicitly, without so much as having seen it, the inscription which that gentleman has written. We are answerable to the memory of our illustrious friend, to the present age, and to posterity: let me add, that we are answerable to another tribunal, without whose approbation of the Epitaph the monument cannot be admitted into St. Paul's Church—I mean, the Dean and Chapter of that Cathedral.

"When Sir Joshua Reynolds asked Dr. Parr to furnish an epitaph, I cannot suppose that he meant to preclude even himself from consideration and all power of objection; far less could he entertain the notion that the other gentlemen, with whom he had conferred on the subject, would be so tied up. He certainly understood that this epitaph, as in all similar cases, was to be subject to revision. He had before him the example of Dr. Johnson himself, who was requested to write Dr. Goldsmith's epitaph. And how did that great man conduct himself? You will find in my octavo edition of his life, vol. ii., p. 248, a letter from him to Sir Joshua, in which he says, 'I send you the poor, dear Doctor's epitaph. Read it first yourself: and if you then think it right, show it to the Club. I am, you know, willing to be corrected.'

"I trust that when Dr. Parr reconsiders his unusual proposition he will be satisfied, and, without any offence to him, it must receive a negative.

"I am, with much regard, dear Sir, your faithful, humble servant, JAMES BOSWELL.

"Great Portland Street, April 13, 1795." *

---

* MS., British Museum.

CHAPTER XXIII.

THE loss of this trusty friend and his advice and direction was a serious one for Boswell. He was now left, uncontrolled, the prey of his own humours, whims, and passions. We can note almost at once the change that took place in his life and habits, which became more lax and unrestrained. The ten years or so that now follow are a piteous and yet instructive record of his vain struggles and broken resolutions, and followed by a gradual, helpless descent into a life of loose pleasures and folly. But for the great task which lay before him, and which seemed, in a measure, to take the place of his lost friend, the spectacle he would have offered would have been more disastrous still. We must, however, admire the resolution and exertion which, in the midst of almost sottish enjoyments, enabled him to rally his efforts and apply himself with painful diligence to his laborious work. This is one of the good notes in Boswell's character, and is an extenuation of his follies.

Making due allowance for the habits of the time, which tolerated drinking and inebriety as a fitting part of social intercourse, it is clear that the cheerful Boswell took a license far in excess of his contemporaries. The consequences were disastrous, not merely to his health, and led to painful and humiliating exhibitions, which made him a sorry spectacle. At one time he was induced by Johnson to become a water-drinker on trial ; but it was only a short experiment.

Almost his first exhibition after the death of his friend was an odd display at Court. There was to be read in the Edinburgh papers : " At the Court of St. James' the following address was presented to the King by James Boswell, Esq., who was introduced by the Lord-in-Waiting. It was most graciously received, and Mr. Boswell had afterwards the honour to kiss his Majesty's hand. This was ' the humble address of the tenants and others residing upon the estate of James Boswell, Esq., of Auchinleck, 289 men, all fit to bear arms in defence of the King and country.' "

But there presently appeared the extraordinary, in-coherent production, before alluded to, from his pen, in which we have the true Boswell before us, viz. a second " Letter to the people of Scotland." Here he chatters away in his most rambling fashion ; diverging from the main topic in hand, literally to say " whatever comes into his head," or whatever vanity or the impulse of the moment prompts. There is now no constraint, no consciousness of being ridiculous ; and, with a curious credulity or self-delusion, he expected that everybody would appreciate, as he did, his bursts about himself, his family, his prospects, and his friends. The latter must have felt humiliated as they read his too rapturous compliments. The most amusing part is the very trans-parent object of the pamphlet, which had little to do with the Scotch judges, and which was really intended to call attention to the neglect of himself, his interests, and his own vast merits—to give the great dispenser of Scotch patronage warning that he was not to be trifled with. It is more interesting, however, as a contribution to the discussion as to what was "Bozzy's" real character: though it seems to make this perplexing question even more perplexing, as here we have the author speaking deliberately, and from his heart, uncontrolled by any restraining influence. It becomes, therefore, more difficult than ever to conceive the writer of this production to be the same man who was presently to be the author of the sensible and judicial life of Johnson, that has been the admiration of the world.

No longer was there the kind, wise friend, of whom he stood in awe, to check and reprove his extravagance. No longer was there one to tell him, roughly but kindly, of his follies, and to lament "that he had not a better bottom." Nothing was less likely to advance him than this pamphlet: he, in fact, made himself "impossible;" for promotion of such a person would have only brought ridicule on the patron. Yet Mr. Dundas, whom he had treated in so free and offensive a style, he continued, after these attacks, to press for preferment—a strange instance of insensibility; and he was in a fury when he found that no notice was taken of his claims.

This appeal was prompted by what he termed "an alarming attempt to infringe the articles of union and introduce a most pernicious innovation in diminishing the numbers of the Lords of Session." As he put it: "What is the crown without subjects? and what are subjects without a good administration of justice?"— *ergo*, the number of judges must not be lessened. This "comes home to our business and bosoms. It is a very serious alarm indeed." The fifteen were to be reduced to ten. The Barons of the Exchequer he did not care about. "Their gowns are of purple cloth and crimson velvet, very gracefully disposed, and they still retain

the sacerdotal badge of a cawl, or pouch. Scandal,
says Mr. Henry Dundas, has been applied to by some
of the judges, who, after feasting at Bayll's French
Tavern, and raising their spirits high with wine, have
formed the lofty wish of severally paying their court to
Regina Pecunia: and Mr. Henry Dundas (sometimes
called Harry the Ninth), very willing to oblige these
senators and make them his devoted humble servants,
has nodded assent."

He then bewailed that all the great and good Scotch
families hung back so lamentably in the matter. "I
remember Archibald, Duke of Argyle, I remember
Stuart Mackenzie, I remember Gilmore, all, in their
turn, bringing the people of Scotland to St. James's, and
the Treasury, as a dalesman drives black cattle to
Smithfield. Poor dumb beasts! why should they not
walk up themselves and bellow as they may incline!
. . . Then came Mr. Henry Dundas, who has made a
distinguished figure at more markets than one. There
was a time when we were flattered there was to be no
monopoly; when that Titus, that delicate humane genus,
the Duke of Portland (I give his Grace as Mr. Burke
gave him me, not having the good fortune to be known
to him), when *he* presided, O then! all was to go well
with Scotland. There was to be no go-between. Nobody to keep back the individuals of that distant part
of the island from fairly asserting their claims of wealth
or merit. But alas! we soon found there was only a
change of Dundases."

This is amusing, and shows transparently what was
working in Boswell's mind, which, as we said, was not the
case of reducing judges, but the neglect of Mr. Boswell
by Mr. Dundas. His extraordinary references to personal friends must have excited roars of laughter; and

so extravagant and excited is the tone of the whole, that one is inclined to think the author must have stimulated his pen by copious draughts of liquor. There are, scattered throughout his account of Johnson, occasional outpourings of Boswellian vanity and complainings, but there is nothing so amusing as what we find here. We have an idea that it must give a good notion of the rambling, ardent style of his talk, when he was well warmed with wine. Both exhibit that glowing and affectionate rapture in which topers extol their friends, the value of which was never so well described as by a French *viveur*, on his deathbed, when he exclaimed impatiently: "*Assez de ces amitiés de Garde Nationale!*" "My amiable and honourable friend Dempster, that *rara-avis* of the Scottish breed, who has sat in Parliament almost as long as our present most gracious Sovereign has sat upon the throne, when I talked to him upon the subject, exclaimed, 'Fifteen too few! I would rather have fifty! They talk of there being only twelve judges in England; I say there are twenty thousand. The juries and our fifteen Lords of Session are all we have for judges in civil causes.' Nobly said! There are 20,000 judges in England, and I hope in God there ever will be, notwithstanding all that the old Conjuror or any of his pupils can do. A few months ago, William Spence, a young man for whom I was Counsel, was indicted by the Lord Advocate for fire-raising. He was prosecuted by his Lordship in person, and the Lord Justice's Clerk gave a charge with all his ability, *to find him guilty!* But a respectable jury acquitted him; and, as I hope for mercy from the Judge of all the earth, had I been one of their number, I should have been clear to join in the verdict. *I will give up my opinion to no human authority.*"

He then asks, " Is a court of ten the same with a court of fifteen ? Is a two-legged animal the same with a four-legged animal ? I know nobody who will defend that proposition gravely, except one grotesque Philosopher whom ludicrous fable represents as going about avowing his hunger, and wagging his tail, fain to become cannibal and *eat his deceased brethren*." He then introduces the patron, on whom his adoring eyes were fixed : " We are his neighbours, we all know what *he* can do, *he* upon whom the thousands depend for three of the elements : *he* whose soul is all great ; whose resentment is terrible ; but whose liberality is boundless. I know that he is dignified by having hosts of enemies. But I have fixed his character in my mind, upon no slight enquiry. I have traversed Westmoreland and Cumberland. I have sojourned at Carlisle and at Kendal : I know of the *Lonsdale Club* at *Lancaster*. Lowther ! Be kindly entreated, come."

He describes the profession and its prizes as " a routine for our sons." " The prime society of Edinburgh is lawyers, they give the tone, they rule the Theatre. They make balls for the ladies. They let the nation know that they can proscribe even a beautiful duchess. Black, *law-black* is the common dress of the gentlemen of Edinburgh, and hence, when Foote was among us, he used to back the Edinburgh Hunt." These little anecdotal touches, however out of place, are welcome and characteristic.

After naming a number of barristers of reputation, he adds, " I could with pleasure give a long list of my deserving brethren. To us it is not fair. As for myself, I do most certainly believe that I am now writing from pure motives, because, at present, *I have no wish for the serious and important office of the Lord of the Session.*

I have a confidence, (perhaps too great a confidence,) in my abilities; and therefore will try my fortune, for some time at least, in a wider sphere. A *gown* in Scotland should be too good a place, lest it become altogether an object of political preferment. Lord Salton might think it a *snug* thing. *My cousin Lord Cathcart* might see it to be better than a regiment.

"I am sorry," he goes on, "Mr. George Byng, I cannot appeal to you at present, as a member of Parliament. For though I differ from you in my political creed, I think you an useful, active, watchman of the state. And I am never unmindful of your civility *to me as counsel,* when you sat as Chairman of the Ayrshire Committee." He then introduces a person who, at the moment, stood in his way, and whom he deals with rather spitefully : "Who seconded the King's Advocates' motion for leave to bring in this odious bill ? It was Sir Adam Fergusson : a man who has vexed me not a little, by his political success in our country, *against my wishes.* Sir A. Fergusson, *as we are told,* made overture to the Earl of Eglintoun. That he was not elected, we know : that he voted for his former opponent, we know : and it is *said* he supports the Earl's friend for one Parliament, and the Earl is to make him member next Parliament—if he can."

After a tissue of insinuations against this gentleman, whom he wished to supplant, he tells us that, "when the report of this curious agreement, burst upon the country, like a bomb, and stunned men of all parties, I made the following *bellman's rhymes* to usher in my friend Colonel Hugh Montgomerie as our representative.

"'Adam, too long you've kept your seat,
    With little for your pains :
Trust me, you'll never make both ends meet,
    Computing loss or gains.

> " 'Surrender then to gallant Hugh,
>   It truly will be best !
>   Bring your mock votes along with you,
>   And laugh at all the rest.' "

Then, turning to Lord Eglinton and his patronage
of Colonel Montgomerie, " his Lordship must not take
it amiss, if some of the best friends of his family should
disdain what they think degrading to him, and obnoxious
to themselves. Amongst these friends, I myself am one
of the warmest, both an enthusiast for ancient attach-
ments and as having the honour and happiness to be
married to His Lordship's relation, a true Montgomerie ;
whom I esteem, whom I love after fifteen years as on
the day when she gave me her hand."

"I myself have reason to hope that many of the
real freeholders of Ayrshire will support me at the
election for next Parliament, against which I have
declared myself a candidate. Colonel Montgomerie has
been chosen by the real Freeholders. May I not have
it in my turn ! I shall certainly stand upon the
interests of the gentlemen of landed property, and if
upon fair trial I should not succeed I have resources
enough to prevent me from being discontented.
Perhaps Sir Alexander Fergusson may support me.
I have asked his vote and interest by a letter. His
answer has neither granted nor refused my application."

He then returns to attack Mr. Dundas, who has
taken very good care of his relations. "And why
should he not, though, to be sure, flesh and blood must
feel his having put his young nephew over, I *know not
how many of us*, as Solicitor General." He was, however,
willing to allow that he was not cruel or vindictive.
Two wrongs he had done, one was the attacking Sir
H. Dundas in his own country, where he was a father
to the people, " *as that hospitable, that splendid, that*

imperial Baronet said to me with tears in his eyes.
The other was, persuading my honoured father, a
venerable judge in the decline of his life, to embark in
county politics, from which he had ceased for twenty
years, and make a parcel of votes to support Sir Adam
Fergusson. I have no more objection to Mr. Dundas's
being made Protector of Scotland than any other man.
Nay I have an interest that he should be in favour, for
there is an hereditary friendship between our families ;
we were at College together, we have often enjoyed ;—

"   'The happier hour of joint pleasure ; '

and I trust to the generosity of his feelings, that, as he
knows he once did me a severe injury, which I have
from my heart forgiven, he will be anxious to make me
full amends, if ever it be in his power. *The desire of
elevation is as keen in me as it is in himself :* though
I am not so well fitted for party exploits."

He then rambles off to the merits of the Judges of
the Session. "Dennis Forbes of Culloden gave every
day, as a toast at table, ' Here's to every Lord of Session
who does not deserve to be hanged.' Lord Auchinleck
and Lord Monboddo, both judges, but *since his time,*
are my authority for this " (these italics are mysterious),
" I do not say that the toast was quite delicate, or even
quite decent." He then quotes a remark, which he says
is not his own : "I owe it to Lord Palmerston, from
whose conversation there is always something to be
borrowed. *I humbly thank His Lordship for it,* and beg
he may pardon my imperfect report of it. He gave it
me at Lord Ossery's; I cannot refrain from mentioning
the *place :* because I am very vain to sit at the table
with a *Fitzpatrick*—the respect for whose ancient and
noble blood is not lessened but increased by the

character of its present representative ; which I feel is
saying a great deal, and flatter myself *Fitzpatrick* was
convinced. If he was, I'll answer for it, all the world
shall not make him flinch."

He then exhorts his countrymen to petition and
address the king. The "English members would
support them ; my old classical companion, Wilkes,
with whom I pray you to excuse my keeping company,
he is so pleasant, did indeed once tell me, when I once
asked him to attend a Scottish contest in the House of
Commons : 'No, no! Damn it! Not I! I'll have
nothing to do with it! I care not which prevails, it is
only Goth against Goth.' I may without offence
account for it by using the very expression of Mr.
Dundas himself, when attacking, at the Bar of the House
of Lords, an address of the Court of Session where I
was Counsel on the other side. *I can swear to the
phrase.* 'They have been seized with some infatuation.' I exhort you, my friends and countrymen, in the
words of my departed Goldsmith, who gave me many
noble truths, and gave me a jewel of the finest water ;
the acquaintance of Sir Joshua Reynolds, I again
exhort you, to fly from petty tyrants to the throne.
While I arraign what strikes me as very wrong in Mr.
Henry Dundas and the Lord Advocate in their public
conduct, I am ready to meet them on friendly but
equal terms in private. To the Lord Advocate I am
willing to allow all his merit : he has risen to the head
of our Bar ; he has made it a Peruvian Profession ;
upon every occasion that I have known him tried, he was
generous ; and he is a very friendly man. I should be
exceedingly ungrateful if I did not acknowledge this."

He next turned to Mr. Burke : "To him I was
much obliged when he was in power ; and it grieved

me that he embraced what, in all sincerity, I thought
such a measure as justified his removal from office;
for his interest is as dear to me as my own." He next
introduces his dear friend, Colonel James Stuart, the
husband of the pretty Mrs. Stuart, "who for sterling
good sense, infinite discernment, humour and honesty
and spirit, is not exceeded by any of them."

"You will be listened to by that brave Irishman,
Captain Macbride, a cousin of my wife, and *the friend
of my heart*, who had come into the House of Commons,
borne upon the swelling bosoms of the worthy electors
of Plymouth. They might also depend upon Mr.
Lee," (Jack Lee) "with whom my intimacy has been
chiefly formed since I made him *dangle* at the end of
a rope in my East India Letter. . . . I love Mr. Lee
exceedingly, though I believe there are not any two
specific propositions of any sort on which we agree; but
the general mass of sense, sociality, toleration, and
religion in each of us produce two given quantities.
which unite and effervesce wonderfully well. . . . I
know few men I would go further to serve than Jack
Lee; *he* whose nobleness of soul has so remarkably
shown how open he is to conviction. I can have
no doubt but that he will send for the Minister for
Scotland and *tell him in a determined tone, 'Dundas!
Dundas! for shame!* Here is a rock on which we
might have split. I'll hear no more of this Court of
Sessions. It is a monstrous measure. Let it be quashed!'
Great god! forgive my thus presumptuously, thus
rashly, attempting for a moment to forge your thunder:
but I conjure you in the name of God, and the King, I
conjure you to announce in your own lofty language,
that there should be a stop put to the conspiracy." All
of which is exquisitely ludicrous, but it is nothing to

what follows. "Believe me sincere," he wanders on, "when I tell you, that, although I, *with all deference, cannot join you in one point*, a reform in Parliament— for the reasons I have given you." Warming up, he bids them,—"Have confidence in Sir Matthew White Ridley, that stately, *that pleasing Northumbrian,*—who exhibits an amount of what it is strange should be rare—independent opulence."

The allusion to the brave Captain Macbride made him speak of the Irish. "I have always stood up for the Irish, in whose fine country I have been hospitably and jovially entertained, and with whom I feel myself to be remarkably congenial." He then quotes a passage in their praise from his book on Corsica, adding that "the Irish were then under a cloud. What a glorious day has burst upon them now!"

Speaking of Mr. Pitt, he exceeded himself in extravagance, uttering a strange, we will not say profane expression; for "Bozzy" would never be profane intentionally: he addressed him in the form used in prayer to the Almighty: "Shall we be so unjust as to apprehend that he will not hear us; he who first took, he who still holds the reigns of Government. Such is my confidence in your talents and virtues; such my sense of the good you have done, that, though not blessed with high blood, but rather I think troubled with a natural timidity of personal danger which it cost me some philosophy to overcome, I am persuaded that I have so much real patriotism in my breast, that I should not hesitate to draw my sword in your defence. It is the *Royal Cause.*" There is another eccentric whose style all this recalls—Elliston, to wit: he, too, fell at times under such strange fits of excitement that the stimulant of a drinking bout seems a sort of sobriety in comparison, when his language assumed a strange heroic, but grotesque inflation.

"In my zeal to prevent what appears to me a most pernicious innovation, I may have been somewhat intemperate in my expression. Though agitated and indignant, I am free from rancour. I write for both sides of the Tweed. It would hurt me very much if, by any misapprehension, it could be thought that any extreme severity in this pamphlet is pointed against the Honourable Judges of the Court of Session, under authority of which I have practised the law for, lo! these nineteen years—

> "'Most potent, grave, and reverend seignieurs,
> My very noble and approved masters;'"

and therefore, I do now in most explicit terms disavow an intention so injurious." Again there must have been much hilarity in all circles as Bozzy's earnest disclaimer was read. There was another whom he had now to commemorate, but with a mixture of awe and fondness. "That great personage who is allowed to have the best memory of any man born a Briton, a sound understanding and a humane heart, may probably recollect that, in a conversation with me, *one of the most zealous Royalists of the age*, he was graciously pleased to give Gen. Paoli, the just praise of putting law into a people who were lawless." This excessive *mystery* of his allusion seems to convey that the secret was between himself, his Majesty, and Dr. Johnson. It suggests Captain Cuttle's confidences with Mr. Carker.

In conclusion, he begs his countrymen to allow him to indulge "a little more in my own egotism and vanity. They are indigenous plants of my mind: they distinguish it. I may prune their luxuriancy, but I must not entirely clear it of them; for then I should be no longer as I am, and perhaps then might be something not so good." This is delightful and was, be it recollected, for the general public. But there is better to come. "I last year claimed, in credit of being no time server: I think I am giving pretty good proof that I am not so this year neither. Though ambitious, I am uncorrupted; and I envy not high situations which are attained by the want of publick virtue. My friend, Lord Mountstuart, flattered me once very highly without intending it. 'I would do anything for you,' said he, ' but bring you into Parliament; for I could not be sure but you might oppose me in something the very next day.' This lord judged well. . . . I cannot exist with pleasure if I have not an honest independence of mind and of conduct; for though no man loves eating and drinking, simply considered, better than I do, I prefer the broiled bladebone of mutton and burnt pork of ' downright Shippen,' to all the luxury of all in station, who play the game through."

CHAPTER XXIV

PUBLICATION OF THE "TOUR TO THE HEBRIDES" AND ITS RECEPTION.

1785.

ON the last page of his strange pamphlet or manifesto, which has long since been forgotten, was an announcement of a far more important work, which showed that he had not lost time in getting ready the venture upon which his heart was set. It was but four months from Johnson's death, yet here was the "Tour" in shape ; and he must have found particular pleasure in issuing this rather piquant notification : "*In the Press and speedily will be published, in one volume octavo.* Printed for Charles Dilly, London. THE JOURNAL of a TOUR to the HEBRIDES with *Samuel Johnson, LL.D.* By *James Boswell, Esq.*

> "O, while along the stream of time, thy Name
> Expanded flies, and gathers all its fame ;
> Gay shall my little bark attendant sail,
> Pursues the triumph, and partakes the gale.

"This journal, which was read and liked by Dr. Johnson, will faithfully and admirably exhibit what he said was the pleasantest part of his life; and which, as it is given with remarks which Mr. Boswell himself was able to make during a very curious journey, will convey a specimen of his conversation, in which wit and wisdom were equally combined."

The "Tour" being virtually ready, took only a few months to pass through the press. He had already shown it to many persons of judgment and distinction, among others to Lord Thurlow, who had been greatly struck, and amused, by it; and it must have been a sore trial to his patience to have been obliged to keep it by him so many years. Now had come his opportunity, and he reasonably reckoned on its having an extraordinary success. It appeared at the end of September, 1785, some nine months after Johnson's death, according to the date of the dedication to Mr. Malone, to whose acquaintance the work introduced him. That gentleman had happened to see a sheet of the book at Mr. Baldwin's press, and was so struck with the style in which Dr. Johnson's character was sketched, that he asked the printer to make him known to the author. Hence one of those fast, firm friendships the warm-hearted Boswell always contrived to bring about. He saw Mr. Malone every day, and, with much good sense and absence of vanity, submitted every page to his revision. In the dedication he handsomely acknowledges how "obligingly he had perused the original manuscript," and could "vouch for the strict fidelity of the present publication." This might seem a little superfluous; for he does not appeal to Malone to vouch for the truthfulness of the incidents or character, but only for the correspondence of his printed text with the manuscript. This seems a curious delusion on Boswell's part; but on it was based his invariable proof of "authenticity" in his various controversies. When his facts were disputed, he would simply say that he had consulted his "original notes," and that he found it as he had stated. This might cause a smile, as it was merely appealing from Boswell to Boswell; but it is proof of the genuine good faith and accuracy of the writer. The note was made on the day in question immediately after the event; and for him it became an independent authority. Not for a moment was he disturbed by the insinuation that it might have been altered in the interval. He felt there was a sacredness in his duty as reporter, and he expected that the world would take the same view.

On the eve of the publication of the "Life," the worthy Mrs. Hannah More happened to meet Mr. Boswell, and a curious conversation took place between them. She wrote an account to a friend, of her sensible appeal to him "to show some reticence," but made in vain: "Boswell tells me he is printing anecdotes of Dr. Johnson. Not his *life*, but, as he has the vanity to call it, his pyramid. I besought his tenderness for our virtuous and most revered departed friend, and begged he would mitigate some of his asperities; he said roughly, he 'would not cut off his claws nor make a tiger a cat, to please anybody.'" The good lady must have been astonished at this rude reception of her appeal. Boswell was later to be irritated by other numerous remonstrances of the same kind. George Stevens wrote thus: "Boswell's book is not yet gone to press. He waits, I believe, till Mrs. Piozzi has published her volumes of Johnson's correspondence with her, which is expected to comprise two hundred letters." Thus, in the "Journal," as well as in the "Life," he was determined to compromise nothing, and not "make a cat of a tiger to please anybody."

On this momentous occasion it occurred to its author that it was high time his lineaments should be portrayed on canvas, by the celebrated artist who had glorified so many of his friends. No doubt he felt it strange that he had not been applied to sit for the celebrated Streatham Gallery, where Murphy, and others of less importance, found a place. Whatever was his feeling, he made this proposal to his friend Sir Joshua :—

Boswell to Sir Joshua Reynolds.

"London, June 7, 1785.

"My dear Sir,—The debts which I contracted in my father's lifetime will not be cleared off by me for some years. I therefore think it unconscientious to indulge myself in any article of expensive luxury. But in the meantime I may die or you may die; and I should regret very much that there should not be at Auchinleck my portrait painted by Sir Joshua Reynolds, with whom I have the felicity of long and social intimacy.

"I have a proposal to make to you. I am for certain to be called to the English Bar next February. Will you now do my picture? and the price shall be paid out of the first fees which I receive as a barrister at Westminster Hall, or, if that should fail, it shall be paid at any rate five years hence by myself, or by my representatives.

"If you are pleased to approve of this proposal, your signifying your concurrence, underneath upon two duplicates, one of which will be kept by each of us, will be a sufficient voucher for the obligation. I ever am, with sincere regard, my dear sir, your faithful and affectionate humble servant, James Boswell."

(Endorsed by Sir Joshua)

"I agree to the above conditions.

"London, September 10, 1785."

He accordingly sat to Sir Joshua, and the result is now to be seen in the National Gallery, to which the picture has found its way from the Peel collection, a not very successful or inspired work. There we see the rather smug and comfortable face, with the double chin, and sensual cast, and an amusing air of dignity. As it is of small size, I am inclined to think it unlikely that the painter accepted payment.*

While preparing his work Boswell must have been disturbed to find that Mrs. Piozzi, who had been for a long time abroad, was likely to anticipate him with her collection. Even more annoying was the knowledge that his enemy, as he considered him, Sir John Hawkins, was also busy with a full life of Johnson, and which he had been commissioned by the booksellers to prepare. Boswell's work, however, was the first to appear. The almost contemptuous manner in which he was alluded to in the lady's book, as though he had had only a trivial connection with Johnson, we must suppose was, in a great measure, the cause of his deep-seated animosity to the author. Still, in the "Tour," he so far restrained himself that he even opened his work with a compliment: "To Mrs. Thrale I was much obliged" (for persuading Johnson to undertake the journey); adding that "her enchantment over him seldom failed." He must have been also annoyed to find that some of the tit-bits he was reserving for the "Life" had been snapped up, such as his verses on Bishop Percy's "Hermit hoar," which had been also taken down by the lady.

* Sir Joshua's legacy to him of £200 looks like a release of the debt. The portrait, consigned to a lumber room at Auchinleck, was sold at his son James's auction. On the title page of the "Tour" was a neatly engraved hawk, with his family crest and motto, "*Vraye foy*," which should certainly be retained in all editions.

This really delightful, genuine book, the best and most artistic of Boswell's efforts, is notable for its clear, unaffected style, its dramatic power, and general spirit of comedy. All the figures are lifelike; and the local colour, the general holiday feeling, the tone of enjoyment and humour are kept up to the end. The cause of this life and spirit is that it was written day by day, when all the incidents were fresh in the author's mind, and on this account it may be considered as unique. The title of the book is, "A Journal, etc.," and the author tells us he had resolved "that the very journal which Johnson read shall be presented to the public. I will not expand the text in any considerable degree, though I may occasionally supply a word to compleat the sense, as to fill up the blanks of abbreviation in the writing: neither of which can be said to change the genuine journal." In his preface he appealed to Malone to vouch for "its strict fidelity;" still, I fancy this only applies to the conversations, and Boswell is likely to have "touched up," or expanded, the descriptive portions. Not less to be admired is the shape which the narrative assumes, and which, though cast in the form of a diary, has none of its stiffness; it is, in fact, a story-book of adventure; controversial notes, therefore, would disfigure it, and are out of place. There is an additional pleasure in reading it in the first edition, which has a quaint, old-fashioned air,* with its monogram, J. B., device, and motto on the title.

* My own copy belonged to Mr. Tasker, who, I fancy, must have been the eccentric personage who read his poem to Johnson. My copy of the "Life" was John Kemble's, and has his notes, but I always lament not having secured Wilkes's copy. Beside the two quartos, I have the rare Dublin edition, and the still rarer second edition of the "Life," in three rather clumsy octavos. I have made a "grangerized" copy of the "Life;" and a most pleasant pastime it is, thus to illustrate almost every page with prints and portraits.

Boswell's art is shown, not only in his treatment of the dialogue and arrangement of the characters, but in his own pleasant sense of comedy, which he " points" by sly comments. Thus, when the travellers were received by Lord Monboddo at his gate, most courteously, who, pointing to the escutcheon, remarked, that " our ancestors were better men than we." " ' No, no, my lord,' said Dr. Johnson, ' we are as strong as they, and a great deal wiser.' This was an assault upon one of Lord Monboddo's capital dogmas, and I was afraid there would have been a violent altercation in the very close, before we got into the house. But his lordship . . . made no reply." This is perfect for its quiet sense of humour, and is a fair specimen of Boswell's happy manner. Even the most carelessly worded scenes are lifelike ; such as that at the opening, where the officials were showing the Library of the Parliament House. Johnson reproached them with the betrayal of Queen Mary. "*Worthy Mr. James Kerr, Keeper of the Records.* ' Half our nation was bribed with English money.' JOHNSON. ' Sir, that is no defence. That makes you worse.' *Good Mr. Brown, Keeper of the Advocates' Library.* ' We had better say nothing about it.' " The incidents at the universities, the dinings with the professors, have a college tone ; while the festive scenes at Dunvegan and other places are exhilarating. No praise, indeed, could be sufficient for this really captivating book. It is, however, rich in the characteristic absurdities of the author. Thus he tells us, they " passed Gordon Castle, which has a princely appearance." He then, in amusing fashion, explains why they were not entertained there : " I am not sure whether the Duke was at home. But not having the honour of being made known to his Grace, I would not have presumed to enter his castle. . . . We were at any rate in a hurry to get forward to the wildness which we were come to see. Perhaps if this noble family had still preserved that sequestered magnificence which they maintained when Catholics, . . . we might have been induced to have procured proper letters of introduction, and devoted some time to the contemplation of venerable superstitious state." One might suspect that Mr. Boswell had met with some rebuff. These remarks are certainly in bad taste.

The appearance of this celebrated book caused much astonishment, anger, and laughter. It may be that a book of such a kind was never issued before. It was amazing to all, to find that living persons were discussed, described, ridiculed even, and calumniated, with the utmost freedom, as if these things were all in the proper course ; while offensive personalities were used in the freest way.* Amusing and original, it certainly was, and the spirit and originality of the conversations were admitted to be as extraordinary as they were novel. Nowadays we have been regularly trained to personality by what are called the " Society papers," in which the names of private persons, as well as their doings, are recorded ; still it would cause a commotion if the conversation of some leading personage were reported, in which persons still living were described in such fashion as this : " A—— is a poor creature: *he has no bottom.*" " B—— is a thorough donkey, talks a good deal of what he *thinks* to be sense," etc.

After recovering from his first surprise at this reception, Mr. Boswell found himself in a very painful predicament. The confessions he had made concerning

---

* So absorbing was this one topic, and so abundant the laughter, that Mrs. Hannah More complained that all conversation was spoiled. " Everybody seems sick of it, though everybody conspires not to let it drop."

himself caused hearty laughter, and ridicule ; while his unbecoming attacks on the living were resented. It was astonishing, indeed, how he escaped personal chastisement.

The first protest came from Mrs. Piozzi. Her "Anecdotes" were issued with extraordinary success, every copy being sold on the day of publication. As Cadell assured her, he had never been so successful with any work. Five editions followed in quick succession. It was mortifying to find that the only allusions to himself in her book were, that Johnson had been in the Isle of Skye "with Mr. Boswell," and, further, an account of how he had been once put down "somewhat roughly" by Johnson, when maintaining "in vino veritas,"—"I fancy," she added maliciously, "Mr. B—— has not forgotten it." Boswell had, moreover, very thoughtlessly reported a speech of Johnson's depreciating Mrs. Montagu, a friend of Mrs. Thrale's, declaring that neither he (the doctor), nor Mr. Beauclerk, nor Mrs. Thrale, "could get through her Essay on Shakespeare." *

* When her book came out she added a note denying this imputation in the strongest terms.

"*Naples, February* 10, 1786.

"Since the foregoing went to the press, having seen a passage from Mr. Boswell's 'Tour to the Hebrides,' in which it is said, that *I could not get through Mrs. Montagu's 'Essay on Shakspeare,'* I do not delay a moment to declare, that, on the contrary, I have always commended it myself and heard it commended by every one else ; and few things would give me more concern than to be thought incapable of tasting, or unwilling to testify my opinion of its excellence."

In his second edition, Mr. Boswell retorted in one of his most characteristic notes :—

"*April* 17*th.*

"Mr. Urban,—No man has less inclination to controversy than I have, particularly with a lady. But as in my 'Journal of a Tour to the Hebrides,' I have claimed, and am conscious of being entitled

The blemishes of the work are these unseemly attacks on persons he disliked, and even on those who had been hospitable to him and his friend. The only

to, credit, for the strictest fidelity, my respect for the public obliges me to take notice of an insinuation which tends to impeach it. . . .

"I might, perhaps, with propriety have waited till I should have had an opportunity of answering this postscript in a future publication ; but, being sensible that impressions once made are not easily effaced, I think it better thus early to ascertain a fact which seems to be denied.

"The fact reported in my Journal, to which Mrs. Piozzi alludes, is stated in these words, p. 299 : 'I spoke of Mrs. Montagu's very high praises of Garrick. JOHNSON. Sir, it is fit she should say so much, and I should say nothing. Reynolds is fond of her book, and I wonder at it ; for neither I, nor Beauclerk, nor Mrs. Thrale, could get through it.'

"It is remarkable that this postscript is so expressed, as not to point out the person who said that Mrs. Thrale could not get through Mrs. Montagu's book ; and therefore I think it necessary to remind Mrs. Piozzi, that the assertion concerning her was Dr. Johnson's, and not mine. The second observation that I shall make on this postscript is, that it does not deny the fact asserted, though I must acknowledge, from the praise it bestows on Mrs. Montagu's book, it may have been designed to convey that meaning.

"What Mrs. Thrale's opinion is or was, or what she may or may not have said to Dr. Johnson concerning Mrs. Montagu's book, it is not necessary for me to enquire. It is only incumbent on me to ascertain what Dr. Johnson said to me. I shall therefore confine myself to a very short state of the fact.

"The unfavourable opinion of Mrs. Montagu's book, which Dr. Johnson is here reported to have given, is known to have been that which he uniformly expressed, as many of his friends well remember. So much for the authenticity of the paragraph, as far as it relates to his own sentiments. The words containing the assertion, to which Mrs. Piozzi objects, are printed from my manuscript Journal, and were taken down at the time. The Journal was read by Dr. Johnson, who pointed out some inaccuracies, which I corrected, but did not mention any inaccuracy in the paragraph in question : and what is still more material, and very flattering to me, a considerable part of my Journal, containing this paragraph, *was read several years ago by Mrs. Thrale herself*, who had it for some time in her possession, and returned it to me, without intimating that Dr. Johnson had mistaken her sentiments.

"When my Journal was passing through the press, it occurred

reason for such outrages on good feeling and decency appears to have been a certain lack of obsequiousness in the victims, in acknowledging the great honour that had been paid them by the visitors. The writer does not appear to have been conscious of his impropriety, and, when vindicating himself, invariably made what he thought an unanswerable excuse—that he was not responsible, for he had referred to his notes, and found that Dr. Johnson had expressed himself in the terms described. Dr. Blagden, a friend of Walpole's, said justly enough, "This is a new kind of libel, by which you may abuse anybody, by saying some dead person said so and so of somebody else."

But his most outrageous breach of decorum was the treatment of Sir Alexander, afterwards Lord, Macdonald. This important personage had met Boswell and Johnson in London, and, by the report of the conversation, is shown to have been an accomplished gentleman, with acute and original views. When the travellers reached Armidale, he and his lady came down to the beach to welcome them, and received them into their house. But Boswell and his friend fancied that their hospitality

to me, that a peculiar delicacy was necessary to be observed in reporting the opinion of one literary lady concerning the performance of another; and I had such scruples on that head, that in the proof sheet I struck out the name of Mrs. Thrale from the paragraph in question, and two or three hundred copies of my book were actually printed and published without it; of these Sir Joshua Reynolds's copy happened to be one. But while the sheet was working off, a friend, for whose opinion I have great respect, suggested that I had no right to deprive Mrs. Thrale of the high honour which Dr. Johnson had done her, by stating her opinion along with that of Mr. Beauclerk, as coinciding with, and, as it were, sanctioning his own. The observation appeared to me so weighty and conclusive, that I hastened to the printing house, and, as a piece of justice, restored Mrs. Thrale to that place from which a too scrupulous delicacy had excluded her.

"On this simple state of facts I shall make no observation whatever. Yours, etc., JAMES BOSWELL."

was not handsome or *empressé* enough, and he gives a most offensive account of his host. What could be more ungentlemanly than this?—"I shall mention," he says, "but one characteristic circumstance. My shrewd and hearty friend, Sir Thomas (Wentworth) Blackett, Lady Macdonald's uncle, who had preceded us on a visit to this chief, upon being asked by him if the punch bowl upon the table was not a very handsome one, replied, 'Yes—*if it were full.*'" Now, repeating such a speech as this must have caused a quarrel between the two gentlemen. But he went on: "Sir Alexander Macdonald having been an Eton scholar, Dr. Johnson had formed an opinion of him, which much diminished when we beheld him in the Isle of Skye, where we heard heavy complaints of rents racked and the people driven to emigration. Dr. Johnson said, 'It grieves me to see the chief of a great clan appear to such disadvantage. This gentleman has talents, nay, some learning; but he is totally unfit for this situation. Sir, the Highland chief should not be allowed to go further south than Aberdeen.'"

This attack on a gentleman of position has always seemed inexplicable. I am inclined to think that Boswell was suffering from a sense of grievance or injury. It will be recollected that, after his failure to gain Miss Blair, he turned his thoughts to Miss Elizabeth Diana Bosville, "the Yorkshire heiress," who, almost immediately, in 1768, was secured by Sir Alexander, an alliance which eventually led to the Yorkshire estate passing to the Macdonald family. This may be doing "Bozzy" an injustice; but his prejudices are likely enough to have been excited by the fact of any one being preferred to himself.

Mrs. Piozzi, when she published her collection of

Johnson's letters, was equally indecorous, though she suppressed the name. There the doctor describes "his host" as having come "from his seat to the middle of the Island, to a small house on the shore, as we believe, that he might with less reproach entertain us meanly. *He had no cook*, nor I suppose much provision, nor had the Lady the common decencies of her tea table. *We picked up our sugar with our fingers.* Boswell waxed angry, and reproached him with his improper parsimony." Later the doctor returned to the subject. Boswell had long before given the nickname of "Sir Sawney" to a rival who had supplanted him; he now transferred it to their host. "I have done thinking," writes Johnson, "of ——, whom we now call Sir Sawney, has disgusted all mankind by injudicious parsimony, and given occasion to so many stories that —— (Boswell) had some thoughts of collecting them, and making a novel of his life."

Boswell, when his book was being printed, seems to have been seized with scruples, and actually cancelled a leaf, which must have contained something actually libellous.*

Now, the injustice of these attacks and charges of meanness is shown by the fact which is stated by Boswell himself, that the family mansion had been burnt down, and the present owner had been obliged to occupy one of their tenants' houses, where they were obliged to receive their ungracious guests.

---

* This must have been done at the last moment, after the book was stitched and bound; for the new leaf is rather clumsily pasted in on the "guard." It will be found between pages 166 and 169. And yet he could complacently write at the close: "Before I conclude, I think it proper to say, that I have suppressed everything which I thought could *really* hurt any one now living." They were, however, "inserted in my journal."

"We attempted in vain to communicate to him a portion of our enthusiasm. He bore *with so polite good-nature our warm,* and what some might call Gothic, expostulations on this subject, that I should not forgive myself were I to record all that Dr. Johnson's ardour led him to say."

But when recording a later period of their travels, the chronicler passes all bounds of decency; he again introduces the gentleman who had the misfortune to have entertained them, with these gross attacks.

"The penurious gentleman of our acquaintance, formerly alluded to, offered us a topic of conversation to-night. Dr. Johnson said, I ought to write down a collection of the instances of his narrowness, as they almost exceeded belief. *Col* told us, that O'Kane, the famous Irish harper, was once at that gentleman's house. He could not find in his heart to give him any money, but gave him a key for a harp, which was finely ornamented with gold and silver, and with a precious stone, and was worth eighty or a hundred guineas. He did not know the value of it; and when he came to know it, he would fain have had it back; but O'Kane took care that he should not. *Col* said, the gentleman's relations were angry at his giving away the harp key, for it had been long in the family. JOHNSON. 'Sir, he values a new guinea more than an old friend.'

"*Col* also told us, that the same person having come up with a sergeant and twenty men, working on the high road, he entered into discourse with the sergeant, and then gave him sixpence for the men to drink. The sergeant asked, 'Who is this fellow?' Upon being informed, he said, 'If I had known who he was, I should have thrown it in his face.' JOHNSON. 'There is much want of sense in all this. He had no business to speak with the sergeant. He might have been in haste, and trotted on. He has not learnt to be a miser; I believe we must take him apprentice.' BOSWELL. " He would grudge giving half a guinea to be taught." JOHNSON. ' Nay, sir, you must teach him *gratis.*' "

It was soon whispered about that Lord Macdonald and Sir Thomas Blackett, " his hearty friend," had called the author to account, and had threatened chastisement. Walcot expressed the general feeling when he wrote—

> " Loud of thy tour, a thousand tongues have spoken,
> And wonder'd *that thy bones were never broken.*"

And again—

> " For thee, James Boswell, may the hand of Fate
> Arrest thy goose-quill and confine thy prate !
> Thine egotism the world disgusted hears—
> Then load with vanities no more our ears.
> Like some lone puppy, yelping all night long,
> That tires the very echoes with his tongue."

This was offensive enough, but it went further :—

> " *Let Lord Macdonald threat thy breech to kick,*
> *And o'er thy shrinking shoulders shake his stick* ;
> Treat with contempt the menace of this Lord,
> 'Tis Hist'ry's province, Bozzy, to record."

Walcot, in his verses and notes, seemed to have collected the most offensive gossip of the day :—

> " Though Wilkes abuse thy brain, that airy mill,
> And swear poor Johnson was murdered by thy grill.
>   ❋   ❋   ❋   ❋   ❋
> What though against thee *porters bounce the door,*
> And bid thee hunt for secrets there no more." ❋

In one of the caricatures, one scene represents our author on his knees, his book open at the offensive

---

❋ " This is literally true, ' Nobody is at home.' So, in London poor Bozzy is in a desert."

pages, 165–167, and Lord Macdonald threatening him
with a stick. Whether there was truth in this painful
incident or not, Boswell made haste, in his next edition,
issued in 1786, to make amends. The more offensive
passages were withdrawn, though much was left that
was offensive enough. He added a vindication of himself
in one of his notes.*

Boswell was, no doubt, much troubled by these
rumours. Yet he took occasion to contradict them
publicly in a "characteristical" letter to the editor of
the *Gentleman's Magazine*, dated March 9, 1786 : " It
having been asserted in a late scurrilous publication that

* " Having found, on a revision of the first edition of this work,
that, notwithstanding my best care, a few observations had escaped
me, which arose from the instant impression, the publication of
which might perhaps be considered as passing the bounds of a
strict decorum, I immediately ordered that they should be omitted
in the subsequent editions. I was pleased to find that they did not
amount in the whole to a page. If any of the same kind are yet
left, it is owing to inadvertence alone, no man being more unwilling to give pain to others than I am. A contemptible scribbler,
of whom I have learned no more than that, after having disgraced
and deserted the clerical character, he picks up in London a scanty
livelihood by scurrilous lampoons under a feigned name, has
impudently and falsely asserted that the passages omitted were
defamatory, and that the omission was not voluntary, but com-
pulsory. The last insinuation I took the trouble publicly to dis-
prove; yet, like one of Pope's dunces, he persevered in 'the lie
o'erthrown.' As to the charge of defamation, there is an obvious
and certain mode of refuting it. Any person who thinks it worth
while to compare one edition with the other will find that the
passages omitted were not in the least degree of that nature, but
exactly such as I have represented them in the former part of this
note, the hasty effusion of momentary feelings which the delicacy
of politeness should have suppressed." It will be noticed that this
vindication, addressed to the Magazine, is very guarded and can
hardly be considered satisfactory. The incriminated passages, it will
be seen, are *deliberate,* and part of the regular narrative : so far
from their having " escaped " him, he cancelled a leaf. His statement, too, that he had added twenty-two pages is also inaccurate,
as, in comparing the editions, I cannot find that he had done more
than add a page or so to the appendix.

some passages relating to a noble Lord, which appeared in my first edition of my journal of a tour in the Hebrides, were omitted in the second edition of that work, in consequence of a letter from his lordship, I think myself called upon to declare that that assertion is false.

"In a note, p. 527, of my second edition, I mentioned that, having found, on a revision of this work, that, notwithstanding my best care, a few observations had escaped me *which arose from the instant impression*, the publication of which might be considered as passing the bounds of a strict decorum, I immediately ordered that they should be omitted in the present edition.

"I did not then think it necessary to be explicit. But as I now find I have been misunderstood by some, and grossly misrepresented by others, I think it proper to add that soon after the publication of the first edition of my work, from the motive above mentioned, without any application from any person whatever, I ordered twenty-six lines relative to the noble lord to be omitted in the second edition, for the loss of which I trust twenty-two additional pages are a sufficient compensation; and this was the sole alteration that was made in my book relative to that nobleman: nor was any application made to me by the nobleman alluded to, at any time, to quote any alteration in my journal.

"To any serious criticism or ludicrous banter, to which my journal shall be liable, I shall never object, but receive both the one and the other with perfect good humour; but I cannot suffer a malignant and injurious falsehood to pass uncontradicted."

Now this had certainly the tone of an apology, and of a humble one. No doubt the Scotch nobleman would not have condescended to require alteration or withdrawal, by a person whom he considered to be

without the manners or feelings of a gentleman; and
he would naturally have felt it beneath him to bring to
account a person who objected to his hospitality.   It
would certainly be impossible to conduct a discussion on
such a topic, or to require a withdrawal, etc.   Boswell,
therefore, was no doubt accurate in saying that no
request of the kind was addressed to him.   But it had
also been stated by Baretti, Walcot and others, that
chastisement was actually threatened.

"Our comic performers," wrote Walpole on April
30, 1786, "are Boswell and Dame Piozzi.   The Cock
biographer has fixed a direct lie on the Hen by an
advertisement in which he affirms that he communicated
his MS. to Mdme. Thrale and she made no objection
to what he says of her low opinion of Mrs. Montague's
book.   It is very possible, but it might not be her real
opinion, but was uttered in compliment to Johnson, or
for fear he should spit in her face if she disagreed with
him."   He also said that Boswell had acted " shamefully " towards Mrs. Piozzi, Mrs. Montague, and Bishop
Percy; and he might have added many more to the
list.

On another occasion he did not conceal his contempt
for the new "Life."   "Have you got Boswell's most
absurd, enormous book ?   The best thing in it is a
bon mot of Lord Pembroke's.   The more one learns
of Johnson the more preposterous an assemblage he
appears, of strong sense, of the lowest bigotry, etc., and
Boswell is the ape of his faults, without a grain of
his sense.   It is the story of a mountebank and his
Zany."

Boswell must have suffered rather acutely from the
pasquinades, pictures, caricatures, which were literally
showered on the town.   One of these, which I possess,

is called "Johnson's Ghost," and depicts the lexicographer appearing to the frightened Boswell, and mournfully reproaching him. A more tremendous attack, however,—unique, perhaps,—is the series of no less than twenty large caricatures, in each one of which he was represented in some ridiculous situation, each sketch, too, having a quotation from his book. These have been supposed to be the work of Rowlandson, but they were by a far inferior artist—Collins.*

Another personage, treated in equally gross fashion, was Sir John Dalrymple, a respectable county gentleman, who, hearing that Johnson was setting off for England, kindly offered him hospitality on his way home. But Mr. Boswell, on a mere report of some utterance of Sir John's, had taken secret offence. "Sir John, I perceived, *was ambitious of having such a guest*; but, as I was well assured, that at this very

---

* Dr. B. Hill has fallen into this mistake. "Collins," says Angelo, "well known in the regions of Covent-garden, and sometime editor of the Public Ledger, was a lively satirist, both with his pencil and his pen. A whole series of designs were published by this witty wag, the heroes of which, or rather the knight and the esquire of his drama, were Johnson and Boswell. The laird of Auchinleck, indeed, had a large collection of these satires upon 'self and company,' as he used facetiously to inscribe them; and boasted at the judge's table, that his *history* would be more copiously illustrated than even the lord high chancellor Clarendon's! Collins, a great tavern goer, and known to all the dons of the green-room, kept late hours. His fate was lamented, he being found dead on the steps of an hotel." These caricatures exhibit Boswell and his wife and family under ludicrous conditions, and are thus described:—"Imitations at Drury Lane Theatre," "The Embrace," "Tea," "Chatting," "Walking in the High Street," "Wit and Wisdom," "Setting out for Edinburgh," "The Procession," "The Reconciliation," "The Dance on Dunvegan," "Veronica's Breakfast Conversation," "The Recovery," "Sailing among the Hebrides," "The Contest at Auchinleck," "The Journalist, with a View of Auchinleck," "Satisfying the Palate," "The Vision," "Lodging at M'Queen's," "Revising for the Second Edition," "All hail, Dablair."

time he had joined with some of his prejudiced countrymen in railing at Dr. Johnson, and had said, 'he wondered
how any gentleman of Scotland could keep company
with him,' I thought he did not deserve the honour:
yet, as it might be a convenience to Dr. Johnson, I
contrived that he should accept the invitation, and engaged to conduct him."

Every word of this was offensive. They were
detained on the way, a delay purposely contrived by
Boswell to affront their host, and during the time he
seemed to have enticed his great friend into ridiculing
the gentleman. Johnson never dreamed that his remarks were to be put into print. "He did not seem
much troubled at our having treated the Baronet with
so little attention to politeness, but when I talked of
the grievous disappointment it must have been to him,
that we did not come to the feast that he had prepared
for us (for he told us he had killed a seven year old
sheep on purpose), my friend got into a merry mood,
and jocularly said, 'I dare say, sir, he has been very
sadly distressed: Nay, we do not know but the consequence may have been fatal. Let me try to describe
his situation in his own historical style: I have as good
a right to make him think and talk, as he has to tell us
how people thought and talked a hundred years ago, of
which he has no evidence.—Stay now.—Let us consider!'—He then (heartily laughing all the while) proceeded in his imitation. 'Dinner being ready, he
wondered that his guests were not yet come. His
wonder was soon succeeded by impatience. He walked
about the room in anxious agitation; sometimes he
looked at his watch, sometimes he looked out at the
window with an eager gaze of expectation, and revolved
in his mind the various accidents of human life. His

family beheld him with mute concern. "Surely (said he, with a sigh), they will not fail me."'"

Friends, in confidence, will often express their opinions freely, and even laugh at the peculiarities of an absent friend. But these are unofficial thoughts, floating in the mind, or impressions which can hardly be checked. They are unregistered. We can quite understand Johnson thus raising his own spirits, and his companion's, by this jocularity; but we can conceive the astonishment and disgust with which their host read this ungracious return for his hospitality. It is suspected, however, that it rather roused wonder and contempt at the unlucky Boswell's fatuity, and dull ignorance of what the ordinary *bienséances* and courtesies of life required.

Further troubles caused by his journal were to come even from those whom he meant to honour. They often found themselves exhibited in some awkward position, and for which no abundance of praise made up. The excellent, much respected Sir William Forbes, of Pitsligo, was introduced and lavishly extolled : " A man of whom too much good cannot be said ; who, with distinguished abilities and application in his profession of a banker, is at once a good companion, and a good christian ; which I think is saying enough." Having given this handsome testimonial at the beginning of the book, at the close he felt he might call on him for one in return, as he had lent him the manuscript to read. The banker acknowledged the favour in a rather cautious and reserved style : " I ought to have thanked you sooner, for your very obliging letter, and for *the singular confidence you are pleased to place in me,* when you trust me with such a curious and valuable deposit as the papers you have sent me. Be assured

I have a due sense of this favour, and shall faithfully and carefully return them to you. You may rely that I shall neither copy any part, nor permit the papers to be seen. They contain a curious picture of society, and form a journal on the most instructive plan that can possibly be thought of; for I am not sure that an ordinary observer would become so well acquainted either with Dr. Johnson, or with the manners of the Hebrides, by a personal intercourse, as by a perusal of your Journal."

Boswell introduced this with a flourish : " It is not for me to boast of my own labours, but I cannot refrain from publishing such praise as I received for, etc." But on the publication the shrewd banker saw at once the position in which he was placed, and that it looked as though he praised because he *had been* praised. He seems to have remonstrated; for in the next edition the author put this note : " In justice to Sir William Forbes and myself, it is proper to mention that the papers which were submitted to his perusal contained only an account of our Tour from the time that Dr. Johnson and I set out for Edinburgh, and consequently *did not contain the eulogium* on Sir William Forbes, which he never saw till this book appeared in print, nor did he even know that this journal was to be published."

But, in truth, at this distance of time we can form but little idea of the general astonishment and anger with which Boswell's work was received. In our day, Mr. Greville's " Memoirs " were thought to be outspoken beyond proper limits, and furnished subject for many a discussion at dinner tables; but it is difficult to conceive what must have been the reception of Boswell's work, where every name, and offensive criticism was given, and spades were called spades, without any consciousness of doing harm. All the persons who suffered being long since dead, we thankfully accept the book without thought of the victims.

Much can be gathered from its effect on the worthy and amiable Dr. Beattie, who was popular and acceptable in all places, particularly with the royal family. There was something engaging in this divine. On the Hebrides tour, it was expected that he would be at Aberdeen to welcome the sage, but he could not attend. Boswell was on the most friendly terms with him ; yet he commonly contrived to set down some trifling uncomplimentary slight to his pride. He tells how Lady Errol presented them with a copy of verses, written by Beattie on her son's birth, and Johnson was asked how he liked them. " Dr. Johnson, who did not admire it, got off very well, by taking it out and reading the second and third stanzas very melodiously." Anything more likely to make Beattie uncomfortable could not be devised, for it compromised him with his patroness, and must have changed his opinion of Johnson. His view of the book, which he wrote to his friend Sir W. Forbes, was not, therefore, very favourable. " He could not," he wrote, " approve the plan of such a work, as it was not quite fair to publish a man's letter without his consent. No doubt he had Johnson's consent for publishing *his* letters and utterances, but Bozzy has published the sayings and doings of other people who never consented to any such thing, and who little thought, when they were doing their best to entertain the two travellers, that a story would be made of it and laid before the public."

He then mentions some things which he thought " highly objectionable,"—such as Johnson saying of the " Man of the World " that he found little or nothing in

it. " Why should this be recorded ? Is it likely to be
of any use ? Of a very promising young gentleman
to whom Johnson was under the highest obligation, for
he had risked his life in his service (" Col "), Dr.
Johnson said, it was a pity he was not more intellectual.
Why should this be recorded ? I will allow that one
friend might say this to another in confidence, but to
publish it to the world shows neither wit nor gratitude.
I am sure Mr. Boswell, who is a very good-natured man,
would have seen it in this light, if he had given himself
time to think. At Aberdeen, where the two travellers
were most hospitably entertained by the professors, they
said to one another, that they had heard at Aberdeen
nothing which deserved attention." He then quotes an
opinion of the Bishop of Chester, who also condemned
the book, saying, " You will wish that many things had
been omitted, and perhaps if they had not existed at
all, it would have been better still." Then, enumerating
all the biographers, Piozzi, Hawkins, Boswell and the
coming " Life," he adds, " Our modest and worthy friend,
Mr. Langton, is the only one who observes a profound
silence on this occasion."

Sir W. Forbes, who had suffered from Boswell's
indiscretion, replied : " I have been accused of being his
adviser to print in book form a letter of mine, *which, by
the by, he inserted without my knowledge or permission* ;
but that letter merely related to a perusal of the MS.,
at a time when I had not the most distant idea of his
printing his journal. I have also been accused of having
written that complimentary letter because of an eulogium
with which he has been pleased to honour me in his book ;
but the passage in which I am mentioned in so flattering a manner, *was* not in his original MS. which I saw."
(This Bozzy was constrained, as we have seen, to insert

in his second edition.) "As his life of Dr. Johnson will probably be a work of a similar nature, I have taken the liberty of strongly enjoining him to be more careful what he inserts, so as not to make himself enemies, or give pain to any person whom he may have occasion to mention; and I hope he will do so, as he seems sorry for some parts of the others." Beattie replied that he, too, was convinced that Bozzy meant no harm. ("I am not convinced of any such thing," wrote Mrs. Piozzi on the margin of her copy; "Boswell meant to gain attention, whether by giving pain or pleasure, he cared not.") *

I am inclined to believe that Boswell had heard, from many quarters, of these severe criticisms of Beattie's. For when the "Life" appeared some years later, Beattie found himself thus "rallied" and girded at, in one of Johnson's letters: "We all love Beattie. Mrs. Thrale says if ever she has another husband, she'll have Beattie. *He sunk upon us that he was married;* else we should have shown his lady more civilities. She is a very fine woman. But how can you show civilities

---

* Sir William Forbes gives this favourable testimonial to his friend: "Mr. Boswell's acquaintance and mine began at a very early period of life, an intimate correspondence continued between us ever after. The circle of his acquaintance among the learned, the witty, and indeed among men of all ranks and professions was extremely extensive, as his talents were considerable, and his convivial powers made his company much in request. His warmth of heart towards his friends was very great, and I have known few men who possessed a stronger sense of piety or more fervent devotion (tinctured no doubt with some little store of superstition, which had probably been fostered by his habits of intimacy with Dr. Johnson), perhaps not always sufficient to regulate his imagination, or direct his conduct, yet still genuine, and founded both in his understanding and his heart. For Mr. Boswell I entertained a sincere regard, which he returned by the strongest proof in his power to confer, by leaving me guardian of his children." ("Pooh, pooh!" writes Mrs. Piozzi in a note in the margin. "It was all affectation.")

to a nonentity ? I did not think he had been married. Nay, I did not think about it one way or the other; but he did not tell us of his lady till late." Many a person, writing to a friend in our own day, might readily indulge in a joke in this way; "What do you think ! ——— actually passed himself off on us as a bachelor—never breathed a word of his wife." But what editor could dream of printing such a statement ! There is certainly high comedy in the situation, as we can imagine the feelings of so revered and much-esteemed divine, the retiring Beattie, so acceptable at court, finding this joke at his expense printed in a large quarto ! Much shocked, he addressed a gentle remonstrance to our author : " I am not sure that I understand *sunk upon us*, which is a very uncommon phrase ; but it seems to me to imply (and others, I find, have understood it in the same sense) *studiously concealed from us his being married*. Now, Sir, this was by no means the case. I could have no motive to conceal a circumstance, of which I never was nor can be ashamed ; and of which Dr. Johnson seemed to think, when he afterwards became acquainted with Mrs. Beattie, that I had, as was true, reason to be proud. So far was I from concealing her, that my wife had at that time almost as numerous an acquaintance in London as I had myself." Boswell inserted this letter, but positively declined to alter, adding a half-contemptuous comment : " I have, from my respect for my friend, Dr. Beattie, and regard to his extreme sensibility, inserted the foregoing letter, though I cannot but wonder at his considering as any imputation a phrase commonly used among the best friends." The truth was, he was not accountable for the expression, which was Dr. Johnson's ; but, in his discretion as editor, it should certainly have been omitted.

Neither had his work given entire satisfaction to Miss Seward, one of that curious Lichfield *coterie* which affected to direct public taste, and to pass judgment on all occurrences in the literary world. Her letters, which were long after collected and published by Sir Walter Scott, are of a rather vapid cast, and full of high-strung rhapsodies. She had been a pretty, interesting woman, but vanity and disappointment had soured her. She was, at first, very friendly and cordial, anticipating no doubt that she would have an important place in the chronicle. Boswell looked to so important a native of Lichfield for valuable assistance, in recovering the traditions of Johnson's early life. He was particularly eager about the doctor's boyish years. Facts, however, were not much in her way; and instead, she could furnish sentiment in abundance, or speculations on the doctor's character. When he consulted her on the point, she told him that she " never heard my dear mother mention any of the *promissary sparkles*, which doubtless burst forth. They are, I fear, like my poor mother, gone to their eternal home, and thus are our *fountains of juvenile intelligence dried up.*" From Miss Lucy Porter, she believed " that not even a *kneeling world* would obtain her the letters." She, however, furnished Boswell with the report of a conversation which she had held with the doctor, on the subject of Mrs. Aston, in which the doctor is made to talk in an extraordinary style, something after the fashion of a Quaker : " When thy mother told thee, . . . thy mother told thee truly, etc." She followed this up with some imaginative stories ; such as that Johnson was first in love with Miss Lucy Porter, his wife's daughter, but was treated by her with disdain, etc.

These communications, on investigation, proved to be apocryphal enough—an opinion which was probably

conveyed to the lady in the author's own blunt style.
In return she gave him her opinion of his " Tour,"
in a tart fashion. ". . . I confess that it was not
without some surprise that I perceived so much exultation avowed concerning the noble blood that flows
in your veins : since it is more honourable for a man
of distinguished ingenuity to have been obscurely
than splendidly descended." She then becomes the
candid friend. " I have, it is true, seen a great deal
of nonsense about your ' Tour,' in the public prints,
and that (*i.e.* the nonsense), *both in its praise* and
abuse. It is hard to say who are most absurd, they who
vilify its entertaining effusions, as vapid and uninteresting : or they who fancy they see a perfect character
in the stupendous mortal whom its pages exhibit, in
lights so striking and so various ; bowing down before
the relics of popish superstition, repaying the hospitable kindness of the Scotch Professors with unfeeling
exultation over the barrenness of their country." She
claims credit for having written " *in a spirit of warm
encomium* " of the " Tour," to the " elegant Bard of
Sussex," Mr. Hayley, and to others.

There were many instances of his indiscretion. In
a discussion on Fingal : " Young Mr. Tytler stepped
briskly forward, and remarked that he had heard it
repeated in the original. Johnson put him down, and
said later : ' Did you observe the wonderful confidence
with which young Tytler advanced, with his front ready
brased ? ' " This impertinence, however, was taken out,
and the name was changed to " a gentleman in company." We cannot help suspecting that there must
have been much apologizing and eating of humble-pie
before Boswell released himself from all these troubles.

CHAPTER XXV.

1786.

HE had now foolishly abandoned the Bar of his native
country, to which he had devoted so many years,
and was speedily to find that he was following a mere
" will o' the wisp," and that neither practice nor success
was to be secured without extraordinary diligence and
close application. Neither of these was he likely to
supply. His unfortunate failings, his lack of restraint
in wine, his lavish confidence to every comer, had de-
veloped with age ; and, with age he became more
provocative of ridicule. Elderly folly is always a direct
challenge; and Boswell at this period had grown "puffy"
of aspect, no doubt owing to his convivial practices, and,
as we can see from the caricatures, offered a self-satisfied
and almost grotesque appearance. It was not until a few
months before Johnson's death, that he was enabled to
accomplish, what had long been his ardent desire, viz.
to join the English Bar, where he conceived his talents
would be properly recognized. This, however, was only
to prove another idle dream. His real aim was, likely
enough, the securing of permanent opportunities for enjoying those London pleasures to which he was so much
attached. The step had been all through discouraged

by his sensible friend, who warned and dissuaded him, perhaps disgusted by his extravagance and perpetual lapses. He had been, accordingly, "called," in Hilary Term, 1786, being now forty-six—an age too late to begin a new career in a profession where a few years give so great an advantage to a professional rival. Unluckily, the younger barristers were inclined to make a "butt" of the new candidate; and, on the circuit, poor "Bozzy" presently became the subject of an amusing hoax, which succeeded so perfectly and unexpectedly, as to prove the victim to be a "*niais*" of the first water. "Bogus" cases, as they might be called, were regularly submitted to him, for his "advice and opinion." He fell into the trap, and drew up elaborate opinions, which caused intense enjoyment to his persecutors. But Lord Eldon recalls an even richer joke of this kind:—"At an assizes at Lancaster," he says, "we found Johnson's friend, Jemmy Boswell, lying upon the pavement, inebriated. We subscribed at supper a guinea for him and half-a-crown for his clerk, and sent him, when he waked next morning, a brief with instructions to move for a writ of what we denominated *quare adhæsit pavimento*, with observations duly calculated to induce him to think that it required great learning to explain the necessity of granting it, to the judge before whom he was to move. Boswell sent all round the town, to attorneys for books that might enable him to distinguish himself; but in vain. He moved, however, for the writ, making the best use he could of the observations in the writ. The judge was perfectly astonished and the audience amazed. The former said, 'I never heard of such a writ; what can it be that adheres to the pavement? Are any of you gentlemen of the Bar able to explain this?' The barristers laughed. At last one of them said, 'My Lord, Mr.

Boswell, last night *adhæsit pavimento*. There was no moving him for some time; at last he was carried to bed, and he has been dreaming about himself and the pavement.'"*

His fitful career at this time is well summarized by a friend who knew him well.† "His beginnings were here also not unpromising. He attended the Judges in pursuit of business upon several of their circuits. He was sometimes retained to plead in a Scottish Appeal. But his habits of conviviality, his character for flighty gaiety, incompatible with eminence in business, the lateness of the time in his life at which he made the attempt, and perhaps also his want of perseverance, soon stopped him short in his career of juridical practice in England as before in Scotland. The publication of his Hebridean Tour, too, as I have been taught to believe, exhibiting him as the minute recorder and retailer of whatever careless conversations might have passed between persons of any eminence in his presence, excited among his acquaintance *a general alarm*, that tended at once to hurt, in some small degree, his practice at the bar, *and to exclude him from some of those social circles in which he had been before a familiar and welcome guest*. His first ardour was gradually extinguished." The passage in italics describes the penalty he had to pay for his free journalization, and has not been before noted. Still he was not disheartened, and his unflagging buoyancy made him reckon on success and " business," and even promotion. "I must be seen," he wrote, "in the Courts, and must hope for some happy openings in causes of importance. The Chancellor, as you observe, has not done as I expected; *but why did I expect it? I am going to put*

* "Life of Eldon," vol. i. p. 130.
† " H." in the *Gentleman's Magazine* for 1803.

him to the test. Could I be satisfied with being Baron of Auchinleck, with a good income for a gentleman in Scotland, I might, no doubt, be independent. But what can be done to deaden the ambition which has ever raged in my veins like a fever?"

He had now brought his children to London—a foolish step,—and the two boys were attending an academy in Soho; but there was no one to look after them, save a couple of Scotch servants. Mrs. Boswell soon after made a trial of London, but she found that it did not suit her, and returned home. He had taken a small house in Queen Ann's Street, at £50 a year, which yet would not accommodate his family. He was going to take chambers, thus adding afresh to his expenses. His hopes were now, however, all in political influence. At this time he had adopted the Utopian scheme of sitting in Parliament, for his own county. There was likelihood of an immediate dissolution, and he began to canvass. In this task he was encouraged by a little local compliment. "At our last general Quarter-Sessions I was appointed Chairman, or Præses, as we call it. I proposed and carried an Address to the Prince of Wales, which I had prepared, expressing a grateful sense of his public conduct with regard to the Regency. . . . I am carrying it up, to be presented by the Earl of Eglintoun, accompanied by such Justices of us as may be in London. This will add something to my *conspicu-ousness.* Will that word do? As to Pitt, he is an insolent fellow, but so able, that upon the whole I must support him against the *Coalition;* but I will work him, for he has behaved very ill to me. Can he wonder at my wishing for preferment, when men of the first family and fortune in England struggle for it? We shall see; meantime the attempt rouses my spirits. What a state is my present !—full of ambition and projects to attain wealth and eminence, yet embarrassed in my circumstances, and depressed with family distress, which at times makes everything in life seem indifferent. I often repeat Johnson's lines, in his vanity of human wishes :—

> " ' Shall helpless man, in ignorance sedate,
> Roll darkling down the torrent of his fate ? ' "

" County of Ayr.

" *Extract from Minute of Quarter Sessions, dated May 5, 1789.*

" To His Royal Highness, George, Prince of Wales, etc., etc. The Humble address of His Majesty's Justices of the Peace for the County of Ayr, met at their general Quarter Sessions. Sir, We, His Majesty's Justices of the Peace for the County of Ayr, now assembled at our first General Quarter Sessions since the happy event of His Majesty's recovery from an alarming indisposition, beg leave to approach your Royal Highness with the most sincere sentiments of Respect and Attachment. From this County your Royal Highness derives the ancient and illustrious title of Earl of Carrick, and many of us hold our lands of the Prince and Steward of Scotland as our immediate feudal Lord. We therefore presume to consider ourselves as having the honour to be peculiarly connected with your Royal Highness.

" While your Royal Father, our beloved Sovereign, was afflicted by an awful visitation of Divine providence, We, Sir, were none of those who pressed forward to worship the appearance of a rising Sun. But now that Almighty God has been graciously pleased to restore His Majesty to perfect health and the full exercise of his Government, we humbly beg leave, from the purest

disinterested motives, to assure your Royal Highness of
the grateful sense which we entertain of your admirable
moderation and truly patriotic conduct.   At a time
when there was not wanting men of different parties
who, in the rashness of their contest for their means of
power, ventured to utter opposite opinions which, if the
heir apparent of the crown had stood forth to resent or
to encourage, the consequences to a nation whose History abounds with civil commotions might have been
dreadfully fatal, your Royal Highness, with a dignified
wisdom and mildness which we never can forget, re-
frained from influencing the deliberations of Parliament.

   " And, Sir, when the result was to constitute a
Regency with just restrictions, as, however, thought
necessary in the calamitous and perplexing state of
public affairs, could not but be ungracious to a noble,
and irksome to an active spirit, your Royal Highness
generously accepted of it, that at least the form of our
most excellent Monarchy might be preserved.   By this
earnest of your regard for the Constitution your Royal
Highness has endeared yourself to all its real friends.
Permit us, Sir, to congratulate your Royal Highness on
the King's Convalescence, by which your Royal Highness
is relieved from a very embarrassing situation, and, as
the earnest concern of His Majesty's subjects during his
illness and fervent rejoicing upon his recovery must have
demonstrated to your Royal Highness, beyond the false
suggestions of frivolous, dissipated, or perverted minds,
what are the qualities by which a Sovereign secures
the reverence and love of a great, free, and enlightened
people, may your Royal Highness steadily observe and
faithfully imitate the great and good example of His
Majesty, and may Heaven grant your Royal Highness
long life and all happiness.   Signed in our presence

and by our appointment at Ayr, the fifth day of May, 1789. Signed, JAMES BOSWELL, P." *

Mr. Boswell fancied he was very "happy" in the wording of this rather ambiguous document, which, however, reflects his discontent at his treatment by Pitt. His complimenting the Prince on his behaviour, after the notorious rapacity he displayed through the whole episode, was certainly as imprudent as it was unneces- sary. It must also have been distasteful to his patron, who was a staunch adherent of Mr. Pitt's. He wrote rather triumphantly to his friends, that the Prince had received the address most graciously; above all, that —" *I am to be presented.*" He accordingly waited to receive an intimation to come to court, but was obliged to depart without it. He was, however, comforted and gratified at receiving a message from the Prince that " he was sorry that Mr. Boswell had been obliged to leave town without waiting on him."

It will be recollected with what importunate eager- ness he had sought to force himself on the first Mr. Pitt's notice; but he was now to exhibit himself with greater absurdity in his efforts to attract the favour of the great minister's son.

It is often a difficult and perplexing question, when we find follies and absurdities mingled in equal propor- tions, to decide which is the true "note" of the character, though the accepted judgment is that where there is wisdom and folly in equal parts the former is held to be the stronger element, and determines the character. It may be said that the sketches given by Miss Burney, by the Irish Dr. Campbell, and by Boswell of himself, certainly exhibit him as a rather ridiculous person.

* This I owe to the courtesy of the secretary of the Grampian Club.

But it was in scenes of conviviality, when surrounded by friends, the glasses and bottles before him, that he seemed to feel that he was most brilliant, and, indeed, at his best. Then "it was all Puff, puff!" and he gave vent to all sorts of ludicrous extravagance. It is Elia who gives warning to beware of the seductive moment when the feelings begin to glow at the sight of the cheerful "materials" spread upon the table; and here the weak resolution of our hero could make little resistance.

He was fond of attending "banquets and city dinners;" and, as he told his friend Taylor, later editor of the *Sun*, "I must keep in with those men." Taylor fancied, and justly, that the reason was that he might have the chance of becoming one of the city counsel, or of attaining some high city honour, "not without the attendant advantage of the good fare connected with such offices." A highly grotesque and amusing scene of this kind has been dramatically described by this gentleman in his lively "Records." Boswell was plunged in grief at the loss of his wife, which had recently occurred, and, perhaps to dissipate it, was induced to attend a Lord Mayor's dinner. "I remember," says Taylor, "dining with him at Guildhall in 1785, when Alderman Boydell gave his grand civic festival on being raised to the mayoralty. Mr. Pitt honoured the table on that occasion with his presence, and, when the company removed to a room, in a short time Mr. Boswell contrived to be asked to favour the company with a song. He declared his readiness to comply, but first delivered a short preface, in which he observed that it had been his good fortune to be introduced to several of the potentates and most of the great characters of Europe, but with all his endeavours he had never been successful in obtaining an introduction to a gentleman who was an honour to his country, and whose talents he held in the highest esteem and admiration. It was evident to all the company that Mr. Boswell alluded to Mr. Pitt, who sat with all the dignified silence of a marble statue, though, indeed, in such a situation he could not but take the reference to himself. Mr. Boswell then sang a song of his own composition, which was a parody on Dibdin's 'Sweet little cherub,' under the title of 'A Grocer of London,' which rendered the reference to Mr. Pitt too evident to be mistaken, as the great minister was then a member of the Grocers' Company. This song Mr. Boswell, partly volunteering and partly pressed by the company, *sang at least six times,* insomuch that Mr. Pitt was obliged to relax from his gravity, and join in the general laugh at the oddity of Mr. Boswell's character. Boswell and I came away together, both in so convivial a mood that we roared out all the way 'The Grocer of London,' till we reached Hatton Garden, where I then resided, to the annoyance of many watchmen whom we roused from their peaceful slumbers, without, however, being taken into custody for disturbing their repose. In the course of the evening Mr. Boswell and I happened to differ about the meaning of a word. I met him the next day about twelve o'clock near St. Dunstan's church, as fresh as a rose. He recollected our dispute, and took me into a bookseller's shop to refer to Johnson's Dictionary, but which of us was right I cannot now recollect."

This ludicrous exhibition was much talked of and laughed at. To heighten the absurdity, his Liberal friends affected to be shocked at his want of principle, in singing praises of the " Grocer," whom he had been heard to abuse. They were enchanted to find him rise to the bait, and thus vindicate himself :—

"Pray let them know that I am vain of a hasty composition which has procured me large draughts of the popular applause in which I delight. Let me add that there was certainly no servility on my part, for I publicly declared in Guildhall, between the encores, 'that this same grocer had treated me arrogantly and ungratefully, but that, from his great merit as a minister, I was compelled to support him.'

"The time will come when I shall have a riper opportunity to show, that in one instance, at least, the man has wanted wisdom."

All this might have passed and been forgotten as a convivial escapade, but poor Bozzy did not dream that his exhibition was to find a place in one of the most popular and satirical poems of the time. Much as Byron gave fame to the poet of the Literary Fund, at the opening of "English Bards," so the lively author of the "Bœviad" led off his rhymes with an account of this incident.

"Though Boswell of a song and supper vain."

"And who has not heard of James Boswell, Esq.? All the world knows, for all the world has it under his own hand, that he composed a ballad in honour of Mr. Pitt, with very little assistance from Mr. Trusler, and still less from Mr. Dibden; which he produced to the utter confusion of the Foxites, and many at the Lord Mayor's table. This important 'state paper' I have not been able to procure, but the terror and dismay it occasioned amongst the enemy, with a variety of other circumstances highly necessary to be known, may be gathered from his letter." *   The satirist, however, recalls him with regret, exclaiming, "Poor Bozzy!" The scene

* This song, with other papers of Boswell, was, I recollect, sold at an auction some years ago, when I had an opportunity of reading it. It was bought, I believe, by the late Lord Houghton.

expresses admirably that curious mixture which makes up Boswell's character : his maudlin state and joviality, his vanity, and credulous belief that he was actually recommending himself to a patron, and securing his favour, by these clumsy forms of compliment, whereas he was only making himself ridiculous ; and the contemptuous encouragement of his friends who led him on to thus exhibit himself. And we feel, all the time, as they did —that here was a " good fellow," after all, who accepted their ridicule in good part. Who could suppose that the laborious and judicious author of a work so full of acute and sagacious remarks, with such tact in the composition, could have taken such a mode of recommending himself to a minister's notice and patronage! Yet it is evident that he thought he was making the deepest impression. It is plain, however, whatever were his chances, that this exhibition must have finished him for ever with Mr. Pitt.

His friend Taylor gives him this pleasant character : " It is no wonder that Mr. Boswell was universally well received. He was full of anecdote, well acquainted with the most distinguished characters, good-humoured, and ready at repartee. There was a kind of jovial bluntness in his manner, which threw off all restraint even with strangers, and immediately kindled a social familiarity." The fatal partiality for liquor, no doubt, disturbed the balance of these agreeable qualities, and turned his genuine good nature into a maudlin benevolence.*

* Burns, in one of his songs, alludes to him rather contemptuously—" gab-like Boswell."

CHAPTER XXVI.

CONVERSATION, WIT, AND "JEUX D'ESPRIT."

IT will have been seen from many passages scattered through "the Life," that the author had a pleasant, careless wit of his own, and loved to take his share in the lively conversation of the hour. We might fairly speculate whether he might not have found an irresistible temptation to heighten or magnify his own contribution, and allot to himself some of the more important sayings; but such an inquiry would be scarcely fair, as he so repeatedly insists on "the authenticity of my journal." He was always gay and lively, and one little trifle will show his agreeable power. "When Dr. Marlay was appointed Dean of Ferns, Burke remarked : ' I don't like the Deanery of Ferns, it sounds so like a barren title.' ' Dr. Heath should have it,' said I. Johnson laughed, and, condescending to trifle in the same mode of conceit, suggested 'Dr. Moss.'" Here Burke was decidedly ponderous, and without fun ; but the other puns were fairly good, and Boswell's certainly the best and readiest.

Mr. Boswell was often ready enough in reply, even to his great friend. Once the latter rather roughly said to him, on his complaining of headache after drinking with him, "Nay, sir, it was not the wine that made your head ache, but the *sense* I put into it." And Boswell replied, "What, sir ! And will sense make the head ache ?" But the doctor was not to be thus disposed of. "Yes, sir," (with a smile) "when it is not used to it." Boswell claims credit for recording this "pleasantry," as he justly calls it, even though at his own expense, and adds, happily, that Johnson having given him £1000 worth of conversation, was entitled to take back a guinea or so.

Often Boswell's utterances in these conversations are gay and lively; but when he invites attention to some sally of his own as specially brilliant, we usually find something flat and foolish. Thus he reminds Johnson of a gentleman who was first talkative from affectation, then silent from the same cause. A nicer discrimination of character was Mrs. Cholmondeley's : "I shall be celebrated as the liveliest man in every company, and then all at once, 'Oh, it is much more respectable to be grave and look wise.' But Boswell must develop." "He has reversed the Pythagorean discipline by being first talkative and then silent. He reverses the course of nature too : he was first the gay butterfly, and then the creeping worm." "Johnson laughed long and loud," he says, "at this expansion and illustration." Nothing could be more ponderous.

It is amusing to find that our author regularly "booked" his own good things, or what he fancied were good. Some of these are respectable. Of a man who exaggerated his stories more and more every time he repeated them, he said that "he *blew* a story to any size, as a man blows figures in a glass-house." Miss Leslie took off a necklace he was admiring, to show it to him, and he said, "It is pretty, even when it is off." Parties of pleasure he had no taste for, but, once engaged, he was like a dog : "I never go into the water of my own accord, but throw me in and I swim well."

The following is agreeably expressed : "There are a variety of little circumstances in life which, like pins in a lady's dress, are necessary for keeping it together, and giving it neatness and elegance."

But a speech which he made when he was on his travels, would have delighted some of his malicious friends : "Boswell said that a dull fool was nothing, as he never showed himself. The great thing, said he, is to have your fool well furnished with animal spirits and conceit, and he'll display to you a rich fund of risibility. He said this at a certain court in Germany."

"Talking of myself to a Corsican priest, the Abbé Cotti, and regretting that the King had not promoted me, I said, ' *Monsieur, il ne manque que la base : je suis déjà la statue.*' " On another occasion, he was so carried away as to make this boast : "Boswell compared himself to the ancient Corinthian brass. 'I am,' said he, 'a composition of an infinite variety of ingredients. I have been formed by a vast number of scenes of the most different natures, and I question if any uniform education *could have produced a character so agreeable.*' " It was speeches such as these that amused his friends, and drew on him many a rude, rough stroke, which he impartially sets down.

At times Boswell could be truly banal, and his sad attempts at puns and wit must have invited ridicule. When he was told that Goldsmith used to earn his travelling expenses abroad by disputing at the Universities, "Well," said Boswell, "that was, indeed, *disputing* his *passage* through Europe." Some one was speaking of a certain general. "Sir," said Boswell, "the gentleman is a general, and I do not choose to enter into particulars."

"Fordyce was much scandalized at a French barber

who shaved him in Paris, and, having caught a fly, call it *cette machine là.* 'Why,' said Boswell, 'in England we call a machine a fly, why may not the French call a fly a machine?'"

A poor minister had his horse seized on some process, it was, however, restored to him. "There was no kindness in it," says Boswell, "for you know the proverb, 'Set a beggar on horseback, etc.'" "Mr. Crosbie was the member of several clubs. I said to him, 'Crosbie, you are quite a club sawyer.'"

Complaining that he had so good a memory for trifles, it prevented his recollecting things of consequence; "My head," said he, "is like a tavern in which a club of confirmed drinkers have taken up the room that might have been filled with lords who drink Burgundy."

But the following is good :—"Sons are truly part of a family; daughters go into other families. Sons are the furniture of your house; daughters are furniture in your house only for sale. Such of them as are well looked are like pictures in the catalogue of the exhibition, those marked thus are for sale. (Or thus, daughters are like certain pictures in the exhibition, those marked thus, &c.)"

So, when he said that the extracts given in a review of a book were often better than the book : "It is like collops well seasoned and served with a good sauce ; and which are better eating than the sirloin or rump from which they are cut."

"Boswell, who had a good deal of whim, used not only to form wild projects in his imagination, but would sometimes reduce them to practice. In his calm hours he said, with great good humour, 'There have been many people who built castles in the air, but I believe I am the first that ever attempted to live in them.'"

"A gentleman was one day making that common serious reflection, 'Time runs.' 'Very well,' replied Boswell, 'let it run, then, for I am sure I shall never try to pursue it.'"

These specimens are not of the highest merit. He was less successful in his "Pun-sauce."

"As a playful instance of the proverb, I said, 'Every man has his price. Lord Shelburne has his price [meaning Dr. Price], whom I love and call *Pretium affectionis.*' (Monday, 18th April, 1785, at Dr. Brock-lesby's.)" This the author must have thought first-rate, from the minuteness of the entries of locality, etc. The next is supremely flat. "Boswell and John Home met with a man in their walk one morning, who said that he was a hundred and three. 'What a stupid fellow,' said Boswell, 'must that be who has lived so long!'"

"A modern man of taste found fault with the avenues at Auchinleck, and said he wished to see stragling trees. 'I wish,' said Boswell, 'I could see stragling fools in this world.'" "The conversation having turned on Andrew Stuart's artful defence of the treacherous conduct of his brother to Lord Pigot, I said, 'He has laid on a thick colouring upon his brother's character. It would not clean; he has died (*sic*) it'" (London, 23rd April, 1779)." "Cullen, the mimick, was excessively ugly, having most horrible teeth, and, upon the whole, a physiognomy worse than Wilkes's. One morning, when he was grinning and pleading a cause, I stood by and observed, 'Whom is Cullen taking off? He is taking off the devil.'"

Again: "Boswell was talking away one evening in St. James's Park with much vanity. Said his friend Temple, 'We have heard of many kinds of hobby-horses, but, Boswell, you ride upon yourself.'" And, on another occasion, " having shown some of his compositions to Lord Kames with the remark that they were were a little dull : ' Yes, yes,' cried Lord Kames, ' *aliquando dormitat Homerus* ' (Homer sometimes nods). Boswell being too much elated with this, my lord added, ' Indeed, sir, it is the only chance you had of resembling Homer.' " This specimen shows that Lord Kames had a " pretty wit of his own." *

Boswell also conceived that he had a particular gift for " throwing off" light epigrams in verse. These we read with amazement, after vainly seeking the point and wondering how they could have been the work of the same being who wrote that delightfully humorous scene when Johnson was seduced into dining with Wilkes. A good specimen, which he appeared to regard with special satisfaction, were some lines on the statue of Charles II. in the Parliament Close, " which some years ago the Provost of the city, from a strange Gothic fancy, had laid over with a thick coat of white paint to make it look white and new. This occasioned the following :—

> " Well done, my Lord, with noble taste,
>   You've made Charles gay as five and twenty.
> We may be scarce of gold and corn,
>   But sure there's lead and gold in plenty.
> Yet for a public work like this
>   I would have had some famous artist,
> Though I had made each mark a pound
>   I would have had the very smartest.

* All these sayings were carefully registered in the commonplace book which the late Lord Houghton allowed to be published. Many years before, he had issued a selection in the "Philobiblon Miscellany," which also included a "folium reservatum" which contained a number of stories in the coarse style of Boswell's day. I may add here my little tribute to this genial, accomplished nobleman, who was glad to place at your service his own knowledge, as well as his stores of papers and letters. He was, perhaps, the last of the old cultured school of literary noblemen.

" Why not bring Allan Ramsay down
    From stately coronet and cushion ?
For he can paint a living king
    And knows the English constitution.
The milk-white steed is well enough,
    But why thus daub the man all over,
And to the swarthy Stuart give
    The cream complexion of Hanover ?

" This statue never gave offence,
    But now, as you've been pleased to make it,
The ladies all will run away,
    Lest they behold a man stark naked,
Stay fair, dissembling cowards ! Stay !
He'll do no harm, you may go near him,
I'll tell you, e'en when flesh and blood
    Some of your grand dames did not fear him."

On another occasion he was joined by his friend
Maclaurin, in some satirical verses on the judges :—

"COURT OF SESSION GARLAND.

" The bill charged on was payable at sight,
    And decree was craved by Alexander Wight ;
But because it bore a penalty in case of failrie,
    It therefore was null, contended Willie Baillie.

" The Ordinary not choosing to judge it at random,
    Did with the minutes make *avizandum ;*
And as the pleadings were vague and windy,
    His Lordship ordered memorials *sine inde.*

" We, setting a stout heart to a stay brae,
    Took into the cause Mr. David Rae ;
Lord Auchinleck, however, repelled our defence,
    And over and above decreed for expense." Etc.

His amatory effusions were of rather a ponderous
sort ; witness the following :—

" ON OBSERVING A LOCK OF MISS B-D-N'S HAIR SEPARATED FROM
HER HEAD-DRESS AND HANGING TOWARDS THE AUTHOR.

" *By James Boswell, Esq.*

" Wild Furies with dishevelled locks are drawn,
    And rustic lassies romping on the lawn ;
But, sweet Eliza, gentle as thou'rt fair,
    Strange that all disordered is thy hair !

> " Sure it has been with calm composure drest,
>   Yet one recreant lock avoids the rest.
>   No more—for I perceive with conscious pride
>   This lovely lock inclining to my side.
>   When such kind partiality I see,
>   Oft may it wander if it strays to me ! "

No author, indeed, supplied so much amusement to the public by fantastic freaks and extravagances, and which he took immense pains to have propagated. Unfortunately, he imagined he had a gift for convivial composition, and indulged in this taste till he died. This same hopeless insensibility and inadmission of the fact that he was making himself ridiculous is more conspicuously shown in this weakness than in any other. A jovial Dr. Lettsom, a man of some science, who used to receive his friends at Grovehill, his villa at Camberwell, where what are vulgarly called "high jinks"— games at bowls, gymnastics, enjoyable days followed by toping nights, went forward.   Hither came various cheerful doctors, some *littérateurs* and publishers, and the ever-convivial Boswell, who, in his relish of these " days and nights of the Gods," wrote a song, which by *banalité*, the unconscious malapropos of the topics, and the exquisite air of sheer nonsense affecting wit, bears fatal testimony to Bozzy's gifts. He was, however, immensely pleased with it.

The author, in his complacency, declared that " he thinks his good friend Dr. Lettsom is in it painted with truth.   It goes admirably to the tune of ' The First Time at the Looking-Glass ' in ' The Beggars' Opera. ' "

" HORATIAN ODE TO CHARLES DILLY.

> " My cordial friend, still prompt to lend
>   Your cash when I have need on't,
>   We both must bear our load of care,
>   At least we talk and read on't.

" Yet are we gay, in every way,
　　Not minding where the joke lies,
On Saturday at bowls we play,
　　At Camberwell, with Coakley.

" Methinks you'll laugh, to hear but half
　　The name of Dr. LETTSOM ;
From him of good,—talk—liquors—food—
　　His guests will always get some.

" And guests has he, in ev'ry degree
　　Of decent estimation :
His liberal mind holds all mankind
　　As an extended nation.

" O'er LETTSOM's cheer we've met a Peer,
　　A Peer—no less than Lansdown :
Of whom each dull and envious cull
　　Absurdly cries, The Man's down.

" Down do they say ?　How then, I pray,
　　His king and country prize him?
Through the whole world known, his peace alone
　　Is sure t' immortalize him.

" LETTSOM we view, a Quaker true,
　　'Tis clear he's so in one sense.
His spirit strong and ever young
　　Refutes pert *Priestley's* nonsense.

" In fossils he is deep we see,
　　Nor knows beasts, fishes ill :
With plants not few, some from Pellew,
　　And monstrous *Mangel Wurzel.*

" West India bred, warm heart, cool head,
　　The City's first physician,
By schemes humane, Want, Sickness, Pain,
　　To aid is his ambition.

" From terrace high he feasts his eye
　　When practice grants a furlough ;
And while it roves o'er Dulwich groves,
　　Looks down—ev'n upon THURLOW." *

　* This song Mr. Nicholls often heard Bozzy troll, with others,
" when exhilarated by moderate potations from a bowl of either
delicious syllabub or generous tortola."

The genial and convival Lettsom, living in such jollity, soon got into difficulties, and was "sold up," as it is called.

This taste for song-writing brings Boswell pleasantly into communication with Goldsmith, there being a favourite song of the poet's which Mr. Boswell used to chaunt upon occasion.*

Here was a "stinging" epigram, as he no doubt fancied it :—

* In a letter to the *London Magazine*, he gives a little history of Goldsmith's pretty song and his own share in its preservation :—

"Sir,—I send you a small production of the late Dr. *Goldsmith*, which has never been published, and which might perhaps have been totally lost had I not secured it. He intended it as a song in the character of Miss *Hardcastle*, in his admirable comedy, *She Stoops to Conquer*; but it was left out, as Mrs. *Bulkeley* who played the part did not sing. He sung it himself in private companies very agreeably. The tune is a pretty Irish air, called *The Humours of Balamagairy*, to which, he told me, he found it very difficult to adapt words; but he has succeeded happily in these few lines. As I could sing the tune, and was fond of them, he was so good as to give me them about a year ago, just as I was leaving London, and bidding him adieu for that season, little apprehending that it was a last farewell. I preserve this little relick in his own hand-writing with an affectionate care. I am, Sir, your humble Servant, JAMES BOSWELL.

"SONG *by Dr.* GOLDSMITH.

" 'Ah me! when shall I marry me?
　Lovers are plenty; but fail to relieve me.
　He, fond youth, that could carry me,
　Offers to love, but means to deceive me.

" 'But I will rally and combat the ruiner :
　Not a look, not a smile, shall my passion discover.
　She that gives all to the false one pursuing her,
　Makes but a penitent, loses a lover.' "

In his praise of this trifle there is a true appreciation which speaks well for Boswell's character.

"EPIGRAM ON THE PUSILLANIMOUS CONDUCT OF THE FRENCH AT TOURNAY.

" By Mr. James Boswell.

" While loyal honour warmed a Frenchman's breast,
    The field of battle was a glorious test;
Nobly ambitious for his King to fight,
    To die or conquer was a *soldier's* right.
A strange reverse the *Democrats* display,
    And prove the right of man to *run away.*"

CHAPTER XXVII.

1789.

In the March of 1789, we find him in town, enjoying himself a good deal, though disturbed by unfavourable accounts of his wife's health. He showed himself ingenious in devising excuses for remaining. It was a remedy for his low spirits. "As London is the best place when one is happy, it is equally so when one is the reverse: for the power of being at once wrapped up in an undisturbed privacy, by not being personally known, and having an influx of ideas by being in the midst of multitudes, cannot fail to dissipate many a cloud which would thicken and augment, and press upon the spirits, in the country." And, following out this acceptable theory, he went out to see the illuminations, with his friend Paoli.

He was, however, induced to linger on, in the hope of receiving better news; or was, perhaps, unwilling to tear himself away from town dissipations, on what might prove to be a false alarm. He was also now engrossed with his great work: he protested that he could not leave London "without stopping what has been delayed too long, and taking myself out of the great wheel of the Metropolis," in which he hoped in time to draw a prize. He was still in low spirits; "I indeed must acknowledge that, owing to the melancholy which ever lurks about me, I am too dissipated and drink too much

wine. These circumstances I must restrain as well as
I can." We thus find him much perplexed and distracted between duty and pleasure, in a very characteristic way : "Supposing that the disease should increase,
and, as sometimes happens, should take a rapid course,
she may be carried off while I am four hundred miles
from her. The alternative is dreadful, and though she,
with admirable generosity, bids me not be in a haste to
leave London (knowing my extreme fondness for it), I
should have a heart hard as a stone were I to remain
here ; and should the fatal event happen in my absence,
I should have a just upbraiding gloom upon my mind
for the rest of my life. I have therefore resolved to set
out early, the day after to-morrow, and take Veronica
with me."

He accordingly left London in April, and returned
to Auchinleck, to the bedside of his dying wife. The
physicians told him there was little hope of her recovery.
She was in fact wasting away. He could only indulge
in maudlin regrets over his past neglect, and console
himself in his own way : "With grief continually at
my heart," he wrote in November, "I have been
endeavouring to seek relief in dissipation and in wine,
so that my life for some time past has been unworthy
of myself, of you, and of all that is valuable in my
character and connections." For five weeks he reluctantly endured his banishment ; when, in spite of all
his poignant self-reproaches, he contrived an excuse for
getting away. His account of this result, and the way
in which he arrived at it, is truly "characteristical,"
and the jumble of affection, self-interest, and self-
indulgence makes up an odd picture. He begins : "No
man ever had a higher esteem or a warmer love for a
wife than I have for her. You will recollect, my Temple,

how our marriage was the result of an attachment truly romantic; yet how painful is it to me to recollect a thousand instances of inconsistent conduct. I can justify my removing to the great sphere of England, upon a principle of laudable ambition; but the frequent scenes of what I must call dissolute conduct are inexcusable; and often and often, when she was very ill, in London have 1 been indulging in festivity with Sir Joshua Reynolds, Courtenay, Malone, etc., etc., etc., and have come home late and disturbed her repose. Nay, when I was last at Auchinleck, on purpose to soothe and console her, I repeatedly went from home; and both on those occasions, and when neighbours visited me, drank a great deal too much wine. On Saturday last, dining at a gentleman's house, where I was visiting for the first time, and was eager to obtain political influence, I drank so freely, that, riding home in the dark without a servant, I fell from my horse and bruised my shoulder severely. Next morning I had it examined by a surgeon, who found no fracture or dislocation, but blooded me largely to prevent inflammation. While I was thus confined to bed, came a letter from Colonel Lowther, one of Lord Lonsdale's Members, informing me that his Lordship would set out for London as soon as I arrived at Lowther, and would be glad to have my company in the carriage with him. I expected such a letter, because I was engaged to appear as Recorder of Carlisle, for the Corporation, in a Cause brought against us in the King's Bench, which I knew was to come on this month or early in June. But I was in a great dilemma what to do. I was afraid I should not be able to travel, and to leave my wife in such a state was severe. She, with a spirit which I cannot enough admire, animated me to set out, which I accordingly did, resolved to return as

soon as the business was over, and bring our two sons
with me, to be some comfort to her, while she can at all
be sensible of it.   His Lordship's *way* is exceedingly
dilatory, so that we have not set out to-day as was proposed, and perhaps we may not go for a day or two
longer.   I philosophically resign myself to what may
happen ; this being (as Governor Penn, the American,
and one of his Members, and a sensible worthy fellow,
says) a school of its own kind.

"My shoulder is more uneasy, and there is now an
extended rheumatism through that arm, and part of the
breast next to it, which I feel acutely, while I cannot
put on and off my clothes without help.   But I will go
forward.   To be *zealous* is, with justice, a strong recommendation ; and such is the great Parliamentary influence, that, be the Minister who will, he may when he
pleases get almost anything for a friend.   I have no
right to expect that he will give me a seat in Parliament,
but I shall not be surprised if he does.   *Entre nous*, my
chance for representing my own County is very small."

From Lowther Castle, though his wife's condition
was not improving, he betook himself to London.
He had hardly been there a fortnight, when a letter
reached him from the doctor, announcing that she was
dying.   He at once set off, taking with him his two
sons.   He accomplished the journey in sixty-four hours,
but, on arriving, found that she had died four days before.
He could only bewail his own neglect in piteous terms.

Poor Boswell had indeed a feeling, affectionate heart :
and, after describing this tragic journey, he says : "But
the fatal stroke had taken place ere I set out.   It was
very strange we had no intelligence on the road, not
even in our own parish, not till my second daughter
came running out from the house and announced to us

the dismal event in a burst of tears." What followed is related pathetically enough. "She continued quite sensible till a few minutes before, when she began to doze calmly, and expired without any struggle" (She died on June 4, 1789). ". . . But alas! to see my excellent wife, and the mother of my children, and that most sensible and lively woman, lying cold and pale and insensible, was very shocking to me. I could hardly bring myself to agree that the body should be removed, for it was still a consolation to me to go and kneel by it and talk to my dear, dear Peggie." He was consoled by the state of the funeral, at which there were nineteen carriages, and many horsemen, with all the tenants walking. He himself read the service to his sons, and "was relieved by that ceremony a good deal;" and, on the Sunday following, his old tutor, Mr. Dun, delivered "*almost verbatim* a few sentences which I sent him as a character of her." *

In this bereavement, he turned for comfort to Lowther, the patron on whom all his hopes were fixed, and whom he had courted with such subserviency. In all his various writings we find many compliments, of a rather fulsome kind, to this great personage. We have seen in what an extravagant and even ridiculous strain he addressed him in his "Letter to the People of Scot-

---

* He nourished these tender recollections in a rather touching way. Johnson, on his wife's death, had prayed that he might have the benefit of her attentions and ministrations, whether exercised by appearance or dreams. On which Boswell tells us he had "a personal motive for presenting it, because it sanctions what I myself have always maintained and am fond to indulge." He then adds, "But I, whom it has pleased God to afflict in a similar manner, have certain experience of benignant communications by dreams." This unaffected confession has more foundation than might be supposed: and many can testify to the vividness of such visions, which bring up the features and tones of voice of the departed, in a way that the waking memory fails to present.

land ;" and when he published his " Tour," he broke
out into an awkward mixture of blame and compliment.
He represents Johnson as saying, "'We have had few
misers in England.' BOSWELL. 'There was Lowther.'
JOHNSON. 'Why, sir, Lowther, by keeping his money,
had the command of the county, which the family has
now lost, by spending it.'"

His literary conscience would not let him suppress
this indiscreet speech, so he added a mollifying note :
" I do not know what was at this time the state of the
parliamentary interest of the ancient family of Lowther ;
a family before the Conquest ; but all the nation knows
it to be very extensive at present. A due mixture
of severity and kindness, economy and munificence,
characterises its present Representative." With much
assiduity he continued to follow this personage ; but all
he obtained was a trifling office—an earnest, as he hoped,
of more substantial promotion. He had particularly
set his thoughts on one of his patron's boroughs, and a
sort of promise, as he fancied, had been given that he
should be elected for one of these. For years he was
beguiled with this hope ; but his patron soon discovered
that poor " Bozzy " in such a position could be of little
use to him, or perhaps only bring ridicule. Boswell's
own indiscretion, too, had the effect of checking his
advance, for we find him, at times, on the point of
writing in opposition to his patron's views. He seems
to have endured much during this time of servitude, for
Lord Lonsdale appears to have been of a rough, coarse
temper, and took care often to remind his dependant of
his position, and of what he had done for him. He
would send for him from Scotland to Carlisle, requiring
his assistance to travel with him, or to wait on him ;
and when he invited him on a visit, he would permit

his friends to make a butt of his guest, or even to play practical jokes on him. It is melancholy to have to admit that it was his own voluntary sacrifice of self-respect and dignity that exposed him to such treatment from those whom he believed to be his admirers and friends. But everything goes down before the laughing contempt which attends the helpless toper—that is, the unhappy being who cannot measure or restrain himself in the presence of drink.

In August, 1789, he was, as we have seen, sunk in grief at the loss of his wife, also at the helpless position in which he found himself; he was, moreover, dreadfully embarrassed, and without assistance to control or guide his large family. The letter which, in this distressed condition of things, he wrote to his old friend Temple offers a truly piteous and genuine picture of grotesquely mingled feelings : its natural and unsuspecting simplicity is also remarkable.

"Almighty and most merciful Father ! let me never impiously repine. May I be enabled by thy grace *really* to submit myself entirely to thy divine Will. Yet, as ' Jesus wept' for the death of Lazarus, I hope my tears at this time are excused. . . .

"How much do I regret that I have not applied myself more to learning. . . . The woeful circumstance of such a state of mind as I now experience is that it *rejects* consolation ; it feels an indulgence in its own wretchedness. O my friend, what would I give for one of those years with my dearest cousin, friend and wife, which are past ! May I not flatter myself with a dawn of hope that I shall be permitted to see her again, aye and to be with her, not to be separated ! What can one think ? what can one do in so wretched a state as this ? She used on all occasions to be my comforter ;

she, methinks, could now suggest rational thoughts to me ; but where is she ?   O my Temple, I am miserable. It is astonishing what force I have put upon myself since her death, *how I have entertained* company, etc., etc. ; but all this makes me worse.   Is it possible that I yet can have any enjoyment in this state of being ? My kindest compliments to all your family.   Value Mrs. Temple warmly while you have her."

In this sad condition he thought he would seek comfort in the jovialities of the circuit, and the society of his patron.   The visit was only productive of a truly farcical incident.   " I left Auchinleck," he writes, " with intention to join the Northern Circuit at Carlisle. I went first to Lowther, the great man having invited me by a letter, to come to him as soon as I should find it convenient.   My mind was so sore from my late severe losses, that *I shrunk from the rough scenes of the roaring, bantering society of lawyers.*   I consulted Lord Lonsdale, who thought I might stay away, as I had a very good excuse.   I accordingly remained at Lowther. Still I was in sad distress, though I forced an appearance of doing wonderfully well."   He describes to his friend the way in which he was treated at Lowther Castle :—

" A strange accident happened : the house at Lowther was so crowded, that I and two other gentlemen were laid in one room.   On Thursday morning my wig was missing ; a strict search was made, all in vain.   I was obliged to go all day in my nightcap, and absent myself from a party of ladies and gentlemen, who went and dined with the Earl on the banks of the lake—a piece of amusement which I was glad to shun, as well as a dance which they had at night.   But I was in a ludicrous situation.   I suspected a wanton trick, which some people think witty; but I thought it very ill-timed to one in my situation. Next morning the Earl and a Colonel, who I thought might have concealed my wig, declared to me upon honour they did not know where it was; and the conjecture was that a clergymen who was in the room with me, and had packed up his portmanteau in a great hurry to set out early in the morning early, might have put it up among his things. *This is very improbable; but I could not long remain an object of laughter*, so I went twenty-five miles to Carlisle on Friday, and luckily got a wig there fitted for me in a few hours. Yesterday I came to this Seat of the Bishop, where I find myself somewhat easier, *there being more quietness.* His Lordship's chaplain read prayers, and preached to us in his chapel to-day. The scene is fine externally, and hospitable and quiet within; but alas! my grief preys upon me night and day. I am amazed when I look back. Though I often and often dreaded this loss, I had no conception how distressing it would be. May God have mercy upon me! I am quite restless and feeble and desponding. I return to Lowther to-morrow for two days, *to show that I am not at all in a pet*, and then I am to return to Auchinleck for a little time.

"Such is my melancholy frame at present, that I waver as to all my plans. I have an avidity for death; I eagerly wish to be laid by my dear wife; years of life seem insupportable. I dread that Eton may make my son expensive and vicious, and it seems hard to send my little daughter two hundred miles beyond London. Every prospect that I turn my mind's eye upon is dreary. Why should I struggle? I certainly am constitutionally unfit for any employment. The Law life in Scotland, *amongst vulgar familiarity*, would now

quite destroy me. I am not able to acquire the Law of
England.   To be in Parliament, unless as an independent member, would gall my spirit; to live in the
country would either harass me by forced exertions, or
sink me into a gloomy stupor.   Let me not think at
present, far less *resolve.*"

In due time the wig was recovered and restored to
him—" found," as his friends chose to describe it; but no
inquiries could discover the mystery of its disappear-
ance; no one being willing, of course, to acknowledge
their share in the "joke."   The mixture of emotion
and grief over a lost wife and a lost wig, is highly
characteristic.

Though he found " that he had but a small party
in Ayrshire, he was determined to keep up a can-
didateship, *as giving consequence.*"   In the following
year he again went down to prosecute his candidature,
but only to have " an unhappy time. . . . O my friend,
this is sad!" is his piteous outburst.   Before this,
however, he had comforted himself with a junketing
to Portsmouth, where he witnessed a review of the fleet.
"I had a most enjoyable time, spending a day and
a night on board the brave Macbride's ship."   Captain
Macbride was his wife's cousin.

The situation in Ayr offered but the most meagre
chance of success.   Three powerful Thanes, Lords
Cassilis, Dumfries, and Glencairn had combined to set
up a candidate of their own.   An independent candidate, one Mr. Whitefood, had also started; and Boswell
had an expectation that he might "slip in."   "Thus the
parties are so poised that I shall have it in my power to
cast the balance; if they are so piqued that either will
rather give the seat to me than be beaten by the other.
Thus I stand, and *I shall be firm.*"   Waxing enthusiastic

as he saw the prospect, he declared that—" should Lord Lonsdale give me a seat, *he will do well.*" As the Regency question was then in agitation, he was inclined to side with the Prince ; for, as he explained naïvely enough, " Pitt has behaved ill in his neglect of me." He was even about to publish a pamphlet on the Prince's side, when it suddenly occurred to him that it might not be acceptable to his patron, who was one of Pitt's supporters ; so he prudently determined to hold his hand. All these turns are highly characteristic.

It was easy to foretell the issue of this connection. The final breach which destroyed the hopes and made void the subserviency of years was a painful one, and is described by him in an admirably vivid way. It occurred in June, 1790, when he was leaving town to attend his patron to the north. He was beginning to tire of waiting. " Seeing me," he says, " by no means in a good humour "—what a trait is here of the arrogance of this " northern tyrant ! "—" he challenged it roughly, and said, ' I suppose you thought I was to bring you into Parliament. I never had any such in-intention.' " He then " expressed himself in a most degrading manner, before a *low man from Carlisle, and one of his menial servants.*" Stung by this coarse attack, poor Boswell turned on him. At this time, he said, the state of his low spirits made him almost " mad under such unexpected insults,"—" and, in my fretfulness, I used such expressions as irritated him almost to fury, so that he used and wrote such language towards me that I should have, according to the irrational laws of honour, been under the necessity of risking my life, had not an explanation taken place." No wonder he thought of this as a most unhappy day, and a most shocking encounter. The grotesque part of the incident

was that he was shut up in the carriage with his patron,
and had to travel with him under these highly awkward
conditions. The journey, as may be conceived, "was
barely tolerable," but when they got to Lancaster they
parted, "in a strange equivocal state," the patron being
"half irritated, half reconciled." Boswell, however,
felt that his behaviour would never be pardoned. As-
suming the airs of independence, he insisted on instantly
resigning his post; but the despot, with a certain
malignity, would not allow of this. As Boswell ruefully
describes it, "He insisted rigorously on my having
solicited the office ; and that I could not, without using
him ill, resign it, until the duties which were now
required of it were fulfilled, and without sufficient time
being given for the election of a successor. *Thus was I
dragged away, as wretched as a convict.*"

Now released from his servitude, his situation
became more pitiable still. "I am alone at an inn, in
wretched spirits, and ashamed and sunk, on account of
the disappointment of hopes, which led me to endure
such grievances. I deserve all that I suffer. I am
quite in a fever. Oh! my old and most intimate friend,
what a shocking state am I now reduced to! I entreat
of you, if you possibly can, to afford me some consola-
lation, and please do not divulge my mortifications. I
will now endeavour to appear indifferent, and, as I now
resign my Recordership, I shall gradually get rid of all
communication with *this brutal fellow.*" Could anything
be more genuine, so heart-rending as these sad jere-
miads ? Here, however, was an end to all his prospects
of promotion, seat in Parliament, and the rest.

CHAPTER XXVIII

His domestic situation was embarrassing. Apart from genuine feeling for the loss of his wife, it was brought home to him in a very inconvenient way. While she lived, as he now found out, " I had no occasion almost to think concerning my family : every particular was thought of by her, better than I could. I am the most helpless of human beings : I am in a state very much like that of one in despair." There were five children to be looked after and controlled, a function for which their erratic father felt himself incapable. His eldest son, who had begun to oppose him, "was at Eton, as discontented and miserable as if at the galleys." On his first visit to the college this pleasantly natural being was quite elated at his reception, which he described in his best style : " I go to Eton to-morrow with my eldest son. I was there last week to prepare matters, and to my agreeable surprise found myself highly considered there, was asked by Dr. Davies, the Head-master, to dine at the Fellows' table, and made a creditable figure. *I certainly have the art of making the most of what I have.* How should one who has had only a Scotch education be quite at home at Eton ? *I had my classical quotations very ready.*

"My second son is an extraordinary boy : he is much of his father (vanity of vanities). He is to be a barrister, and I am very desirous to train him properly. He is of a delicate constitution, but not unhealthy, and his spirit never fails him. He is still in the house with me ; indeed he is quite my companion, though only eleven in September. He goes in the day to the academy in Soho Square, kept by the Rev. Dr. Barrow, formerly of Queens', Oxford, a coarse north-countryman, but a very good scholar ; and there my boy is very well taught. After the holidays I am to take resolution and board my little James *somewhere*, for while under my roof he passes his time chiefly with my old housekeeper and my footman. What shall I do? Soho is a competently good place, there are few boys there but of an inferior rank ; in justice to a good master, should I remove my son ? The boy wishes much to go to Eton, because his brother is there ; I, on the other hand, think it better they should be separate, and wish to place him at Westminster. To that there is the objection of danger to his morals, which however is answered by the boys there not being worse than at other schools, and by the first people in the nation continuing to keep their sons there. The *éclat* of Westminster, I think, would be of service to him, and I have a great respect for Vincent, the present Head-master."

But what to do with his motherless daughters was even a greater difficulty. The eldest, Veronica, was placed with a lady in London, but he foresaw that she would not stay there long. The second, as he oddly put it, " must escape from school in a year." Another of his daughters was at Edinburgh, under the inspection of her grandmother, Lord Auchinleck's widow, who, Boswell is constrained to admit, " was exceedingly good to her."

" How much better," he then says, " is it that I am on decent terms with that lady ! "

Presently, he had forgotten all his sorrows, and, in the early part of the year 1790, the widower, now fifty years old, recurred to his old pursuit of heiress-hunting. In this way he hoped to repair his tottering fortunes. But here he was indulging in his usual sanguine dreams. It was, in fact, the same old Boswell that had courted Miss Blair.

" While in the North, I got such accounts of the lady of fortune, whose reputation you heard something of, that I was quite determined to make no advances. Whether I shall take any such step I doubt much. *The loss I have experienced is perpetually recurring* ; and, though there might be comforts in what you suggested, I fear there would be troubles." Nothing more was heard of this lady of the North. But in the following year he heard of another likely candidate, and, as usual, considered the thing as good as settled, even before he had seen her ! These objects of his choice were ladies of fortune. One of them he sought in the true spirit of the fortune-hunter. Alas for poor Peggie Montgomerie !

" I am to dine with Sir William Scott, the King's Advocate, at the Commons to-morrow, and shall have a serious consultation with him, as he has always encouraged me. It is to be a family party, where I am to meet Miss Bagnal (his lady's sister) who may probably have six or seven hundred a year. She is about seven and twenty, and he tells me lively and gay—a Ranelagh girl—but of excellent principles, insomuch that she reads prayers to the servants in her father's family every Sunday evening. ' Let me see such a woman,' cried I ; and accordingly I am to see her. She has refused young and fine gentlemen. ' Bravo,' cried I, ' we see then what her taste is.' Here then I am, my Temple, my flattering self! A scheme—an adventure seizes my fancy. Perhaps I may not like her; and what should I do with such a companion, unless she should really take a particular liking to me, which is surely not probable; and, as I am conscious of my distempered mind, could I *honestly* persuade her to unite her fate with mine? As to my daughters, did I see a rational prospect of so good a scheme, I should not neglect it on their account, though I should certainly be liberal to them."

" *You must know,*" he writes, "*I have had several matrimonial schemes of late.* I shall amuse you with them from Auchinleck. One was with Miss Miles, daughter of the late Dean of Exeter, a most agreeable woman ' d'un certain âge,' and with a fortune of £10,000; she has left town for the summer. It was no small circumstance that she said to me, ' Mr. Temple is a charming man'" As this scheme also proved fruitless, he became discouraged.

At this time he broke out into one of those unaccountable freaks or exhibitions—the result of some whim or humour, and which once more shows his lack of good common sense. He had conceived a vehement objection to the abolition of slavery, and had written a poem which, however, he hesitated to publish. It had the extraordinary title, "No Abolition of Slavery, or the Universal Empire of Love." Unable to resist his longings for publicity, he issued it in 1791. No copy is found in the libraries, nor have I ever seen one offered for sale, and it seems not unlikely that he suppressed it. Some fragments, however, are found in the various reviews, where the critics treated it with scant courtesy and contemptuous good-humour, declaring that an allusion to the "Ancient Baron of the Land"

" proves the author to be *aut Boswell aut* ——." But as all Boswell's writings have a certain personal cast, we come, at the close to some forty very coarse lines in praise of his reigning mistress, and which had no connection with the subject of the poem. Indeed, there must be some mystery connected with this little piece, for there is a rambling incoherence about it; and as it vehemently ridicules some political doctrines which were held by some of his patrons, it is likely enough to have been withdrawn.

> " Dolben would destroy
> *Both slavery and licentious joy.*
> Foe to all sorts of planters, he
> Will suffer neither bond nor free."

He then addresses Mr. Pitt :—

> " Accept fair praise, but while I live
> Your Regency I can't forgive.
> My Tory soul with anger swells
> When I the parcelled crown beheld,
> Prerogative put under hatches,
> A monarchy of shreds and patches.
> Thurlow, forbear thy awful frown ;
> I beg you may not look me down.
> My honest fervour do not scout ;
> I too, like thee, can be devout.
> O never let Majesty suppose
> The Prince's friends must be his foes ;
> There is not one among you all
> Whose sword is readier at his call.
> An ancient Baron of the land,
> I by my King shall ever stand ;
> But when it pleases Heav'n to shroud
> The royal Image in a cloud,
> That image in the heir I see."

Nor does he spare his friend Burke :—

> " BURKE, art THOU here too ? thou whose pen
> Can blast the fancied *rights of men ;*
> Pray, by what logic are those rights
> Allow'd to Blacks—deny'd to *Whites ?* "

Nothing could be more curious than the contrast between Boswell's figure, as displayed in his own pages, when he appears as the humble disciple of the master, seeking instruction, and gravely deploring the follies of other men, and the melancholy display of weaknesses now exhibited in his soiltary course. We always find, at least, good impulses, and a yearning for a better mode of life, which he had not strength to pursue. No creature was ever so pitiably helpless in regard to resolutions, and he seemed to have consoled himself with the placid theory that it was not he that was responsible, but his own fallible nature. Later this took the odd shape of a complete laxity in practice, neutralized by sound moral and even pious sentiments.

Bishop Butler, in a well-known passage on habits, has well explained the working of this fatal combination. Passive and active habits, he points out,—that is, sentiment and action,—are opposed or mutually destructive. Thus the indulgence in feelings of compassion or pity, unsupported by action, eventually destroys the exercise of charity; while indulgence in practical habits of charity equally destroys sentiment. Thus, charitable people appear insensible, and "sentimentalists" seem selfish. It is easy to apply this to the case of Boswell, whose indulgence in good impressions, without restraint on his actions, ended in destroying all effort at reform. There is nothing more melancholy than the tracing of this decay, and the failure, in morals and manners, of Johnson's favourite pupil. In this view, a further interest is found in his great and interesting life of Johnson, which, as I have before hinted, offers ingeniously disguised references to Boswell's own life. All through, Boswell felt the pricks of conscience, and the poignant sense of his own degradation. We can follow the little arts by which he pleaded, as it were, for himself, and put forward the weaknesses of his great friend in extenuation of his own weaknesses.

The picture drawn by a friend of the closing portion of his life is truly a melancholy one. The ordinary sensualist runs his course to the end with a stolid or reckless infatuation; but in the nature of Boswell there was implanted good instincts, and, it would seem, an ever-reproaching conscience.

" In the last years of his life, Boswell still continued to frequent the societies in which he had been wont to delight. But death carried away, one after another, many of his dearest companions. The fickle multitude of unattached acquaintance deserted him from time to time for newer faces and less familiar names. His joke, his song, his sprightly effusions of wit and wisdom, were ready, but did not appear to possess upon all occasions their wonted power of enlivening convivial joy. He found that fortune, professional connexions, great expence, and the power of promoting or thwarting people's personal interests, are necessary to give, even to the most polished and lively conversational talents, the power of pleasing always. His fits of dejection became more frequent, and of longer duration. Convivial society became continually more necessary to him, while his power of enchantment over it continued to decline. Even the excitement of deep drinking in an evening became often desirable to raise his spirits above melancholy depression. Disease, the consequence of long habits of convivial indulgence, prematurely broke the strength of his constitution. He died before he had yet advanced to the brink of old age, and left, assuredly, few men of worthier hearts or more obliging manners behind him.'

During Mrs. Boswell's illness Johnson prophetically warned him, " In losing her you *will lose your anchor,* and be tost without stability on the waves of life ;" on which Boswell, " *The truth of this has been proved by sad experience*"—a strange confession.

After these mortifications and failures, we are not surprised to find him indulging in a burst of pious sentiment. In July, 1790, he writes some wholesome sentiments to his friend: "Surely, my dear friend, there must be another world in which such beings as we are will have our misery compensated. But is not this a state of probation? and if it is, how awful is the consideration! I am struck with your question, 'Have you confidence in the Divine aid?' In truth I am sensible that I do not sufficiently ' *try* my ways' as the Psalmist says, and am ever almost inclined to think with you *that* my great *oracle Johnson did allow too much credit to good principles, without good practice.*" How characteristic is this laying the blame of his own " divarications " on Johnson! But nothing could be more unjust. Again and again had the sage warned him " to beware of impressions." Indeed, if there was a favourite doctrine of his, it was that a life of practical virtue was worth all the most pious sentiments in the world.

While he was thus pursuing various schemes, he was distracted by the embarrassments of his home. In a truly piteous letter, which is really full of tragedy, he is led on to bewail the failure of all his hopes. What to do with his children was still his embarrassment. "What is to become of them?" he asked. "I am utterly at a loss. They cannot live with satisfaction, or even propriety, in a house here with me, as I am very little at home, cannot afford to keep a carriage, and have nobody to take them out to visit, or to public places.

Undoubtedly, my having a house in Edinburgh would be best for them ; but, besides that my withdrawing thither would cut me off from all those chances which may, in time, raise me in life, I could not possibly endure Edinburgh now, unless I *were to have a Judge's place to bear me up;* and even then I should sigh deeply for the Metropolis. Malone advises me to find some respectable elderly lady, who, though well bred and well connected, has little fortune, and would be glad to be a companion and superintendent of them, from the consideration of being comfortably accommodated, and having £30 or £40 to buy clothes. But *my* daughters are not what girls of fifteen and sixteen commonly are ; they are exceedingly advanced for their years, and would not submit to such a woman, nor have I almost any authority over them. Is not this a sad situation ? I have no guess what will be done.

"I have given up my house, and taken good chambers in the Inner Temple, to have the appearance of a lawyer. *O Temple ! Temple ! is this realizing any of the towering hopes which have so often been the subject of our conversations and letters ?* Yet I live much with a great man, who, upon any day that his fancy shall be so inclined, may obtain for me an office which would make me independent. The state of my affairs is very disagreeable, but be not afraid for your £200, as you may depend upon its being repaid. My rent-roll is above £1,600 ; but, deducting annuities, interest of debts, and expenses absolutely necessary at Auchinleck, I have but about £850 to spend. I reckon my five children at £500 a year. You see what remains for myself. I am this year to make one trial of the Lord Chancellor. In short, I cast about everywhere. I do not see the smallest opening in Westminster Hall ; but I

like the scene, though I have attended only one day this
last Term, being eager to get my 'Life of Johnson'
finished. And the delusion that practice may come
at any time (which is certainly true) still possesses
me."

He could not refrain from putting on record in his
great work this naïve plea for his lack of success at the
Bar. "Now, at the distance of fifteen years since this
conversation passed, the observation which I have had
an opportunity of making in Westminster Hall has
convinced, the same certainty of success cannot now
be promised to the same display of merit. The reasons,
however, of the rapid rise of some, *and the disappointment of others equally respectable,* are such as it might
seem invidious to mention, and would require a larger
detail than would be proper for this work." The reasons
for the disappointment of one, at least, of the "respectable" persons, could be readily found in a neglect of
business, and a too great indulgence in social pleasures.
Boswell felt even more acutely the rise of some of his
competitors.

We should be inclined to suppose, with Dr. Johnson,
that Boswell's perpetual complaining of low spirits was
a sort of affectation, that they could be dispelled by
manly exertion of the will. It is clear, however, that
poor Boswell was all his life a victim to this hateful
malady, from which he fled to a remedy that only
inflamed the disease. Most dreadful was his state:
"I have for some weeks had the most woeful return of
melancholy, insomuch that I have not only had no relish
of anything, but a continual uneasiness, and all the prospect before me for the rest of life has seemed gloomy
and hopeless. The state of my affairs is exceedingly
embarrassed."

"Fling but a stone, the giant dies," was alas! not the remedy sought by Boswell. The cheerful glass—the pleasant night among gay friends, such was the remedy that for the time gave him relief. It will be noted in some of his letters the almost frantic eagerness with which he tried to collect companions of an agreeable kind to attend some dinner at a friend's house. So zealous was he in this way, that Mr. Dilly and others regularly employed him to arrange their dinners and collect their guests. This is evidenced by some of his unpublished letters to Wilkes.

While thus engaged, news reached him which appeared to be of immense importance. This was the death of his old tutor, Mr. Andrew Dun, the Minister of Auchinleck. The choice of a successor appeared of such moment, that he posted down to his country seat, and, on the eve of his departure, in February, 1793, addressed his friend Temple in solemn terms on the serious duty he was about to undertake : " I am within a few hours of setting out for Auchinleck, honest David having secured me a place in the Carlisle coach to Ferry Bridge, that I may have an opportunity to stop should I be too much fatigued. It is quite right that I should now go down. The choice of a minister to a worthy parish is a matter of very great importance, and I cannot be sure of the real wishes of the people without being present. Only think, Temple, how serious a duty I am about to discharge ! I, James Boswell, Esq.—you know what vanity that name includes." He was resolved, however, to leave the choice to the parishioners, and this he announced to them formally.

For forty years this worthy Mr. Dun had exercised his functions in Auchinleck, and looked back with pride to his long service, and to the day of his " call " by the

Presbytery in 1752.* He appears to have had his share of rough quaintness, evidenced by the two volumes of sermons with notes which he published at Kilmarnock in 1790, and which he dedicated to " the man whom I have known to be always diligent and just," viz. Lord Auchinleck.

An "advertisement," prefixed to one of these sermons, shows his character in a pleasing way. It was preached " at the wish of Lady Elizabeth Creighton, the only child of the Earl and Countess of Dumfries." "The young lady had been seriously ill of a fever at London, from whence, after her recovery, the order was sent, with a donation of £5 from the parishes. The author's heart was gladdened one Tuesday, a very cold, frosty, but fine, clear, sunny day, to see columns of smoke ascending from so many huts, the homes of the poor now warmed with the young lady's bounty and that of the parents. While writing this, what pleasing thoughts crowd into the mind! a young lady thus educated, what a blessing to society, etc." This " etc." is very quaint. But what was this to the very original dedication of the sermon, to the young lady herself! " Madam, I will pay you no compliments until you are got out of leading strings, and are your own governess. You have reason to thank God in this modern age that you have *such Parents,* parents entrusted with an heiress; a child taken by wise men from her nearer friends and connections to them. I rejoice to hear of the dawnings of wisdom, and to see the progress of Humanity in you. Continue, *my dear young creature,* continue to increase in wisdom and favour with God and man. That the Lord may give you the generosity and taste of your grand-uncle,

* The " call " was signed, first by Lord Auchinleck as patron, and by two Boswells, John and Alexander, as heritors and elders.

the Earl of Dumfries and Stair; the piety of his lady, of the family of Aberdeen; the wisdom and charity of the Countess, your Mother; with the honest, warm, friendly heart of the Earl, your Father, is the constant prayer of, etc.,"—all of which·is simple and droll.

In some of the notes to the sermons we find some personal recollections as odd as those of his pupil. He tells how he was once "convoying a cousin to her father's house. A witch, she was; I had formerly felt her power, as had fifty others. She did not wound us with pins, but with darts. Smile not, for it is said the man who ever was in love, has long ears. A man visits, and with formality proposes marriage, once or twice a year. So these *formulists* remain bachelors all their days, or stumble into matrimony. Reader, be not sour; all now said is consistent with piety, unless you think that piety consists in saying continually with the monks, *mementoo moori, mementoo moori.*"

He has quaint anecdotes too. "A curate who had been called to pray with a dying man, grievously gored by a bull, after tossing the leaves of the Common Prayer Book, said, 'Upon my word, I cannot find a prayer for *bull-goring,* in all the Prayer Book:' so went off." He recalls, too, a Presbyterian, praying publicly for the Royal Family, who said, "O Lord, bless the King, our Sovereign, and the Queen, his Sovereign."

CHAPTER XXIX.

PREPARING FOR THE "LIFE OF JOHNSON."

WE are now approaching that momentous period when
Boswell was making ready to give the world that great
book which has made him famous.   In the midst of his
pleasures, follies, and day dreams, he had been busy
with this really huge enterprise, and had contrived to
prosecute the gigantic task of bringing into order the
vast mass of materials he had collected.   It is extraordinary to find that this was successfully accomplished
within a period of little over six years.   The difficulties
were enormous : for he had not only to arrange his own
personal recollections, to rewrite or " Johnsonize " as he
called it, innumerable notes of conversation, but to
collect all the facts or incidents of Johnson's life, most
of which were unfamiliar to him.   No laborious scholar
working in his study, undistracted by social pleasures,
could have been more successful in this part of the
scheme.

   There were others, besides Mr. Malone and Mr.
Boswell, who had been thought of as biographers of
Johnson.   Among these was his friend and executor,
Sir W. Scott, afterwards Lord Stowell, who was pressed
by Mr. Twiss to undertake the task.   "I think I
should not have troubled you with a letter at this
time," he wrote in 1784, "had I not been more than

JAMES BOSWELL.

From a sketch by Sir Thomas Lawrence.

commonly anxious to renew my solicitations with you
to become the biographer of your friend Dr. Johnson.
When I formerly mentioned this matter to you at Coles-
hill, and wished you to be collecting proper materials,
your answer that Dr. Percy was already engaged in the
business by no means satisfied me, nor am I better
pleased with the report that Sir John Hawkins or *Mr.
Boswell* would perform the task : I do not think either
of them equal to the work ; the one is a puppy, the
other a pedant : suffer not, I beseech you the life of so
excellent a man to be written by such puny fellows :
more abilities are required than possessed by all three :
rescue his memory from all such mean hands." This not
very sagacious person was happily not to have his way ;
but the appeal is valuable, as showing what was the
general feeling as to Boswell's fashion of dealing with
biography. A more serious mortification, however,
was the selection by the united booksellers of London
—nearly fifty in number—of Sir John Hawkins, Knight,
as the biographer of Dr. Johnson. In spite of the
success of the "Tour" these practical men could not
accept Mr. Boswell seriously. Hawkins's work deserves
praise, and was really of some aid to Boswell, in
laying out, as it were, the life of Johnson, fixing dates,
events, etc.

Boswell was an enthusiastic author, and during his
life projected a vast number of works, all on interesting
subjects, which he would no doubt have treated with the
honest labour, and pleasant earnestness that was habitual
with him. He had made "collections" for a history
of "The Beggar's Opera," to be issued in a great quarto,
which would no doubt have dealt with the history of
the performers and the curious controversies that arose
out of it. He had talked much with the old Duke of

Queensbury, who had seen the first representation, had heard anecdotes at second hand from Quinn and others. Besides, he delighted in the subject; and, as he says in his natural way, "their very tunes never failed to render me gay, because they are associated with the warm sensations and high spirits of London." With this view he had been attending the executions at Newgate, and had cemented a friendship with Mr. Akermann, the Governor.

Another of his schemes was an account of his travels on the continent, for which he had collected materials, but Johnson dissuaded him, saying he would lessen his reputation. "What can you tell of countries so well known?" "But," said Boswell, sensibly enough, " I can give an entertaining narrative, with many incidents, anecdotes, and remarks, so as to make very pleasant reading." We heartily wish he had not attended to the sage's advice, for his observations would have been shrewd and agreeable. Another of his plans is disclosed in a letter to Bishop Percy, to whom he applied for aid. " I wish to publish, as a regale to him, a neat little volume, 'The Praises of Doctor Johnson by contemporary writers.' It will be about the size of Selden's 'Table Talk,' of which your lordship made me a present. Will your lordship be at the trouble to send me a note of the writers you recollect, who have praised our much respected friend." His extraordinary intimacy with the notorious Mrs. Rudd led him to set down her conversations and the odd incidents she related to him, which he contemplated publishing. From this he was fortunately dissuaded. Yet another scheme was a life of Lord Kames, for which he had been making " collections," some items of which were used in the " life " executed by Lord Woodhouslee. There are a few anecdotes and

professional recollections which Boswell took down.
He was tempted to undertake an account of General
Oglethorpe, attracted by some anecdotes which the
general recounted to him. But the general died before
he was able to undertake the duty. He also proposed
to write the life of " the learned and worthy Thomas
Ruddiman," in which he was encouraged by his mentor.
" I should take pleasure in helping you to do honour to
him." He made " collections " on the antiquities of
Scotland. But Boswell had reasonable doubts as to
the use of such a thing. A more curious scheme was a
" Dictionary of Words peculiar to Scotland : " as also a
new edition of his father's " Anacreon ; " a work on
Addison ; an edition of " Johnson's Poems ; " a history of
Sweden ; a history of the '45 Rebellion ; a life of
Sir R. Sibbald ; a history of James IV. ; a work on
Scotch charters ; an account of his family ; a descrip-
tion of the Isle of Man ; a sort of story based on the
parsimonious habits of Lord Macdonald ; and a defence
of his great work, with a reply to Dr. Parr's attacks.
He had also a vague idea of editing Walton's " Lives."
This was a large programme.

With a view to make his book as full and as complete
as possible, Boswell spared himself no trouble of inquiry
or investigation, plying every one likely to contribute
information with questions, or invitations to give him
assistance. With this view he made an expedition down
to Windsor, to try and extract something from the
vivacious Miss Burney, who describes his attack in the
most amusing style.

"And now for a scene a little surprising. The beautiful chapel of St. George, repaired and finished by the
best artists at an immense expense, which was now
opened after a very long shutting up for its preparations,

brought innumerable strangers to Windsor, and, among others, Mr. Boswell.

"This I heard, in my way to the chapel, from Mr. Turbulent [the Rev. Mr. La Giffardière], who overtook me, and mentioned having met Mr. Boswell at the Bishop of Carlisle's the evening before. He proposed bringing him to call upon me; but this I declined, certain how little satisfaction would be given here by the entrance of a man so famous for compiling anecdotes. But yet I really wished to see him again, for old acquaintance' sake, and unavoidable amusement from his oddity and good humour, as well as respect for the object of his constant admiration, my revered Dr. Johnson. I therefore told Mr. Turbulent I should be extremely glad to speak with him after the service was over.

"Accordingly, at the gate of the choir, Mr. Turbulent brought him to me. We saluted with mutual glee: his comic-serious face and manner have lost nothing of their wonted singularity; nor yet have his mind and language, as you will soon confess.

"'I am extremely glad to see you indeed,' he cried, 'but very sorry to see you here. My dear ma'am, why do you stay?—it won't do, ma'am! you must resign!—we can put up with it no longer. I told my good host the Bishop so last night; we are all grown quite outrageous.'

"Whether I laughed the most, or stared the most, I am at a loss to say; but I hurried away from the cathedral, not to have such treasonable declarations overheard, for we were surrounded by a multitude.

"He accompanied me, however, not losing one moment in continuing his exhortations:

"'If you do not quit, ma'am, very soon, some violent measures, I assure you, will be taken. We shall

address Dr. Burney in a body; I am ready to make
the harangue myself. We shall fall upon him all at
once.'

"I stopped him to inquire about Sir Joshua; he
said he saw him very often, and that his spirits were
very good. I asked about Mr. Burke's book.

"'Oh,' cried he, 'it will come out next week: 'tis the
first book in the world, except my own, and that's
coming out also very soon; only I want your help.'

"'My help?'

"'Yes, madam; you must give me some of your
choice little notes of the Doctor's; we have seen him
long enough upon stilts; I want to show him in a new
light. Grave Sam, and great Sam, and solemn Sam, and
learned Sam—all these he has appeared over and over.
Now I want to entwine a wreath of the graces across his
brow; I want to show him as gay Sam, agreeable Sam,
pleasant Sam: so you must help me with some of his
beautiful billets to yourself.'

"I evaded this by declaring I had not any stores at
hand. He proposed a thousand curious expedients to get
at them, but I was invincible.

"Then I was hurrying on, lest I should be too late.
He followed eagerly, and again exclaimed:

"'But, ma'ma, as I tell you, this won't do—you
must resign off-hand! Why, I would farm you out myself for double, treble the money! I wish I had the
regulation of such a farm—yet I am no farmer-general.
But I should like to farm you, and so I will tell Dr.
Burney. I mean to address him; I have a speech ready
for the first opportunity.'

"He then told me his 'Life of Dr. Johnson' was
nearly printed, and took a proof-sheet out of his pocket
to show me; with crowds passing and repassing, know-

ing me well, and staring well at him ; for we were now at the iron rails of the Queen's Lodge.

" I stopped ; I could not ask him in ; I saw he expected it, and was reduced to apologise, and tell him I must attend the Queen immediately.

" He uttered again stronger and stronger exhortations for my retreat, accompanied by expressions which I was obliged to check in their bud. But finding he had no chance for entering, he stopped me again at the gate, and said he would read me a part of his work.

" There was no refusing this ; and he began, with a letter of Dr. Johnson to himself. He read it in strong imitation of the Doctor's manner, very well, and not caricature. But Mrs. Schwellenberg was at her window, a crowd was gathering to stand round the rails, and the King and Queen and Royal Family now approached from the Terrace. I made a rather quick apology, and with a step as quick as my now weakened limbs have left in my power, I hurried to my apartment.

" You may suppose I had inquiries enough, from all around, of ' Who was the gentleman I was talking to at the rails ? ' And an injunction rather frank not to admit him beyond those limits.

" However, I saw him again the next morning, in coming from early prayers, and he again renewed his remonstrances, and his petition for my letters of Dr. Johnson."

He also determined to extract all that he could from Dr. Percy, the bishop of Dromore, who had shown him much kindness and hospitality. " My talent," wrote Boswell, " for recording conversation is handsomely acknowledged by your Lordship upon the blank leaf of Selden's ' Table Talk,' with which you were so good as to present me." He then begs for assistance in the shape of recollections, notes, etc. "You must certainly recollect a number of anecdotes. *Be pleased to write them down,* as you so well can do, and send them to me." The prelate kindly set to work, and sent him some useful particulars. Boswell had allowed nearly a year to elapse before acknowledging these communications, "which, though few, are valuable," pleading a sort of Johnsonian excuse. "Procrastination we all know increases, in a proportionate ratio, the difficulty of doing that which we might have once done very early." He then gives an account of his progress and method. "I am ashamed that I have yet" (it was then February 7, 1788) "seven years to write of his life. I do it chronologically, giving year by year his publications, his letters, his conversations, and everything else I can collect. It appears to me that mine is the best plan of biography that can be conceived; for my readers will, as near as may be, accompany Johnson in his progress, and, as it were, see each scene as it happened." He then speaks of the long delay which he fears may be prejudicial to the work, but means "to do his duty as well as he can." It has been thought that Boswell's animosity to Mrs. Thrale was occasioned by her attempted, anticipated publications. But here, at least, we find him speaking of her project good-naturedly, as if he were pleased. "It will be," he says, "a rich addition to the Johnsonian Memorabilia." His curiosity, too, tempted him into a violation of printing-office etiquette. "I saw a sheet there yesterday," he says, "and observed letter 350, so we may have much entertainment."

"Your Lordship would, I am sure, be glad to see that I was lately elected, in February, Recorder of Carlisle. Lord Lonsdale recommending me to that office was an honourable proof of his Lordship's regard

for me, and may hope that this may lead to future promotion. I have indeed no claims upon his Lordship,
but I shall endeavour to deserve his continuance."
Then, recalling the past, he says, he recollects "with
fondness the happy mornings I passed in the capital
and elsewhere. Does not your Lordship sometimes wish
to be in old England again?" The Bishop, in replying,
exhibits his reverence for the great Lord Lonsdale :—

"I felicitate you most sincerely on your growing
interest with so warm and generous a patron as Lord
Lonsdale, whose generous attachment to his friends has
always been a distinguished feature in his character, and
who, I doubt not, will be glad to introduce into Parliament a member of your abilities, and active exertion.
I must myself acknowledge with gratitude that, during
my residence in that country, I always received very
flattering instances of his Lordship's polite attention ;
and I have great pleasure in seeing you so agreeably
connected with his Lordship, who shows a discernment
rarely seen in men of great fortunes, in looking out and
attracting to himself men of distinguished talents, as he
has lately manifested in his patronizing of you and
Dr. Douglas." Dr. Percy was a courtly prelate, and
had due deference for all personages with political influence. He therefore added, "I have heard with great
pleasure, the important part you lately acted in the
north. You are now connected with a nobleman, who
serves his friends with zeal and spirit, which I hope will
be attended with the happiest consequences to your
establishment in England. I already anticipate his
bringing you into the House of Commons as an event
no less certain, than splendid to your fortunes." It was
no wonder that Mr. Boswell took this prophecy as fresh
encouragement for his sanguine hopes. It was charac-

teristic, however, that Boswell had never thought of sending his episcopal friend a copy of his book, expecting, no doubt, that he ought to purchase it. When, however, the volumes were before him, the bishop found himself pictured as a time-serving prelate, ridiculously obsequious to a duke, with whose family he is represented as being nervously anxious to establish a relationship.

With the same maladroitness Boswell recounts, " Dr. Percy humorously observes that Levett used to breakfast on the crust of a roll which Johnson, after tearing out the crumb, threw to his humble friend." It must have been very offensive to the bishop to be represented as making a jest of such an incident, if true. But it is likely that it was a mere fanciful speculation.

At the end of the third edition of the "Tour," Mr. Boswell made fresh announcement of the great work which he was planning. In the first edition he had given a short statement to the same effect, which has been quoted, and this he now expanded. It is in his own clear and precise style, and drawn up with his usual sagacity. It will be seen that it by no means expresses the large and ambitious scale which his work was afterwards expanded to, and he did not propose to extend it beyond the dimensions of a single quarto volume :—" Preparing for publication, in One Volume Quarto, ' The Life of Samuel Johnson.'

" Mr. Boswell has been collecting materials on this work for more than twenty years, during which he was honoured with the intimate friendship of Dr. Johnson, to whose memory he is anxious to erect a literary monument, worthy of so great an author and so excellent a man. Dr. Johnson was well informed of his design, and obligingly communicated to him several curious particulars. With these will be interwoven the most authentic accounts that can be obtained from those who knew him ; many sketches of his conversation on a multiplicity of subjects, with various persons, some of them the most eminent of the age ; a great number of letters from him at different periods, and several original pieces dictated by him to Mr. Boswell, distinguished by that peculiar energy which marked every emanation of his mind. Mr. Boswell takes this opportunity of gratefully acknowledging the many valuable communications which he has received to enable him to render his 'Life of Dr. Johnson' more complete. His thanks are particularly due to the Rev. Dr. Adams, the Rev. Dr. Taylor, Sir Joshua Reynolds, Mr. Langton, Dr. Brocklesby, Rev. Thomas Weston, the Rector of Birmingham, Mrs. Porter, and Miss Seward. He has already obtained a large collection of Dr. Johnson's letters to his friends, and shall be much obliged for such others as still remain in private hands, which he is the more desirous of collecting, as all the letters of that great man which he has yet seen are written with peculiar precision and elegance, and he is confident that the publication of the whole of Dr. Johnson's epistolary correspondence will do him the highest honour."

Naturally we have an interest in the publisher selected by Boswell, Dilly, at whose house the famous dinner to Wilkes and Johnson took place. He cordially esteemed his client, and brought out all his works in handsome style. He lived in "the Poultry," and was a very hospitable man. His brother was "Squire Dilly," who was sheriff of his county. Beloc, the strange "Sexagenarian," describes Charles Dilly as the "queer Bookseller," and as having peculiar dryness of manner.*

* "This epithet" of the Queer Bookseller, he says, " is not intended to express the smallest disrespect, but the person in ques-

Never was a work written under such struggles and depressing conditions. He had, however, the most

tion was characterized by a dryness of manner peculiarly his own. He was seldom betrayed into a smile, nor did he ever appear particularly exhilarated, even when the greatest wits of the day assembled at his house. He had to boast of the familiar acquaintance of Wilkes and Boswell, and Johnson and Cumberland, and Parr and Steevens, and a numerous tribe of popular writers. No one could exercise the rites of hospitality with greater liberality, and when enabled from success to retire from the world with great opulence, he retained his kind feelings towards those who had formerly been connected with him as authors, and gave them a frequent and cordial welcome at his table.

" But to evince the powerful effect of habit, he retained so strong a partiality for the situation in which he had passed the greatest part of his life, and where he had accumulated his wealth, that though it was in the very noisiest part of the noisiest street in the city, he invariably, and for ever afterwards, made it the standard by which he estimated how far any thing was handsome, convenient, or agreeable. 'My house in the city,' comprised every thing which was animating and delightful without, and comfortable and exhilarating within.

" With the dry manner above described, there was united an extraordinary simplicity, which, where this individual's better qualities were not very well known, frequently gave offence. Our friend had never any intercourse with him on matters of business but once. In conjunction with a friend, whose works are now under more solemn and awful criticism elsewhere, he was prevailed upon to print a book on speculation, presuming, which indeed turned out to be the fact, that the booksellers would subscribe for the impression. The dry bookseller was, among others, applied to, but he returned the letter of application to the writer, simply writing under it, 'A. B. will not subscribe.'

" Upon another occasion an author who lived at a distance from the metropolis, at that period a great patriot, and flaming politician, had written a book of biography, the sale of which was to pour unheard-of riches into his bosom; guineas, for it was then the time of guineas, glittered in brilliant heaps before his warmed imagination. He employed a common friend to entreat the interposition of the Sexagenarian with some publisher, as being better acquainted with the nature of such negociations.

" The office was readily accepted, and this same Queer gentleman was the person fixed upon to become the purchaser of the copyright of this inestimable treasure. A meeting was appointed, the circumstances explained, the copy produced, was cast off, and agreed to be comprised in an octavo volume. Then succeeded the extraordinary faith in its success, and long hesitated about accepting an offer made to him of £1000 for it. But it would go to his heart, he said, to accept such a sum, which he considered far too low. Robinson, the publisher, was the person who made him this proposal. As he got near the close of his labours, his pecuniary difficulties became dreadfully complicated. In January, 1791, we find him writing to his friend Malone : "I have been so disturbed by sad money-matters, that my mind has been quite fretful; £500, which I borrowed and lent to a first cousin, an unlucky captain of an Indiaman, were due on the 15th to a merchant in the city. I could not possibly raise that sum, and was apprehensive of being hardly used. He, however, indulged me with an allowance to make partial payments; £150 in two months, £150 in eight months, and the remainder, with the interest, in eighteen months. How I am to manage I am at a loss, and I know you cannot help me. So this, upon my honour, is no hint. I am really tempted to accept of the £1000 for my ' Life of Johnson.' Let me struggle and hope. I cannot be out on *Shrove Tuesday*, as I flattered myself. P. 376 of Vol. II. is ordered for press, and I expect another

anxious moment of expectation of the reply to be given to, " How much will you advance for the copy-right ? "

" The author had doubtless heard of the large sums given per volume to Gibbon, Robertson, Blair, Beattie, and other writers of that calibre; and though perhaps neither his pride nor his ambition carried his expectations quite so far as to suppose that he should be placed on a parallel with these illustrious names, yet his disappointment (and disappointment is always in proportion to the hopes indulged) cannot easily be described, when, in a dry, grave, and inflexible tone, he heard the words, 'Twenty pounds and six copies.'

" Thus was the flattering hope of authorship nipped in the bud, the labour of many successive months, in a moment rendered unavailing, and the fond dreams of fame and emolument made to vanish as by the wand of a sorcerer."

proof to-night. But I have yet near two hundred pages of copy besides letters, and *the death*, which is not yet written. My second volume will, I see, be forty or fifty pages more than my first. Your absence is a woful want in all respects." Yet, under this pressure, he had foolishly incurred fresh obligations, to gratify his family pride, and could not resist purchasing back a portion of the family estate, which cost him £2500, fifteen hundred of which was borrowed on the mortgage, but the rest he could not conceive a possibility of raising, except on the ruinous system of annuity. "It was," he wrote, "imprudent in me to make a clear purchase at a time when I was sadly straitened, but if I had missed the opportunity it never again would have occurred, and I should have been vexed to see an ancient appanage, a piece of, as it were, the flesh and blood of the family in the hands of a stranger. In this situation, then, my dear sir, would it not be wise in me to accept 1000 guineas for my ' Life of Johnson,' supposing the person who made the offer should now stand to it, which I fear may not be the case ; for two volumes may be considered as a disadvantageous circumstance. Could I indeed raise £1000 upon the credit of the work, I should incline to *game*, as Sir Joshua says, because it may produce double the money, though Steevens *kindly* tells me that I have over printed, and that the curiosity about Johnson is *now* only in our own circle. In my present state of spirits I am all timidity. I have now desired to have but one compositor. Indeed I go sluggishly and comfortlessly about my book. As I pass your door I cast many a longing look." These confidences are touching enough, and must have enlisted sympathy.

He then thought of a lottery venture, and invested seventeen guineas in a share ; it, however, came out a blank. In his despair he wrote : "Oh, could I but get a few thousands, what a difference it would make upon the state of my mind, which is harassed by thinking of my debts. . . ." He could see no issue, nor could he make up his mind what course to take as to the *magnum opus.*

In April he was writing to Temple, that he was almost in sight of land. He was correcting the last sheet. "I really hope to publish it on the 25th current;" but in this he was too sanguine. "I am at present in such bad spirits that I have fear concerning it—that I may get no profit, nay, may lose—that the public may be disappointed, and think that I have done it poorly—that I may make many enemies, and even have quarrels. But, perhaps, the very reverse of all may happen." It is curious to read this modest, doubtful speculation, "*But perhaps the reverse of all this may happen.*" He frankly told Temple that he and other friends must not expect to receive presents of copies, as in the case of the "Tour," it being a so much larger and more expensive work. But he was now as elated as he had been before depressed. "I really think it will be the most entertaining collection that has appeared in this age. When it is fairly launched, I mean to stick close to Westminster Hall."

He was also perplexed by the typographical difficulties, arising from the fact that he actually was writing the work as it was being printed. This led to the second volume being considerably larger than the first. "Nothing short of divination can equalize the volumes in such a case, or else there must be a sacrifice of important matter—which, for the author, would be like parting with his heart's blood." However, "the Councillor" (Malone) had devised an ingenious way to

thicken the first volume by prefixing the index. Ingenious as this was, it was but a clumsy device, as any
one can see by looking at the volumes. It may be
added that the book was badly printed, and worse
"read." It is full of mistakes, omissions of words and
letters, owing, no doubt, to the hurried fashion in which
the author revised all his proofs. Even the title-page
exercised him a good deal, and it was long before he
could perfectly satisfy himself.*

In the agreeable letters, first published by Mr.
Croker, we read the whole story of his progress, his
hopes and wretched fears, his uncertainty as to what
course he should take—whether "to game," as he called
it, with his book, or dispose of it. "You cannot imagine
what labour, what perplexity, what vexation I have
endured in arranging a prodigious multiplicity of
materials, in supplying omissions, in searching for
papers, buried in different masses, and all this besides
the exertion of composing and polishing. *Many a time
have I thought of giving it up.*" He little thought when

---

* He had at first intended it to be very short and summary :—
"It appears to me that mentioning his studies, works, conversations, and letters, is not sufficient; and I would suggest, 'comprehending an account, in chronological order, of his studies, works,
friendships, acquaintances, and other particulars; his conversation
with eminent men; a series of his letters to various persons; also
several original pieces of his compositions never before published.
The whole, etc.' You will probably be able to assist me in expressing my idea and arranging the parts. In the advertisement I
intend to mention the letter to Lord Chesterfield, and perhaps the
interview with the King, and the names of the correspondents, in
alphabetical order. . . . Do you know that my bad spirits are returned upon me to a certain degree; and such is the sickly fondness for change of place, and imagination of relief, that I sometimes
think you are happier by being in Dublin, than one is in this great
metropolis, where hardly any man cares for another. I am persuaded I should relish your Irish dinners very much. I have at
length got chambers in the Temple, in the very staircase where
Johnson lived."

he penned this careless sentence, how much really depended on it. But we may doubt if he could ever have brought himself to abandon his scheme. " It will certainly be to the world a very valuable and peculiar volume of biography, full of literary and characteristical anecdotes, told with authenticity, and in a lively manner. Would that it were in the booksellers' shops!"

On the 8th of February, 1790, he had written: " I am within a short walk of Mr. Malone, who revises my ' Life of Johnson' with me. We have not yet gone over quite a half of it, but it is at last fairly in the press. I intended to have printed it upon what is called an *English* letter, which would have made it look better. I have therefore taken a smaller type, called *Pica*, and even upon that I am afraid its bulk will be very large."

In excellent terms with himself, and rejoicing in his literary aptitude, he thus addresses Mr. Temple on the 13th of February: "I dine in a different company almost every day, at least scarcely ever twice running in the same company, so that I have fresh accessions of ideas. I drink with Lord Lonsdale one day; the next I am quiet in Malone's elegant study revising my ' Life of Johnson,' of which I have high expectations, both as to fame and profit. I surely have the art of writing agreeably. The Lord Chancellor told me he had read every word of my Hebridean Journal; he could not help it."

On the 4th December we find him writing: " The *magnum opus* advances. . . . The additions which I have received are a Spanish quotation from Mr. Cambridge, an account of Johnson at Warley Camp from Mr. Langton, and Johnson's letters to Mr. Hastings —three in all,—one of them long and admirable; but what sets the diamonds in pure gold of Ophir is a letter from Mr. Hastings to me, illustrating them and their writer. I had this day the honour of a long visit from the late Governor-General of India. There is to be no more impeachment. But you will see his character nobly vindicated, depend upon this."

By December he had revised to page 216. At one of the club dinners he sat next young Burke, who talked of his great father. "I mentioned Johnson, to *sound,*" says Boswell, thinking of his book; "he made none." Edmund Burke he met soon after, when "I at him again:" he heard much which pleased, and "took care to write down soon after."

A few weeks before the publication we find revived the Mr. Dempster of the old days, who had so scandalized the doctor at one of the early meetings. To him poor Boswell writes out of his heart, and his letter is a good specimen of the simple confidence, of the little devices of affection, dejection, and buoyant spirits which worked in his breast. "We must not entirely lose sight of one another," he wrote; "two such old friends, who have always lived pleasantly together, though of principles directly opposite. I was happy that your accepting one of Mr. Pulteney's seats proved a false rumour, for it would have been a sad degradation. I some time ago resigned my Recordership of Carlisle. I perceived that no advantage would accrue from it. The melancholy event of losing my valuable wife will, I fear, never allow me real comfort. You cannot imagine how it hangs upon my spirits; yet I can talk, and write, and, in short, *force* myself to a wonderful degree. . . . I am sadly straightened in my accounts. I can but *exist* as to *expense;* but they are so good to one here, that I have a full share in the metropolitan advantages. My *magnum opus,* in two volumes quarto, is to be published on Monday, 16th May. I really think it will be the most entertaining collection that has appeared in this reign. When it is fairly launched I mean to stick close to Westminster Hall, and it will be truly kind if you recommend me appeals, or things of that sort."

CHAPTER XXX.

IN the year 1791, on the eve of the publication of his great work, Mr. Boswell found it essential to let the public have an authentic account of its author, and accordingly prepared for the *European Magazine* a minute account of his own life, which it is difficult to read without a smile. He tells all the world about himself, his education, the general pleasure he imparted to all, the favour with which he was ever received, and in the most amusing fashion. One distinction should be noted in the difficult matter of appraising Boswell's character : where he speaks of his great subject, *there* he is usually grave and impartial, moving, as it were, in fetters ; where he has to speak of himself and give himself due credit, his nature naively breaks out, or in, and carries him away. Who would not recognize " Jamie Boswell " in this passage : " In giving an account of this gentleman there is little occasion to make private enquiries, as, from a certain peculiarly frank, open, and unostentatious disposition which he avows, his history, like that of the old *Seigneur* Michel de Montaigne, is to be traced in his writings " ?

The appearance of this extraordinary book produced quite a sensation. Nothing like it had hitherto been known, for the common official "life," in two volumes quarto, to which the public was well accustomed, was usually a dry ponderous record, after the pattern of historical memoirs, without the vivacity supplied by conversations, or description of dramatic scenes, dinner parties, routs, and travelling excursions; all of which were considered to be beneath the dignity of the subject. Boswell's first performance, the "Tour," was merely the description of an episode, and an accurate report of conversations, etc., and in form was not exactly biographical.*

There is a curiously prophetic passage in the preface to the account of Corsica. "For my part," he says, "I should be proud to be known as an author: and I have an ardent ambition for literary fame, for of all possessions I should imagine literary fame to be the most valuable. A man who has been able to furnish a book which has been approved by the world, has established himself as a respectable character in distant society, without any danger of that character being lessened by the observation of his weaknesses. ... The author of an approved book may allow his natural disposition an easy play, and yet indulge the pride of superior genius when he considers that by those who

* It would be interesting to ascertain the exact day on which this famous work appeared. His preface is dated April 20th. He "hoped" to publish on the 25th. But when he fixed this date, which was on the 6th, he had some corrections to make. Then there was the binding to be done. It seems likely therefore that it appeared on May 16th. Seventeen hundred copies were printed, of which twelve hundred were sold within three months. The edition was exhausted before the end of the year. When, however, we consider the expense he was at for corrections, engravings, cancels, etc., it may be doubted if this edition brought him the anticipated thousand guineas.

know him only as an author he never ceases to be re-spected. Such an author, when in his hours of gloom and discontent, may have the consolation to think that his writings are at that very time giving pleasure to numbers ; and such an author may cherish the hope of being remembered after death."

His address, or "advertisement," to the public is interesting, and as genuine as it is interesting. There is a true ring in its acknowledgments, and an affec-tionate tone in the gratitude expressed to friends, as well as in his laments for their loss.*

---

* In speaking of his own share, too, there is a sober sadness : "I at last deliver to the world a work which I have long promised, and of which, I am afraid, too high expectations have been raised. The delay of its publication must be imputed, in a considerable degree, to the extraordinary zeal which has been shown by dis-tinguished persons in all quarters to supply me with additional information concerning its illustrious subject ; resembling in this the grateful tribes of ancient nations, of which every individual was eager to throw a stone upon the grave of a departed hero, and thus to share in the pious office of erecting an honourable monument to his memory.

"The labour and anxious attention with which I have collected and arranged the materials of which these volumes are composed, will hardly be conceived by those who read them with careless facility. The stretch of mind and prompt assiduity by which so many conversations were preserved, I myself, at some distance of time, contemplate with wonder ; and I must be allowed to suggest, that the nature of the work, in other respects, as it consists of innumerable detached particulars, all which, even the most minute, I have spared no pains to ascertain with a scrupulous authenticity, has occasioned a degree of trouble far beyond that of any other species of composition. Were I to detail the books which I have consulted, and the inquiries which I have found it necessary to make by various channels, I should probably be thought ridiculously ostentatious. Let me only observe, as a specimen of my trouble, that I have sometimes been obliged to run half over London, in order to fix a date correctly : which, when I had accomplished, I well knew would obtain me no praise, though a failure would have been to my discredit. And after all, perhaps, hard as it may be, I shall not be surprised if omissions or mistakes be pointed out with invidious severity. I have also been extremely careful as to the

This great book, it would be vain to praise : it is more and more appreciated every year. It is curious, however, that, not until some fifty years had passed over, was it accepted seriously as a really great book : it being hitherto considered merely a work of entertainment. Mr. Croker, with Macaulay and Carlyle, did much to settle its place. Lord Macaulay's essay is somewhat " patronizing " and a good deal contemptuous : and this tone we now feel to be out of place ; but it was not out of keeping with the limited knowledge of Boswell, and comparative indifference to his work, that then obtained. It is impossible, too, to resist the impression that Macaulay relished the subject because it was adapted to his brilliant and, as it now seems, rather theatrical style. Mr. Carlyle's essay, though it seems to plead too much for Boswell, making too ample

exactness of my quotations ; holding that there is a respect due to the public, which should oblige every author to attend to this, and never to presume to introduce them with, ' I think I have read,' or ' If I remember right,' when the originals may be examined.

" I beg leave to express my warmest thanks to those who have been pleased to favour me with communications and advice in the conduct of my work. But I cannot sufficiently acknowledge my obligations to my friend Mr. Malone, who was so good as to allow me to read to him almost the whole of my manuscript, and made such remarks as were greatly for the advantage of the work ; though it is but fair to him to mention, that upon many occasions I differed from him, and followed my own judgment. I regret exceedingly that I was deprived of the benefit of his revision, when not more than one half of the book had passed through the press.

" Such a sanction to my faculty of giving a just representation of Dr. Johnson I could not conceal. Nor will I suppress my satisfaction in the consciousness, that by recording so considerable a portion of the wisdom and wit of ' the brightest ornament of the eighteenth century,' I have largely provided for the instruction and entertainment of mankind.

" J. BOSWELL.

" London, April 20, 1791."

acknowledgment of his foolishness,* is a far more robust and exact appreciation of Boswell's character than Macaulay's.

Too much cannot be said of Boswell's *style*. We may well wonder where he obtained this happy, judicious power of narrative, so limpid and unaffected, and without the least literary realism, or attempt at colouring and " word painting." His phrases and words are admirably chosen, clear and direct, without the least pretence. In particular passages, there is dramatic grouping of the highest kind. I have alluded, however, to the curious blending of two currents of narrative : one of which is historical, in which the author describes what he has obtained at "second hand;" the other dramatic, in which he describes present impressions and

---

* His main argument for Boswell's subservience to Johnson always appears rather a weak one. He urged that if Boswell were as sycophantic as he was popularly thought to be, he would have selected some conspicuous personage, high in politics or in the State, and not an old "dominie." From such he would have obtained more profit for his devotion. But Boswell was sagacious enough to see that he had chosen exactly the sort of idol that would furnish him with what he sought—on the assumption, that is, that he had interested views of the kind. As it was, he tried to attach himself to patrons of another kind, but without happy result. The intimacy brought him both present and posthumous fame. It is, of course, with diffidence that I venture this objection, for I think with pleasure of the talk I had with this great man on the subject, not very long before his death, and when he good-humouredly allowed me to try my 'prentice hand on a bust of him. And here, too, I feel some pride in inserting the dedication of my edition of that life : " Dear Mr. Carlyle, you were kind enough to encourage me to undertake the task of restoring the text of Mr. Boswell's great biography; and, in addition, have allowed me to inscribe the work now completed to you. That my humble labours will be found worthy of such encouragement, I will not venture to affirm ; but it, at least, has been directed by a reverential feeling ; and, above all, is conceived in the spirit of that admirable view of Boswell's work and character, which you gave to the world many years ago."

the incidents in which he himself took part. These
styles do not harmonize artistically. That Boswell was
in some sense conscious of this, is shown by his styling
the Hebridean expedition "A *Journal* of a Tour:" which
it was in the strictest sense, being written down from day
to day—excepting the last few pages. This alone might
have been a warning to Mr. Croker against the blunder
of incorporating it into the "Life."

It would be difficult to give an idea of the dramatic
art shown in his various sketches and touchings, without
quoting to an inordinate length. One specimen will
suffice—the scene in which Johnson, as the whole company gathered round, declared of a certain lady: "The
woman had a bottom of good sense." "The word *bottom*
thus introduced was so ludicrous when contrasted with
his gravity, that most of us could not forbear tittering
and laughing; though I recollect that the Bishop of
Killaloe kept his countenance with perfect steadiness,
while Miss Hannah More slily hid her face behind a
lady's back who sat on the same settee with her. His
pride could not bear that any expression of his should
excite ridicule, when he did not intend it: he therefore
resolved to assume and exercise despotic power, glanced
sternly around, and called out in a strong tone, 'Where's
the merriment?' Then collecting himself, and looking
awful, to make us feel how he could impose restraint,
and as it were searching his mind for a still more
ludicrous word, he slowly pronounced, 'I say the
woman was *fundamentally* sensible;' as if he had said,
Hear this now, and laugh if you dare. We all sat composed as at a funeral." The "glosses" here given by
the author—his reading and interpretation of the turns
in Johnson's mind—are truly admirable. This is part
of Boswell's artistic system, and in his analysis of

mental changes, as well as in the command of suitable expressions, he seems unrivalled.*

The noise or fuss which the author had made over his work attracted attention and expectation ; even at Court there was some curiosity as to his proceedings. The Queen made inquiries of the lady-in-waiting. "Miss Burney, have you heard that Boswell is going to publish a life of your friend Dr. Johnson ?"

"No, ma'am."

"I tell you as I heard. I don't know for the truth of it, and I can't tell what he will do. He is so extraordinary a man, that perhaps he will devise something extraordinary."

When the book appeared, his Majesty—"told me once, laughing heartily, that, having seen my name in the Index, he was eager to come to what was said of me : but when he found so little, he was surprised and disappointed. I ventured to assure him how much I had myself been rejoiced at this circumstance, and with what satisfaction I had reflected upon having very seldom met Mr. Boswell, as I knew there was no other security against all manner of risks in his relations."

---

* There is a most perplexing passage in the " Life " which it is almost impossible to make clear. A discussion arose at Dilly's on toleration, when "a gentleman" asked whether preaching against the Trinity, for instance, might be allowed. Johnson said, "I wonder how a gentleman of your piety can introduce such a subject in a mixed society." The gentleman, who was certainly Langton, said deferentially that he only wished to hear Johnson on the subject. A short time after, we find that he had taken serious offence, and left town in dudgeon without seeing Johnson—nay, refused to be reconciled for a long time. It appears, however, that he walked to the club with Johnson, and had him to dine a day or two later ! If this account be accurate, it is impossible that this can be the correct order of events : as the dinner must have condoned the offence. So I am inclined to believe that Boswell may have "mixed up" his notes on this occasion.

His Majesty often talked it over with her. "The King, who was now also reading the work, applied to me for explanations without end. Every night, at this period, he entered the Queen's dressing-room and delayed her Majesty's proceedings by a length of discourse with me upon the subject. . . . The Queen frequently condescended to read over passages and anecdotes which perplexed or offended her. Little did I think it would ever fall to my lot to vindicate him to his King and Queen." She also adds, "These occasional sallies of Dr. Johnson, all related verbatim by Mr. Boswell, are filling all sorts of readers with amaze, except the small party to whom Dr. Johnson was known, and who, by acquaintance with the power of the moment over his unguarded conversations, know how little of his solid opinions was to be gathered from his accidental assertions." No doubt this lively lady had thought over his Majesty's suggestion that she had not figured in the narrative as she ought: which seems unreasonable, as she had met Boswell's applications for aid in a very repelling manner.*

* In his "Tour" Boswell hints mysteriously at the king's approval of his calling the Pretender " Prince." "I *know*," he says, "and exult in having it in my power to tell that *the only* person in the world, etc., thinks as I do." It seems he actually talked with his Majesty on the subject, as Dr. Lort repeats the story (in Nichols's "Illustrations," vol. vii.). He writes : " Boswell's book, I suppose, will be out in the winter. The king, at his Levee, talked to him, as was natural, on this subject. Boswell told his Majesty that he had another work on the anvil— a 'History of the Rebellion in 1745 ; ' but that he was at a loss how to style the principal person who figured in it. 'How would you style him, Mr. Boswell ? ' 'I was thinking, sire, of calling him the grandson of the unfortunate James the Second.' 'That I have no objection to ; my title to the crown stands on firmer ground—on an Act of Parliament.' This is said to be the substance of a conversation which passed at the Levee. I wish I was certain of the exact words." It must have been a sore trial to Boswell to have to suppress the details of this conversation, which

About a year after the appearance of the work, Miss Burney met the author at a breakfast party given by Miss Dickenson, and where the " guests were Mr. Langton, Mr. Foote, Mr. Dickenson, jun., a cousin, and a very agreeable and pleasing man ; Lady Herries, Miss Dickenson, another cousin, and Mr. Boswell.

" He entertained us all *as if hired for that purpose*, telling stories of Dr. Johnson, and acting them with incessant buffoonery. I told him frankly that, if he turned him into ridicule by caricature, I should fly the premises : he assured me he would not, and indeed his imitations, though comic to excess, were so far from caricature that he omitted a thousand gesticulations which I distinctly remember.

" Mr. Langton told some stories himself in imitation of Dr. Johnson ; but they became him less than Mr. Boswell, and only reminded me of what Dr. Johnson himself once said to me—' Every man has, some time in his life, an ambition to be a wag.' "

As was to be expected in the case of so novel and interesting a work, the newspapers unceremoniously helped themselves to the most striking passages and " tit-bits," serving up large extracts for the benefit of their readers. The author did not relish this free and easy appropriation of his labours, and at once took legal measures to stop this system of piracy. He was, however, not inclined to be severe, and readily accepted their excuses on promise of future amendment, and in July, 1791, he drew up a form of apology which answered very well as an advertisement, and which he required to be inserted in the newspapers.*

may have occurred when he presented the address of his tenants (see *ante*, p. 16).

* " From a desire to furnish interesting entertainment to our

With his vast amount of accumulated material, the thought of one danger always made him nervously apprehensive. During the long process of preparation he knew that other pens were working diligently, inquiring, gathering up anecdotes and stories of the great man, which publications would forestall much of the interest of his own work. Mrs. Piozzi was the most dreaded of these "interlopers," and she had already issued her little volume of piquant anecdotes, and two substantial volumes of letters. The latter was the more serious interference. These works had now appeared, and offered a substantial contribution to Johnsonian biography. In them, too, there were many anticipations of curious facts which Boswell had set apart for his own use.

Of all Boswell's contemporaries, Mr. Walpole, per-

readers, we inserted Dr. Johnson's conversation with His Majesty, and his celebrated letter to Lord Chesterfield, which we extracted from Mr. Boswell's ' Life of Johnson.' We had not the smallest apprehension that we were invading literary property, which we hold sacred. But it seems these two valuable articles were entered at Stationer's Hall as separate publications, which were advertized in some of the newspapers ; but the advertisement escaped us. We are very sorry for the mistake ; but Mr. Boswell is too candid to take any advantage, and upon our assuring him of the fact, has declared he will not prosecute." Considering Boswell's jealous guard over his copyrights, it is difficult to understand how he could have tolerated such audacious piracies as the following : " The Life of Dr. Samuel Johnson, carefully abridged from Mr. Boswell's larger work, by F. Thomas, *fine front, entitled Dr. Johnson's politeness to Madame Boufflers, by Isaac Cruikshank.*" This was issued in 1793, some two years after the appearance of the " Life." In the same year also appeared " The Witticisms, Anecdotes, Jests, & Sayings of, during the whole course of his Life, with a full account of Dr. Johnson's Conversation with the King, to which is added a great number of Jests, in which the most distinguished Wits of the present Century have a part, by J. Merry, *front. by Cruikshank (The Elder) Representing Mrs. Thrale's Breakfast Table with portraits.*" Here, it will be noted, was reproduced the cherished " conversation with the King."

haps, showed the greatest contempt for his character and general follies. He seemed almost to detest him. This shows rather a narrow-minded view, and was really taking Mr. Boswell too seriously. Johnson, too, he equally disliked. This openly expressed feeling had no effect on the insensible author. When Johnson was busy with his "Lives of the Poets," Mr. Boswell officiously intruded himself on Walpole to beg for some anecdotes of Mr. Gray. " I said,"—Walpole is describing the scene,—" very coldly, that I had given what I knew to Mr. Mason. Boswell hummed and hawed, and then dropped, 'I suppose you know Dr. Johnson does not admire Mr. Gray?' Putting as much contempt as I could into my look and tone, I said, 'Dr. Johnson don't! —Humph!' and with that monosyllable ended our interview."

On another occasion the great letter-writer's dislike was shown in even more amusing fashion. " T'other night," he says,—it was in the June of 1785,—" I was sitting with Mrs. Vesey; there was very little light; when there arrived Sir Joshua Reynolds and a person whom I took for Mr. Boswell. I *sewed* up my mouth, and, though he addressed me two or three times, I answered nothing but yes or no. Just as he was going away I found out that it was Mr. Richard Burke, and endeavoured to repair my causticity." "Sewed up my mouth" is good.

When the great book appeared he wrote: " I never would be in the least acquainted with Johnson, or, as Boswell calls it, I had not a just value for him; which his biographer imputes to my resentment at the doctor's putting bad arguments, purposely, out of Jacobitism, in speeches which he wrote fifty years ago for my father in the *Gentleman's Magazine*, which I did not read then, or ever knew Johnson wrote, till he died, nor have looked at since."

"If Johnson's opponents were weak, he told them they were fools ; if they vanquished him, he was scurrilous ; to nobody more than to Boswell himself, who was contemptible for flattering him so grossly, and for enduring the coarse things he was continually vomiting on Boswell's own country. Boswell's book is gossiping ; but having a number of proper names, would be more readable, at least by me, if it were reduced from two volumes to one, but there are woeful *longueurs* both about his hero and himself, the *fidus achates* about whom one has not the smallest curiosity."

When he was applied to, to subscribe for Johnson's monument, "an ambling letter," as he called it, "was left, signed by Burke, Sir Joshua, and Boswell. This he treated as an impertinence, for they must have known his opinion : "I would not deign to write an answer, but sent down word, by my footman, as I would have done to parish officers, with a brief answer that I would not subscribe." This seems rather petty. The incident is significant as showing what Boswell must have exposed himself to.

CHAPTER XXXI

CRITICISMS AND CONTROVERSIES.

THE enormous number of persons, living and dead, who were introduced, the allusions to facts that many remembered or were familiar with, naturally gave rise to protests and rectifications, which brought much embarrassment to the writer. The wonder is that among so many dangerous pitfalls he escaped so well, and this shows how carefully and surely he had steered his way. On the whole, he got off very well, though not without a share of virulent controversy.

Now was to set in the reign of controversies, attacks and recriminations. His first trouble came from his old ally, Miss Anna Seward, the literary spinster of Lichfield. This lady, as we have seen, was but little pleased with the "Tour." When writing the "Life" he had asked her assistance, and she had supplied him with contributions, which, as may be imagined by those familiar with her style, proved to be of no value. As soon as she had read the volumes, the lady began the attack, in an indignant protest addressed to the *Gentleman's Magazine*.

"I have very recently seen a pamphlet entitled 'The Principal Corrections, etc.' It surprised me to find my name very impolitely introduced in the first page. When Mr. Boswell was collecting materials for his work, he desired me to give him all the assistance in my power. I made every effort to oblige him, and, though the anecdotes he had from me were not numerous, yet I covered several sheets of paper on the subject for his use." She then goes on to repeat and justify her statement as to the "Sprig of Myrtle" which her mother had told her was addressed to Miss Porter. Johnson, she said, might not strain at a little fiction, "and this," adds the bitter and inflamed spinster, "was a very slight untruth compared with the unquestionably conscious falsehood of some other assertions of his."

Our author was not slow to reply; indeed, was eager for the contest. Her work, he said, contained more of "fine writing," and "elegant reflections" than those hard facts which would be useful to a Biographer. Such would seem to have been the character of many "sheets of Johnsonian narrative" furnished him. There were two notable incidents on which she had descanted, namely, the story of the "Verses on a Duck," which Johnson was reported to have written at three years old, as well as the incidents connected with some lines on "A Sprig of Myrtle."

"This anecdote of the duck, though disproved by internal and external evidence, has, nevertheless, upon supposition of its truth, been made the foundation for the following ingenious and fanciful reflections of Miss Seward, amongst the communications concerning Dr. Johnson with which she has been pleased to favour me. . . . *This is so beautifully imagined, that I would not suppress it.* But, like many other theories, it is deduced from a supposed fact which is, indeed, a fiction."

How Boswellian is this! Her facts prove to be unreal, but her reflections on the false facts are " beautifully imagined." It was scarcely surprising that the lady was hurt at so grotesque a shape of compliment. As to the "Sprig of Myrtle" verses, in his first edition he had said, "I am assured by Miss Seward that he conceived a tender passion for Miss Lucy Porter, daughter of the lady whom he afterwards married. . . . And he addressed to her the following verses on her presenting him with a nosegay of myrtle."

Boswell was the more pleased with this story, as it enabled him to deal contemptuously with Mrs. Piozzi, who had reported the anecdote in another shape. "Mrs. Piozzi, in her anecdotes, asserts that Johnson wrote this effusion of elegant tenderness not in his own person but for a friend, who was in love. But the lively lady is as inaccurate in this instance as in many others, for Miss Seward writes to me," etc.

It may be conceived what was Mr. Boswell's disgust in finding that he had been altogether misled by Miss Seward, and that Mrs. Piozzi, whom he had attacked so wantonly, was correct! He had received a communication from a gentleman for whom the verses were actually written. Could anything be so mortifying! But he did what was his duty manfully and conscientiously.

In his quarto supplement of "Corrections and Additions," which he issued before publishing the second edition, he struck out the passage about Miss Porter. "Instead of, 'and I am assured,' etc., to the end of the paragraph, *read*, 'but with what felicity he could warble the amorous lay will appear from the following lines which he wrote for his friend, Mr. Hector.'" Then he makes the *amende* to Mrs. Piozzi. "In my first edition I was induced to doubt the authenticity of her account, by the following circumstantial statement in a letter to me from Miss Seward, of Lichfield : ' I *know*, etc.'

"Such was Miss Seward's statement, which I make no doubt she supposed to be correct ; but it shows how dangerous it is to trust too implicitly to traditional testimony and ingenious inference ; for Mr. Hector has lately assured me that Mrs. Piozzi's account is, in this instance, accurate, and that *he* was the person for whom Johnson wrote these verses, which have been erroneously ascribed to Mr. Hammond. I am obliged, in so many instances, to notice Mrs. Piozzi's incorrectness in relation, that I gladly seize this opportunity of acknowledging that, however often, she is not always, inaccurate." This last venomous stroke is admirable.

Now began the entertainment. Miss Seward, stung by this treatment, and inexpressibly mortified, wrote some letters to the *Gentleman's Magazine*, abusing Johnson and the " too invidious comments " of his biographer. Before she had seen his supplementary notes her friends had expressed their indignation " at what they termed the ungrateful rudeness with which I was treated on his first page." As to the verses, she simply " declined to resign her conviction." She added in plain terms, that Johnson had asserted such falsehoods as that " Buchanan was the only man of genius Scotland had produced," and that her facts were for the most part well known in Lichfield. Boswell replied in his happiest style :

"Miss Anne Seward, in a letter in your last Magazine, seems to apprehend that I have not treated her well in the first page of what she denominates a *pamphlet*. ... As I should be sorry to be thought thus deficient in politeness, much more in justice, to any person, but particularly to a fair lady, I think it necessary to answer a charge thus hastily brought against me.

"This lady, as she herself has stated, did indeed cover *several sheets of paper* with the few anecdotes concerning Dr. Johnson, which she did me the honour to communicate to me. They were not only poetically luxuriant, but I could easily perceive were tinctured with a very strong prejudice against the person to whom they related. It, therefore, became me to examine them with much caution. One of them, the idle and improbable story of his making verses on a duck when he was but three years old, which good Mrs. Lucy Porter, among others, had credulously related, he himself had enabled me unquestionably to refute; notwithstanding which, Miss Seward adheres to her original tale, and, in the letter now under consideration, still refers to them as his composition. Another story which she sent me was a very extraordinary fact, said to have been mentioned in a conversation between his mother and him on the subject of his marrying Mrs. Porter, which appeared to me so strange as to require confirmation. Miss Seward having quoted as her authority for it a respectable lady of Lichfield, I wrote to that lady, without mentioning the name of the person from whom the report was derived, inquiring fully into the authenticity of it. The lady informed me she had never heard of the fact alluded to. If my book was to be a *real history*, and not a *novel*, it was necessary to suppress all erroneous particulars, however entertaining. I was, therefore, obliged to reduce into a very narrow compass indeed, what Miss Seward's fluent pen had expanded over many sheets. The account, however, which she gave, in contradiction to that of Mrs. Piozzi, of the circumstances attending Johnson's writing his beautiful 'Verses to a Lady on receiving from her a Sprig of Myrtle,' seemed so plausible that I with confidence inserted it in the first edition of my book, nor had I any doubt of it till Mr. Hector spontaneously assured me, by letter, that the fact was as Mrs. Piozzi had represented it.

"Miss Seward says, that 'I ought in justice, as well as common politeness, since I mentioned her testimony, to have stated the reasons she gave for that different evidence.' Now, Sir, *this I have done*. In the first edition these reasons are fully stated. It was not necessary that the Corrections and Additions—which are not, as she imagines, a *distinct pamphlet*, but *supplemental* to that edition, and *to be taken along with it*—should contain a repetition of the grounds of her testimony. It was enough that a refutation of them was there exhibited. But in the second edition itself, after stating these grounds in her own words, *I let my fair antagonist down as softly as might be*—thus:" (He then quotes the passage).

"Miss Seward surely had no occasion to say one word to guard against her being suspected of 'averring a conscious falsehood.' No such suspicion was ever insinuated. Undoubtedly it *was* indifferent to her whether Dr. Johnson's verses were addressed to Lucy Porter or written for Mr. Hector; therefore when she made her statement of the case she had no motive of vanity or interest. Now it may, perhaps, not be indifferent, because she seems exceedingly zealous that her statement should be thought right. But there is no question either as to conscious falsehood or conscious truth; it is merely a matter of argument upon evidence, and, I think, a very plain one. I hope, then, Mr. Urban, this fair lady will be convinced that I have neither been unpolite nor unjust to her. But from the veneration and affection which I entertain for the character of my illustrious friend, I cannot be satisfied without expressing my indignation at the malevolence with which she has presumed to attack that great and good man.'

"So far from having any hostile disposition towards this lady, I have, in my 'Life of Dr. Johnson,' spoken of her in as handsome terms as I could; I have quoted a compliment paid by him to one of her political pieces; and I have withheld his opinion of herself, thinking that she might not like it. I am afraid it has reached her by some other means; and thus we may account for various attacks by her on her venerable townsman since his decease, even in your Magazine, where I have been sorry to see them,—some avowed, and with her own name, and others, as I believe, in various forms and under several signatures. What are we to think of the scraps of letters between her and Mr. Hayley, impotently endeavouring to undermine the noble pedestal on which the public opinion has placed Dr. Johnson? But it is unnecessary to take up any part of your valuable miscellany in expressing the little arts which have been employed by a cabal of minor poets and poetesses, who are sadly mortified that Dr. Johnson, by his powerful sentence, assigns their proper station to writers of this description." This is trenchant enough: but touch any of the good-humoured Boswell's writings, or his great friend, and he was "alive all over."

Miss Seward again replied, making allusion to "what Mr. Boswell has *generously* recorded concerning her father, at whose house he has been frequently entertained with the most friendly hospitality."

In reply, Boswell wrote :—

"Great Portland Street, January 20, 1794.

"Mr. Urban,—Having been too hastily charged in your Magazine, by Miss Anna Seward, with *want of politeness and even common justice* towards her, I was naturally anxious to vindicate myself, which I accordingly did in November last, by showing, in the most satisfactory manner, that I had been careful to express myself with due delicacy when obliged to correct an error into which she had been led, as to the true history of Dr. Johnson's writing the verses on a sprig of myrtle. I refer to my statement—I trust it with confidence to the candour of all who are capable of reasoning and judging of evidence.   I, at the same time, could not but discover some indignation at the malevolence with which that fair lady had presumed to attack the great and good Dr. Johnson, whose character was altogether unconnected with the inconsiderable matter in question. Whether he wrote those beautiful verses for himself or for a friend, his merit as a poet must be the same.   The investigation of their history was important only for the sake of truth, and in fairness to another lady, whom Miss Seward had induced me to contradict on grounds sufficiently probable, as I admitted in my additional note, I should have thought that there was no occasion for any more writing upon the subject; but I am sorry to find that our poetess has made a second attack, at great length, and in such a temper as must be very uneasy to a gentle bosom.

"Miss Seward may be assured that she is as much mistaken as to me as she is as to Dr. Johnson.   I am not her *foe*, though I committed to the flames those sheets of '*Johnsonian Narrative*' with which I was favoured by her, among the almost innumerable communications which I obtained concerning the illustrious subject of my great biographical work. I, however, extracted from those sheets all that I could possibly consider to be authentic. Nay, so desirous was I to give Miss Seward every advantage, that, after refuting the *impossible* legend of Johnson's verses on a Duck when he was but three years old, to which, for *a woman's reason*, she still pertinaciously adheres, I preserved the ingenious reflections which she, supposing it to be true, had made on that idle tale. I am not her *foe*, though I cannot allow that the censure of BACON by POPE, that Prince of Poets, who could

'Expatiate free o'er all this scene of man,'

is any reason why it is not presumptuous in Miss *Nancy Seward* to judge and condemn DR. JOHNSON, 'the brightest ornament of the eighteenth century,' as Mr. Malone has truly and elegantly described him. I am not her *foe*; though instead of joining in the republican cry as she does, that Johnson has been unjust to Milton, I declare my admiration of his very liberal and just praise of that great Poet, who was the most odious character, both in public and private, of any man of genius that ever lived; in public, the defender of the murderers of his sovereign, the blessed martyr; in private, the sulky tyrant over his own wretched, uneducated, and helpless daughters.

" Why should I be my fair antagonist's *foe?* she never did me any harm, nor do I apprehend that she ever can. She protests against entering further into a *paper war* with me. It there be such *war* it is all on one side, for it is not in my thoughts. That kind of conflict is not what I wish to have with ladies, and I really must complain that my *old friend* (if she will forgive the expression) should represent me so unlike myself.

"The lady quotes as genuine a sarcasm of Doctor Johnson on Lord Chesterfield, in these words : 'He is a wit among Lords, and a Lord among wits,' which, it seems, she has heard repeated by numbers. Here is a proof of the justice of the late Mr. Fitzherbert's observation that it is not everyone that can carry a *bon mot*. This representation of Johnson's saying is flat and unmeaning, indeed. What he did say is recorded at p. 238, vol. i. of my book, which Miss Seward handsomely, and I believe sincerely styles, 'interesting memoirs.' 'This man I thought had been a Lord among wits ; but I find he is only a wit among Lords.' It would, therefore, be better if Miss Seward would not boast of all the communications concerning Johnson, as 'conveying strong internal evidence of their verity from characteristic turn of expression ;' nor would it be any disadvantage to her if she should sometimes distrust the accuracy of her memory (I seriously protest, I mean no more).

"The detection of so considerable a mistake should make Miss Seward not so sure of having read, either in Dr. Johnson's works or in the records of his Biographers, an assertion concerning Dr. Watts, which she calls 'a base stigma and slander, and unchristian-like ;' and pours forth in her customary manner a profusion of words and abuse. It is not in the life of that excellent man ; and if Miss Seward has read it anywhere, she has read what was not true. That poets and poetesses also have too often been not of the most exemplary lives, is universally known ; but Dr. Johnson never uttered such a sentence as Miss Seward imputes to him. She, indeed, seems doomed to perpetual error, for she mentions a sentence quoted by her anonymous correspondent from Warburton, which she, with all imaginable ease, calls impious ; when, in truth, that admirable sentence is not quoted from Warburton, and was not written by Warburton, but by a most distinguished author now alive.*

"Miss Seward dreams that I have insinuated 'envy and selfish prejudice against her,' in my defensive letter; for this, after reading it over again and again, I cannot perceive the smallest foundation. She may make herself quite easy on that head, for I don't even suspect that my fair antagonist ('herself all the nine,')† envies any human being. Neither am I at all conscious of 'heroical attempts to injure a defenceless female (meaning herself), with which she charges me.

"'How canst thou, lovely Nancy, thus cruelly——?' Is it an injury to mention in civil terms that she has been misinformed as to a fact? Is it an injury to reprehend with generous warmth, her malevolent attacks on 'my Guide, Philosopher, and Friend'? Would that she were *offenceless! defenceless* she is not; as she now avers that she can at pleasure put on the masculine attire, and lay about her as a second Drawcansir, armed *cap à pied*, in the masked character of *Benvolio.* She modestly wishes that the strictures under that signature should be 'recurred to and considered well.' She may rest satisfied that they have been well and truly tried, and that the verdict of ineffectual ill-nature will ever be set aside. I wonder at her seeming to glory in such effusions. And now to put an end to all future disputation on the mighty points of the *Duck* and the *Myrtle,* which have been the causes of this *War;*

'This tumult in a vestal's veins.'"

Thus pleasantly does Boswell rally the fair combatant.

* Bishop Hurd.
† "See a short dialogue, in verse, between her and Mr. Hayley, written by Professor Porson."

Miss Seward presently retorted :—

"*Oct.* 14, 1793. The letter from Mr. Boswell is too
invidious not to require some comments. In these
Johnsonian narratives which he requested and obtained
from me, I neither invented nor embellished anything,
or felt or expressed resentment that he suppressed some
of them. Very different were his acknowledgments to
me at the time they were received. Before I had seen
Mr. Boswell's notes several of my friends expressed
indignation at what they termed the ungrateful way
in which I am introduced on the first page. Dr. Johnson's frequently expressed contempt for Mrs. Thrale, on
account of this want of veracity which he imputes to
her, at least as Mr. Boswell has recorded, either convicts
him of narrating what Johnson never said, or Johnson
himself of insincerity. I smile at Mr. Boswell's word
'presume,' as if it were more presumptuous to speak of
Dr. Johnson as he was, than of the illustrious Lord
Bacon. . . . Those with whom I have conversed were
too polite or too good-natured to inform me of one of
those many things which, I doubt not, he said to my
disadvantage. It cannot be pleasant to any person to
know that they must go down to posterity with the
arrows of his detraction sticking about them. It is,
however, of many of my superiors, both in merit and
talents, through Mr. Boswell's rage for commemoration,
which politeness and benevolence I once and long
believed inherent in his mind, ought on several instances to have been restrained; when they operated
in my favour I was obliged to him; but what he un-
generously says on that subject entirely cancels that
obligation, and proclaims him the foe of her whom he
has so often called friend. Of envy and selfish prejudice, insinuated against me by Mr. Boswell, I shall

be acquitted by all who know my disposition and the habits of my life."

Before the controversy began, there had been appearing in the magazines some rather malignant attacks signed "Benvolio," which Boswell charged the lady with writing. She wrote to the editor and acknowledged herself as the author: "The letters signed Benvolio are mine; I avowed them to almost all my friends, and I think to Mr. Boswell. The only occasion on which I declined to acknowledge them was in a literary circle in London, May, 1786, when I heard the first two pronounced the most equitable balance of Dr. Johnson's good and ill qualities which had appeared. They were too highly spoken of to permit my owning them, as the company were chiefly strangers to me. Who it was that took the unwarrantable liberty of sending to your Reporters these extracts from Mr. Hayley's letters and mine, without the consent of their authors, I have to this hour no guess. They were never intended for the public, but made and transmitted to some friend for his amusement." *

* Porson wrote some amusing lines upon the interchanges of compliments between "the Bard" and the lady.

"Miss SEWARD *loquitur.*

Tuneful Poet, Britain's glory,
Mr. Hayley that is you.

HAYLEY *respondet.*

Ma'am, you carry all before you,
Trust me, Lichfield Swan, you do.

Miss SEWARD.

Ode, didactic, epic, sonnet,
Mr. Hayley you're divine.

MR. HAYLEY.

Ma'am, I'll take my oath upon it,
You yourself are all the Nine."

Another of his antagonists was Bishop Percy. As some of the speeches and retorts addressed to him by the sage were of rather an offensive kind, the bishop, with a sagacious mistrust that he was not likely to figure with dignity in the chronicle, took care, in sending to Boswell a number of communications filled with details of Johnson's early life, to request that his name might not be mentioned in the work. But Boswell felt that the incidents in which Dr. Percy took part were among the most piquant of his collection, and refused to comply, declaring that it was a duty he owed "to the authenticity of his book, to its respectability, and to the credit of his illustrious friend, to "—and the reader will wonder what was the shape of this sacred obligation — "introduce *as many names of eminent persons as I can.*" "Believe me, my lord," he goes on, "you are not the only Bishop in the number of great men with which my pages are graced. I am quite resolute in this matter." The prelate had no redress. There was something, indeed, ungracious in the gusto with which Boswell recorded Johnson's speeches and sneers at the expense of his episcopal friend, as in the "History of the Grey Rat," and the warm discussion on Pennant—one of the most dramatic in the book. Unfortunately the bishop had been indiscreet enough to confide to Boswell that he "was uneasy at what had passed," for a person had witnessed the scene, a friend of the Duke of Northumberland, who would of course report how contemptuously the friend of Johnson had been treated. On this very natural speech the busy Boswell proceeded to work, and, as I said, exhibits his mind and its processes to posterity in a most original fashion. We can imagine the bishop's feelings as he read the opening words. "There was a man," he was made to say, " who had recently been admitted into the confidence of the Northumberland family, *to whom he hoped to appear more respectable* by showing him how intimate he was with the great Dr. Johnson, and now the gentleman would go away with an expression much to his disadvantage, as if Johnson treated him with disregard, which might do him an essential injury." On this rather sycophantic and candid confession of motives it is evident a warm remonstrance and even contradiction must have followed; for we find in later editions that " the gentleman recently admitted, etc.," becomes merely " acquainted with the Northumberland family," and the " essential injury " that might follow is omitted. While the phrase " the *great* Dr. Johnson," which suggests the idea that Percy had been boasting in the country of his intimacy, was toned down to " Dr. Johnson."

Boswell having duly reported the bishop's complaint to Johnson—who remarked that " this only came of stratagem "—a fresh, indirect reflection on the bishop, the doctor proceeded to speak of Dr. Percy " in the handsomest terms "—or " manner," as Boswell chose to alter it later: " Then, Sir," said I, " may I be allowed to suggest a mode by which you may effectually counter-act any unfavourable report of what passed ? I will write a letter to you upon the subject of the unlucky contest of that day, and you will be kind enough to put in writing, as an answer to that letter, what you have now said, and as Lord Percy is to dine with us at General Paoli's soon, I will take an opportunity to read the correspondence in his lordship's presence." This friendly scheme was accordingly carried into execution without Dr. Percy's knowledge. . . . I contrived that Lord Percy should hear *the correspondence. Our friend*

Percy was raised higher in the estimation of those by
whom he wished most to be regarded. I breakfasted
the day after with him, and informed him of my scheme,
and its happy completion, for which he thanked me in
the warmest terms, and was highly delighted with Dr.
Johnson's letter in his praise, of which I gave him a
copy.

The passage in italics must have also given offence :
for "our friend" Boswell later shaped it "Thus every
unfavourable impression was obviated that could possibly have been made on those by whom," etc. As
Johnson's letter was warm and handsome in its terms,
and would have been a testimonial to his merits in the
eyes of Lord Percy and the other guests, naturally Dr.
Percy was grateful and pleased at the idea, and at its
being so successfully carried out. But the meddling
Boswell took care not to show him the letter to which
Johnson's letter was an answer ; and in which *he* had
written :—"My dear Sir,—I beg leave to address you
in behalf of our friend Dr. Percy, *who was much hurt
by what you said to him* that day we dined at his house
. . . Percy is sensible that you did not mean to injure
him ; but he is vexed to think that your behaviour to
him on that occasion may be interpreted *as a proof that
he is despised by you,* which I know is not the case. . . .
Earl Percy is to dine with General Paoli next Friday ;
and I should be sincerely glad to have it in my power
to satisfy his lordship how well you think of Dr. Percy,
who, I find, apprehends that your good opinion of him
may be of very essential consequence ; and who assures
me that he has the highest respect and the warmest
affection for you."

Now, it will be noted that the italicized passages are
put in the most awkward and needlessly emphatic mode

that can be conceived. It was bad to read all this in the "Life," but it would seem that Mr. Boswell actually read it aloud at the dinner *in presence* of Lord Percy: for he used the phrase, "read the *correspondence*," thrice to Johnson : but when writing to Percy he takes care to say that he only "read Johnson's *answer*." Finally, at the close of his characteristic episode he adds a kind of disclaimer to this effect :—"Though the Bishop of Dromore kindly answered the letters which I wrote to him, relative to Dr. Johnson's early history ; yet, in justice to him, I think it proper to add, that the account of the foregoing conversation, and the subsequent transaction, as well as of some other conversations in which he is mentioned, has been given to the public without previous communication with his lordship." The meaning of which is that the bishop was no party to the publication of portions of this little history: though Boswell was so dull as not to see that he was making his friend ridiculous.

That the bishop's remonstrances on the way he was mentioned in the work were rather "tart," is evident from a passage or two later introduced by Boswell. In the amusing passage about Dr. Grainger and his heroic introduction of "Let's sing of Rats !" (changed from *mice*, as "more dignified ") Percy had originally furnished a defence of his friend—which Boswell introduced in a note. In his second edition, Boswell maliciously supplies the following from his recollection :—"Dr. Johnson said to me, 'Percy, sir, was angry with me for laughing at his "Sugar Cane ;" for he had a mind to make a great thing of Grainger's rats '—and, further, adds this comment to the bishop's original defence of his friend : 'The above was written by the Bishop when he had not the poem itself to recur to ; and though the

account given of it was true at one period, yet, as Dr.
Grainger afterwards altered the passage in question, the
remarks in the text do not now apply to the printed
poem.'" No wonder Dr. Percy wrote to his friend
Anderson—"Boswell's ludicrous account of the 'Sugar
Cane' deserves no attention." And his disgust at
this treatment is shown in other comments; the account of the manner of writing the dictionary, "as
given by Mr. Boswell, is confused and erroneous, and
a moment's reflection will convince every person of
judgment, could not be correct." And again he adds:
"Mr. Boswell describes Levett as a man of a strange
grotesque appearance. This is misrepresented." "Mr.
Boswell objects to the title of the Rambler, etc. These
are curious reasons." As to Savage—"This, if true,
Johnson was not likely to have confessed to Mr. Boswell, and therefore must be received as a pure invention
of his own." This seems pretty sharp.

Boswell was to excel himself in one surprising indiscretion, which is, in the common phrase, Boswell "all
over." When Johnson and Wilkes, after their reconcile-
ment, were sitting talking in almost affectionate terms,
Boswell declared it suggested the lion lying down with
the lamb. "When I mentioned this (the speech about
the lion and lamb) to the Bishop of Killaloe (Dr.
Bernard), '*With the goat*,' said his lordship:" a very
offensive remark, and never, of course, meant by the
prelate to be repeated or printed. Yet the passage
must have been read by both Wilkes and the bishop.
He then adds: "Such, however, was the engaging
politeness and pleasantry of Mr. Wilkes, and such the
social good-humour of the bishop, that when they dined
together at Mr. Dilly's, when I also was there, they were
mutually agreeable." Boswell, according to his favourite

recipe, fancied he thus completely neutralized the mischief. It is only fair to add, however, that Boswell's enthusiasm for his great work, and "the authenticity of my journal," was such that he could not bring himself to sacrifice any effective detail, and thought by compliment to make up for indiscretion.

But it is his behaviour towards Mrs. Piozzi that seems most wanton, and, it must be said, ungrateful. For at Streatham he had been welcomed with hospitality as Johnson's friend.

The reason of this unbecoming dislike is to be found, as it appears to me, in Boswell's annoyance and mortification at discovering that some of the very best of his anecdotes—the choicest almost of Johnson's good things, and some of the most piquant sayings, uttered in *his* presence as well as in hers—had been noted by the "lively lady" and published. He had been forestalled. She was, therefore, a greater offender than Hawkins; and it does seem, moreover, that her having fallen under public odium might encourage Mr. Boswell in his attacks.*

In this "no case," all that was left to him was "to abuse the plaintiff"—that is, to break out into those

---

* The following will show that Mrs. Thrale had secured a good deal of what may be called the "cream." The remark on "Kelly" and Dodd; the "*Strong* Facts" in the Ordinary of Newgate's account; the Siamese sending ambassadors to Louis XIV.; the going to church; the lines "Hermit Hoar;" "talked about Tom Thumb;" "a good hater;" "the dead wit;" "just enough to light him to Hell;" remarks on being able to dispense with dress; Goldsmith and Doctor Minor; Hannah More "choking him with her flattery:" the gentleman that said but one word, "Richard;" the story of his reading when he met Mr. Cholmondeley; the retort on *in vino veritas;* the Scotchman's "finest prospect;" a ship being a jail; the "many men, many women;" "knowledge in Scotland being like food in a besieged city;" all these racy anecdotes had been anticipated.

perpetually recurring attacks on her inaccuracy, in which, it must be owned, he did not succeed. At the very end of his work, he brings in his friend Malone to abuse the lady—"Two instances of inaccuracy," he says, "are particularly worthy of notice." One night they were both abusing Mrs. Thrale, and Boswell could not resist reporting their discourteous remarks, the publication of which Johnson would never have sanctioned. "He showed me to-night his drawing-room, very genteelly fitted up ; and said, '*Mrs. Thrale sneered*, when I talked of my having asked you and your lady to live at my house. I was obliged to tell her, that you would be in as respectable a situation in my house as in hers. Sir, the insolence of wealth will creep out.' BOSWELL. 'She has *a little both of the insolence of wealth, and the conceit of parts.*' JOHNSON. 'The insolence of wealth is a wretched thing ; but the conceit of parts has some foundation. To be sure, it should not be.'"

But his dislike, and venom even, were chiefly displayed against Sir John Hawkins. When Sir John's "Life of Johnson" appeared, Boswell was stung by the way in which he was mentioned : "He had *long been sollicited by Mr. Boswell, a native of Scotland*, and one that highly valued him, etc." Miss Hawkins says that she well remembered "the first introduction of Boswell on what may be called the Johnsonian stage. What is ludicrously called his *earwigging*, began to attract notice ; and my father inquired of Mr. Langton, who this novel performer was, meaning rather, I believe, to be on good terms with him, as a frequenter in Bolt Court. The answer he received was a caution against opening his door to him. Not only were his visits described to be long, but he was

known to carry, as was said, perhaps by way of
metaphor, his night-cap in his pocket, and to be blind
to all inconvenience, and deaf to all hints, when at
leisure. My father and he, however, grew a little
acquainted; and when the 'Life' of their friend came
out, Boswell showed himself very uneasy under an
injury, which he was much embarrassed in defining.
He called on my father, and being admitted, complained
of the manner in which he was enrolled amongst
Johnson's friends, which was as 'Mr. James Boswell
of Auchinleck.'

"Where was the offence? It was one of those,
which a complainant hardly dares to embody in words,
he would only repeat, 'Well, but, *Mr. James Boswell,*
surely, surely, *Mr. James Boswell*——'

"My father relieved him by guessing with some
humour, that the distinction bestowed on a public
singer or dancer, would have better satisfied him. 'I
know,' said he, 'Mr. Boswell, what you mean; you
would have had me say that Johnson undertook this
tour with THE Boswell.' He could not indeed absolutely
covet this mode of proclamation; he would, perhaps,
have been content with 'the celebrated,' or 'the well-
known,' but he could not confess quite so much; he
therefore acquiesced in the amendment proposed, but
he was forced to depart without any promise of correction in a subsequent edition."

This version seems to be true; and the idea of Mr.
Boswell placidly accepting the idea of being described
as "*the* Boswell" is quite characteristic. But he
registered the insult, especially when he found that the
new edition had appeared without alteration. Two
years afterwards, in 1789, he was at work revising the
first pages of his book, and had a Roland for the

knight's Oliver ready. "Pray," he wrote to his friend, "by return of post, help me with a word. In censuring Sir J. Hawkins's book, I say, 'There is throughout the whole of it a dark, uncharitable cast, which puts the most unfavourable construction on my illustrious friend's conduct.' Malone maintains *cast* will not do; he will have 'malignancy.' Is that not too strong? how would 'disposition' do? Hawkins is no doubt very malevolent. *Observe how he talks of me as quite unknown.*"

It will hardly be credited that only a few weeks before this consultation Mr. Boswell had breakfasted with the knight, and our author was writing to his friends that he was, "he believed, a good man, but very mean for his fortune." And later, within a week or two of the little plot, he was declaring that they were "in good social plight" together, and exceedingly well —that he had entertained Hawkins, and Hawkins him. All the winter, too, he said, they had been intimate. Yet, all the while he was putting down the most extraordinary accusations—charges of theft, etc. Hawkins was in bad health, and died soon after, otherwise these accusations and insinuations could not have been published.

One would be inclined to suppose that these were owing to the promptings of Mr. Malone, who seemed to have loathed Hawkins, calling him "a detestable fellow," accusing him of stealing Johnson's watch, stick, etc., and of lying. Some of these comments show a strange spirit of perversion. Thus Boswell says, "I cannot trace the least foundation for the following dark and uncharitable assertion by Sir John Hawkins :— 'The apparition of his departed wife was altogether of the terrific kind, and hardly afforded him a hope that she was in a state of happiness." Terrific may be too

strong a word, but we certainly find Johnson perpetually praying for *the repose* of his Tetty's soul—"and
that she might finally be received into eternal happiness."

It is almost amusing to follow the stages of Boswell's
animosity; he admits, however, that in Sir John's
" *compilation* "—not " life," mark !—there were " some
passages of unquestionable merit." Hawkins, when
dealing with Johnson's love for his antique wife, speculates that it was " dissembled," *i.e.* assumed or learned
by rote. On this Boswell says, this view probably arose
" *from a want of similar feelings* in his *own breast.*" (!)
Boswell's dislike, it seems, made him allude in this
unbecoming way to a malicious story, that was circulated,
that he had " married an old woman for the sake of her
money." Miss Hawkins vindicates her father, and
assumes too hastily that Boswell had actually set this
charge down in words, and also that " he was the son of
a carpenter," in which she was mistaken. " Unless,"
she adds, " marrying a very pretty woman twenty-six
years of age, when he himself was seven years older,
can in any way be distorted into this baseness. Nor
can I admit that my father married even for the sake of
her money. He had been the favourite of her father,
Peter Storer, of Highgate."

" Here," says Boswell, " I am enabled to refute a
very unjust reflection against Johnson and his faithful
servant Francis Barber, by Sir John Hawkins, as if he
had been unjust towards one Heely, whom Sir John
chooses to call a *relation* of Dr. Johnson's." For he
explains that Heely had been married only to Johnson's
cousin. It will hardly be credited that Hawkins states
that Heeley's relation to Johnson was *by marriage.*
He further adds that Johnson had been " very liberal to

him." And he does not vindicate Barber at all. In another point, too, Boswell was singularly unfair. The deceased knight, in his second edition, had altered and softened many of the passages, to which our biographer takes exception ; yet in many instances Boswell quotes from the first, ignoring the alterations in the second. Again : " Sir John Hawkins has given a long detail of it, in that manner vulgarly, but significantly, called *rigmarole ;* in which, amidst an ostentatious exhibition of arts and artists, he talks of ' proportions ' of a column being taken from that of the human figure, and *adjusted by nature.* . . . To follow the Knight through all this would be an useless fatigue to myself, and not a little disgusting to my readers." When Sir John makes some errors in transcribing from one of Johnson's notebooks, he says, " It would have been better to have left blanks than to write nonsense." In a note he describes him as " Mr. John Hawkins, an attorney," " who upon occasion of presenting *some* address to the King, accepted the *usual offer* of knighthood. By *assiduous attendance* upon Johnson in his last illness, he obtained the office of one of his executors, *in consequence* of which the booksellers employed him to publish an edition of Johnson's works, and to write a preface." Now all this ingenious depreciation is distorted by animosity. Hawkins was one of Johnson's oldest friends, and nearly a year before his death (in February, 1784,) had been asked by him to prepare his will and act as his executor. The description " an attorney " was studiously offensive, and a retort for " Mr. Boswell, a native of Scotland." The choice of the booksellers, who sent a deputation to him on Johnson's death, was a deep mortification to Boswell.

But Boswell's final assault was reserved for the end

of the knight's book. The important part the latter took in the closing scenes of Johnson's life must have filled him with annoyance and mortification, and he went as far as to accuse him of stealing Johnson's property! Hawkins, it seems, observing two MS. volumes of Johnson's lying about, put them in his pocket, declaring that he wished to keep them from falling into the hands of persons whom he suspected might take them. When Johnson asked for them, he gave them up. It must be recollected that he was Johnson's executor. This explanation he gave in his second edition, no doubt obliged to do so by the malignant reports of Malone, who in his "Diary" charges Hawkins with stealing a walking-stick and other articles. Boswell, all through, was inspired by Malone. The droll part of it is that Boswell himself had read these valuable papers, and had actually been inclined to steal them. Further, Hawkins expressly says that he told "those around him, particularly Mr. Langton and Mr. Strahan, that I had got both volumes, with my reasons for thus securing them." Here falls to the ground the charge of Hawkins's animosity to Barber, and to Heely who "detected" him. Mr. Croker falls into the mistake of saying that Hawkins was forced into making this explanation by Boswell's notice of the affair in his book. But Boswell's book was not published until some years after Hawkins' death.

Boswell's dislike of Hawkins and Mrs. Piozzi is, as we have said, founded on their having forestalled him in his task. Both had been kind and hospitable to him; and it is not too much to say that, in Hawkins's case, certainly an action for libel would have gone against Boswell, so blind and blundering are his attacks.

It would take a volume to show the indiscreet

strokes, sketches, and sayings of persons living and dead
which the author scattered through his book.   Again
we wonder that he escaped personal chastisement.   Even
ladies like Lady Diana Beauclerk found their careless
remarks recorded.   But there was a more redoubtable
adversary, Dr. Parr, whom a statement of the author's
now brought into the field.   Boswell had described
Johnson's indignation at Dr. Priestley's name being
mentioned in his presence ; and, in a note, the chronicler
made allusion to a recently published tract of Dr. Parr's,
in which the latter appeared "to suppose that *Dr.
Johnson had not only endured, but almost solicited an
interview with Dr. Priestley.*   In justice to Dr. Johnson
I declare my firm belief that he never did.   My illustrious friend was particularly resolute in not giving
countenance to men whose writings he considered as
pernicious to society."   He then tells how he had seen
Dr. Johnson leave the room at once when Dr. Price
came into the company : *   "Much more would he have
reprobated Dr. Priestley.   Whoever," he goes on,
"wishes to see a perfect delineation of *this literary
Jack of all trades* may find it in an ingenious tract
entitled, etc."   Boswell's vindication of Dr. Johnson
might have been readily disposed of by merely quoting
the meeting at dinner with Wilkes, whose writings
certainly were "pernicious to society," meetings which
he himself had contrived.

Dr. Parr replied, and, as may be imagined, "demo-
lished" Mr. Boswell.   "Through the bluntness of
Mr. Boswell's language, I am unable to collect precisely
the extent of his meaning.   He might mean to say that

---

* This, by the way, shows that Boswell has omitted to give
an account of some dramatic incidents in his hero's course.   We
should have been glad to have had a description of this curious
scene.

Dr. Johnson and Dr. Priestley had not met at all; or he might mean to say only that Dr. Johnson had not 'almost solicited the meeting.'" He was, however, not in a hostile mode; indeed added, "he hoped to give him no offence" by the answers he had obtained to his inquiries. A Mr. E. Johnstone, it seems, had been the person to whom Dr. Priestley had told the tale that he had met Johnson; who said that, knowing Dr. Johnson's prejudices against himself, he had never sought that interview; that he had met Dr. Johnson under the idea that Dr. Johnson wished to see him, and that Dr. Johnson's behaviour was very civil, and seemed to him very respectful. "I particularly remember the word *respectful;* and it is so marked a word from so plain a man, that I can know. I must and do appeal to you for the correctness of my statement." Another gentleman, Mr. Edward Bearcroft, probably the eminent counsel, wrote that he had heard, in April or May last, Dr. Priestley relate the story of his meeting with Johnson, describing also "the particular civility with which the doctor had treated him when they dined together at Mr. Paradise's. The writer had that very evening reminded Mr. Paradise of the incident, who said he remembered very well that Johnson had been previously told that Priestley was to be one of the company, and that he manifested great civility to him upon that occasion." More interesting to us is the testimony of one who is remembered by some of our time. "I heard," wrote Samuel Rogers, "of the interview between Dr. Johnson and Dr. Priestley, from Dr. Priestley himself. I have heard it mentioned more than once. I understood that it was not solicited by Dr. Priestley; and that if any overture was made for that purpose, it came from Dr. Johnson. I found that Dr. Priestley thought that Dr. Johnson's behaviour was such as it ought to have been from one man of letters to another. Johnson was very civil."

Most people will agree with Dr. Parr in his logical comments upon these testimonies. "The dispute," he says, "now lies between Mr. Boswell and Dr. Priestley; between firm belief, on the one hand, and positive assertion on the other; between Mr. Boswell's inference from his knowledge of Dr. Johnson's general disposition, and Dr. Priestley's account of Dr. Johnson's behaviour in a particular case. Mr. Boswell cannot imagine that I was capable of overlooking the guarded and ambiguous language in which he represents me as *appearing to suppose* what in truth I believed, and still continue to believe very firmly, what I recollected very distinctly, and stated very unreservedly. He will not be displeased with me for declaring that in my tract I meant no dishonour to Dr. Johnson's memory, while I allow that he intended to do what he thought justice to Dr. Johnson's memory by his note. . . . Should Mr. Boswell be pleased to maintain that Dr. Johnson rather *consented* to the interview than *almost solicited it*, I shall not object to the change of expressions. If Dr. Johnson met Dr. Priestley, and if he previously knew that he was to meet him,—if, upon meeting him, he behaved to Dr. Priestley with particular civility,—he did what Mr. Boswell represents as unlikely, indeed as unfit to have been done by so exact and inflexible a moralist towards a writer whose opinions he thought pernicious to society. I reverence Dr. Johnson not less than Mr. Boswell does; and if I respect Dr. Priestley more than he seems to do, I am not entirely without the hope of being approved by some who are wise and many who are good. The chief purpose, however, for which I desire you, Mr. Editor, to insert what I am now writing to you, is neither to defend Dr. Priestley, nor to censure Dr. Johnson, but to show that when I was speaking in my tract of two men, who have deservedly so large a share of public attention, I possessed a sort of evidence which even Mr. Boswell himself, when he knows it, will have too much candour to slight. That evidence, though it should fail to convince Mr. Boswell, is, at all events, sufficient to justify me."

This is in the doctor's best style. Mr. Boswell was not inclined to sit down quietly under this chastisement, and he set to work to answer it, but was interrupted by his last illness.*

It would be difficult to give an idea of the number of persons who must have taken offence at the way they were introduced, and to whom some sort of *amende* had to be made in the second edition. This could only be shown by a collation of the editions. Some of his friends took offence at the fashion in which they were introduced. Amongst them was Sir William Scott, Johnson's executor. The good-humoured Boswell soothed him in his persuasive way.

". . . Be so good as to recollect that I have not published any of *your* folly, for a very obvious reason ; and what I have published of your share in the 'Johnsonian Conversations' was revised by yourself, upon which occasion I enjoyed one of the pleasantest days I ever passed in my life. *You*, therefore, my good Sir William, have no reason even to *grumble*. If others, as

---

* The editor of the *Gentleman's Magazine* had his say in a curt note : "To the communications of our correspondents, relative to our late worthy friend, James Boswell, Esq., we have to add that he was preparing, at the time he was taken ill, a general answer to the letter from the Ajax of literature, in which he proposed also to notice the attacks of his more puny antagonists."

well as myself, sometimes appear as shadows to the Great
Intellectual Light, I beg to be fairly understood, and
that you and my other friends will inculcate upon
persons of timidity and reserve, that my recording the
Conversations of so extraordinary a man as Johnson,
with its concomitant circumstances, was a peculiar
undertaking attended with much anxiety and labour,
and that the conversations of people in general are by
no means of that nature as to bear being registered, and
that the task of doing it would be exceedingly irksome
to me.   Class me then, my dear Sir, with none but who
are clear of a prejudice which you see may easily be
cured : I trust there are enough who have it not.   I can
return you the compliment, that I should certainly
consider a quarrel with you as a real misfortune.   I
now do not apprehend that there can be even any cold-
ness. . . ." etc.*

We have shown how many allusions Boswell made
to his friend Wilkes, some of a rather awkward and
offensive kind ; though the good-natured Wilkes was
not the man to take offence.†

* Letter in Messrs. Sotheby's Catalogue, November 27, 1889,
dated April, 1791.

† In Mr. Walford's " Antiquarian " is given an interesting
account of the copy which the author presented to Mr. Wilkes,
which I myself had once the opportunity of purchasing : " In the
cover of each volume there was a book-plate, with the owner's
coat of arms and name—'John Wilkes, F.R.S.,' and with the
motto, '*Arcui meo non confido.*'   At the bottom of the blank
reverse of the last leaf of the Dedication to Sir Joshua Reynolds
is an autograph inscription in the handwriting of James Boswell:—

" ' To John Wilkes, Esq :
from his much obliged friend,
The Authour.
' *Nil ego contulerim jucundo sanus amico.*'

" There is a printed list of ' Corrections and Additions which
the Reader is requested to make with his Pen, before perusing the

It must have needed all Wilkes's *bonhomie* and good humour to have passed over the style in which

following Life.' These, which are twenty-four in number, Wilkes has carefully attended to, down to the minutest particulars.

"But the chief interest centres in two original notes in Wilkes's handwriting, the first of which supplies the *ipsissima verba* of Johnson, misreported by Boswell.

"In vol. i., p. 107–108 (under date 1749, when Johnson was forty years old, and when Garrick was in the full flush of his early fame), the following passage occurs in the text :—

" ' He [Johnson] for a considerable time used to frequent the *Green Room*, and seemed to take delight in dissipating his gloom by mixing in the sprightly chit-chat of the motley circle then to be found there. Mr. David Hume related to me from Mr. Garrick that Johnson at last denied himself this amusement, from considerations of rigid virtue ; saying, " I'll come no more behind your scenes, David ; for the silk stockings and white bosoms of your actresses *excite my amorous propensities.*' "

"Whether the four words in italics were substituted by Hume, as a sacrifice to the proprieties, in relating the story to Boswell, or were a polite periphrasis of Boswell himself, mindful for once of what was due *virginibus puerisque*, cannot now with certainty be determined. Wilkes informs us, on the authority of Garrick himself, to whom the utterance was addressed, what those words actually were. We are unable to reproduce them here ; but they will be forthcoming to such students as may communicate privately with the writer of this paper, or with the editor or publisher of the Magazine.

"At vol. ii. p. 141, occurs this passage in the text :—' Johnson gave us this evening, in his happy discriminative manner, a portrait of the late Mr. Fitzherbert, of Derbyshire.'

"To this Wilkes has appended the following manuscript note at the foot of the page :—' Lady Vane described Mr. Fitzherbert well. She said that he was very *dry*, very *shy*, and very *sly*.'

"It was with some disappointment that I found no marginalia or annotations against the passages where Wilkes himself personally figures as one of the *dramatis personæ* of Boswell's narrative ; but against his name in the index, Wilkes has enumerated other pages where it is incidentally mentioned or introduced either by the biographer or by Johnson and his interlocutors. He has also added to the index a reference to ' WOMEN,' ii. 501,'—the passage where Johnson declares that ' ladies set no value on the moral character of men who pay their addresses to them ; the greatest profligate will be as well received as the man of the greatest virtue,' " etc. Wilkes, when he had read it, declared to the

he was exhibited in Boswell's work. No worse
specimen of indiscretion could be found than this. He
reports Johnson as saying: "It is wonderful to think
that all the force of government was required to
prevent Wilkes from being chosen the chief magistrate
of London, though the liverymen knew he would rob
their shops, knew he would debauch their daughters."
This was gross, especially as it was published at a
moment when the world was beginning to forget and
condone Wilkes's follies. To this he added his comment
in a note: "I think *it incumbent on me* to make some
observation on this strong satirical sally on my classical
companion, Mr. Wilkes. Reporting it lately from
memory, *in his presence,* I expressed it thus: 'They
knew he would rob their shops *if he durst,* they knew
he would debauch their daughters *if he could,*' which,
according to the French phrase, may be said *renchérir*
on Dr. Johnson; but on looking into my Journal, I
found it as above, and would by no means make any
addition. Mr. Wilkes received both readings with a
good humour that I cannot enough admire. Indeed,
both he and I are too fond of a *bon mot,* not to
relish it, though we should be ourselves the object of
it." Here he not only repeats Johnson's offensive and,
it must be said, unfounded criticism, but adds of his
own motion something to make it still more offensive.
On referring to his note for the true version he takes
credit for not altering it: "would by no means make
any addition."

The tolerance or indifference of Wilkes is shown in
the total absence of comment on the passages referring

author, "It is a wonderful book." Next day Boswell wrote to him
to have this opinion in writing. "Do confirm this to me, so that
I may have your testimonies in my archives at Auchinleck."

to himself. We find that Wilkes had even helped his friend with a timely loan :—

Mr. Boswell to Mr. Wilkes.

" DEAR SIR,—Notwithstanding a late seasonable relief I am not yet free from vexatious embarrassments. But I should be very uneasy if I could not restore what was put into my hands upon the most liberal terms, when it is of any consequence to you, and still more, when I am informed that at this moment trifles are of importance. I am very sorry to find that I cannot command it till next week. But you may depend upon its being thus gratefully returned. I am, dear sir, your obliged friend and humble servant, JAMES BOSWELL.

"Great Portland Street, Dec. 24, 1792." *

Boswell to Wilkes.

" Mr. Boswell presents his compliments to Mr. Wilkes—an invitation to dinner will not do. The Laird of Auchinleck is not hungry, and *he* does not want wine, but wit. In short, he must have a pleasant apology for *putting him in fear* of Dr. Johnson's displeasure on account of a certain Epithalamium, or there must be an end to a certain classical and gay connection.

"No. 22, Poultry, March 26, 1783." †

To the Same.

" DEAR SIR,—As I undertook to be the negociator of the dinner at your house, The High Sheriff of

* MS., British Museum. † Ibid.

Pembrokeshire, his brother Mr. Charles Dilly, and an old *Vesuvius* fellow traveller, I beg to know if next Sunday will be convenient for the Chamberlain of London. This is '*omnia magna coquens.*' My best compliments to Miss Wilkes. She knows my conditional threating that you should have been *mon beau père. Vale at me ame.* JAMES BOSWELL.

"General Paoli's, South Audley Street, May 12th."

A good instance of Boswell's unbecoming indulgence in his dislikes of persons is the following. He praised Mr. Maclaurin's argument for the negro, and the motto prefixed, "*Hominum* ne crede colori," which he called "happily chosen." This it certainly was not, for "color" would refer to the negro's tint, which we are invited not to trust. It proved, however, that he had made a complete mistake, and that the "happily chosen" motto was "Quamvis ille niger, etc." He then adds, "a circumstance not less strange than true, that a brother advocate in considerable practice, but of whom it certainly cannot be said 'ingenuas fideliter didicit fideliter artes,' asked Mr. Maclaurin, *with a face of flippant assurance,* 'Are these words your own?'" Could anything be more indecorous or foolish? Again, "Tom Tyers," a great friend of Johnson's, "was exceedingly obliging" to Mr. Boswell, a claim certainly, to forbearance. He dared, however, to publish a short biography of Johnson; on which Boswell proceeds to describe him as "eccentric," running about the world amusing everybody with his desultory conversation. "He abounded in anecdote, but was not sufficiently attentive to accuracy. I therefore cannot venture to avail myself much of his biographical sketch which he published, *being one among the various persons* ambitious of appending their *names to that of my illustrious friend.*" This was his most contemptuous mode of disparaging competitors.

We have seen that his old enemy Walcot's attacks were in a coarse vein. On these a happy parody was written by Mr. Chalmers, which is witty, and not ill-natured. In his copy of the "Life," we find this note : "This imitation I printed in the *Morning Herald*, in July, 1791. When Boswell discovered I had written it, he often took an opportunity in my company to praise it, and had once an intention to have printed it in his octavo edition, but was dissuaded. To all appearance he took it, as it was meant, in good part, and was after very friendly with me." How creditable is this to Bozzy's good nature and good humour ! For he was so pleased with the wit of the thing, that he could condone the ridicule of himself.

"*P. P.:* ' Pray, Doctor, what is your opinion of Mr. Boswell's literary powers ? '

"*Johnson:* ' Sir, my opinion is, that whenever Bozzy expires, he will create no vacuum in the region of literature—he seems strongly affected by the *cacoëthes scribendi;* wishes to be thought a *rara avis,* and in truth so he is—your knowledge in ornithology, sir, will easily discover to what species of bird I allude.' Here the Doctor shook his head and laughed.

"*P. P.:* ' What think you, sir, of his account of Corsica ?—of his character of Paoli ? '

"*Johnson:* ' Sir, he hath made a mountain of a wart. But Paoli hath virtues. The account is a farrago of disgusting egotism and pompous inanity.'

"*P. P.:* 'I have heard it whispered, Doctor, that should you die before him, Mr. B. means to write your life.'

"*Johnson :* 'Sir, he cannot mean me so irreparable an injury—which of us shall die first is only known to the Great Disposer of events : but were I sure that James Boswell would write *my* life, I do not know whether I would not anticipate the measure by taking *his.*' (Here he made three or four strides across the room, and returned to his chair with violent emotion.)

"*P. P. :* 'I am afraid that he means to do you the favour.'

"*Johnson :* 'He dares not—he would make a scarecrow of me. I give him liberty to fire his blunderbuss in *his own* face, but not murder *me*, sir. I heed not his αυτος εφα. Boswell write my life ! why, the fellow possesses not abilities for writing the life of an ephemeron.'"

There are also numbers of allusions and incidental notices which have a slightly offensive tone, and which are contrived to make the persons named feel "awkward." Here is one example : Lord Hailes, whom Boswell troubled a good deal, had said of Johnson's legal argument that "it was pleasantly and artfully composed." On which Boswell says in a note, "Why his Lordship uses the epithet *pleasantly* when speaking of a grave piece of reasoning I cannot conceive. But different men have different notions of pleasantry." He then tells of a gentleman at the opera, who, when Medea was about killing her children, "turned to me with a smile and said, 'Funny enough.'" Lord Hailes could not have been pleased with this similitude.*

* From the redoubtable Dr. Farmer he received some rough treatment : "After wondering how a Scotch advocate should be so perfectly uninformed as to know nothing of the best edition and the best modern editor of Demosthenes, I will only say of him what Dr. Taylor himself probably would, had he seen the strange passage—at least I have heard him say it of many similar geniuses,

One distinction, at least, that was secured to him by the publication of his volumes was his election by the Royal Academy to the honorary office of Secretary for Foreign Correspondence. To his great gratification he was now, at last, taken seriously—like Goldsmith, Burke, and other friends; and he wrote his letters of thanks in three languages.*

'The fellow! why would he go out of his way to make such blundering work?' I sent this to Nichols; and he returned Boswell's note of his readiness to correct.—T. F." Boswell, it seems, had described Taylor as the translator of Demosthenes; but he altered the word to "editor."

* Not, as Dr. B. Hill says, because he was so proud of his knowledge, but to show the Academy that he was fitted for the office.

I.

"October 31, 1791.

"*To the President and Council of the Royal Academy of Arts in London.*

"GENTLEMEN,—Your unsolicited and unanimous selection of me to be Secretary for Foreign Correspondence to your Academy, and the gracious confirmation of my election by his Majesty, I acknowledge with the warmest sentiments of gratitude and respect.

"I have always loved the arts, and during my travels on the Continent I did not neglect the opportunities I had of cultivating a taste for them. That taste I trust will now be much improved, when I shall be so happy as to share in the advantages which the Royal Academy affords; and I fondly embrace this very pleasing distinction, as giving me the means of providing additional solace for the future years of my life.

"Rest assured, Gentlemen, that as I am proud to be a member of an Academy which has the peculiar felicity of not being at all dependent on a minister, but under the immediate patronage and superintendence of the Sovereign himself, I shall be zealous to do everything in my power that can be of any service to our excellent institution. I have the honor to be, Gentlemen, your much obliged, faithful, humble servant, JAMES BOSWELL."

II.

"*A messieurs le Président et les autres membres du Conseil de l'Académie Royale des Arts à Londres.*

"MESSIEURS,—C'est avec la plus vive reconnaissance que j'accepte la charge de Secrétaire pour la Correspondance Étrangère de votre

Académie, à laquelle j'ai eu l'honneur d'être choisi par vos suffrages unanimes, gracieusement confirmés par sa Majesté.

"Ce choix spontané, Messieurs, me flatte beaucoup ; et m'inspire des désirs les plus ardents de m'en montrer digne, au moins par la promptitude avec laquelle je saisirai toute occasion de faire ce que je pourrai pour contribuer à l'avantage des Arts et la célébrité de l'Académie. J'ai l'honneur d'être, avec toute la considération possible, Messieurs, votre serviteur très-obligé, très-humble et très-fidèle, BOSWELL."

III.

" Agli illustrissimi Signori il Presidente e Consiglieri dell' Academia Reale delle arti in Londra.

"Avreste forse, illustrissimi Signori, potuto scegliere molte persone piu degne dell' Officcio di Segretario per la correspondenza straniera ; ma non sarebbe, son certo, stato possibile di trovar alcuno dal quale questa distinzione sarebbe stata piu stimata. Sento con un animo molto riconoscente la parzialita che l'Academia a ben voluto mostrar per me ; e mi conto felicissimo che la mia elezione sia stata graziosamente confirmata dalla sua Mæsta, lo stesso Sovrano che a fondato l'Academia e che si è sempre mostrato il suo beneficente Prottetore. Vi prego, Signori, di credere que porro ogni mio studio a contribuire tanto che potro alla prosperita della nostra instituzione ch' è già arrivata ad un punto si respettevole. Ho l'onor d'essere, illustrissimi Signori, vostro umilissimo e devotissimo servo, GIACOMO BOSWELL."[1]

---

[1] "Life of Johnson," edited by Dr. B. Hill.

CHAPTER XXXII

THERE is nothing more sad or piteous than the following this pleasant being to his disastrous end, and marking the decay of the once cheerful, good-natured Boswell : with the gradual change from the sympathizing follower of Johnson into the maudlin creature who had to revive his spirits of nights by the bottle. The truth was, before his death poor Bozzy had become something very near what may be called " a sot." It was humiliating that his friends should have often to interpose to try to rescue him from this fatal vice, by persuading him to enter into compacts—as a favour—with them, not to drink more than a very liberal allowance for a certain number of weeks or months. No one, indeed, felt so acutely as the poor toper the sadness of his situation, or the precipice to which he was hurrying, and he clutched vainly at straws in the hope of saving himself. Like most weak mortals, he must take the world into his confidence, and, as if to guarantee his reform of life, told as many persons as possible how he had registered these vows to give up drinking.

His old friends, Paoli and Temple, and later Mr. Courtenay, had all good-naturedly tried to help him in this way. But such devices could have little result. In the case where he thus obliged his friend, Mr. Courtenay, he confessed that he had broken the pledge nearly a week before the time, but did not appear to think that this amounted to an infringement of the bargain.

It was in 1792 that Mr. Wilberforce was setting off for Bath, in a highly strung religious mood, and wishing to do good to all men. He went a little out of his road to call upon Sir W. Young, driving to his house, and staying the night. He found there " our own Boswell," as Johnson styled him : certainly " not a godly company, and opposed to the abolition of slavery. Bozzy talked of Johnson. Sat up too late." Next day he " had some serious talk with Bozzy, *who admitted the depravity of human nature.* Last night he expressed his disbelief of eternal punishment. He asked me to take his bag home, and walked off into the west of England, with two shirts and a nightcap in his pocket *sans servant.*" " Poor Boswell!" wrote Wilberforce, so late as 1832, recalling this scene ; " I once had some curious conversation with him ; he was evidently low and depressed, and appeared to have many serious feelings. He told me that Johnson had assured him that he was never intimately acquainted with one religious clergyman."

There is something pathetic in the struggle which he was making in these declining days, and in which he felt himself almost helpless.

In June, 1793, as he was coming from some revel, and scarcely in a condition to protect himself, he was set upon in the streets, knocked down, and robbed. He was much cut about the head, and confined to his bed for many days, " in pain and fever, and helpless as a child." This discreditable incident he determined, alas ! too late, should be a " crisis in my life : I trust I shall henceforth be a sober, regular man. Indeed, my indulgence in wine has, of late years especially, been excessive. You remember what Lord Eliot said, nay, what you, I am sorry to think, have seen. Your suggestion as to my being carried off in a state of intoxication is awful. I thank you for it, my dear friend. It impressed me much, I assure you." Mr. Elwin had seen a passage in the letters, omitted from the published volume, which was even more significant. His friend Temple relates : "On Sunday Boswell and I communicated. You know we dined at Forster's : he drank too much Madeira, and got intoxicated, and was seen staggering on the ramparts." Alas! Boswell has registered a saying of his own, but intended for others, " A drunken fellow is not honest." " A stick," said I, " kept always moist, must become rotten."

And now the inevitable result of these long-sustained excesses was to appear. No constitution could have withstood so disorderly a life ; and the poor, weak, helpless Boswell was at last to be called upon for the final penalty.

In April, 1794, his friend Temple had a fall from his horse, which suggested serious and anxious thoughts indeed to his friend. " In a moment," he moralized, "the awful separation which we so much dread might have taken place." This solemn reflection was at the opening of the letter ; but at its close, we have this strange mundane confidence : "You seem too violent against D——— on account of Miss M——. I have heard *alteram partem ;* but I will try to persuade him to get her apothecary's bill paid for her. You must not consider her by any means as having these extraordinary strong claims on the Admiral. The £40 annuity will, I doubt not, be certain."

This significant transaction, into which Boswell entered with a strong *goût*, or sympathy, shows that, to the very last, his ideas of rectitude were curiously warped.

On the eve of his last illness, we find him busy at his great work. The second edition of the book, "revised and augmented," had been called for in 1793, and made its appearance in three stout and rather unwieldy octavos.* This had not gone off at his death in 1795, so it had taken some four years to exhaust two editions. This shows that the success of the book was not quite so rapid as is commonly supposed.†

* At the end of the second volume a number of letters are added, thus introduced : "After the first two volumes of this work were printed off, my worthy friend, Mr. Langton, in searching among his papers, found the following valuable letters of Dr. Johnson, beginning with the first which that gentleman received from him. Though it is impossible, in the present edition, to insert them in chronological order, I cannot withhold from my readers so great a satisfaction as the perusal of them offered."—It may be said here that Boswell always showed much artistic instinct in his selection of the Johnsonian letters. He was anxious to have such only as were associated with the leading figures of his narrative ; whereas it is now the fashion to suppose that *any* unpublished Johnsonian letter may be appropriately introduced.

† His preface to the new edition is most interesting, written in his clear, admirable style ; a little exultant too. But there is no exaggeration in the terms used to describe the reception and actual position of his work. We must always admire in our author this measured and judicious tone of his language. "That I was anxious for the success of a work which had employed much of my time and labour, I do not wish to conceal ; but whatever doubts I at any time entertained, have been entirely removed by the very favourable reception with which it has been honoured. That reception has excited my best exertions to render my book more perfect ; and in this endeavour I have had the assistance not only of some of my particular friends, but of many other learned and ingenious men, by which I have been enabled to rectify some mistakes, and to enrich the work with many valuable additions. These I have ordered to be printed separately in quarto, for the accommodation of the purchasers of the first edition. May I be permitted to say that the typography of both editions does honour to the press of Mr. Henry Baldwin, now Master of the Worshipful Company of Stationers, whom I have long known as a worthy man and an obliging friend.

"In the strangely mixed scenes of human existence, our feelings

He was now busily engrossed, preparing his third edition, assisted by his friend Malone, who states that

are often at once pleasing and painful. Of this truth, the progress of the present work furnishes a striking instance. It was highly gratifying to me that my friend, Sir Joshua Reynolds, to whom it is inscribed, lived to peruse it, and to give the strongest testimony to its fidelity; but before a second edition, which he contributed to improve, could be finished, the world has been deprived of that most valuable man; a loss of which the regret will be deep, and lasting, and extensive, proportionate to the felicity which he diffused through a wide circle of admirers and friends.

"In reflecting that the illustrious subject of this work, by being more extensively and intimately known, however elevated before, has risen in the veneration and love of mankind, I feel a satisfaction beyond what fame can afford. We cannot, indeed, too much or too often admire his wonderful powers of mind, when we consider that the principal store of wit and wisdom which this work contains was not a particular selection from his general conversation, but was merely his occasional talk at such times as I had the good fortune to be in his company; and, without doubt, if his discourse at other periods had been collected with the same attention, the whole tenour of what he uttered would have been found equally excellent.

"His strong, clear, and animated enforcement of religion, morality, loyalty, and subordination, while it delights and improves the wise and the good, will, I trust, prove an effectual antidote to that detestable sophistry which has been lately imported from France, under the false name of philosophy, and with a malignant industry has been employed against the peace, good order, and happiness of society, in our free and prosperous country; but, thanks be to God, without producing the pernicious effects which were hoped for by its propagators.

"It seems to me, in my moments of self-complacency, that this extensive biographical work, however inferior in its nature, may in one respect be assimilated to the Odyssey. Amidst a thousand entertaining and instructive episodes, the hero is never long out of sight; for they are all in some degree connected with him; and he, in the whole course of the history, is exhibited by the author for the best advantage of his readers:

"—Quid virtus et quid sapientia possit,
Utile proposuit nobis exemplar Ulyssen

" Should there be any cold-blooded and morose mortals who really dislike this book, I will give them a story to apply. When the great Duke of Marlborough, accompanied by Lord Cadogan, was one day reconnoitring the army in Flanders, a heavy rain came

it was almost ready for press, when the author was
seized with his last illness. This must always be regarded as a literary misfortune; for Malone was so
industrious a commentator, that we are inclined to
suspect that, as he was uncontrolled, he must have made
abundant changes. At all events, it is difficult to
distinguish between the author's work and his.

Boswell had received one warning, in the shape
of an attack of weakness early in April, when he

on, and they both called for their cloaks. Lord Cadogan's servant,
a good-humoured alert lad, brought his lordship's in a minute.
The duke's servant, a lazy sulky dog, was so sluggish, that his
grace, being wet to the skin, reproved him, and had for answer,
with a grunt, 'I came as fast as I could;' upon which the duke
calmly said, 'Cadogan, I would not for a thousand pounds have
that fellow's temper.'

"There are some men, I believe, who have, or think they have,
a very small share of vanity. Such may speak of their literary
fame in a decorous style of diffidence. But I confess, that I am so
formed by nature and by habit, that to restrain the effusion of
delight, on having obtained such fame, to me would be truly painful. Why then should I suppress it? Why 'out of the abundance
of the heart' should I not speak? Let me then mention with a
warm, but no insolent exultation, that I have been regaled with
spontaneous praise of my work by many and various persons, eminent for their rank, learning, talents, and accomplishments; much
of which praise I have under their hands to be reposited in my
archives at Auchinleck. An honourable and reverend friend
speaking of the favourable reception of my volumes, even in the
circles of fashion and elegance, said to me, 'You have made them
all talk Johnson.' Yes, I may add, I have *Johnsonised* the land;
and I trust they will not only talk but think Johnson.

"To enumerate those to whom I have been thus indebted would
be tediously ostentatious. I cannot however but name one, whose
praise is truly valuable, not only on account of his knowledge and
abilities, but on account of the magnificent, yet dangerous embassy,
in which he is now employed, which makes everything that relates
to him peculiarly interesting. Lord Macartney favoured me with
his own copy of my book, with a number of notes, of which I have
availed myself. On the first leaf I found, in his lordship's handwriting, an inscription of such high commendation, that even I,
vain as I am, cannot prevail on myself to publish it.   J. BOSWELL.

"1st July, 1793."

returned from his club, "quite spent and languid." We learn nothing of his state until a week later, when, on April 8th, he sat down to write to his old friend, and thus began :—

"My dear Temple,—I would fain write to you in my own hand, but really cannot——" (These words are in faltering characters, and scarcely legible, showing that he was completely prostrated. His son James then took the pen.) "Alas! my friend, what a state is this. . . . The pain which continued for so many weeks was very severe indeed, and when it went off, I thought myself quite well; but I soon felt a conviction that I was by no means as I should—so exceedingly weak, as my miserable attempt to write to you afforded a proof. All, then, that can be said is, that I must wait with patience. But O! my friend, how strange is it that at this very time of illness you and Miss Temple should have been in such a dangerous state. Much occasion for thankfulness is there, that it has not been worse with you. Pray write, or make somebody write, frequently. I feel myself a good deal stronger to-day, notwithstanding this scrawl. God bless you, my dear Temple! I ever am your old and affectionate friend, here, and I trust hereafter, James Boswell."

At the end, his son James added a postscript to say that the situation was grave, and his father ignorant of his dangerous condition. They had hopes, however, as he was able to take nourishment, that his strong constitution would carry him through. In a day or two he rallied considerably, after remaining in "an extraordinary state of pain and weakness." He had the best advice—that of Dr. Warren and Mr. Earle, the surgeon, and his recovery was now looked for. But ten days later he relapsed, was taken with a fever, shivering fits, and other disorders.

Another letter, written from his death-bed, has a pathetic interest. It shows the warmth of his heart, even under such trying conditions, and which he retained to the last.

Boswell to Warren Hastings.

" Mr. Boswell presents his respectful compliments to Mr. Hastings.

" He has ever since Tuesday se'night been close confined to bed with a severe and alarming fever, which has deprived him of being present at Mr. Hastings' honourable acquittal, and of offering him in person his sincere and warm congratulations which he thus conveys.

" Dr. Warren now gives him the pleasing assurance that his sufferings are now at an end. The moment that he is able to go abroad, he will fly to Mr. Hastings, and expand his soul in the purest satisfaction.

" Considering the very powerful influence which has been shamefully used to aid the rancorous prosecution, there is no wonder that some effect was produced ; but it is to the credit of the Lords that it was within narrow limits. There appears, however, an accumulated baseness almost beyond credibility.

" Great Poland Street, April 24, 1795." *

His brother, the former Spanish merchant, was now with him, and witnessed the departure of poor " Bozzy." It was he who had the sad duty of writing to Mr. Temple on May 19, 1795, that the good, " flighty,"

* MS., British Museum.

clever, warm-hearted " Bozzy " had ended his fitful course.

" MY DEAR SIR,—I have now the painful task of informing you that my dear brother expired this morning at two o'clock: we have both lost a kind, affectionate friend, and shall never have such another. He has suffered a great deal during his illness, which has lasted five weeks, but not much in his last moments. May God Almighty have mercy upon his soul, and receive him into his Heavenly Kingdom.

" He is to be buried at Auchinleck, for which place his sons will set out in two or three days. They and his two eldest daughters have behaved in the most affectionate and exemplary manner during his confinement; they all desire to be kindly remembered to you and Miss Temple, and beg your sympathy on this melancholy occasion.

" I am, my dear Sir, your affectionate, humble servant, T. D. BOSWELL."

The remains of the poor " Baron of Auchinleck ' were taken down to the family seat. So passed away one to whom readers are under deep obligation, and who has certainly increased the harmless gaiety of the nation.*

---

* In the papers was to be read : " At three o'clock this morning, at his house in Great Poland-street, in the 55th year of his age, after an illness of five weeks (an intermitting fever at first), James Boswell, esq., whose death will be most sincerely regretted by all who really knew him. We have not room this month to do justice to his merits; but a full account of him shall be given in our next.

" His remains were carried to Auchinleck; and the following inscription is engraved on his coffin-plate :

" ' JAMES BOSWELL, Esq. died 19 May, 1795, aged 55 years; '

Mr. Boswell left a will, which is a characteristic document, written in the year 1785, in London. He confesses that he has prepared it "under the apprehension of some danger to his life, which, however, may prove a false alarm." * This was, no doubt, an attack of serious illness, and not, as Dr. Rogers supposes, an impending duel, which was hardly in Bozzy's way.†

over which, in a shield, are the initials J. B. between two strips of laurel; and his crest, On a wreath Argent and Sable, a hawk with a hood on all proper.   Motto, over the crest, v r a y e   f o y.—The arms borne by Mr. B. (in virtue of a grant in Scotland 1780) were, Quarterly, 1 and 4, Argent, on a fess Sable three cinquefoils of the field, a canton Azure charged with a galley, sails furled, with a tressure Or.   2 and 3, quarterly, 1 and 4, Argent, a lion rampant Azure ; 2 and 3, Or, a saltire and chief Gules ; over all, a cross engrailed Sable.   Crest as above."

* The paper seems to have been prepared without the assistance of a Scotch practitioner, and I fancy that any English or Scotch lawyer would pronounce that it was impracticable.   The dispositions beyond being mere wishes seem worthless.

† Dr. Rogers indeed speculates that he was expecting a challenge from Lord Macdonald, for the libels in the "Tour," but he forgets that the book was not published until the following year.

Dr. Rogers has published this will from the Commissariat Register of Glasgow, preserved in the General Register House, Edinburgh, vol. 74, p. 194 :—

"I James Boswell Esquire of Auchinleck having already settled everything concerning my Landed Estate so far as is in my power as an heir of Entail, so that my mind is quiet respecting my dear wife and children, do now when in perfect soundness of mind but under the apprehension of some danger to my life which however may prove a false alarm, thus make my last Will and Testament containing also clauses of another nature which I desire may be valid and effectual.   I resign my soul to God my almighty and most merciful Father trusting that it will be redeemed by the awfull and mysterious Sacrifice of our Lord Jesus Christ and admitted to endless felicity in heaven.   I request that my body may be interred in the family burial place in the church at Auchinleck.   I appoint my much valued spouse Mrs. Margaret Montgomerie and my worthy friend Sir William Forbes of Pitsligo, Baronet, to be my Executors and in case of the death of either of them the office shall devolve solely to the survivor.   And whereas my honoured and pious grand mother Lady Elizabeth Boswell devised to the heir succeeding to the barrony of Auchinleck from

It will be seen that the notion of "granting" deeds
of entail, to be executed, and leases to be given to

generation to generation the Ebony Cabinet and the dressing plate
of silver gilt, which belonged to her mother Veronica, Countess of
Kincardine, leaving it however optional to her son my father that
entail thereof or not as he should think fit, and he having neglected to do so, whereby the said Ebony Cabinet and dressing plate
are now at my free disposal, I do by these presents dispose the
same to the heir succeeding to the barrony of Auchinleck from
generation to generation. And I declare that it shall not be in
the power of any such heir to alienate or impignorate the same on
any account whatever. And I do hereby dispose to the said heirs
of Entail in their order, all lands and heritages belonging to me,
in fee simple, after payment of my debts, but under this provision,
that in case any of them shall alienate the said Ebony Cabinet and
dressing plate, the person so alienating shall forfeit the sum of
One Thousand Pounds sterling, which shall be paid to the next
heir succeeding by entail. And I declare that the heir of Entail
first succeeding to these my unentailed lands, shall within six
months after his succession thereto execute a deed of Entail thereof
to the same series of heirs with that in the Entail executed by my
Father and me, which if he fails to do they shall then go to the
next heir of Entail, and it is also an express condition that he
shall divest himself of the fie thereof and reserve only his life-rent.
I mean this to apply to the said first succeeding heir. Further-
more as my late honoured Father made a very curious collection
of the classics and other books, which it is desireable should be
preserved for ever in the family of Auchinleck, I do by these
presents dispose to the successive heirs of Entail of the barrony
of Auchinleck" [here there is a word torn off] " Greek and Latin
books, as also all manuscripts of whatever kind, lying in the house
of Auchinleck, under the same conditions and under the same
forfeiture as I have mentioned with regard to the Ebony Cabinet
and dressing plate, and all my other moveable Estate or Executory
I leave equally among my other children, the furniture in the
house of Auchinleck to be valued by two sworn appreazers, and
the heir to keep it at that value and pay the same to my younger
children, excepting however all my pictures which I dispose to the
said successive heirs of Entail under the same conditions and
forfeiture as above mentioned, and excepting also the furniture in
my house at Edinburgh which I bequeath to my dear wife. I
bequeath one hundred pounds sterling to my dear brother Thomas
David Boswell Esquire banker in London, to purchase a piece of
plate to keep in remembrance of me in his family and to my dear
brother Lieutenant John Boswell being a batchelor, I bequeath
Fifty Guineas to purchase a ring or whatever other thing he may

tenants, after the owner's death was Utopian enough ;
as well as the device for "curing" the absence of a
proper stamp.

like best to keep for my sake. To my friends the Reverend Mr.
Temple in Cornwall, John Johnstone Esquire of Grange, Sir John
Dick Baronet, Sir William Forbes of Pitsligo, Baronet, Captain
John Macbryde of the Royal Navy, and Mr. Charles Dilly of
London, bookseller, Alexander Fairlie of Fairlie, Esq. and Edmund
Malone Esq. of the kingdom of Ireland, The Hon. Colonel James
Stewart and George Dempster Esquire, I bequeath each a gold
mourning ring, and I hereby leave to the said Sir William Forbes,
the Reverend Mr. Temple and Edward Malone Esquire all my
manuscripts of my own composition, and all my letters from
various persons to be published for the benefit of my younger
children, as they shall decide, that is to say they are to have a
discretionary power to publish more or less. I leave to Mr. James
Bruce my overseer Twenty Pounds yearly during his life and if
he shall continue to reside at Auchinleck I leave to him the house
he now possesses with his meal and all other perquisites. And to
Mrs. Bell Bruce my housekeeper I leave Ten pounds yearly during
her life with two pecks of meal weekly in case of her not liveing
in the family of Auchinleck.   Lastly, as there are upon the estate
of Auchinleck several tenants whose families have possessed their
farms for many generations, I do by these presents grant leases
for nineteen years and their respective lifetimes of their present
farms to John Templeton in Hopland, James Murdoch in Blacks-
town commonly called the Raw, James Peden in Old Byre,
William Samson in Mill of Auchinleck, John Hird in Hirdstown,
William Murdoch in Willocks town, and to any of the sons of the
late James Caldow in Stivenstown whom the ministers and elders
of Auchinleck shall approve of, a lease of that farm in the above
terms, the rents to be fixed by two men to be mutually chosen by
the laird of Auchinleck for the time and each tenant. I also grant
a lease in the like terms to Andrew Dalrymple in Mains of Auchinleck, my Baron officer.   And I do beseech all the succeeding heirs
of Entail to be kind to the Tenants and not to turn out old pos-
sessors to get a little more rent. And in case my nomination of
Tutors and Curators to my children being written upon unstamped
paper should not be valid, I here again constitute and appoint my
dear wife, Mrs. Margaret Montgomerie and my worthy friend Sir
William Forbes of Pitsligo, or the survivor of them, to the said
office with all usual powers and with the recommendations contained in the said unstamped deed. In witness whereof, these
presents written with my own hand (of which I consent to the
registration in the books of Council and Session that they may
have full effect and thereto constitute my procurators) are sub-

Boswell left all his papers, and letters from eminent persons, journals, travels, etc., to his three

scribed by me at London this twenty eight day of May, One thousand Seven hundred and Eighty five, before these witnesses Mr. Edward Dilly bookseller there, and Mr. John Normaville his clerk. (signed) James Boswell. Chs. Dilly witness, John Normaville witness."

Dr. Rogers has also obtained the inventory of Boswell's personal estate :—

" In the first place there pertained and belonged to the said defunct at the time aforesaid of his death, the articles aftermentioned of the values underwritten, whereof the Executor herein gives up in inventary the sum of Twenty Shillings sterling of the value of each article viz., Imprimis Four hundred and eighty three pounds fourteen shillings as the amount of sales of furniture books pictures &c. in the defunct's house in London. Item, Five hundred and Seventy six pounds eight shillings and two pence as the value of furniture in the house of Auchinleck estimated by two sworn appraisers. Item, One hundred and five pounds as the value of silver plate at Auchinleck exclusive of the family plate devised to the heir estimated at or near the bullion value. Item, One hundred pounds supposed about the value of the books at Auchinleck per catalogue in the hands of the Executor exclusive of Greek and Latin classics and manuscripts there, also left to the heir. Item, Seventy seven pounds three shillings as the value of cattle and stocking at Auchinleck per estimate in the hands of the Executor. Item, Three hundred pounds as the value of the remaining copies of the Life of Dr Johnson written by the defunct and sold to Mr. Dilly bookseller. And One hundred pounds as the supposed value of manuscripts left by the defunct.

" In the second place there was indebted and owing to the said defunct at the time aforesaid of his death, the sums of money after mentioned for the reasons after specified, viz., One Pound sterling part of the sum of Ninety Seven Pounds eight shillings and Eleven pence sterling being a balance of cash in the hands of Mr Thomas David Boswell brother to the defunct per accompt. Item, One pound sterling, part of the sum of Ninety one pounds sixteen shillings and six pence being a claim Mr Alexander Boswell the heir for cash advanced to him by Mr Thomas David Boswell at the time of the defunct's death and credited to Mr Thomas David Boswell in his account with the Executor. Item, One pound Sterling part of the sum of Two hundred and twenty five pounds fourteen shillings and three pence as arrears of rent of the estate of Auchinleck for accounts transmitted by the factor. Item, One pound sterling part of the sum of Nine hundred and forty two pounds six shillings and seven pence sterling as the executors, with a strict injunction that they should be published " for the benefit of his younger children." The only discretion allowed them was as to *selection.* The executors, however, transferred this discretion to Sir Alexander, who, it is said, destroyed them. Dr. Birkbeck Hill speaks of the " brutish " conduct of the family ; but it may be questioned if there was anything really worth preserving. A book, founded on such materials by Boswell himself, would have been welcome, but in other hands would have had little value. At all events, poor " Bozzy's " Utopian notion of providing for younger children out of the two or three hundred pounds that would be obtained as " copy money " was absurd. It is likely enough the heir purchased these scraps, and thus carried out the directions of the will.

claim against the heirs of said estate under the Entail act for three fourths of the defunct's expenditure in improving the Entailed estate bearing interest from Martinmas seventeen hundred and ninety five. Item, One pound sterling, part of the sum of nine hundred and fifty pounds sterling as half a year's rent of said estate due to the Executor by law for the year Seventeen hundred and ninety five, being the year in which the defunct died per rental furnished by the factor. Item, one Pound sterling part of the sum of forty two pounds nine shillings and one penny being a balance of account due by Mr. Dilly, bookseller. Item, One pound sterling, part of the sum of six hundred and eighty four pounds sixteen shillings and eight pence being debt due by Captn Bruce Boswell of Calcutta of Principal and Interest paid to the Executor since the defunct's death. Item, One pound sterling, paid of the sum of one hundred and ninety five pounds sterling being a balance of debt due by the Trustees of the late Mr Johnston of Grange, as stated by the defunct in a holograph view of his affairs made out by him, as at the first day of January Seventeen hundred and ninety five. And One pound sterling, part of the sum of seven hundred pounds sterling and upwards of debts due from various turnpike roads in Ayrshire for money advanced by the late Lord Auchinleck.'

BEFORE considering the character of this remarkable being, we shall follow the fortunes of the unhappy children of an unhappy father. He was succeeded in his title and estate by his eldest son, Alexander, who had been educated at Eton. Some of his precocious sayings were thought worthy of being recorded in his parent's note-book :

"My son Alexander, one day in December, 1783, when in a passion at his sister Phemie for something she had said, used this strong expression, 'Phemie, if your tongue be not cut out, it will soon be full of lies.'" —"January 7, 1784. He understood that there was a violent opposition to the king ; and he imagined Sir Philip Ainslie was on that side. He said the king should send messengers to discover all that are against him. That would soon turn Sir Philip Ainslie's brain right."—"January 10th. He complained that his brother James beat him. Grange said he should not mind him, as he was but a child. 'Ay,' said he, 'but he must not be a big man to me' (alluding to the weight of his blows)."

After his father's death, Sir Alexander, the new laird of Auchinleck, made the grand tour of Europe, and cultivated his foreign tastes. He turned out a

rather remarkable character, devoting himself to the
study of old Scotch literature, attracting the notice
of Sir Walter Scott.   He had a taste for writing Scotch
ballads, intended to be coarsely humorous and satirical,
a taste that brought him a disaster.   He also indulged in the costly luxury of a private printing press
at Auchinleck, whence issued reprints of old, rare
Scottish tracts.   Mr. Lockhart, who knew him, declares
"that he had all his father, Bozzy's, cleverness, good
humour, and joviality, without one touch of his meaner
qualities."   His song, "Jennie the Weaver," was often
called for, and "he sang it capitally."

"The late Sir Alexander," wrote Sir Walter to Mr.
Croker, "was a proud man, and, like his grandfather,
thought his father lowered himself by his deferential
suit and service to Johnson.   He disliked any allusion
to the book or to Johnson himself, and I have observed
that Johnson's fine picture by Sir Joshua was sent
up stairs out of the sitting apartments at Auchinleck.
Sir Alexander differed from his father in many particulars; he was a very high-spirited man, whereas in
James's heirs the blood of Bruce flowed faintly and
sluggishly, though he boasted so much of it.   Indeed,
with the usual ill-hap of those who deal in *mauvaise
plaisanterie*, old Bozzy was often in the unpleasant
situation of retreating from expressions which could not
be defended."

One son, David, died early in the year 1777.   The
other son, James, was a serious character, and had a
reputation for well grounded learning and knowledge.
His career was most creditable.   He entered Oxford in
1797, where he obtained a fellowship, and, on leaving,
devoted himself to the study of old English literature, editing, etc.   "In the investigation of any

subject, his inductive judgment and discrimination were equally remarkable; his memory unusually tenacious and accurate, and he was always ready to communicate what he knew." When Mr. Malone died, leaving his great Shakespeare incomplete, he chose Mr. Boswell as his literary executor, and he accomplished the great task in a very workmanlike and satisfactory way.

He was quite as fond of London as his father. His social gifts made him sought as an agreeable and acceptable guest, and his really good heart, and the warmth of his friendship when a call was made upon it, was the most remarkable feature of his character.

As his friend, Mr. Taylor, tells us: " He was more cautious in conversation, but not less disposed to partake of social enjoyment. Indeed, he inherited the father's love of convivial pleasure. He was a barrister, and generally reputed to be a man of learning. His merit entitled him to all the friends of his father, particularly Mr. Malone, Mr. Windham, General Paoli, and the present Marquis of Lansdown. He devoted a great part of the morning to reading, but from his habits, and the general tenour of his conversation, I rather think more for literary gratification than for the study of his profession. His knowledge of the floating literature of the day, particularly any interesting poetry or striking novels, was evident; and referring to any works from his recommendation, I had always reason to respect his taste and to rely upon his judgment.

" When he had ended his morning studies, or rather amusements, he used to sally forth, and pay a round of visits to his friends, as he used freely to say, in hopes among them 'to spring a dinner,' for he 'strolled a bachelor's merry life,' as the song has it. He lived very retired in the morning at his chambers in the Temple, and very few, if any, of his friends were admitted when they called. It is very probable that he never dined in his chambers during the whole year, as he was fond of company, and always a welcome guest at any friend's table."

Towards the end of his life, he obtained a Commissionership of Bankrupts, a coveted form of provision, then attainable without much difficulty. His friend asking him, had it turned out profitable, he answered pleasantly, "Not very, as yet, but we trust to the hops." *

He died in the Temple on Feb. 24, 1822.

Among the mourners at his funeral in the Temple, was his brother Alexander; and no one could have imagined that within a month he was to follow this brother to the grave. Disaster thus seemed to pursue the ill-fated family. One of the daughters,

---

* The catalogue of his library, which was disposed of at his death, is a curious and even entertaining one. The books were sold by Mr. Sotheby in May, 1825, and comprised over three thousand two hundred lots, bringing £2045. It was the library of a scholar, stored with classics, modern Latin writers, curious, rare, old English poetry, early French, scarce quarto plays, and manuscript fragments. Some of these rarities were sold at prices that would excite astonishment now, the first edition of Shakespeare's "Richard III." bringing but eight shillings. Kemble's folio of 1623 fetched 100 guineas. He seems to have inherited all his father's Johnsonian papers, and the description of some of these are not without interest, as, for instance, "a letter of Mr. Byng's to Mr. Malone, describing Johnson's last moments;" the register of the baptism of Johnson's father, endorsed "Father's Register;" Johnson's manuscript notes on Lord Hailes's proof-sheets; the two plans for the Dictionary, and "copy from memory by Mr. Jephson of Johnson's letter to Lord Chesterfield," which Mr. Boswell had, no doubt, found useful, though he does not mention it. More interesting to us are the following: "Proof-sheets of the first edition of Boswell's 'Johnson,' corrected in Mr. Boswell's hand, with some remarkable variations, and a parcel of letters and memoranda relating to the 'Life,'" which brought £9. Also a dictionary of the Scottish language in manuscript, by James Boswell, Esq., sen., estimated, alas! at only sixteen shillings.

Veronica, Johnson's pet, lost her life, it is said, from her affectionate assiduity in attending her father. She died on September 26, 1795. The second sister, Euphemia, appears to have been slightly deranged. She left her family, wrote operas and verses, and seems to have been constantly begging assistance from royal personages, once on the ground "that she had pledged her piano-forte." She charged her family with casting her off, though it seems without reason, and desired that she might be buried next Dr. Johnson.

"In 1820, party spirit was extravagantly inflamed in Edinburgh, and a newspaper called 'The Beacon,' subsidized by the Tory faction, was so personal and violent in its tone, that a Whig, Mr. Gibson, boldly attacked its unseen proprietors, and, announcing that he would call some of them to account in the field, suc-ceeded in extinguishing it. It was, however, in a short time followed by a new paper no less violent, called *The Sentinel,* which was encouraged and supported by the same party. Rancour and deadly feud raged afresh between the factions, and Mr. Stuart, a well-known gentlemen of the time, took an action for libel against the editors, Alexander and Borthwick. These men, being intimidated, offered, if the action were dis-continued, to give up the names of the writers of the attacks on Stuart. He set off for Glasgow to receive this acknowledgment, and, to his astonishment, found that the worst and most personal of the attacks were written by a relation of his own, Sir Alexander Boswell of Auchinleck, with whom he had always been on ex-cellent terms. The hand was disguised, but the spirit was malevolent." There was something in this transac-tion that suggested his father. Indignant and shocked, Mr. Stuart returned to Edinburgh to await the arrival

of Sir Alexander, who was in London.   The latter, when
he heard of the papers being given up, knew what was
in store for him, and selected his friend, suggesting the
possibility of a trip to the Rhine, "in case he should be
the successful shot."   As soon as he arrived, Lord
Rosslyn came to him to arrange preliminaries.   He
avowed himself the author of the article, an offensive
song in which his friend was spoken of as a coward.

"They met," says Lord Cockburn, "near Auchter-
pool, in Fife, on March 22, 1822.   Stuart, an awkward,
lumbering rider, had never fired a pistol but once or
twice from the back of a horse in a troop of yeomanry.
He stopped at his beautiful Hillside, near Aberdeen, to
arrange some settlements.   Boswell, who was an expert
shot, told his second, Mr. Douglas, later Marquis of
Queensberry, that he meant to fire in the air.   He fell,
however, at the first fire.   Stuart told me that he never
was more thunderstruck than when, on the smoke clearing away, he saw his adversary sinking gently down.
Sir Alexander died in two days.*   Stuart fled at first
to France, but returned to stand his trial, when he was
acquitted."

Lord Cockburn draws this character of him :
"Boswell was able and literary, and, when in the
humour of being quiet, he was agreeable and kind.
But in general he was overbearing and boisterous, and
addicted to coarse personal ridicule.   With many respectable friends his natural place was at the head of a
jovial board, when every one laughed at his exhaustless
spirits, but each trembled lest he should be the object

---

* The ball struck him in the shoulder and shattered the blade ;
it was supposed to have entered the spine, as the limbs were quite
paralyzed.   The unfortunate gentleman was carried to Balmuto
House, where he was attended by his wife, Professor Thomson,
and several surgeons of eminence.

of the next story or song. He even was a short time in Parliament. It is curious, but it was he who introduced, or at least took charge, of the Act which abolishes one old Scottish statute against fighting a duel or sending a challenge." *

Sir W. Scott, on learning the tragic result, wrote to Miss Edgeworth : " The sudden death of both the Boswells, and the bloody end of one, have given me great pain." He was, indeed, warmly attached to them both. Sir Alexander had dined with him in Castle Street only two days before the casualty. That evening, as Mr. Lockhart recalled, " was the gayest he ever spent under Scott's roof. And though Charles Matthews was present, and in his best force, poor Boswell's songs, jokes, and anecdotes showed no eclipse. It turned out that he had joined the party he had thus delighted immediately after completing the last arrangements for his duel. Several circumstances of his death are exactly reproduced in the Duel Scene in ' St. Ronan's Well.' "

James Boswell's third daughter Elizabeth had a happier fate than her sisters, and was married to Dr. Boswell's grandson William, an advocate, who became sheriff of Berwickshire. It will be interesting to trace the direct descendants of James Boswell. Sir Alexander, in 1799, married Miss Cumming, the daughter of an Edinburgh banker, belonging to the good and ancient family of Erenside, by whom he had a son and three daughters. One daughter died ; the others were married, to Sir W. Elliot and General Vassall. Sir Alexander's son James, born in 1806, married in 1830, his cousin, a daughter of Sir James Cunningham of Corsehill, who was most probably a descendant of the hero of the desperate

* " Memorials of his Time," p. 396.

duel that we have described. But he had daughters
only. But now was to occur a proceeding enough to
make the old judge, his ancestor, "turn in his grave."
So lately as 1850, his anxious longings to exclude
female issue from the entail were frustrated by an over-
sight. "In 1850, Sir James Boswell instituted a legal
process to prove the invalidity of the Auchinleck entail.
He was opposed by Thomas Alexander Boswell, of
Crawley Grange, next heir-male, but it was held by the
judges that as the material word 'irredeemably' was
written upon an erasure, the entail was inoperative.
Relieved from the settlement of 1776, Sir James Boswell
bequeathed Auchinleck to his two daughters as co-
heiresses. Sir James died in 1857, when the baronetcy
became extinct. Julia, his eldest daughter, married
George Mounsey, solicitor, Carlisle, sometime mayor of
that city. Emily Harriet, the younger daughter, married
in 1873, the Hon. Richard Wogan Talbot, eldest son of
Lord Talbot de Malahide."

After allowing all credit to Boswell for his admirable,
artistic workmanship, and judicious arrangement of his
materials, it must be admitted that there are some
blemishes which mar the general symmetry, and are
difficult to account for. Nothing can be better than the
general vivacity and the evenness of the narrative;
which makes us wonder the more at the introduction of
certain ponderous disquisitions and discussions, which,
besides being uninteresting, seem out of place, and
disturb the interest of the story. At one exciting and
critical passage—the touching account of Johnson's
death—this intrusion becomes *mal à propos.* Thus,
when he had begun to describe Johnson's last illness, his
approaching end, and his dignified preparation for the
same: "Soon after Johnson's return to the metropolis

both the asthma and the dropsy became more violent
and distressful, etc. :" the author stops to supply a long
list of his various literary schemes : then goes on to give
a short disquisition on his knowledge of Greek, taking for
his text, " during his sleepless nights, he amused himself
by translating Latin verse from the Greek." Then, to
our astonishment, he breaks off altogether. " I shall
now fulfil my promise of exhibiting "—it would be difficult to conceive what—"specimens of various sorts
of *imitations of Johnson's style ;* " and so introduces,
under headings, the Irish Academy, Dr. Robertson, Miss
Burney, and so on for several pages, returning to
Johnson's death-bed, as abruptly as he had left it :
" Johnson's affection for his departed relatives seemed
to grow warmer as he approached the time, etc." These
wanderings really destroy much of the effect of a
natural, well-written episode. Another intrusion was
the long disquisitions on the meaning of classical passages,
to which a mere allusion occurs in the text. Such as
that on the line " difficile est communia, etc.," and the
" quem Deus vult perdere," discussed at inordinate
length. In these, there can be little doubt, it was
Malone who was thus airing his antiquarian knowledge.
Other ponderous episodes are those " opinions " on Scotch
points of law, which Boswell " worried " out of his " all
knowing " friend ; such as the " case of the negro," " the
case of the schoolmaster," etc. This was an adroit mode
of flattering Johnson, for his " opinions " could have had
no practical value, from his ignorance of Scotch law, and
were mere academical exercises. Boswell does not say
positively that any use was made of them in the causes,
and he no doubt considered them as so much useful
" copy." It is amusing to find Lord Hailes and other
luminaries affecting to take these productions " au grand

serieux" and describing them as "valuable contributions" to Scotch law.

In a preceding page I have noticed that, in strict
view of form, Boswell's work is faulty, and its artistic
construction open to criticism.   He had undertaken
two duties or offices which seem rather incompatible,
or, at least, do not harmonize together.   He was the
chronicler of Johnson's life and proceedings; standing,
as it were, apart, gathering up facts and dates at second
hand, and surveying the Johnsonian *coterie* from a
distance, and impartially.   Yet he was one of the *coterie*
himself, in intimate connection with the subject of his
memoir, and bound up with the thoughts and feelings
and expressions of the great man.   Thus, there are two
different points of view from which he regarded his
hero, and, also, two different methods of narrative; and
he had somewhat awkwardly to shift from one to the
other as the occasion required.   The style of writing, at
one moment becomes dramatic, recording what is passing
before the writer, but presently sinks into historical
narrative, as though the writer had no personal connection with his subject.*

The question of deciding on Boswell's character—
whether he was sensible, or a fool, or a combination of
both, is one of the most intricate and most "knotty"
points conceivable.   Lord Macaulay's harsh and rather
coarse judgment is well known, and has done poor
Bozzy's memory much harm.   But by this time the great

---

* Equally to be condemned are his profuse alterations, amend-
ments, and additions; for, before getting ready a second edition,
he issued a sort of quarto pamphlet—entitled "Corrections and
Additions," with new paragraphs, letters, etc., whose places were
marked by reference to the proper page.   This clumsy and
rather confusing arrangement he fancied would be welcomed by
the purchasers of the first edition, who were to bind this supplement up at the end of their copies.

essayist's glittering and theatrical method, which sacri-
ficed so much to brilliant antithesis, is well understood.
In fact Boswell's character was exactly suited to his
method; here he could introduce his "school-boy" and
apply his favourite form, "no man was ever so, etc.,
and yet no man was so, etc." with telling effect.

Can a man be sensible, shrewd, clever in one
department, and at the same time, be ridiculous, foolish,
and unconscious of his folly in another? It is too
often assumed that there must be a sort of homo-
geneousness in human character, and that intention con-
trols every act. No doubt this can be, and is, so in
many cases; but, as a general rule, there is usually a
failure in some direction. Who so clever, brilliant, and
sagacious in many ways as Fox or Sheridan; yet who
so foolish and reckless in others? Many of Sheridan's
acts seemed those of an insane man. Goldsmith was
called an inspired idiot. Leigh Hunt, La Fontaine,
Fontenelle, and others, displayed an amount of simplicity, almost childish, and that seemed irreconcilable
with cleverness and genius.

Mr. Elwin—too long lost to the world of criticism—
was perhaps the first,—Carlyle's essay being, rather,
metaphysical and controversial,—to put the matter
in a true light. One of Macaulay's most startling
statements was, that for such a creature to have written
one of the best books in the world, is a strange, inexplicable phenomenon. Mr. Elwin says happily, that
it is not merely strange, nor a phenomenon, but simply
impossible. Macaulay's Boswell was a fantastic personage
that never existed—a fool *in omnibus*, who worked
mechanically. "Could such a book be written without
judgment and discrimination, or without some knowledge of the course of an infinite variety of curious and

important topics discussed in it? The authorship of a book giving decided proof of intellectual power, discrimination, or capacity, is a positive fact which cannot be neutralized, or set aside by any number of weak actions, or silly speeches. It is just as logical for a mass of admirers or apologists to infer from his writings that he possesses knowledge and judgment, as for his assailants to conclude from his conduct or conversation that he is a fool. Are not the inconsistencies and contradictoriness of human nature a by-word?" *

In the same spirit, a sensible writer in Chambers' Encyclopædia has said, "The remarkable merit of the book has led many to wonder how it could have been written by a man of such egregious weakness and vanity as Boswell. Indeed Macaulay advanced the preposterous paradox that it was because of his unrivalled qualities as a fool, that its author had written the best life in existence. The true explanation, however, is that this vanity and folly by no means make up the whole mental equipment of Boswell, and these unenviable qualities in his character have merely become so conspicuous because he has so much less reticence than ordinary men.

"Nor could the most veracious fool have written such a dexterously artistic book: nothing has suffered in his hands, he adds not one word too much, but gives us the most vivid dramatic pictures by a few simple but subtle strokes. This is not the work of memory nearly so much as of artistic production; it is not photographic and realistic half so much as it is idealistic and creative: we have here a special literary faculty, and, moreover, one of the rarest. He had in him something of the true Shakespeare secret."

* *Edinburgh Review,* v. 105.

The truth is, there is "a peccant part"—to use Johnson's phrase—in most clever persons. The balance is often disturbed by enthusiasm or excitement, and also by a craving for sensual enjoyments, the pleasures of conviviality, talk, love of expense, etc. These were accountable for most of Boswell's foolish acts. He was *tête montée* to an extravagant degree. In estimating character, it is no bad test to look round upon our acquaintances, where we are likely enough to find types of character that correspond with the one we are investigating. Who has not met persons who, when talking of subjects they are interested in, kindle, as it were, into a sort of extravagance, and form speculations perfectly Utopian and improbable? Some public personage has done something that pleases them, and their tongue "grows absolutely wanton in his praise;" they pierce into the future; they see amazing and immediate results; everything becomes grand, splendid, and fruitful, to a degree that is astonishing to cooler natures. Boswell had this turn for exaggerated appreciation, and it is very common. Vanity, too, is another disturbing element. Indulged in, it seems to blunt all fine sensibility to ridicule.

Mr. Croker's estimate of him is judicious, and happily expressed.

"It was a strange and fortunate concurrence, that one so prone to talk and who talked so well, should be brought into such close contact and confidence with one so zealous and so able to record. Dr. Johnson was a man of extraordinary powers, but Mr. Boswell had qualities, in their own way, almost as rare. He united lively manners with indefatigable diligence, and the volatile curiosity of a *man about town* with the drudging patience of a *chronicler*. With a very good opinion of himself, he was quick in discerning, and frank in applauding, the excellencies of others. Though proud of his own name and lineage, and ambitious of the countenance of the great, he was yet so cordial an admirer of *merit*, wherever found, that much public ridicule, and something like contempt, were excited by the *modest assurance* with which he pressed his acquaintance on all the *notorieties* of his time. His contemporaries indeed, not without some colour of reason, occasionally complained of him as vain, inquisitive, troublesome, and giddy ;. but his vanity was inoffensive—his curiosity was commonly directed towards laudable objects—when he meddled, he did so, generally, from good-natured motives—his giddiness was only an exuberant gaiety, which never failed in the respect and reverence due to literature, morals, and religion.

" Mr. Boswell's birth and education familiarized him with the highest of his acquaintance, and his good-nature and conviviality with the lowest. He describes society of all classes with the happiest discrimination. Even his foibles assisted his curiosity ; he was sometimes laughed at, but always well received ; he excited no envy, he imposed no restraint. It was well known that he made notes of every conversation, yet no timidity was seriously alarmed, no delicacy demurred ; and we are perhaps indebted to the lighter parts of his character for the patient indulgence with which everybody submitted to sit for their pictures."

CHAPTER XXXIV

WE now approach an interesting portion of our inquiries. Boswell's record is one of the most astonishing monuments of accuracy and memory; and there has been much speculation as to what could have been the method adopted by him in his system of reporting, and how he contrived to expand and manipulate his notes. In April, 1778, he himself explains that, " though I did not write what is called stenography, or short-hand, in appropriate characters devised for the purpose, I had a method of my own of writing half words and leaving out some altogether, so as yet to keep the substance and language of any discourse which I had heard so much in view, that I could give it very completely soon after I had taken it down." He must, therefore, have always had his note-book in his pocket, and it may be imagined that from practice he could set down the few " catch words" that might be necessary without interrupting the conversation. Mr. Barclay had seen Boswell lay down his hat and take out his note-book to record. At Streatham, and at houses where he was well known, he did not scruple to *report* regularly, and it would almost seem that he took so little share in what was going on, or was so privileged, that his proceedings caused as little *gêne* as a professional stenographer would to a practised speaker.* Mrs. Piozzi, however, when she found how she had suffered from his note-taking, inveighed severely against what she calls " a trick, which I have seen played on common occasions, of sitting steadily down at the other end of the room to write at the moment what should be said in company, either *by* Dr. Johnson or *to* him. There is something," she adds, "so ill-bred, and so inclining to treachery in this conduct, that were it commonly adopted, all confidence would soon be exiled from society, and a conversation assembly-room would become tremendous as a court of justice." Another witness, Miss Burney, gives a truly ridiculous portrait of the faithful reporter at his work : " As Mr. Boswell was at Streatham only upon a morning visit, a collation was ordered, to which all were assembled. Mr. Boswell was preparing to take a seat that he seemed, by prescription, to consider as his own, next to Dr. Johnson ; but Mr. Seward, who was present, waved his hand for Mr. Boswell to move further on, saying, with a smile, ' Mr. Boswell, that seat is Miss Burney's.'

" He stared, amazed, . . . but, after looking round for a minute or two, with an important air of demanding the meaning of this innovation, and receiving no satisfaction, he reluctantly, almost resentfully, got another chair, and placed it at the back of the shoulder of Dr. Johnson, while this new and unheard of rival quietly seated herself as if not hearing what was passing ; for she shrunk from the explanation that she feared might ensue, as she saw a smile stealing over every countenance, that of Dr. Johnson himself not excepted, at the discomfiture and surprise of Mr. Boswell. . . . In truth, when

* Of his " Tour " he says, " I will not expand the text in any considerable degree, though I may occasionally supply a word to compleat the sense, as I fill up the blanks of abbreviation."

he met with Dr. Johnson, he commonly forbore even answering anything that was said, or attending to anything that went forward, lest he should miss the smallest sound from that voice to which he paid such exclusive, though merited homage. But the moment that voice burst forth, the attention which it excited in Mr. Boswell amounted almost to pain. His eyes goggled with eagerness; he leant his ear almost on the shoulder of the Doctor; and his mouth dropt open to catch every syllable that might be uttered; nay, he seemed not only to dread losing a word, but to be anxious not to miss a breathing; as if hoping from it, latently, or mystically, some information.

"But when, in a few minutes, Dr. Johnson, whose eye did not follow him, and who had concluded him to be at the other end of the table, said something gaily and good-humouredly, by the appellation of Bozzy; and discovered, by the sound of the reply, that Bozzy had planted himself, as closely as he could, behind and between the elbows of the new usurper and his own, the Doctor turned angrily round upon him, and, clapping his hand rather loudly upon his knee, said, in a tone of displeasure, 'What do you do there, Sir?—Go to the table, Sir,' Mr. Boswell instantly, and with an air of affright, obeyed; and there was something so unusual in such humble submission to so imperious a command, that another smile gleamed its way across every mouth, except that of the Doctor and of Mr. Boswell, who now, very unwillingly, took a distant seat.

"But, ever restless when not at the side of Dr. Johnson, he presently recollected something that he wished to exhibit, and, hastily rising, was running away in its search: when the Doctor, calling after him, authoritatively said: 'What are you thinking of, Sir? Why do you get up before the cloth is removed?—Come back to your place, Sir!'"

One of his note-books came into Lord Houghton's possession, who states that it contains "several sheets filled with anecdotes and observations of the most various character, written without order, and generally without dates. At the end are inserted many scraps of paper and backs of letters, on which Boswell has jotted down memoranda of stories and reflections." *

Dr. Birkbeck Hill has offered on this rather perplexing subject some acute speculations, and supposes that these rough notes were the basis of his regular diary. But it will be found that this was a collection of stories, etc., made for a special purpose, and having nothing to do with the " Life." There are, indeed, a few Johnsonian remarks and anecdotes, which appeared in the " Life ;" but they are few, not more than half a dozen at most.

As Dr. B. Hill has clearly explained,† when Boswell was gathering his recollections from Langton, the latter did not produce any notes, but simply related his anecdotes *viva voce.* " I found," says his friend, " in conversation with him, that a good store of Johnsoniana was treasured in his mind. The authenticity of every article is unquestionable. For the expressions, I, who wrote them down in his presence, am partly answerable."

" It is quite clear from this," adds Dr. Birkbeck Hill, " that Boswell had, to use his own word, ' Johnsonised ' the stories with which Mr. Langton supplied him. His friend gave him the substance of what Johnson had said, and Boswell then gave it a Johnsonian turn." In fact,

---

* A selection was published in the miscellanies of the Philobiblon Society. The whole was later printed at the end of Dr. Rogers' " Life of Boswell," issued by the Grampian Club.

† " Dr. Johnson, his Friends, etc." p. 191.

there is in existence one of the little books which Boswell
used in his records, and which is distinct from the one
described by Lord Houghton. In Mr. Pocock's Johnsonian catalogue there was "A note-book in which Boswell jotted down from day to day the actual sayings and
doings of the eminent Lexicographer. This volume contains literary opinions and aphorisms peculiar to this great
man, and of which many have never been published.
He gives a specific account of the manner in which he
compiled the Dictionary, and relates other matters of
interest bearing on his long literary career and contemporaries." But I can illustrate this point in a still more
curious way. All readers will recall Johnson's powerful
letter to Macpherson which begins :—

"MR. JAMES MACPHERSON,—I received your foolish
and impudent letter. Any violence offered me I shall
do my best to repel ; and what I cannot do for myself,
the law shall do for me. I hope I never shall be deterred
from detecting what I think a cheat, by the menaces of a
ruffian." Now, this was written down by Boswell at Johnson's dictation ; Johnson, however, may not have recalled
the exact words, for he endorsed it, "This, I *think*, is a
true copy." One cannot be certain that Boswell may not
have "touched up" what was thus dictated. However
this may be, that industrious collector, Mr. Pocock,
actually came into possession, not of Boswell's copy, but
of the *original* letter itself.

"MR. JAMES MACPHERSON,—I received your foolish
and impudent *note*. *Whatever insult* is offered me, I
will do my best to repel, and what I cannot do for myself,
the law will do for me. *I will not desist* from detecting
what I think a cheat *from any fear* of the menaces of a
ruffian." The words in italics are the variations ; the
date is January 20, 1775.

But how are the different shapes of the same story in the printed version and in Boswell's notes to be accounted for? It is clear that Boswell took the stories directly from this collection, and the "collection" being for the most part written in the early part of the acquaintance with Johnson, an interval of many years elapsed before their being used in the "Life." Did Boswell "work them up," as it is called, when he addressed himself to the task of writing the "Life," or did he copy them directly from his notes? As we understand the account, what Boswell took down in his peculiar "short-hand" was the substance of a sentence, its meaning, the forcible words used; but when he came to compose, he found repetitions, the same idea or the same argument being repeated in different words. Here was shown Boswell's admirable power of selecting the essence, not merely of the argument, but even of the expression, and he knew how to add strength by discarding what seemed *de trop.* This, itself, would be evident, even from the text itself, which never could have represented the talk as it came from Johnson's lips. The whole is too deliberate, too close, and too well winnowed, as it were. A few specimens will show, in a sufficiently convincing manner, I think, the nature of the process adopted by Boswell, which consisted of two distinct modes of treatment; viz., 1st, compressing, combining, and giving the essence; and 2nd, "touching up," and substituting, and making more forcible, but keeping *within* the form used by his friend.

"'Mr. Sheridan, though a man of knowledge and parts, was a little fancifull in his projects for establishing oratory and altering the mode of British education. Mr. Samuel Johnson said, "Sherry cannot abide me, for I allways ask him, 'Pray, Sir, what do you propose to

do ?'" (From Mr. Johnson.)' 'Boswell was talking to
Mr. Samuel Johnson of Mr. Sheridan's enthusiasm for
the advancement of eloquence. "Sir," said Mr. Johnson,
"it won't do. He cannot carry through his scheme. He
is like a man attempting to stride the English Channel.
Sir, the cause bears no proportion to the effect. It is
setting up a candle at Whitechapel to give light at Westminster." '"

"In the 'Life,'" says Dr. B. Hill, "these stories about
Mr. Sheridan are not only run into one, but they are also
not a little altered. Boswell writes : 'He now added,
"Sheridan cannot bear me. I bring his declamation to
a point. I ask him a plain question : What do you mean
to teach ? Besides, Sir, what influence can Mr. Sheridan
have upon the language of this country by his narrow
exertions ? Sir, it is burning a farthing candle at Dover
to show light at Calais." '"

Now, here is dropped out the words "It won't do.
He cannot carry through his scheme. He is like a man
attempting to stride the English Channel. Sir, the cause
bears no proportion to the effect." It is evident that
Boswell did not, when revising, *recall* a more correct
version, for the result shows that a process of selection
took place. Johnson must have used the illustration of
Westminster and Whitechapel, but the allusion to "the
Channel" suggested Calais, and it occurred to Boswell
that it might be more forcible to substitute "Calais and
Dover" in the candle illustration ; and it must be
admitted, there was a gain of effect.

Again : "In the 'Boswelliana' we have the following
anecdote : 'Boswell asked Mr. Samuel Johnson what
was best to teach a gentleman's children first. "Why,
sir," said he, "there is no matter what you teach
them first. It matters no more than which leg you

put first into your bretches. Sir, you may stand disputing which you shall put in first, but in the meantime
your legs are bare.   No matter which you put in first,
so that you put 'em both in, and then you have your
bretches on.   Sir, while you think which of two things
to teach a child first, another boy in the common course
has learnt both."   (I was present.)'

"This is thus given in the 'Life' in a much more
pithy form : 'We talked of the education of children,
and I asked him what he thought was best to teach them
first.   Johnson. "Sir, it is no matter what you teach
them first, any more than what leg you shall put into
your breeches first.   Sir, you may stand disputing which
is best to put in first, but in the meantime your breech is
bare.   Sir, while you are considering which of two things
you should teach your child first, another boy has learnt
them both."' "

But there is one passage which supports this view in
a very conclusive way, and exhibits Boswell's process of
"touching up :" "Johnson had a sovereign contempt
for Wilkes and his party, which he looked upon as a
mere rabble.   'Sir,' said he, 'had Wilkes' mob prevailed
against Government, this nation had died of *phthiriasis.*'
Mr. Langton told me this."   Boswell then adds a sort
of colloquy with himself.   "The expression *morbus
pediculosus,* as being better known, *would strike more.
Lousy disease* may be put in a parenthesis."   Here he
reveals his method.   The obscurer Latin word was not
likely to *tell.*   The substituted one, and its explanation,
he considered, was in the spirit of what Johnson had
said, but more intelligible to the crowd.   This will be
shown from yet another instance which I have discovered.

"A dull country magistrate gave Johnson a long

tedious account of his exercising his criminal jurisdic-
tion, the result of which was his having sentenced four
convicts to transportation. Johnson, in an agony of
impatience to get rid of such a companion, exclaimed,
' I heartily wish, Sir, I were a fifth.' " From the " Boswelliana " we learn that the scene was at Windsor, and
the hero the mayor, with whom he dined. " But the
fellow (said he), not content with feeding my body,
thought he must feed my mind too, and so he told me
a long story how he had sent *three* criminals to the
plantations.' Tired to death with his nonsense, ' I wish'
(to God), said Johnson, ' that I was the fourth.'—
MR. SHERIDAN."

Now here Boswell made the criminals *four*, and
Johnson the fifth, to give an idea of greater tediousness
to the narrative. But as he had it at second hand, and
the *ipsissima verba* of Johnson were not reported to
him, he felt entitled to tell it in his own way, and the
improved shape in which he has presented it shows his
artistic power. His making it general, with the suppression of the verbiage, give dignity to Johnson's remark.
This, too, makes quite clear his mode of dealing with
communicated anecdotes such as those of Langton,
which, as I have shown, he put into language such as
would best express the tone of thought of his friend.
" The authenticity of each article is unquestionable.
For the expressions, I who wrote them down in his
presence am partly answerable." See how carefully
accurate he is : "*partly* answerable"—that is, where
they seemed to be in Johnson's style, he accepted
them : when not, he " edited " them.

Even after the publication of his first edition he
could improve and strengthen a story. Thus: " A
foppish physician imagined that Johnson had animad-

verted on his wearing a fine coat, and mentioned it to
him. 'I did not notice you,' was his answer. The
physician still insisted. 'Sir' (said Johnson), 'had
you been dipped in Pactolus I should not have noticed
you.'" Now the point of Johnson's answer does not
come with much comedy effect; and indeed, the supposition that Johnson had "animadverted" on his coat,
seems to show that the physician did not deserve such
a retort. This is mended in the second edition, possibly
because another version was given to Boswell, or because
he recalled the true one himself. "A foppish physician
once *reminded Johnson of his having been in company
with him* on a former occasion. 'I do not remember it,
sir.' The physician still insisted, adding, that *he that
day wore so fine a coat that it must have attracted his
notice.* 'Sir,' said Johnson, 'had you, etc,'" How
infinitely superior this version!

It is remarkable, by the way, that Mr. Boswell must
have reported some of these speeches in social meetings,
and did not suppress a good thing of the kind, even if
directed against himself. For, in a selection of "Johnsoniana" in the *European Magazine,* published before
the appearance of the "Life," we find Johnson's retort
on Boswell as to his "coming from Scotland," and which
the editor says had been communicated to him by Mr.
Boswell, as if for publication.

Sometimes Boswell "nods," and does not improve
his story, as in this instance in the "Life:"—"I mentioned that Sir James had said to me, that he had never
seen Mr. Johnson, but he had a great respect for him,
though at the same time it was mixed with some degree
of terror. JOHNSON: 'Sir, if he were to be acquainted
with me, it might lessen both.'" In the note-book it
runs: "Boswell told Mr. Samuel Johnson that Sir James

Macdonald said he had never seen him, but he had a great respect for him, though at the same time a great terror. 'Were he to see me,' said Johnson, 'it would probably lessen both.'"

"Boswell was saying that Derrick was a miserable writer. 'True,' said Mr. Samuel Johnson, 'but it is to his being a writer that he owes anything he has. Sir, had not Derrick been a writer, he would have been sweeping the crosses in the streets, and asking half-pence from everybody that passed.'" (Note-book.)

In the "Life": "But you are to consider that his being a literary man has got for him all that he has. It has made him King of Bath. Sir, he has nothing to say for himself but that he is a writer. Had he not been a writer, he must have been sweeping the crossings in the streets, and asking halfpence from everybody that passed."

"Dr. Johnson desired me to tell Sheridan he'd be glad to see him and shake hands with him. I said Sheridan was unwilling to come, as he never could forget the attack. 'But it was wrong to keep up resentment so long,' said the Doctor; 'the truth is, he knows I despise his character; 'tis not all resentment; partly out of habit, and rather disgust, as at a drug that has made him sick.'" (Note-book.)

In the "Life:" "On Saturday, May 17, I saw him for a short time. Having mentioned that I had that morning been with old Mr. Sheridan, he remembered their former intimacy with a cordial warmth, and said to me, 'Tell Mr. Sheridan, I shall be glad to see him and shake hands with him.' BOSWELL: 'It is to me very wonderful that resentment should be kept up so long.' JOHNSON: 'Why, Sir, it is not altogether resentment that he does not visit me; it is partly falling out of the habit,—partly disgust, such as one has at a drug that has made him sick. Besides, I used to laugh at his oratory.'" Here we see that Boswell knew by heart Johnson's "common forms." He allots to himself the passage about "resentment," and knows by instinct that the doctor would have answered him, "Why, sir, it is not altogether, etc."

Boswell at times, when he has been negligent in his diary, presents a sort of miscellany or collections of "odds and ends" of his great friend's remarks, which he introduces with some such phrase as "I shall here insert some particulars which I collected at various times." There appeared in several numbers of the *European Magazine* for 1785, shortly after Johnson's death, a number of "Johnsoniana," many of which are met again in the "Life." These were republished in a little volume by Kearsley, now very scarce indeed. Some of these are in the form of conversations, which Boswell, in his book, represents as having taken place with *him.* Could he have adapted them or artfully manipulated them; or did he incautiously repeat them to some second Boswell, who took them down and made this use of them?* These are perplexing speculations.

---

* In this collection there are about twenty stories which Boswell used. Such as the sayings of Lord Bolingbroke not having courage to "let off" his work during his lifetime; the precedence between a louse and flea; Macklin's conversation being a "renovation of hope;" his proposal to Mrs. Macaulay to illustrate true equality; the likening Scotch learning to a ship's crew on short allowance; Lord Chesterfield being a wit among lords, etc.; Ossian being capable of being written by many men, many women, etc.; Sheridan being "dull," naturally dull; the retort on the fine prospects in Scotland; the king's compliment, "If you had not written so well;" "Who drives fat oxen;" his speech to the lady who was flattering him, "Consider what it is worth;" the epigrammatic criticism on Lord Chesterfield's letters; his reason for not giving a list of subscriptions. So with the likening of a *congé d'élire* to throwing a person out of a window and re-

The despised Hawkins' "Life" he must have found very serviceable, as here all the *official* acts of Johnson were regularly traced. Boswell did not disdain using a good many passages.

To Mr. Malone, a practised critic, and *littérateur* well *répandu,* his obligations were very great. From Malone's notes, some of which are found in the "Maloniana," he sometimes copied *verbatim.* Malone's judgment directed the whole arrangement of his book, and, we may be certain, secured the omission of much indiscreet matter. In fact, as the book stands at present, it is difficult to say what additions may not have been made by him, for Mr. Boswell died when the third edition was being got ready, which was then being directed by Malone. There is, indeed, to be noticed all through the work traces of another style or control, especially in the more historical portions where the judicial or critical faculty was requisite.

commending him to fall soft; the declaring that fame was a shuttlecock to be kept up by abuse as well as praise; the reply to the gentleman who did not think himself *honoured* by his conversation; the ridicule of simple ballads at Miss Reynolds's, "As with my hat upon my head;" and finally at his death-bed, the declaration of an attendant's activity being that of a turnspit, etc. All these Mr. Boswell adapted from their often unmeaning shape in Mr. Kearsley's little book, and gave them their present point and effect.

CHAPTER XXXV.

BOSWELL'S SECOND THOUGHTS.

CAREFULLY and deliberately as he prepared his volumes, he found himself obliged for various reasons to make alterations, having, as we have seen, embroiled himself with various persons who clamoured loudly against some too candid statements that affected their reputation. For it does seem as though Mr. Boswell had been guided in his revelations by a sort of graduated measure; such as fear of the consequences; the being indifferent when the persons were weak, as in the case of women and clergymen, or of those whom he disliked and despised, as rivals or competitors in the task he had on hand; or in the case of those who were dead and could make no sign. In most cases he kept these considerations before his eyes, and in most instances this "canny" view was borne out by the event.

A collation of the two editions—all he lived to publish—and a view of the "second thoughts" which rose in his curious mind will now be found entertaining, though it will be impossible to give more than a few specimens.

To these second thoughts we owe some pleasant touches—such as in the description of Lord Errol: "From perhaps a weakness, or more fancy and warmth of feeling than is quite reasonable, I could expatiate on

Lord Errol's good qualities." This seemed an odd way to be affected by a Scotch nobleman—as it was, no doubt, pointed out to him. Our author amends it by making it more general, and perhaps more absurd, by inserting after "reasonable," "my mind is ever impressed with admiration for persons of high birth," and Lord Errol's "agreeable look" was changed into *manners*. When the account of the battle of Culloden was given to him, he says, "I *several* times burst into tears," which later became "I could not refrain from tears." After declaring that Johnson was courted by "all the great and all the eminent persons of his time," he altered "great" to "high"—thinking, perhaps, that great and eminent were synonymous. "High and eminent," however, seemed strange, so he eventually reverted to "great." Mr. Capel Lofft, he declared, had "a mind so much exercised in various *exertions*"—not an unhappy word, and of some force. But he changed it to "departments." "Births are nothing," he makes Johnson say, but which he changed to "the register of births proves nothing." He quotes Warton's account of Johnson at Oxford: "I once had been a whole morning sliding [skating] in Christchurch meadow," etc., the meaning of which is that Boswell had left both words until he could ascertain from Mr. Warton which was correct. It now stands "sliding."

Some of the corrections arise out of Boswell's own eagerness to correct others. As when he quotes a letter of Cave's, suggesting to Birch that "your society should buy it," *i.e.*, "Irene." "It is strange," says Boswell, "that a printer who knew so much as Cave, should conceive so ludicrous a fancy as that the Royal Society should purchase a play." In his new edition he writes, "*Dele* note, and read as follows:—'Not the Royal

Society, but the Society for the Encouragement of Learning;" the "ludicrous fancy," therefore, being his own. Mentioning some praise of Johnson in *The Champion*, he says, "This paper is well known to have been written by the celebrated Henry Fielding. But, I suppose, Johnson was not informed of his being indebted to him for this civility; for, if he had been apprised of that circumstance, as he was very sensible of praise, he probably would not have spoken with so little respect of Fielding, as we shall find he afterwards did." Discovering that the passage was written by Ralph, he erased these remarks. In the passage in which he mentions Hooker and other lights of the English Church as "giants, as they were well characterized by one whose authority, were I to name him, would stamp a reverence on the opinion," he alters "one" to "A GREAT PERSONAGE," meaning, of course, the King. Mr. Croker says that "some of his Majesty's illustrious family have condescended to permit these inquiries to extend to them," and without result. It is certainly not likely that the old Dukes of Sussex or Gloucester would be likely to know to what person or on what occasion the happy expression was used.

Further illustrations can be given of Boswell's eager care, particularly in the correction of his work. He mentioned one Rolt:—"This was a sufficient specimen of his vanity and impudence. But he gave a more eminent proof of it in our sister kingdom, as Dr. Johnson informed me. When Akenside's 'Pleasures of the Imagination' first came out, he did not put his name to the poem. Rolt went over to Dublin, published an edition of it, and put his own name to it. Upon the fame of this he lived for several months, being entertained at the best tables as 'the ingenious Mr. Rolt.'"

Boswell had originally set down this proceeding as " a literary fraud." But he grew nervous as he was going to press. " It has occurred to me," he wrote to Malone, " that when I mention ' a *literary fraud*,' by Rolt, I may not be able to authenticate it, as Johnson is dead, and he may have relations who may take it up as an offence, perhaps a *libel*. Courtenay suggests, that you may perhaps get intelligence whether it was *true*. The Bishop of Dromore can probably tell, as he knows a great deal about Rolt. In case of doubt, should I not cancel the leaf, and either omit the curious anecdote, or give it as a story which Johnson laughingly told as having circulated ? "

It was finally put in the form of a note :—

" I have had inquiry made in Ireland as to this, etc."

Boswell's reports of his great friend's conversation we have tested by comparing them with his own notes.* It will be interesting to put them beside the notes of another reporter far less skilful. Among the *dramatis personæ* of these various scenes was an " Irish Dr. Campbell," as he was called, a cheerful, light-hearted man, who seemed to say " whatever came into his head," and was acceptable enough to Johnson. He is well described by Boswell, who introduced him at various parties; of these Campbell set down notes, which in some cases are fuller than those of the great note-taker himself.† Of one dinner at General Oglethorpe's he gives a long report; but it will be seen that, though Boswell's is not nearly so full, it more exactly expresses the tone of the scene, and the impressions left on his

---

* Mr. Croker mentions, without giving any particulars, that he had seen the original MS. of the " Life." This must now be in existence.

† These notes found their way to New Zealand, where they were printed many years ago in a little volume.

own mind. "On Monday, April 10," says Boswell, "I dined with him at General Oglethorpe's with Mr. Langton and the Irish Dr. Campbell, whom the general had obligingly given me leave to bring with me. This learned gentleman was thus gratified with a very intellectual party. I must, again and again, intreat of my readers not to suppose that my imperfect record of conversation contains the whole of what was said by Johnson or other eminent persons who lived with him. What I have preserved, however, has the value of the most perfect authenticity"—an exordium which shows in what a veracious spirit Boswell did his work, for on this day his report is very meagre, and much interesting matter is left out. The truth was, Boswell, having held out the prospect of a great treat to his friend, attempted to stir up "the old lion" and make him roar, as it were : but with the result of only irritating him.

"He this day enlarged upon Pope's melancholy remark,

"'Man never *is*, but always *to be* blest.'

He asserted that *the present* was never a happy state to any human being; but that, as every part of life of which we are conscious, was at some point of time a period yet to come, in which felicity was expected, there was some happiness produced by hope. *Being pressed upon this subject,* and asked if he really was of opinion that though, in general, happiness was very rare in human life, a man was not sometimes happy in the moment that was present, he answered, 'Never, but when he is drunk.' He urged General Oglethorpe to give the world his Life. He said, 'I know no man whose Life would be more interesting. If I were furnished with materials, I should be very glad to write it.' Mr. Scott of Amwell's Elegies were lying in the room. Dr. Johnson observed, 'They are very well; but such as twenty people might write.' Upon this I took occasion to controvert Horace's maxim, etc. Johnson repeated the common remark, that ' as there is no necessity for our having poetry at all, it being merely a luxury, an instrument of pleasure, it can have no value, unless when exquisite in its kind.' *I declared myself not satisfied.* 'Why, then, Sir, (said he,) Horace and you must settle it.' He was not much in the humour of talking."

This is meagre enough : and we now turn to the Irish doctor's account of the same scene :—

"Dined with General Oglethorpe. Dr. Johnson pressed him to write his life, adding that no life in Europe was so well worth recording. The old man excused himself, saying the life of a private man was unworthy public notice. He, however, desired Boswell to bring him some good almanac, that he might recollect dates, and seemed to excuse himself on the ground of incapacity ; but Boswell desired him only to furnish the skeleton, and Dr. Johnson would supply bones and sinews. 'He would be a good Doctor,' said the General, ' who would do that.' 'Well,' says I, ' he *is* a good Doctor ; ' at which he, the Doctor, laughed very heartily. Talking of America, it was observed that his works would not be admired there. 'No,' says Boswell, ' we shall soon hear of his being hung in effigy.' 'I should be glad of that,' says the Doctor, ' that would be a new source of fame,' alluding to some conversation on the fulness of his fame, which had gone before. 'And,' says Boswell, 'I wonder he has not been hung in effigy from the Hebrides to England.' 'I shall suffer them to do it corporally,' says the Doctor, ' if they can find a tree to do it upon.' Boswell asked if he had ever been under the hands of a dancing master. 'Aye, and a dancing mistress too,' says the Doctor, 'but I own to you I never took a lesson but one or two; my blind eyes showed me I should never make a proficiency.' Boswell led him to give his opinion of Gray. He said there were but two good stanzas in all his works, viz. the Elegy. Talking of suicide, Boswell took up the defence for argument's sake, and the Doctor said that some cases were more excusable than others, but if it were excusable, it should be the last resource. 'For instance,' says he, 'if a man is distressed in circumstances, (as in the case I mentioned of Denny) 'he ought to fly his country.' 'How can he fly,' says Boswell, 'if he has wife and children?' 'What, sir,' says the Doctor, shaking his head as if to promote the fermentation of his wit, 'doth not a man fly from his wife and children if he murders himself?' *Boswell desirous of eliciting his opinion upon too many subjects, as he thought,* he rose up and took his hat. This was not noticed by anybody, as it was nine o'clock, but after we got into Mr. Langton's coach, who gave us a set down, Langton said, 'Boswell's conversation consists entirely in asking questions, and is extremely offensive.' I defended it upon Boswell's eagerness to hear the Doctor speak."

This shows how Boswell contrived to arrange or soften down his own reports. His "pressing him" on the subject, and later declaring himself "not satisfied," which provoked the reply, "Then you and Horace must settle it," are revelations, made quite unconsciously, of his highly impolite system; and it is evident from Boswell's closing remark, "Johnson was not much in the humour for talking," that he did not perceive, what everyone else did, that he had actually driven the doctor away by his persistence. We are inclined to suspect, too, from his complete forgetfulness of the most striking speeches and incidents, that the chronicler had taken too much wine ; to which Johnson's remark, " Never, but when he is drunk," may have referred. It is likely that he exhibited himself unfavourably, and when he returned home was not in a state, or not disposed, to sit down and record what had occurred.

Dr. Campbell's accounts are also curious, as showing us what was the general estimate at this time of Boswell. It would seem that his attendance on Johnson was a subject of delight to the wags of the coterie, who hugely relished the rude snubs which he encountered. These were actually retailed in his own presence to strangers, as " capital things :" as on another occasion when everything that could be offensive was retailed to the stranger.

"April 1, 1775 " writes the Irish doctor, " dined at Mrs. Thrale's. There was Murphy, Boswell, and Baretti, the two last, as I learnt just before I entered, are mortal foes, so much so that Murphy and Mrs. Thrale agreed that Boswell expressed a desire that Baretti should be hanged upon the unfortunate affair of his killing, etc. Upon this hint I went, and without any sagacity it was easily discernible ; for upon Baretti's entering, Boswell did not rise, and upon Baretti's descry of Boswell, he grinned a perturbed glance. Politeness, however, smoothes the most hostile brows, and theirs were smooth. Johnson was the subject both before and after dinner. His *bon mots* were retailed in plenty. . . . Boswell arguing in favour of a cheerful glass, adduced his maxim ' in vino veritas.' 'Well,' says Johnson, 'and what then, unless a man has lived a lie ?' B. then urged that it made a man forget all his cares. 'That to be

sure,' says Johnson, 'might be useful if a man sat by
such a person as you.' . . . It is ridiculous to pry so
nearly into the movements of such men, yet Boswell
carries it to a degree of superstition. The Doctor, it
appears, has a custom of putting the peel of oranges in
his pocket, and he asked the Doctor what use he made
of them ; the Doctor's reply was, that his dearest friend
should not know that. This has made poor Boswell
unhappy, and I verily think he is as anxious to know
the secret as a green love-sick girl. The book with
which Johnson presented a Highland girl was Cocker's
Arithmetic. . . . Boswell, desirous of setting his native
country off to the best advantage, expatiated upon the
beauty of a certain prospect, particularly upon a view
of the sea.   'Sir,' says Johnson, 'the sea is the same
everywhere.' " Murphy, then, to further entertain his
guest, told another comical story, also at Boswell's
expense, of his interview with Johnson—"upon his
earnest desire of being known to the doctor," about his
coming from Scotland.   Fairly as Boswell has related
this amusing scene, it seems likely that, from his nervous-
ness and *gaucherie* he committed a good many
absurdities.   Boswell mentions none of these topics,
and represents the discussion as turning on public
speaking, statutes against bribery, and the like.

    "*April* 8.   Dined with Thrale, when Dr. Johnson
and Boswell (and Baretti as usual) were there. The
Doctor was not in as good spirits as he was at Dilly's.
He had supped the night before with Lady ——, Miss
Jeffreys, one of the maids of honour, and Sir Joshua
Reynolds, at Mr. Abington's.   He said Sir C. Thompson
and some others who were there spoke like people who
had seen good company, and so did Mrs. Abington herself, who could not have seen good company.   He seems

fond of Boswell, and yet he is always abusing the Scotch
before him, by way of joke. Talking of their nationality,
he said they were not singular, the negroes and Jews
being so too. Boswell lamented there was no good map
of Scotland. 'There never can be a good map of
Scotland,' says the Doctor, sententiously. This excited
Boswell, who asked wherefore. 'Why, sir, to measure
land, one must go over it; but who could think of going
over Scotland!'

"When Dr. Goldsmith was mentioned, and Dr.
Percy's intention of writing his life, he expressed his
approbation strongly, adding, that Goldsmith was the
best writer he ever knew, upon every subject he wrote
upon. He said that —— had borrowed all his
dictionary from him. 'Why,' says Boswell, 'every
man who writes a dictionary must borrow.' 'No, sir,'
says Johnson, 'that is not necessary.' 'Why, says
Boswell, 'have you not a great deal in common with
those who wrote before you?' 'Yes, sir,' says Johnson,
'I have the words, but my business was not to make
words, but to explain them.' Talking of Garrick and
Barry, he said he always abused Garrick himself, but
when anybody else did so, he fought for the dog like a
tiger; as to Barry, he said, he supposed he would not
read. 'And how does he get his part,' says one. 'Why,
somebody reads it to him,' and yet I know he says that
he is very much admired. Mr. Thrale then took him by
repeating a repartee of Murphy's. Setting Barry up
in competition with Garrick is what irritates English
critics, and Murphy standing up for Barry, Johnson
said he was fit for nothing but to stand at an auction-
room door with his pole. Murphy said Garrick would
do the business as well, and pick the people's pockets
at the same time. Johnson admitted the fact, but said

Murphy spoke nonsense, for the people's pockets were not picked at the door, but in the room. Then said I, he was worse than the pickpockets. This went off with a laugh."

This story Boswell also reports, but all through he takes care to omit Dr. Campbell's jocose remarks. But it is impossible not to be struck by the infinite superiority of Boswell's method, beside which Campbell's report seems cold and lifeless. Boswell courageously discards trivial details, and with his masterly touch " dashes in " the doctor's manner and expression. He had in truth the art of the practised comedy writer, who can " abstract " and put before his audience the essentials only.

CHAPTER XXXVI.

BOSWELL SELF-REVEALED.

In various portions of this work I have alluded to Mr. Croker's theory that an examination of Boswell's work undertaken with reference, not to Johnson, but to Boswell himself, would furnish new and expected lights in the direction of psychological study. He, indeed, anticipated that one result would be the discovery that Boswell was *insane;* but this seems rather a fantastic conclusion, and is really only one more of the many extravagant speculations with which his laborious and ingenious commentary is stored. But the inquiry he suggests will be found to open up more reasonable, and interesting questions, supplying the key to his abundant disquisitions on religion, and to his pleadings for lapses in morality, so often introduced without apparent purpose. In this view, it will be found, that he was pleading for himself. Boswell had the strongest religious instincts, and a very firm faith ; he was even super-stitious to a degree ; his superstition was, further founded on a wholesome terror of punishment in a future state. Yet, as I have shown, he was enslaved to his vices, and his life exhibited extraordinary " laxity." This inconsistency he was always striving to hide from himself by ingenious arts and excuses. He felt, too, that his homilies and moralities must have impressed his friends much as the "sentiments" of Joseph Surface did his brother Charles. Yet from beginning to end he persisted in enunciating his approval of a correct life, of faith, and of religion, in all sorts of shapes and forms. What, then, was the mystery, or meaning of his system?

The truth seems to be, it was an *apologia pro vita sua*, a vindication or palliation of himself, carried through steadily to the end, with much practical ingenuity. Nor is he so much pleading before the public, as pleading for himself to himself. His nervous anxiety as to his spiritual interests—his consciousness that he was helpless in controlling himself, that he was following evil while he knew what was good—made him seek feverishly and even artfully for every aid of extenuation—so that he might finally plead : " I have at least taught what was good. I have had the sanction and indulgence of my great friend. I have not shrunk from ridicule ; and I have registered for future generations my own inconsistency." He found comfort in this method, and hoped thus to encourage himself to a reform.* These excuses and palliations he also sought in the shape of little parables, as it were : he would dwell on the failings of others ; he would quote some dictum of his great friend which seemed to favour his own case. This uneasy state of mind must excite our sympathy and interest, and lead us to take a kindly view of poor Boswell and his struggles.

A fair specimen of these fluctuations is his tendency to Catholic doctrines, of which he had never divested himself. We find him persistently introducing the

---

* Readers will recall his curious story of the seducer, which need not be quoted in full, but which ends, " I would not debauch her *mind*,"—which seems to exactly express his own view.

subject under a pretext of extracting Johnson's opinions, and, though he appears to put forward objections, it is plain he is eager to obtain favourable answers. To the Catholic he suggests the type of the lax Catholic rather than of the lax Protestant ; he rests on ritual observances, and longs to go up to town to worship in the cathedral at Easter, etc. He had a true reverence for " the sacrament," which, he more than hints, he accepted in the Catholic sense. There is no more singular instance of his " crazy piety," as Johnson termed it, than the one he furnishes of his own devout " impressions."

When they were at Southhill in 1781, on the first Sunday of the month, Boswell stayed to partake of the sacrament, and Johnson praised him, saying, " You did well to stay. I had not thought of it." Boswell speculates that he did not feel himself sufficiently prepared ; and then, as though quite pleased with his own piety, expounds the different opinions of " good men " on the subject. " A middle notion I believe to be the just one," a " long train of preparatory forms is not necessary, but neither should they rashly venture upon so awful and mysterious an institution." Here the well-intentioned Boswell was eager to proclaim this " set off " to his failings. And he still feels, even when writing the account, a piously complacent satisfaction, and tells us that, " being in a frame of mind which I hope, for the felicity of human nature, many experience, *in fine weather, at the country house of a friend, consoled and elevated by pious exercises* " (how droll and yet natural is this jumble !), " I expressed myself with an unrestrained fervour to my Guide, etc. . . . My dear sir, I would fain be a good man : and *I am very good now.* I fear God and honour the King ; I *wish* to do no ill, and to be *benevolent* to

all mankind." Then it was that Johnson gave him
sound advice about not "trusting to impressions," or
to benevolent feelings of the kind. This picture of a
soul which fancied itself religious because it was a fine
day, at a pleasant country house, and then "felt good,"
was characteristic. It is odd to find that the sage rather
encouraged this superficial form of piety in his pupil by
an awkward example. He said he was afraid Dr. John
Campbell "has not been inside of a church for many
years, but he *never passed one without pulling off his
hat*," adding that "he was a good man—a pious man."
This cue was enough for Boswell, who was delighted to
enforce and improve the precedent; "Though Milton,"
he says, "could absent himself from public worship, *I
cannot*." He then repeats that his friend Campbell was
"a sincerely religious man," and, apparently, for this
reason,—he once found him "reading a chapter in
the Greek Testament," which was "his constant practice." So the idea of mere ritual observance was very
acceptable to Boswell. He himself "read Ogden's
Sermons," and recommended them constantly. On
another occasion, speaking of his uncle Dr. Boswell's
death, and describing his lax life, he added, fervently,
that "he believed he was now in Heaven." All which
reveals to us the state of Boswell's conscience, and the
anxiety he had to quiet its prickings.

He always shrank from what he called "the dreadful
doctrine of an eternity of punishment," which he hoped,
but did not believe, was "figurative, and would not literally be executed." This comfortable theory is what a man
of pious instincts, but of free life, would cling to ; the
dread of punishment would be always before him. He
was also artfully trying to extract comfort from his
friend. Johnson's religious counsels to him were excel-

lent, judicious, and full of good sense, and, we may fancy, did the pupil much good. As he later said, he talked to him on "this awful and *delicate* question in a gentle tone, as if afraid to be decisive."

We must often admire the easy power with which Boswell analyzes mental processes and emotions; and this was owing to his study of himself and to the absence of affectation. Such is his comment on Johnson's confession of melancholy at Ranalagh: "The feeling of languor, which succeeds the animation of gaiety, is itself a very severe pain; and when the mind is then vacant, a thousand disappointments and vexations rush in and excruciate. Will not many even of my fair readers allow this to be true? I suggested that, being in love, and flattered *with the hopes of success*, or having *some favourite scheme in view for the next day*, might prevent that wretchedness." Here is a delicate touch and most naïve revelation of character to which many would not be equal. But it was Boswell "all over"—some little "favourite scheme in view for the next day," or "being in love," would put all "the fumes" to flight. "While Johnson and I," he goes on, "stood in calm conference by ourselves in Dr. Taylor's garden at a pretty late hour, in a serene autumn night, looking up to the heavens, I diverted the discourse to the subject of a future state." This shows how picturesque was Boswell's nature, and with what artistic feeling he could introduce a subject.

But we now come to a more delicate matter. Readers will have been struck by the frequent and persistent way in which Boswell introduces the subject of unfaithfulness in wedded life. On one notable occasion he urged that the "laxity" of the husband released the wife from the contract; and, in support of this doctrine, he quoted a lady, whom his friends would have found no difficulty in recognizing. His theories and speculations on this point are singular from the *naïveté* and earnestness with which they are put forward. At one time he was eager to show that Johnson considered it a fair matter for discussion. At another time, he took the side of strict morality. Here can be applied the principle that we have been considering, that Boswell had his own practice before him, and by this airy treatment was extenuating it to himself or to his friends. In another discussion on the same subject, Boswell shows his own mixed feelings. " I mentioned to him a dispute between a friend of mine and his lady " on this point of infidelity, " which, my friend maintained, was by no means so bad in the husband as in the wife." Johnson maintained that the friend was in the right. " Between a man and his Maker it is a different thing." BOSWELL. " To be sure, there is a great difference," etc. JOHNSON. " The difference is boundless." This must have been acceptable to Boswell ; and, as the acceptable or convenient view was supported on such high authority, he felt that he might consequently support the other side ; and so we find him gravely doubting if this was " entirely in the right." " Still, it may be maintained that, independent of moral obligations, *it is by no means a light offence*, because it must hurt a delicate attachment." Then he thinks that some allowance must be made for people living laxly in the world, that it may be the wife's fault, who is too straitlaced, or wanting in *tact*. So we find him putting this gloss on his friend's doctrine : " Here he discovered that acute discrimination, that solid judgment and knowledge of human nature, for which he was so remarkable. Taking care to keep in view the moral and religious view, he showed clearly from reason and good sense, the greater degree of culpability in the one sex, deviating from it, than the other ; and, at the same time, inculcates a very useful lesson as to *the way to keep him*." Again and again, Boswell contrived to start this rather unpleasant topic, which, on one occasion at least, he treats very broadly. "Our conversation to-day," he says, "turned (I think for the only time at any length during our long acquaintance)," etc. There is something apologetic in this, and he winds up : "It would not be proper to record the particulars of such a conversation in moments of unreserved frankness, when nobody was present on whom it could have any hurtful effect. That subject, when *philosophically treated*, may surely employ the mind in as curious discussion and as innocently as anatomy, *provided that those who do treat it, keep clear of inflammatory incentives*."—a "characteristical" passage. He was longing to give the whole, and had to content himself with a sort of abstract, which was coarse enough.

On one most singular passage I have already dwelt, namely, Boswell's exaggeration of the failings with which Johnson charged himself on his deathbed. This, as Mr. Croker pointed out, was certainly intended as palliation of Boswell's own follies.

Excess in drinking, with arguments in favour of drinking and against it, are repeatedly introduced with the same personal reference. His introduction even of Johnson's careless charges against Reynolds, in this respect, was an ingenious insinuation to show how general was the indulgence in liquor. Once Boswell was emboldened to declare when told that Hawkins Browne drank freely, and wrote his poems : "I listened to this with the eagerness of one who, conscious of being himself fond of wine, is glad to hear that a man of so much genius and good thinking had the same propensity." *

A still more curious passage is his comment on Johnson's gloomy view of life, in "Rasselas." After declaring that Johnson "had less enjoyment than I have," he devised an ingenious theory of responsibility, to justify lax behaviour. A Turkish lady, it seems, told him, that "being well depended on the way our blood circulated. This I have learned from a pretty hard course of experience; and would, from sincere benevolence, impress upon all who honour this book with a perusal : *that until a steady conviction is obtained that the present life is an imperfect state, and only a passage to a better, if we comply with the divine scheme of progressive improvement,*—and also that it is a part of the mysterious plan of Providence that intellectual beings must ' be made perfect though suffering,'—there will be a continued recurrence of disappointment and uneasiness. But if we walk in the mid-day sun of revelation, our temper and disposition will be such that the comforts and enjoyments in our way will be

---

* It is sad to think that both master and pupil may be said to have shortened their days, by indulging their unrestrained appetites, the one for eating, the other for drink. No one was so eager as Johnson in warning Thrale that he was sacrificing his life to greed for food; yet he himself, almost up to the time of his death, was literally "gorging" himself at dinner-parties. Yet he had had a paralytic stroke, was suffering from dropsy, asthma, and other afflictions, for which the only alleviation was to be found in strict temperance. This strange weakness in so good a man is extraordinary, and was quite as censurable as Boswell's failing for drink; nay, he even quarrelled with his lifelong friend Dr. Taylor, for pressing on him the necessity of temperance, "by which alone," as Mrs. Thrale says, "his life could have been saved." Any one that could eat as Johnson did, "gobbling" his food until the veins in his forehead swelled, and the perspiration broke out, was placing himself in hourly danger of sudden death, or of fits of apoplexy.

relished, while we patiently support the inconveniencies and pains. Let us cultivate, under the command of good principles, '*la theorie* des sensations agréables,' and, as Mr. Burke once admirably counselled a grave and anxious gentleman,"—Boswell himself, no doubt, "'Live pleasant.'"

When Boswell went to see the silk-mill at Derby, it suggested to him some singular reflections on low spirits—singular, because they appear to have no àpropos. He says he had learnt from Dr. Johnson on this occasion, "not to think with a dejected air of indifference of the works of art and the pleasures of life." He then gives a most wholesome "preachment," on taking unselfish views of life. "We are apt to transfer to all around us our own gloom. Before I came into this life, in which I have had so many pleasant scenes, have not thousands and ten thousands of deaths and funerals happened? But have those dismal circumstances at all affected me? Why, then, should the gloomy scenes which I experience affect others?" This very natural passage shows that Boswell was trying to encourage and reassure himself for the future, by writing down this comforting reasoning.

Another of these harmless devices was a sort of apologetic method. He knew that his friends made merry over his weaknesses, and that when he attempted to vindicate himself only laughed the louder. But in his book he would appeal to a higher Court—to his readers. Thus, in the "Tour," when he and his friend talked of going to see the King of Sweden, Johnson doubted if he would speak to them. "'I am sure,' said Colonel M'Leod, 'Mr. Boswell would speak to *him*.' But, seeing me a little disconcerted by his remark, he politely added, 'and with great propriety.'" Satisfied with this halting *amende*, poor Boswell offers a short defence of this propensity : "It has procured me much happiness. I hope it does not deserve so hard a name as either forwardness or impudence.   If I know myself, it is nothing more than an eagerness to share the society of men distinguished either by their rank or their talents, and a diligence to attain what I desire."   It is hard to resist this pleading, and it is, no doubt, the true explanation.   It shows that he was well aware of the rather ill-natured view that was taken of his "propensity;" and that he was not to be laughed out of his purpose.   On another occasion he tells that in approaching the great, he was always for " trying "—that is, for making advances.   In the same spirit, when Johnson declared that no one ought to praise or censure himself, because he does the latter " in order to show how much he can spare," Boswell urged : " It may proceed from a man's strong consciousness of his faults being observed.   He knows that others would throw him down, and therefore he had better lie down softly of his own accord."   Can we not see here that he is confessing to a device of his own?

We find Boswell also revealing his own whims, prejudices, and humours in an amusing way.   These were not tolerated in society, so he found this fashion of making a protest.   In one of the notes there is a pettish explosion against the introduction of children into company!   He is glad to have Johnson's authority against having "children too much about you."   "The common custom of introducing them after dinner is highly injudicious; . . . they should not be suffered to *poison* the moments of festivity by attracting the attention of the company, and, in a manner, compelling them, for politeness, to say what they do not think."   This vexation is characteristic, but we can read between the lines

—he had been interrupted; the attention of the company diverted from *him*, by the noisy irruption of the children. He complains that parents "are too apt to indulge their fond feelings *at the expense of their friends.*" Yet this was apropos of Langton's children—the friend who had helped him so cordially and so abundantly in his work, and who must have been amazed to find himself and his family held up to the public under a perfectly recognizable shape. This offers a fair specimen of this very entertaining fashion of reading our "Boswell"—if only as a study of character.

There is a passage in the "Tour to the Hebrides," which betrays rather significantly enough what an opinion Boswell had of himself and his position, at a time when he had not made his reputation. Johnson had said that it was advantageous for an author to be attacked as well as praised, like a shuttlecock which must be struck at both ends. On which Boswell: "Often have I reflected on this since, and, instead of being angry at those who have written against me, have smiled to think *that they were unintentionally* subservient to my fame, by using a battledore to make me *virorum volitare per ora.*" When this was written, of course neither the "Tour" nor the "Life" had appeared, and yet the author speaks of "*my fame,*" and of being in the mouths of men. He could not refer to his Corsican travels, which were twenty years old and forgotten; his pamphlets had been little noticed; it was therefore of himself as a personage—as Dr. Johnson's attendant—that he must have been thinking. One would be inclined to fancy, however, that he foresaw the real fame which his great books would bring, and was transported, as it were, into the future; and most natural and well warranted, too, was this faith.

Boswell's rather childish practice of "trying" his friend's regard, by long protracted silences when he was at a distance, has been mentioned. This is a really unhealthy note of character, indicating a sort of morbid, diseased state. It is likely that the first suggested motive was not the real one. He really shrank from encountering his great friend, even in a letter, or was brooding over some imagined offence. Then would come a sudden violent impulse to return to his old state of affection. Most persons have encountered persons of this disposition, and they are usually odd, uncertain characters, slightly unhinged. There is one episode of this kind. On May 3, 1779, he left London on the best and most affectionate terms with Johnson, and for more than two months would not write him a line—he says, "trying how he would be affected by my silence." Johnson wrote in wonder and alarm to know the reason for his silence, which Boswell answered in a rather strange explanation, saying that it was owing to "a supine indolence of mind" which had been his "state of existence since his return." Somewhat ashamed, however, he retorts upon Johnson, that—"in a livelier state, I had often suffered severely from long intervals of silence on your part, and I had even been chid by you for expressing my uneasiness." He wished, then, to—"try whether an unusual silence would make you write first." However, it was now all restored by the receipt of Johnson's letter : he was—"beginning to grow tender, and upbraid myself, after having dreamt, two nights ago, that I was with you." He would never again put him to that test.

A week later Johnson wrote, "a letter full of particulars." But he, it seems, had not attended to it, for Johnson wrote him "an angry reproachful letter : "—

" Are you playing the same trick ? Remember that all tricks are either knavish or childish." But he would not be cheated again, etc. Johnson's letter is dated Sept. 9th, nearly seven weeks after the receipt of Boswell's. So the latter was now jealously requiring that there should be strict reciprocity, and that every letter should have its answer. This letter he answered after a week's delay, and in an odd strain : "Pray let us write frequently. A whim strikes me that we should send off a sheet once a week, like a stage-coach, whether it be full or not ; nay, though it should be empty." A lively image ; but the whole transaction shows a morbid, unbalanced mind, and it is clear that, during the few years before Johnson's death, the sage suffered from these humours ; I have shown that Boswell was actually indulging in them when Johnson was in his last sickness ; and it seems likely enough that, from disgust at this treatment, he forbore to name him in his will.

Yet another interesting topic, suggested by the study of Boswell's character, is the curious one, that a predominating " hobby " will engender a whole tide of passions, which will exhibit themselves in connection with that hobby. Bozzy was eminently good-natured : he had no malice or ill will ; he was good-humoured and forgiving. Yet in connection with his book and the " god of his idolatry " he was full of hatred, malice, envy, and all the meaner passions. I suppose no more ingeniously venomous display could be conceived than his attack on Mrs. Thrale. I have dealt with this already ; but I will analyze one specimen more. Malice often supplies ingenuity and even wit ; and Boswell exulted himself in the variety and contrivance of his strokes against this lady. She had published the great collection of Johnson's letters, " hugely to the detriment " of his work, as he fancied it. Among them were some of her own—which the lady, as he hinted, had revised, if not rewritten. So we have it ingeniously suggested— " I shall present my readers with one of her original letters to him at this time, which will amuse them, probably, more than those well-written but studied epistles which she has inserted in her collection ; . . . it is also of value as a key to Johnson's answer, *which she has printed by itself* "—i.e. had suppressed her own letter. Accordingly, we are given it, and it certainly, as he says, contrasts with her formal " cooked up " productions—and is full of sharp strokes : " There was Mr. Melnoth. I do not like him," etc., " he hates the Bishop of Peterborough. Mrs. Montagu flattered him finely." Then her flatteries of Johnson, which Boswell was anxious to bring out. "You would hardly forget me . . . for I felt my regard for you in my face last night, when the criticism was going on." Then she says that her husband cannot live " unless his mouth be sewed up." What can she do ? " He will eat, I think."

There is one curious instance of Boswell's frankness and truth in his narration. When he said that Caligula wished that the people of Rome had but one neck, etc., General Oglethorpe corrected him, saying, " It was of the Senate he wished that ; " and Boswell records his error and its correction, without comment. Yet it turns out that Boswell was right, after all.

Here is a very natural and pleasant confession. One night he owns that " he missed that awful reverence with which he used to contemplate Mr. Samuel Johnson," and lamented it. " I have a wonderful superstitious love of *mystery :* when, perhaps, the truth is that it is owing to the cloudy darkness of my own mind. . . . My dissatisfaction to-night was foolish. Would

it not be foolish to regret that we shall have less
mystery in a future state? This reflection, which I thus
freely communicate, will be valued by the thinking
part of my readers," etc. This is an extract from his
journal, which must have been interesting enough. For
he was thus following Johnson's advice to keep a record
of the state of his mind.

I have mentioned that Boswell was good-naturedly
accustomed to tell people any good that was said of them
by another. This he practised on principle. " I think,
sir, it is right to tell one man of such a handsome thing,
which has been said of him by another. It tends to
increase benevolence. JOHNSON: Undoubtedly it is
right, sir." Johnson had just been told of a most
handsome thing said of him by a very distinguished man.

Boswell, has scarcely obtained sufficient credit for
his sense of *humour*, and his dramatic art in telling a
story. His nice and delicate instinct in seeing weakness of character, yet without insisting on it, leaving it to
make its impression on the reader, is extraordinary. I
cannot resist giving two instances, familiar as they are,
which illustrate this power in an extraordinary degree.*

"A foreign minister, of no very high talents, who had
been in his company for a considerable time quite over-

---

* I often think that one of the most delightful, natural "touches"
in Boswell's work is this. When they were shown over Lord
Bute's seat, Luton Hoo, " As we entered the Park, I talked," says
Boswell, " *in a high style*, of my old friendship with Lord
Mountstuart, and said ' *I shall probably be much at this place.*' The
sage, aware of human vicissitudes, gently checked me : ' Don't you
be too sure of that.' " The extraordinary thing here is, that, while
Boswell records his own exuberant anticipations, he should be
quite conscious of their futility. He is, as it were, pointing the
moral ; and does not mind furnishing himself as an instance.
Numbers of these pleasant passages could be quoted, and, as I
said before, it is in this direction that Boswell's work can be
studied with most enjoyment.

looked, happened luckily to mention that he had read some of his 'Rambler' in Italian, and admired it much. This pleased him greatly ; . . . and, finding that this minister gave such a proof of his taste, he was all attention to him, and, on the first remark which he made, however simple, exclaimed 'The Ambassador says well. His Excellency observes——' And then he expanded and enriched the little that had been said, in so strong a manner, that it appeared something of consequence. This was exceedingly entertaining to the company who were present, and many a time afterwards it furnished a pleasant topic of merriment. *' The Ambassador says well,'* became a laughable term of applause when no mighty matter had been expressed." Here is a genuine touch of comedy ; for there is no ill nature, and yet there is presented a little amiable weakness of Johnson in a very amusing way. Another truly delightful sketch, done in the most delicate way, and proving Boswell to have been an acute observer of character, is the discussion between Johnson and Lord Newhaven. It was on the Middlesex Election—a point on which Johnson was always vehement and intolerant. " Lord Newhaven took the opposite side, but respectfully said : ' I speak with great deference to you, Dr. Johnson ; I speak to be instructed.' This had its full effect on my friend. He bowed his head almost on the table, *to a complimenting nobleman ;* and called out ' My lord ! my lord ! I do not desire all this ceremony : let us tell our minds to one another quietly.' After the debate was over, he said, *' I have got lights on the subject to-day,* which I had not before.' This was a great deal from him, especially as he had written a pamphlet, etc." The charm here is the good-natured way in which Boswell exhibits his friend, yet with the full consciousness of the result of the nobleman's flattery. And there is a sly reserve in the way he so simply records Johnson's speech, "I have got lights, etc." One can read these two anecdotes again and again, and always with a smile.

I may add here, that what most excites our astonishment and admiration is the skilful, adroit, unflagging way in which Boswell *conducted* his great enterprise. For some twenty years, he, as it were, supervised every conversation, led it, made skilful suggestions, and added his own contribution. It is wonderful with what cleverness he would "introduce a subject," as he called it, or divert it; how ready he was with a quotation, or some scrap of knowledge aptly introduced; he confesses sometimes that he would assume an air of ignorance, and put a question innocently, to get his friend to talk. His latest editor, Dr. B. Hill, makes the surprising statement that "*Boswell was no reader*," the truth being that he was a man of the most varied and extensive reading. And there can be little doubt that, without this starting of topics, this careful thought beforehand, and watchful selection of subjects, the talk would have languished or died out. Again, in a work of such proportions—there are close on two thousand octavo pages in the "Life"—made up chiefly of conversation, and perpetually recurring conversation, it would have seemed almost impossible to avoid monotony, or a certain "scrappiness;" yet in nothing is Boswell's art shown so conspicuously as in the *variety*, the brightness, the ever-changing methods and devices for introducing these "talks." They come about in the most easy, natural way. There is no "piecing" them together, and each presents itself with an air of novelty.*

* Some years ago there appeared a chronicle of this kind, which minutely recorded the sayings and doings of Prince Bismarck during

This praise is not exaggerated; indeed a volume could be filled with specimens of this sort of analysis. I am tempted, however, to supply a few more, and thus to invite the Boswellian student to follow up this new and entertaining subject of inquiry.

Boswell was so " penetrated " with his subject, that we can almost always trace in his depreciation of various persons some connection or interference with his cherished project. Of this he was, no doubt, unconscious. We find, in these cases, some indirect competition with him, or entering on the same line. Even an attempt at self-vindication was an attack on his text; and any one who wrote an account of Johnson, however trifling, he managed to depreciate.

This is shown in the case of one Tom Tyers, of the Vauxhall Gardens, whom he thus sketches : " He was bred to the law, but, having a handsome fortune, vivacity of temper, and eccentricity, he could not confine himself to the regularity of practice." Thus was he like J. Boswell, Esq., himself. " He therefore *ran about* the world with a pleasant carelessness, amusing everybody by his desultory conversation." So far, this was delightfully contemptuous. " He abounded in anecdote, but was not sufficiently attentive to accuracy ; I therefore

the Versailles occupation—a journal laboriously kept by his secretary, Dr. Busch. It is full, and appears to be accurate; but Dr. Busch possessed no Boswellian gift of abstraction, or selection. He set down everything : with the result, to say nothing of the stupidity, of leaving a very unfavourable impression of the conversation of the great man ; for, as we have seen, not everything that is spoken is suitable for record. The same principle directs what is called the " Society journalism " of our day ; and we have " topical interviews "—descriptions of persons " at home "— with the most trivial remarks duly recorded. It is curious that the result of this minature " photographic " treatment should be to supply no real portraiture, for such details have no genuine significance whatever.

cannot venture *to avail myself much of a biographical
sketch of Johnson* which he published, being one among
the various persons ambitious of appending their names
to that of my illustrious friend. The sketch, is, however,
an entertaining little collection of fragments." He then
praises another work of Tyer's, and adds : " This much
I may be allowed to say of a man who *was exceedingly
obliging to me.*" Any student of character will be
amused with the little struggle between evident jealousy
and the sense of obligation, presented here in so natural
and transparent a way.

One of the best, most dramatic conversations
recorded by Boswell—and in which the characters sustain
their parts in the most brilliant way, are fully discrimi-
nated, and hold our attention to the end—is the dinner
at Dilly's on April 15, 1778, where were Mrs. Knowles,
" the ingenious quaker lady ;" Miss Seward ; Dr. Mayo,
and others. Boswell is at his best, and never flags for
an instant. That Johnson shone in the conversation is
evident, and we cannot but admire how Mrs. Knowles
"held her own" against the sage. Boswell has caught the
tranquil, quakerish " note " of the lady. How dramatic is
Johnson's attack on the young quaker convert : " She is
an odious wench ! " etc. Mrs. Knowles afterwards published a report of this little discussion—which, as any one
can see, is unfaithful ; but Boswell disposes of it in a note,
which is admirable for its studied impertinence, and dis-
paragement, though couched in a strain of affected respect. Here he felt, as I have shown, that his record—
made almost on the spot—had a sort of sacred authenticity.
" Mrs. Knowles—*not satisfied with the fame of her needle-
work*, in which she has indeed displayed much dexterity ;
nay, with the fame of reasoning better than women
generally do, as I have fairly shown her to have done,—

communicated to me a dialogue of considerable length, which, after many years had elapsed, she wrote down as having passed between her and Dr. Johnson at this interview." We are thus prepared by this artful mixture of praise and depreciation. " *As I had not the least recollection of it,* and did not find the smallest trace of it in my *record* taken at the time, I could not, in consistency with my firm regard to authenticity, insert it in my work. . . . It chiefly relates to the principles of a sect called quakers ; *and no doubt the lady appears to have greatly the advantage of Dr. Johnson, both in argument as well as expression.* From what I have now stated, and from the internal evidence of the paper itself, *any one, who may have the curiosity to peruse it,* will judge whether it was wrong in me to reject it, however willing to gratify Mrs. Knowles." It would be difficult to comprise within a small space so much that was contemptuous. But she was one of those who had dared to write of Johnson, and on one of Mr. Boswell's own topics.

A young clergyman wrote, in the ' Transactions 'of the Edinburgh Royal Society, a very temperate criticism of Johnson's line, " Panting time toiled after him in vain." Boswell talks of his " presumptuous petulance," " cloudy confluence of words," assumes that he is " a very young man, *though called Reverend;*" and concludes, " The learned Society, *under whose sanction such gabble is* ushered into the world, would do well to offer a premium to any one who will discover its meaning ! "

Another worthy Scotch clergyman, Mr. Burrowes, had written a criticism on Johnson's style, to which Boswell gave some praise for its acuteness, and other merits. Still this person was a trespasser, so he must point out with gusto that "the *critick of the style* of Johnson says 'they are *called on* by every *tye,* etc.'"

Dr. Douglas, the Bishop of Salisbury, having ventured to doubt the accuracy of a report of a remark of his own, was roughly treated. In a discussion, he had urged that a work of Swift's contained "strong facts," when Johnson turned on him and ridiculed his phrase: "housebreaking is a strong fact, and murder is a mighty strong fact, etc." Not pleased at being thus exhibited, he remonstrated with the reporter. He must have been disagreeably surprised to see that his position was made rather worse. "My *respectable friend* . . . observed that he must have said . . . 'strong facts well arranged.' His lordship, however, knows too well the value of written documents to insist on setting his recollection against my notes taken at the time. He does not attempt to traverse the record" (which was true; for the Bishop says, "he *must* have said"). Boswell, however, concedes, that "it might be that the words escaped him," or that Johnson did not allow the Bishop to finish—which amounts to no more than that he *intended* to add the words, but did not.

We have seen with what pleasant old-fashioned hospitality Lord Monboddo welcomed the travellers. He put such restraint on himself that he allowed some of his favourite doctrines to be attacked. Johnson, at least, always spoke kindly of him, calling him "Monny," though in private he laughed at his theories. On one occasion he said that some one "talked nonsense," but that he was afraid Monny "did not *know* he was talking nonsense." Boswell tells us that, "His lordship having frequently spoken in an abusive manner of Dr. Johnson in my company, I, on one occasion *during the lifetime of my illustrious friend*, could not refrain from retaliation, and repeated to him this saying. He has since published I don't know how many pages in one of his curious books, attempting, in much anger, but with pitiful effect, to persuade mankind that Johnson's fame was undeserved," etc.   It is difficult to realize the cool insensibility of the man who could repeat such an impertinence to an old venerable judge ; and we can understand how it must have inflamed him against Johnson.   Boswell's enmity he was likely enough to have incurred by some expressed contempt.

Other of Boswell's notes are marvels of sly malice. Dr. Johnson was reading Dr. Watson, the Bishop of Llandaff's " Chemical Essays ; " on which Boswell, gratuitously : " One of the *poorest* bishopricks in this kingdom. His lordship has written with much zeal to show the propriety of equalizing the revenues of Bishops."   This is good.   " He has informed me that he has burnt all his chemical papers.   The friends of our excellent constitution would have less regretted the suppression of some of his lordships other writings."   Imagine the surprise or rage of the bishop as he read !   He, no doubt, had met Bozzy at some dinner-party, and told him familiarly that he had burnt his chemical papers, a confidence reproduced in this offensive shape.

At one dinner was Mrs. Hall, a worthy, pious lady, the sister of John Wesley, whom he knew ; yet he describes her as " *lean, lank, preaching Mrs. Hall.*" " Manners, sir," said Johnson to him once, " that is your want."   And yet he was eager to know her brother, John Wesley, and waited on him.

Most readers will have noticed how persistently Boswell contrives to depreciate Goldsmith, recording every little weakness or blunder that can make him ridiculous.   There is an amusing tone of superior patronage.   But Boswell seems to vindicate himself, as who should say, " Here is a man of genius, admired,.

sought, and followed; yet he is laughed at, 'talks like poor Poll,' and made a butt of. The same people laugh at *me*, James Boswell, Esq.: so I cannot complain, etc."

The observant reader will discover for himself abundant instances of the kind.

CHAPTER XXXVII.

BOSWELL'S EDITORS.

Mr. Boswell issued two editions of his book, the first in 1791, the second in 1793. He had begun to prepare the third, when he was interrupted by death. Neither of these were in such shape as would have satisfied his critical taste, much new matter having reached him too late, which he was obliged to insert out of its proper place ; and, as he had now leisure sufficient, there is little doubt that the third edition would have been a very complete and finished production. At his death, when the revision was about half done, Mr. Malone took up the task. As he had diligently co-operated in the preparation of the work, no one could have been better fitted to take the author's place ; and under his supervision no less than four editions were issued, in the course of which many changes and material alterations came to be made. The sixth, or fourth from the author's death, was issued in 1811, and was the last superintended by Malone, who died in that year.* From the date of his death, this edition became the standard one, and was regularly reprinted until the year

---

* To Mr. Tedder, we are indebted for a very full and accurate bibliography of the "Life" and the "Tour," which the true Boswellian will find an excellent aid to his studies. It will be found in the first volume of my own second edition of the "Life," 1888.

1831, when it may be said to have been supplanted by Mr. Croker's important edition in five volumes, which, under various forms, has held its place until the present moment. There have been other reprints, upon which various editors have exercised their taste and judgment.

For exactly one hundred years, therefore, has this genuine and seductive book furnished occupation to innumerable students and commentators. But though the reprints have been innumerable, the list of regular, official editions is a small one. They are as follows :— 1. Mr. Malone's four editions, viz., in 1799, 1804, 1807, and 1811. 2. Dr. Chalmers's, in 1822. 3. Mr. F. Walesby's, in 1826, which is the fine Oxford edition. 4. Mr. Croker's, in 1831, in 1835 (with Mr. Knight's aid), and in 1848. These three Crokerian editions, as Mr. Tedder points out, differed from each other in shape, matter, and arrangement. 5. Mr. Carruthers's, in 1852-3. 6. Mr. Percy Fitzgerald's first edition in 1875, second edition in 1888. 7. Rev. A. Napier's, in 1884. 9. Dr. G. Birkbeck Hill's, in 1887. There are, of course, many *arrangers* of editions, rather than editors.

A curious phenomenon in literary history is the treatment under which this great work has suffered at the hands of those who professed to illustrate it. Editors of ordinary works usually show restraint, and aid the author by clearing up doubtful points, obscure allusions, and the like. But in Boswell's case almost every editor, since Chalmers, has handled the book without restraint, has altered it, as it were, and in some cases seems to have substituted himself for the author. The want of taste in this procedure was extraordinary, for it was forgotten that Boswell's book is an agreeable and dramatic *narrative*, and its pleasant form and tone is outraged when it is overlaid with controversies and profuse noting. Boswell, by his own notes, prescribed the pattern that was to be followed, thus clearly showing that any additional note was meant to be curt, and to the point, furnishing a name, or explaining an allusion. This would exclude all "parallel passages," illustrations, quotations, discussions, reprovings of the author, and the like.*

It was Malone who first began the system of revision and addition, feeling, no doubt, that he was privileged to carry out, after the author's death, the control he had been allowed to exercise during the author's life. New letters were inserted as they came to hand, and the fashion was introduced of adding notes, supplied by Johnson's friends and others, in the shape of correction or illustration. Malone, however, exceeded the privileges of his executorship, in often converting notes into text, and *vice versâ*, in shifting the place of notes, and in "revising" the text itself. These changes were not very material as to substance, but still such a mode of "settling the text," pursued through a whole series of editions, could only have resulted in serious departure from the original. He also announced that "every new remark, not written by the author," together with "the letters now introduced, are carefully included within crotchets, that the author may not be answerable for anything which has not the sanction of his approbation." This wholesome caution was respectful to the author and his work, his own notes being left undistinguished by any sign. That system, however, has long since been abandoned, and in the modern editions we find the author jostled by a crowd of competitors,

* It may be urged that, in my own edition, I have exceeded in this way; but it will be seen that any comments I have made are "fenced off," as it were, from Boswell's text and notes, and may be passed by at will.

his annotations being labelled with his name, as though he himself had been an intruder.

After Malone came Mr. Croker. Not only did he make interpolations in the text on a vast scale, but he overloaded the whole with a huge bulk of elaborate notes. Obscure allusions guessed at, biographies furnished, blanks filled up, speculations offered, opinions either of Boswell or of Johnson refuted in controversial style, contemporary authors quoted largely, and political opinions and prejudices duly ventilated,—these were but a tithe of his contribution, which, save by a few men of true critical instinct, who made early protest, was accepted as a valuable resetting of the old Boswellian gem. For more than forty years has Boswell's work remained embedded in this mass of concrete and rubble. This treatment was long ago good-humouredly exposed. "Four books," says Mr. Carlyle, " Mr. Croker had by him wherefrom to gather light for the fifth, which was Boswell's. What does he do now, in the placidest manner?—slit the whole *five* into slips and sew them together into a *sextum quid*, exactly at his own convenience. Not till after consideration can you ascertain now, when the cup is *at* the lip, which liquid it is you are imbibing—whether Boswell's French wine, which you began with, or some of Piozzi's ginger-beer, or Hawkins' entire, or perhaps some other great brewer's penny swipes." As, however, Mr. Croker admitted his mistake, and in a later edition withdrew the bulk of the intruded matter, it would not be fair to say more on this point. Yet he could not bring himself to sacrifice the whole of the foreign element; and his work, which still includes masses of Thrale and other letters, diaries, and the like, is no longer Boswell's " Life of Johnson," but Boswell's " Life of Johnson, altered and enlarged by Croker." The editor did not stop there, but proceeded to make serious alterations in the text. Letters were transposed, and shifted here and there, on account of some inconsistency; dates were altered, notes rewritten, cut up, and distributed, or altogether omitted; while good old-English adjectives, of a somewhat coarse flavour, were struck out, and others substituted. Italics were removed with loss of point, and the arrangement of paragraphs altered, several being fused into one. What, too, can be said for consigning to an appendix, established especially for the purpose, the various legal "arguments," quotations, letters, which had been fixed in their proper places by the author himself. Such removal does violence to the text; passages such as, "Dr. Johnson then dictated to me the following argument for the negro," having to be altered to suit the omission. But it is strange that it did not occur to Mr. Croker that there was a special interest connected with these essays, from the fact of their having been *dictated* by Johnson, and taken down on the occasion described. They are, therefore, a faithful record of the situation: we seem to hear the great sage rolling forth his full periods; we see his follower recording; and it must have been an obtuse sense which could not see that the removal of such pieces left so many blanks in the text. Still, as I said, it might have been better, if the author had omitted or condensed them, as they are far too long. Not less to be reprobated is the rude disruption of the narrative about the middle, for the purpose of arbitrarily inserting the "Tour to the Hebrides." This is defended on the ground of chronological symmetry; but the result, even in this view, is, as may be imagined, clumsy and confused. By this arrangement the reader is given the sketch of Dr. Johnson's character, habits, etc., with which the "Tour" commences, though this has been already given at great length; and when the "Life" is once more resumed, a sort of epitome of Johnson's proceedings in Scotland follows, so that the ground is in each case gone over twice. Moreover, to smooth the joinings, the editor took it on himself to alter various phrases; but the fact that the "Tour" had been written many years before the "Life," in the shape of a diary, while the "Life" was cast in a grave and judicial key, ought to have at once shown that the two works could never have been made to harmonize. This is a more serious objection than Lord Macaulay's, viz., that the "Tour" had been perused in manuscript by Johnson, whereas the "Life" had not. Finally, the various advertisements to the "Tour," as well as the dedication to Malone, together with the characteristic abstract of contents, quite Boswellian in its way, are all suppressed, while the text he selected for the "Tour" is a sort of mongrel one, compounded from the first, second, and third editions.

It might be urged, however, that interpolation should be tolerated to a certain degree, at least as regards letters of Johnson's bearing on transactions incompletely dealt with by Boswell. Malone inserted several under their proper dates, notably the interesting and affectionate letters written by Johnson when his mother was dying. These Boswell had tried to obtain and failed, and they would probably have been arranged by him in the very places they now occupy. Yet, even in these cases, a distinction should be taken between the materials for a "Life," and the disposition of such materials. Mr. Boswell was, in his way, an artist; nothing is more remarkable in his great book than the tact, the self-denial, the power of selection, and the rejection of all that is surplusage.

Boswell's life and character, and his peculiar rela-
lation to his great friend, have become so interesting,
that the extravagances of editors may be a little excused
or justified as excessive zeal. Everything that con-
cerns the pair has been explored and winnowed and
hunted out, and the process still goes on merrily. The
study of Boswell's character and humours has really
something fascinating, on the ground that in no other
instance has such ample materials been presented to
work on. I may claim, however, to being the first to
work out a true psychological method for pursuing this
interesting inquiry. This is to trace the working of
his mind and whims, by following the changes in his
three editions. The motives for such changes are often
quite transparent, and the author made them supposing
that they would be unnoticed, and thus reveals himself
very candidly. It occurred to me, therefore, that a
reprint of his first edition, with notes in which these
changes were marked, would be a useful contribution
and entertaining addition to Boswellian literature. There
is also the satisfaction of having before us the original
text of Boswell's first edition, exactly as it was printed
—with the old spelling, punctuation, paragraphs—and
without any of the shapings and polishings which have
been found necessary to give it the air of a modern
work. The breaking up of the text into chapters, with
headings of the contents, had something to commend
it on the score of convenience; but it was a departure
from the author's intention. Chapters are not to be
formed after a work is completed, by the mechanical
process of cutting it into fairly-proportioned lengths;
for the artistic writer who employs such a form of construction works to the close of a particular episode,
when he rests, as it were, before coming to a new point

of departure. On this ground I was careful to restore the original form. In the "Tour" such an arrangement is actually inconsistent with the author's divisions, which are in diary shape, each day's proceedings being complete. Here, too, the original punctuation is specially characteristic ; the profuse "dashes," the use of capitals after colons and semi-colons, show the irregular nature of the entries—which were indeed "extracts from his journal," presented almost in the state in which they were jotted down.

This edition had also the merit of allowing Boswell to speak, unencumbered or jostled by a crowd of commentators. His work—text, notes, and alterations —were for the first time given complete, distinct, and fenced off, as it were, from all notes and illustrations supplied from other sources. Thus the author, with the results of his labour, is preserved from that "encumbering with help" with which the zeal, and perhaps the sense of self-importance, of friendly coadjutors has hitherto oppressed him.

Now, in illustrating a book of the character of Boswell's "Johnson" for the use of a generation living subsequent to the author's time, it would seem that, at the outset, certain limitations for illustration should be fixed, and a principle sought for. Otherwise, in a large work of the kind, filled with names and local allusions, the stock of newly discovered information, gathering as it goes, will become inexhaustible. If all that *can* be told about such subjects is to be told, or even abstracted, the tide of commentary will rise higher and higher, until it at last will fairly submerge, or at least inundate, the text. A simple rule would be to put the question —Is this particular allusion or passage sufficiently intelligible as regards the purpose for which it was introduced ? Does it illustrate, not Johnson's life, but Boswell's view of that life ? Would the information or details have been adopted by the biographer himself ? These tests, fairly applied, would dispose of a vast amount of useful, but, as it would seem, impertinent information which has adhered to the sides and bottom of Mr. Boswell's fine vessel, and has certainly impeded its sailing powers. Thus the innumerable biographies, births, and deaths of numberless obscure individuals, or of writers quoted in the text, the contemporary accounts or illustrations of a transaction which add little to the version in the text, with, above all, controversy, or refutation of opinions of Boswell or Johnson, which forms so important a portion of a commentator's notes—would be excluded by putting the questions just given. Further, passages in Johnson's life omitted by Boswell should not, on the same principle, be supplied, or should at most be touched in the lightest and briefest fashion. For the fallacy that has misled so many editors is, that they believe themselves called on to supply, not *Mr. Boswell's " Life of Johnson*," but *a* life of Johnson—a fallacy founded on an inartistic appreciation of the nature of a written " life," which consists in the use of particular materials, the rejection of others, from which is educed a purpose, harmony, or theory, directed by a single mind.*

When I wrote of this anticipation, that Boswell would be submerged in the notes and comments of his editors, I did not dream that the foreboding would be so speedily justified : nor did I forecast that Dr. Birkbeck Hill and his six great volumes were at hand.

In 1887 the Oxford University Press projected an

---

* It should be stated that a good deal of the above is taken from the introduction to my edition.

issue of Boswell's " Life of Johnson," to be edited by
Dr. G. Birkbeck Hill, of Pembroke College.   No expense
or trouble was spared.   The work was fifteen months in
passing through the press ; *carte blanche* was given to the
editor for illustrations, *fac-similes*, etc. ; and the handsome volumes at last emerged from the press, finely
printed, on fine paper, in " Roxburghe binding."   Here
was, at last, the long-expected final edition of " Boswell,"
and the critics expatiated on the research, the labour,
the ingenious discoveries of the laborious editor.   Yet,
in this cordial reception one thing was to be noticed,
significant of the superficial character of our time.
There was hardly a single attempt to deal critically
with the work.   No effort was made to discuss the
editor's conclusions, or to test their value.   All was
accepted on his statements, and on the faith of his
position as a professional critic.

In his preface the editor explained how, from his
youth, he had been drawn to this fascinating subject.
When he first went to college, " by a happy chance he
turned to the study of the literature of the eighteenth
century," owing to a sort of theme, set regularly every
week, and which consisted in turning into Latin a
passage from *The Spectator*.   From Addison, in the
course of time, he " passed on to the other great writers
of his and the succeeding age."   Yet " many and many,"
never destined to edit Boswell have, somehow, gone
through this training during their undergraduate course ;
in fact, have pursued the ordinary college education.
But a solemn moment was at hand—and the account
recalls the agitated passage in which Gibbon describes
his walk in the garden after penning the last sentence
of his monumental work.   " A happy day came just
eighteen years ago, when in an old shop, under the

shadow of a great cathedral," our doctor was enabled to secure that uncommon stall-book, " a second-hand copy of a somewhat early edition of 'the Life' in five well-bound volumes." The discovery of this rarity produced quite a revolution in our student. As he made his way, he began almost unconsciously, as it appeared to him, to edit. And how? " Before long I began to note *the parallel passages and allusions,* not only in their pages, but in the various authors whom I studied." Other preparation for the task was also going on all the time. Once, when Dr. Birkbeck Hill had to criticize a rival edition—my own, I fancy—he read it through notes and all, to fill two columns of a weekly newspaper! Everything in his reading that " bore " on the subject was all the time being carefully " noted," until he felt that it was about time " to begin to raise the building "—that is, the note-books were filled with heterogeneous matters that remotely " bore " upon the subject. Then, unfortunately, his health broke down, and he had to go abroad. But, "ever in the sleepless hours of the night I almost forgot my miseries in the delightful pages of Horace Walpole, and, with pencil in hand, *managed to get a few notes."* There we have the system—noting Walpole! The delusion that such could be " editing Boswell " is extraordinary.

In his tremendous preface of nineteen closely printed pages, Dr. B. Hill, with tremulous pride, proclaims a number of various and startling discoveries. As a composer gathers up his leading " motives " in the overture, so the editor, with pride and triumph, invited special attention to some selected specimens. He is almost exultant over one " find : " " That I have lighted upon the beautiful lines which Johnson quoted when he saw the Highland girl singing at her wheel, and have

found out who 'one Giffard a parson' was, is to me *a source of just triumph.* I have not known many happier hours than the one in which, in the Library of the British Museum, my *patient investigation* was rewarded and I perused 'Contemplation.'" We can readily sympathize with the author's transports on thus discovering the name of the poem so little known, and perhaps uncared for. Curious to ascertain whether the same triumph could not be obtained without any labour at all, I took up the index to our old friend, the *Gentleman's Magazine*, which Dr. B. Hill has consulted hundreds of times, and was referred to vol. lxxvii., p. 1, p. 477, where, to my astonishment, is a short account of this very "Giffard a parson," with this passage :—
"One small poem of his, entitled 'Contemplation,' was printed in 1752, which attracted the notice of Dr. Johnson, who has quoted it in his Dictionary." Next I turned to Nichol's "Literary Anecdotes and Illustrations," an equally useful and often consulted *vade mecum.* There, again, was "Contemplation" revealed ! But further : we might expect that a poem so appreciated by Johnson would be found in his dictionary ; and there accordingly it is, "Contemplation," under the word "wheel."

A fresh "discovery," on which our editor plumes himself in his preface, so far from being a discovery at all, is only a very serious misapplication of the meaning of the text. A gentleman talked of "retiring." "Never think of that," said Johnson. The gentleman urged, " I should then do no ill." " No, nor good either. Sir, it would be a civil suicide." Dr. B. Hill even thinks that Burke was present, though Boswell speaks of his hopes from his patronage. He even fancies that Burke was meant ; and that by retiring he meant resigning office.

Burke was not resigning, though in one of his speeches he did say that, if the House of Commons persisted, he was prepared to bow to their will. But any reader of ordinary acumen will see that this word " retiring " is here used in the sense of withdrawing from the world. But what is conclusive is, that, in the " Tour," a Mr. Nairne talks of " retiring " and Johnson approved, " when he had done his duty to society."

Another discovery, which yet again proves to be no discovery at all, refers to the well-known rather scurrilous passage in the " Tour," relating to Lord Macdonald, which Boswell suppressed in a later edition. The editor tells us that he had " *discovered*, though too late to be mentioned in its proper place, that there had been a cancel of a leaf containing pages 167, 168." He then states how, " in my own copy, I noticed between pages 168 and 169 a sort of guard on which the new leaf had been pasted," on which both binders and printers were agreed. This is a slight inaccuracy, for it will be seen from Dr. B. Hill's own statement that the guard, or cancelled leaf, must have been between pages 166 and 169 ; and so it is in " my own copy." But we " discover " that the " discovery," cancel and all, such as it is, is due to Mr. Croker's ingenuity, and was made over forty years ago !

There is one more of Dr. B. Hill's " discoveries " for which he takes due credit. Here it is. He is afraid that ardent advocates of total abstinence will not be pleased at finding that " I have been obliged to show that Johnson thought that his gout was due to his temperance." To this special attention is called in the preface. But, on returning to the body of the work, it is seen that it was pointed out by a correspondent of *Notes and Queries.*

It is only right to acknowledge that Dr. B. Hill has gathered much curious and interesting matter; but it seems truly a problem why he should, with pride, direct attention in his preface to such trivial "discoveries" as these, which, on investigation, break down. Thus he speaks of "the light I have thrown" on the incident of Johnson engaging in politics with "single speech" Hamilton. It was well known that Johnson had formed this connection, and wrote for him a work on "Corn." "But," said the editor, "I suspect there was more than this," as now we shall hear. In the spring of the year 1766, "Burke separated from Hamilton," and it seems to Dr. B. Hill "highly probable" that Hamilton then sought Johnson's assistance. In almost the next sentence we are told that Hamilton, "on losing Burke, wrote on February 12, 1765," etc.; though, we have just been told, he did not lose Burke until a year later. Then we learn that Chambers was looked for to supply Burke's place, though we have been assured that on "losing Burke" Johnson was applied to. But leaving aside this confusion, we are still in the dark as to "the discovery" made by Dr. B. Hill, or "the light" he has "thrown" on the matter. We hear of Warton, Chambers, Burke, Hamilton, but nothing new about Johnson, except that "I think it highly probable."

In a passage in the preface he tells us: "Johnson, I fondly think, would have been proud could he have foreseen this edition. Of Boswell's pleasure I cannot doubt." He then proceeds to give proof. "How much he valued any tribute from Oxford" (whence the edition issued) "is shown by the absurd importance he gave to a sermon preached by Mr. Agutter:" and the performance was so contemptible that it could only have been admiration for Oxford that permitted him to admit it. But what are the facts? Boswell was enumerating minutely what he calls the "accumulation of literary honours" which were heaped on his hero after his death, among which was the high compliment of a sermon in memory of Johnson, preached before the University. Could he with propriety have omitted such an honour? The mention of it, and the quotation from it, was simply historical, and had nothing to do with personal liking for Oxford. The editor must therefore find some other reason why Boswell should be pleased with his edition. Nearly all Dr. B. Hill's discoveries dissolve in this way, and are mere fancies.

"I hope," says the editor, speaking rather mysteriously of his index, "I have shown that I am not unmindful of all I owe to men of letters." This means, I presume, that he has mentioned their names and works. But if he be thus indebted, what does not the existing generation owe to *him*? "Some relief," he adds, "is obtained from the burthen (of gratitude to the dead) if we, in our turn, make the men of our own time *debtors to us.*" The passage is obscure, and may refer to the writers enshrined in his index, who are thus laid under heavy obligation to Dr. B. Hill by being mentioned.

With regard to the text he has chosen, an all important matter, the editor is rather misty and uncertain. He tells us that he settled on the third edition, which the author was preparing at his death, but did not publish. Yet it seems in the earlier portions he adopted the *second* edition. As Malone had prepared and edited the third edition, Dr. B. Hill was eager to distinguish the additions made by him from those of Boswell. "I felt it my duty," he then tells us, with solemnity, "to have the whole second edition read aloud to me, for comparison with the third," which still would hardly help him to discriminate between Boswell's and Malone's work ; "but, as I read on, *I was convinced* that *about all* the verbal alterations were Boswell's own." This "being convinced" is not much aid. "I have retained Boswell's spelling" (such as "aweful," etc.), the editor tell us, "for the reason that Boswell, in another work, had said that in case of a reprint he hoped that care would be taken of his orthography." On turning to the work, published twenty-three years before, we find that Boswell was only speaking of two forms of spelling, the addition of the "k" to "public," and of "u" to such words as "humour," and he trusted that these forms would be adhered to. Dr. B. Hill is scarcely justified in forcing or enlarging the meaning in this way.

I have also to complain that our editor is capricious in the application of his system. Thus he points out about a dozen instances where Boswell has made alterations in the first edition of his text. Now, as it seems to me, this should have been carried out consistently, and *every* change have been noted, or else the matter have been left alone. I may add that in my own edition I have collated the two editions and noted these alterations, many of which are truly characteristic and even amusing, as they show that Boswell had acted under pressure of some sort.

The last of the six great volumes is almost entirely devoted to Indexes and Abstracts. It is, indeed, a perfect "curio" in its line. Everything is odd and confounding. Thus, as we open it, we unfold what looks like a weather map, a strange mystery or diagram with crossed lines, and figures, and colours, and columns, which is described as, "*A chart of Dr. Johnson's Con-*

temporaries, drawn up by Margaret and Lucy Hill, on the model of a chart in Mr. Ruskin's Ariadne Florentina." Diable ! Recovering from this, we pass on to "Titles of many of the Works quoted in the Notes," filling twelve closely printed pages. Next we come upon what is called "Addenda :" scraps from a number of Johnson's letters, which, it seems, were sold at Sotheby's some years ago, all more or less trivial ; such as an account of "Young Strahan at College," having no relevancy to Boswell's "Life of Johnson," where Dr. B. Hill rambles off on his own account ; "My friend, Mr. C. J. Faulkener, Fellow and Master of University College, has given me the following extracts," —which are concerned with the election of this young George Strahan to the Bennett Scholarship ! This strangely leads to a disquisition on the value of the Bennett Scholarship in 1764—how much was the emolument, etc. Next we come to an index of these "Addenda ;" and then to the gigantic general index, which consists of no less than 288 pages, or nearly 600 columns ! It has indexes within indexes—indexes to Johnson's and Boswell's lives, to Scotland, Ireland, etc. Yet another index follows, oddly denominated "Dicta Philosophi," or a concordance of Johnson's sayings ; with a third. We may contrast with this bulk Mr. Croker's simple, admirable index, which fills not quite thirty pages.

After all this labour, the editor "will be greatly disappointed if actual errors are discovered." We point out a few. Looking at the first of the two indexes to Boswell—the "Chief events of his life," the other a general one to his sayings and doings—the eye falls on one of his juvenile productions, "*The Club at New-market*, I. 383." Turning back to the page, again it

stands, " The *Club*," etc. Boswell had indeed written a
foolish piece of doggrel, called " The Cub at Newmarket,"
the title whereof is characteristic, as he intended it as a
description of himself, thus early showing his lack of
self-respect. A printer's very natural " slip," it will be
said, Cub and Club being so like. But we cannot allow
the editor this excuse. Has he not said that he verified
every authority, in person, twice over, once in MS., once
in proof? The fact is, there is the same error in
Boswell's letters to Temple; and this our doctor copied.

One sort of reference in his index the editor is partial
to. Yet it seems but a crabbed form. We turn to
" Bute " and find : " BUTE, third Earl of, Adams, the
architect, patronises, II. 325." This seems an odd sort
of " Pigeon " English. Adam, by the way, and not
Adams, is the architect's name.

In spite of the editor's boast, we have found other
errors of reference, paging, etc., and he himself confesses that though, under the headings of America,
Oxford, London, Ireland, etc., he sets out all that falls
under such heads, somehow " the provincial towns of
France, by some mistake, I did not include in the
general article." The following is grotesque enough.
Under " Port," we find " it is rowing without a port,"
i.e., without an object ; on which the editor refers us,
" See Claret." Some of the Johnsonian dicta are not
Johnsonian at all, and would appear to have slipped
into the list from the general index. Thus we have
Cibber's old jest about the pistol missing fire ; and
under " *quare*," " A writ of *quare adhæsit pavimento*
(*Wags of the Northern Circuit*), III. 261," which refers
to the well-known hoax upon Boswell. We have also
Mrs. Salisbury's sayings : with the one about " No tenth
transmitter of a foolish face," etc. ; and finally the

quotations—" Live pleasant, *Burke ;* " with Quin's and Lord Auchinleck's speeches about kings, and " Boswell's description of himself as ' Baro,' " all which are classed as " sayings of Johnson."

Everything in his edition, according to our editor's preface, is astonishing and *hors ligne.* It is hard not to smile at the following : " In the forward-references, in the notes, to other passages, *the reader may be surprised* to find that, while often I only give the date under which the reference will be found, frequently I am able to give the page and volume." I doubt if this phenomenon has struck any reader. " But," goes on our doctor, " the explanation is *a simple one.* Two sets of compositors were generally at work, and two volumes were passing through the press simultaneously." Thus is the mystery of the " *See post's* " explained. To be logical, this " *See post* " system should be carried out consistently ; but by the editor's own admission, it could only be adopted where the reference happened to be in one of the volumes which were being printed simultaneously.

Boswell's title-page, reproduced here, is surely misdescribed as " Boswell's Life of Johnson, including Boswell's Journal of a Tour to the Hebrides, and Johnson's Diary of a Journey into North Wales." Boswell's " Life of Johnson " does *not* include either of these things. His Journal was a separate work, and with the Diary he had nothing to do.

In the mechanical disposition or arrangement of his work, the editor is scarcely orthodox. I have just shown how his title-page does not faithfully represent Boswell's. A more serious blemish is the arrangement of the notes. When a work of this kind is illustrated with additions and comments by another " hand," such matter should, of course, be marked with the writer's name, so as to distinguish them from the author's. Here, strange to say, Dr. B. Hill's numerous notes are unsigned, and, at first sight, appear to be the legitimate notes of the text. We find every one of poor Boswell's notes marked "Boswell," as though he were some intruder or outsider. A man in his own house has no need to label his property with his name; if anything be labelled, it should be the effects of strangers. Malone, when preparing the third edition, was careful to mark every additional note by brackets and initials. Mr. Croker marked, with suitable reverence, all his own very voluminous notes, "Croker." Dr. B. Hill also thrusts passages of his own composition into Boswell's notes. thus spoiling their symmetry. Boswell, for instance, furnished a business-like list of Johnson's residences: "1, Bolt Court; 2, Gough Square; 3, Johnson's Court," etc. This becomes, under our editor's treatment: "17, Bolt Court, No. 8 (he was here on March 15, 1776, *ante* II. 427). From about 1765 (*ante* I. 493) to Oct. 7, 1782 (*post*) he had, moreover, an apartment at Streatham." But Boswell was speaking of *London* residences. Then, with more detail, we are told that "he had a room either in Grosvenor Square or Argyll Street," that is, with the Thrales, which were not his "residences" in Boswell's sense. We must doubt, too, the propriety of introducing a head-line over every page, of the editor's composition, which affects to describe the subject-matter of each page. This was not, at all events, Boswell's idea. Another adornment, which shows a lack of delicate instinct, is the supplying an elaborate modern engraved map for the "Tour." Now, Boswell gave a very clear outline map, without any shading of mountains, etc.—a plan or diagram of the tour, as it were, which has a quaint, antique look. This should surely have been reproduced. Even in the matter of the portrait which faces the title-page, the editor has gone astray. Boswell selected a rather characteristic likeness, representing the doctor at his desk, pen in hand, and this we find preserved in all the many editions down to Mr. Croker's. Boswell had good reason for his selection, as we find under it the inscription, "From the Portrait in the possession of James Boswell, Esq." Dr. B. Hill, however, has, for some reason, substituted the well-known Peel portrait. Again, Boswell, in all the titles of his "Tour," seemed to pride himself on a piquant little device, which he had specially engraved, his crest, a hawk, and motto, "*Vraye foy.*" This is missing in Dr. Hill's edition. Again, Boswell gave fac-similes of Johnson's writing at different periods of his life, which he placed on a single page for convenience of comparison. But Dr. B. Hill supplies various huge fac-simile letters at full length, which have to be folded and refolded and unfolded, and which give a clumsiness to the volume. It is the same with the subject of the many fine prints which are introduced, but after a capricious principle. Thus, because Sir William Scott had presented a print of his friend Johnson, after Opie, to his college—where it is to be seen now—the editor thought fit to have it engraved for this trivial reason.

Boswell, in his third edition, as the editor points out to us, had altered the word "forenoon" into "morning," on which he adds: "The correction being made in one of his letters renders it likely that he corrected them before publication." This seems confused, for he has just told us that the correction was not made until the third edition, so the letter must have been published in the first and second without correction.

One of the long appendices is devoted to an account of George Psalmanazar and his character. Other remarkable, curious, and eccentric personages alluded to in the text might have equal claim to this separate form of treatment. But will any one guess what was our editor's reason for selecting Psalmanazar? Not the importance of the adventurer; not the editor's own judgment, but this: "I have complied with the request of an unknown correspondent ('query, anonymous'), who was naturally interested in the history of that strange man." This mysteriousness is extraordinary. Granting that the unknown one was "naturally interested," was he therefore to be attended to? He was not even one of our "valued correspondents" who supply materials. He had nothing to offer but his "natural interest." The editor himself apparently had not judged the matter worthy of treatment, but yielded to this probably flattering application.

So much for the form and arrangement of Dr. B. Hill's work. It would take long to examine his notes, which, we grieve to say, all through the book, lack relevancy, and, in many instances, are founded upon complete misunderstanding of the text. Here is a typical specimen, and dozens of the same kind could be supplied. Johnson had suggested to Cave various subjects for essays, such as "Forgotten Poems," or "Loose Pieces like Floyer's," a mere illustration of his suggestion. Boswell does quite enough in supplying this note: "Sir John Floyer's treatise on the Cold Bath, *Gentleman's Magazine*, 1734, p. 197," his purpose being to mark one of Johnson's contributions. "His letter," says the editor, "shows *how uncommon a thing a cold bath was.*" Floyer, it seems, after recommending a "general method of bleeding and purging before the

patient uses the cold bath," continues: "I have commonly cured the rickets by dipping children, etc., etc.
(For mention of Floyer, see *ante*, etc., and *post*, etc.)."
Having started this topic of bathing, we then go back
to Locke, who, in his "Treatise on Education," had
recommended cold bathing for children : "Johnson, in
his review of Lucas' 'Essay on Waters' (*post*, 1756),
thus attacks cold bathing," etc. (passage quoted). Then
we have Dr. Lucas himself: "The old gentleman," he
says, "that uses the cold bath," etc.—*Literary Magazine*, p. 229. After which we turn back to the text, and
find that Johnson was not thinking of any of these things
or persons, but had merely suggested the *subject* for a
paper! Again, Cave writes that "he had received the
reports of the speeches, some by hand, others by penny
post." Prepared as we were, we never expected that
our editor would actually pause here to describe the
origin of the Penny Post. But such is duly set out,
with an extract from the "Reports of the Commis-
sioners, 1837." A reference to "suburbs" is made
which sends our editor straying away on another tack.
The word "suburbs" must have had a very limited
signification, "for," etc. And here 1 must venture to
repeat that, of all known methods of illustrating or
commentating Boswell, the most profitless and unmeaning is that of supplying "parallel passages," or extracts
from other works. In the case of some great classic
where the meaning is obscure, this is a well-recognized
system, but in a record of conversations, which Boswell's
work virtually is, the opinions and sentiments are the
opinions and sentiments of the moment, and are to be
accepted *quantum valeant*. Johnson has declared that
every work dealing with manners would require notes
after a long interval of years; meaning clearly that

an obscure allusion, say to some custom grown obsolete, or to some name or fact long forgotten, should be explained. Nor would we exclude, as I have shown, discussions of personal character, as in the case of Boswell himself, or that of his hero ; though it may be questioned whether this should strictly find a place in a commentary.

After these specimens of the editor's oppressive " parallel passage " or " notebook " system, we shall find quite " a superfetation of suggestion," as Johnson might put it, in the different fashions of considering this famous work. Students of all tastes will discover what is suited to their individual tastes—the study of character, the study of manners, and the like. How extraordinary is the phenomenon, for instance, of two gentlemen meeting every day for the strict purpose of conversation—for the discussion of the *belles lettres* and the " musical glasses " ! and how strange it now seems that the chief talker should be willing to talk without an audience, and that the other should not be bored ! This sort of thing seems out of nature in our day. No elderly man of such gifts would be content to expend them on a younger man, however assiduous he might be. There is one point recorded, in the way of manners, which has always seemed to my mind curious and even mysterious. Johnson once looked into a new book before a dinner-party began, and, we are told, took it in with him to table, kept it open on his knees, and read occasionally! This apparently excited neither astonishment nor remark. Again, at the dinner where he met Wilkes, he appears to have entered the drawing-room unnoticed, though he was the " great man " of the party, and to have read books in a corner until dinner was announced.

Numerous little touches of this kind have surely significance.*

The "Pickwick Papers," written fifty years before, offers an extraordinary picture of obsolete manners, customs and allusions, which must seem almost unintelligible to the young generation of our day; and some years ago the author's son supplied an edition with notes and comments. The effect was incongruous, as the grave notes and explanations seemed hostile to the pleasant levity of the text. It is the same with the "Life;" and no one would have made such vehement protest as Boswell himself against the overloading his lively text with this inappropriate lumber.

But here we must pause. In concluding, we may join in one aspiration, that some great and competent critic would arise to furnish light on this interesting study. The subject is of extraordinary interest. The taste for Boswellian study is growing, edition after edition appears, yet we look in vain for direction or for any of those "exegetical" principles which direct other investigations of the same class. I have alluded to the strange fact that, when the University issued their important and ambitious edition, under Dr. Birkbeck Hill's editorship, not a single really critical examination of it appeared, though there were "notices" in

---

* We wonder, too, occasionally, if Johnson always went in a hackney coach to his numerous dinners? How curious, too, the tavern life of that day! It would almost seem that no man who was "in town" dined at home. The Duke of Norfolk was to be found regularly at the Bedford Head in Covent Garden. We can recall these taverns which are found in "Nickleby" and "Pickwick," and naturally seem to suggest adventures that could not occur under other conditions. Even so lately as thirty or forty years there were places of this kind—like the Clarendon in Old Bond Street—where people dined and supped in a stately way. To the rising generation the tavern suggests the public-house.

abundance. Mr. Elwin, the last of the good school of critics, is the one best qualified for such a survey. In default of such guidance, I have made an attempt in these past chapters to indicate, rather than expound, some principles of criticism; and no one will welcome more gladly than I shall the advent of some sound, well-cultured Boswellian guide.

APPENDIX.

CATALOGUE RAISONNÉ OF BOSWELL'S WORKS.

An Ode to Tragedy. 1761.

Elegy upon the Death of an Amiable Young Lady, 1761. With commendatory letters from A. E[rskine], G. D[empster], and J. B[oswell]. 1761.

Contributions to a collection of original poems by Dr. Blacklock and other Scottish gentlemen.

The Cub at Newmarket: a tale. 4to. 1762.

Critical Strictures on Mallet's " Elvira," by A. Erskine and J. Boswell.

Letters between the Honourable Andrew Erskine and James Boswell, Esqr. 1763.

An Account of Corsica, the Journal of a Tour to that Island, and Memoirs of Paoli. By James Boswell, Esq. Illustrated with a new and accurate map of Corsica. 1768. Printed by the Fowlis. Published by the Dillys.

The translations of Seneca's epigrams are by a correspondent, the author having made public appeal for this assistance in the *London Chronicle.* Of the several translations sent he chose those signed " Patricius," who proved to be the well-known Thomas Day. The book was revised by Lord Monboddo, Lord Hailes, Rev. Mr. Wyvil, and Rev. Mr. Temple. Count Rivarola also assisted. The Rev. Mr. Burnaby, English Chaplain at Leghorn, who travelled through Corsica in 1766, with the eccentric Bishop of Derry, lent his journal, of which Mr. Boswell made use. Mr. John Dick the Consul at Leghorn, Casa Bianca, Buttafoco, and the Abbé Rostini also gave their aid. The book concludes with a remark of Mr. Pitt's, made no doubt to the author, at their interview : " It may be said of Paoli, as the Cardinal de Retz said of Montrose : He is one of those men who are no longer to be found but in the 'Lives of Plutarch.'" It will be noted that Boswell, in both his books of travels, used the phrase, "Journal of a Tour *to* the Island," and " Journal of a Tour *to* the Hebrides." This would appear to be the use of the stricter sense of the word " tour," as " excursion or journey to."

Essence of the Douglas Cause. 1767.

Previously published in the *Scots Magazine*. I have never seen a copy of this little volume.

Dorando : an allegory. 1767.

An Account of Corsica. Second Edition. Dillys. 1768.

An Account of Corsica. Third Edition, corrected. 1769.

Often described in booksellers' lists as wanting passages contained in the first two editions, but it has exactly the same number of pages as the preceding one, viz. pp. xxii., 384.

British Essays in Favour of the Brave Corsicans. By several hands. Collected and published by James Boswell. 1769.

A reprint of letters that appeared in the newspapers.

The Decision of the Court of Session . . . in the cause of J. Hinton . . . pursuer, against A. Donaldson. Published by J. Boswell, Esq. 4to. 1774.

A Letter to the People of Scotland on the Present State of the Nation. Edinburgh. 1783.

Another Edition. London. 1784.

A Letter to the People of Scotland on the alarming attempt to infringe the Articles of the Union, and introduce a most pernicious innovation by diminishing the number of the Lords of Session. Dated May, 1785.

Journal of a Tour to the Hebrides with Samuel Johnson, LL.D., by James Boswell, Esq. Containing some poetical pieces by Dr. Johnson, relative to the Tour, and never before published : a series of his Conversation, Literary Anecdotes, and Opinions of Men and Books. With an

authentick account of the Distresses and Escape of the Grandson of King James II. in the year 1746.

> " And while along the stream of time, thy name
> Expanded flies, and gathers all its fame,
> Say, shall my little bark attendant sail,
> Pursue the triumph and partake the gale? "
>
> Pope.

Under which is a "device," "Vraye Foy," over a hooded hawk, with "J. B." underneath. London, printed by Henry Baldwin for Charles Dilly in the Poultry. 1785.

There is a dedication to Malone of three pages, dated September 20, 1785. And on the verso a character from Baker's Chronicle. There are 524 pp., and thirteen lines of trifling errata. Under which is the advertisement of the forthcoming life, already quoted in the text.

On the title-page of the "Life" Boswell announced a "series" of his "conversations," not "conversation," as here.

Journal of a Tour, etc. (a piracy). Dublin. Byrne, &c. 1785.

Journal of a Tour, etc. Second Edition, revised. 1785.

Boswell professes that, in spite of omissions, this edition contains over twenty pages of additional matter—which is a serious exaggeration, as there are not more than three or four additional pages. In this a copperplate "device" was substituted for the rude wood block. At the end is an appendix containing Dr. Blacklock's letter and Lord Macdonald's Latin verses. To this edition was added the pleasant and dramatic abstract of each chapter, which lightens up the whole. It is a pity, however, that an index was not supplied. There is no book in which it is so difficult to find any particular passage: such almost seems to hide itself perversely, and the only way is to begin at the first page and go "doggedly" through.

Journal of a Tour, etc. Third Edition, revised. 1786.

This contained an "advertisement to the Third Edition," dated August 15th, in which he speaks of "two large impressions" which had been exhausted, and of a defence which a gentleman had written of the work—I presume the one that appeared in the *Gentleman's Magazine.*

No further edition was called for during the rest of Boswell's lifetime —for some seven years. But when the "Life" appeared in May, 1791, he made this announcement:—

"At the same time will be published The Journal of a Tour, etc., the Third Edition corrected, to which is now added a map describing the route of the travellers. N.B. The map may be had separately, price 6*d.*, to accommodate purchasers of the former editions." This was, no doubt, some of the old "stock" of the Third Edition, still on hand, that was to "partake the gale" of the "Life," which was "swelled" by the map.

A German Translation of the "Tour:" Tagebuch einer Reise nach den Hebridischen Inseln mit Doctor S. Johnson. Nach der Sweyten Ausgabe aus denn Englischen übersetzt. A. Willenberg. Lubeck. 1786.

A Conversation between his Majesty George III. and Samuel Johnson, illustrated with observations by J. B. 4to. 1790.

The Celebrated Letter from Samuel Johnson to Philip Dormer Stanhope, Earl of Chesterfield. With notes by J. B. 4to. 1790.

These leaves were published at the prohibitory price of half a guinea, Boswell wishing to protect himself against being anticipated. The "conversation," as is shown in the "Life," was made up from the reports of many persons, and was likely enough to get abroad. In the letter to Lord Chesterfield, Boswell surely could have had no property.

No Abolition of Slavery; or, the Universal Empire of Love. A Poem. 1791. (Probably suppressed, as it is *introuvable.*)

———

We now come to the "Life of Johnson." It will be interesting to turn to the advertisements in the *London Chronicle, Public Ledger*, and other journals. On April 28th, we read that—"On Monday the 16th May will be published, in two volumes, quarto, price two guineas in boards, (dedicated to Sir Joshua Reynolds) and illustrated with the following plates :—Dr. Johnson, by Heath, from the large picture painted by Sir Joshua Reynolds in 1756, being the first, and never before engraved; Fac-similes of his handwriting at different periods; and a Round Robin addressed to him concerning his letter on Dr. Goldsmith. 'The Life of Samuel Johnson, LL.D., comprehending," etc. (the title-page reproduced).

"*⁎* The extraordinary zeal which has been shown by distinguished persons in all quarters in supplying additional information, authentic manuscripts, and singular anecdotes of Dr. Johnson, has occasioned such an enlargement of this work, that it has been unavoidably delayed much longer than was intended.

"At the same time will be published 'The Journal of a Tour, &c.' The 3rd edition, corrected. To which is now added a Map" (quoted before).

The Life of Johnson. The First Edition. The Life of Samuel Johnson, LL.D., comprehending an account of his studies and numerous works, in chronological order; a series of his epistolary correspondence and conversations with many eminent persons; and various original pieces of his composition, never before published. The whole exhibiting a view of literature and literary men

in Great Britain for near half a century during which
he flourished. In two volumes. By James Boswell, Esq.

"—— quò fit omnis
Votiva pateat veluti descripta tabellæ
Vita senis."—Horat.

Volume the first. London : Printed by Henry Baldwin, for Charles Dilly, in the Poultry. mdccxci.

In two volumes quarto. Portrait of Johnson at his table writing, after
Sir Joshua Reynolds, engraved by J. Heath. Dedication i, vii. pp.
Advertisement ix.-xii. Alphabetical table of contents to both volumes,
also an index, 15 pp., but unpaged. Corrections and addition 1 p. Vol. I.
516 pp.; Vol. II., 588 pp. Facsimiles of Dr. Johnson's handwriting—three
specimens on one page, a copperplate. There are strange mistakes in the
printing, wrong paging, omission of pages, etc., of which the great
exemplar is the first Shakespere Folio.

The Principal Corrections and Additions to the First Edition of Mr. Boswell's Life of Dr. Johnson. London. Printed by Henry Baldwin for Charles Dilly, in the Poultry. mdccxciii. Price two shillings and sixpence. 42 pp. quarto.

This was issued for the convenience of purchasers of the quartos, and
is sometimes found bound up with the volumes. It is a confused
perplexing mass.

The Life of Johnson, etc. Three volumes octavo. Dublin. 1792.

Issued by J. Exshaw and twelve other piratical booksellers. A
brightly printed, acceptable edition. Its handy size must have suggested
the form of his Second Edition to the author.

The Life of Johnson. Second Edition.

Title-page the same as the first, except after " flourished." " The
Second Edition, revised and augmented. In three volumes octavo.
Portrait, reduced from that of the First Edition. Dedication, pp. i.-
xvi. Advertisement to the First Edition, pp. vii.-xii. Advertisement to the Second Edition, p. xiii.-xviii. Additions to Dr. Johnson's
life, recollected and received after the Second Edition was printed,"
p. *i., *xxii. A chronological catalogue of the prose works of Samuel
Johnson, LL.D., *xxiv., xxxi. (There is no folio *xxiii.) Corrections
*xxxiii., *xxxvi. Additional corrections. " Additions prefixed to Vol. I.,
p. *x., instead of ' Talking reverently, etc.,' *xxxviii. (no folio *xxxvii.).
An alphabetical table of contents, pp. xvii., xxxix.; on verso of xxxix.
Motto and note. Vol. I., pp. 603. Vol. II., 634. Vol. III., 711. In Vol.
III. the alphabetical table of contents is repeated. (It is plain that the
author found himself in a sad state of confusion among his various " additions and corrections," to which he yet had to add fresh " additions and
corrections." Vol. I. is not creditable, in this view, as a specimen of
typographical arrangement).

The Life of Johnson. The Third Edition, revised and augmented, in four volumes. Printed by E. Baldwin and Son, for Charles Dilly, in the Poultry. 1799.

Advertisements to First, Second, and Third Editions. The last is by Malone, and dated April 8, 1799. In this is carefully distinguished the little share Boswell had in the revision. He had pointed out the places where some of the letters, introduced in the "addenda" of the preceding edition, were to be inserted. "All the notes that he had written in the margin of the copy which he had in part revised, are faithfully preserved." Burney, Blakeway, Boswell the son, Bindley, and Malone himself furnished a few notes, not of much value. With this edition begins the series of regularly *edited* issues of Boswell's work, and I may refer the reader to the excellent bibliography of Mr. Tedder, F.S.A., Librarian of the Athenæum Club, who has enumerated the various editions of the "Life." I will only add a list of the more important editions that have been "edited" in regular form. The bulk of the editions are mere re-issues, trade editions, etc.

The Life, etc. By John Wilson Croker. In five volumes, 8vo. 1831.

With this he incorporated Mrs. Piozzi's "Recollections," the "Tour in Wales," and Mr. Courtenay's "Poetical Review." For this work Mr. Murray paid him the sum of £1000. There is an interesting account of it in the "Croker Papers."

The Life, etc. Ten vols. Edited by T. Knight. 1835. With additions from Hawkins, Piozzi, Murphy, Tyers, Reynolds, Steevens; with notes by various hands, Chalmers, Malone, Croker.

The Life, etc. Edited by Croker, but revised and enlarged by J. Wright, with many engravings, and the "Johnsoniana," a collection of miscellaneous anecdotes, and of the sayings of Dr. Johnson. Ten vols. 1850.

The Life, etc. A new Edition of Croker's, thoroughly revised, with much additional matter, portraits, etc. Ten vols. 1860.

(3) The Life, etc. Edited by R. Carruthers, in five volumes, including the "Tour." Sm. quarto. 1851.

A very pretty and interesting edition, which will always be a favourite one, owing to its profuse and happily selected illustrations, portraits, localities, etc. Unhappily the blocks have been much "worn," and it is only the first impressions that are tolerable. The printing is bright and good, and the editing most judicious and reserved. Mr. Carruthers' accounts of the Scotch families in the Hebrides, of Rasay, and others, are excellent. For years I have been pressing on Messrs. Cassell the propriety of issuing a popular edition of the great book, to be circulated broadcast, and to be illustrated with abundance and intelligence from their great storehouse of blocks. But I am always met with the *non possumus*, "It would never pay."

(4) The Life, etc. Together with a Journal of a Tour, etc. A reprint of the First Edition, to which are added Mr. Boswell's corrections and additions issued in 1793; the variations of the Second Edition, with some of the author's notes prepared for the third; the whole edited, with new notes, by Percy Fitzgerald, M.A., F.S.A., in three volumes. 1874.

With a dedication to Mr. Thomas Carlyle, followed by "Proposals" justifying the issue of an edition on a new system, and dealing chiefly with Mr. Croker's erroneous views and treatment. The intention was to supply the "original Boswell" of the first edition, so that the reader might have before him the book as it left Boswell's hands, unadulterated and unburdened with notes. The amusing and interesting changes made by the author were duly marked.

The Life, etc. Second Edition. With a preface by the Editor, and a Boswell bibliography by H. R. Tedder, F.S.A. 1888.

The preface reviewed the efforts of various editors who had "treated" Boswell since 1874. It also enumerated some of the more striking changes make by Boswell in his editions. The Bibliography followed the preface. Then came the original title-page, dedication, advertisements, etc.

(5) The Life, etc. By the Rev. A. Napier. In five vols. 1884.

Mr. Napier was a judicious Boswellian scholar, and for many years was engaged on this work. Mr. Murray, with his accustomed good nature, allowed him to use the illustrations, notes, etc., of Mr. Croker's edition. He added Dr. Campbell's Diary, with copious extracts from Miss Burney, etc., and reprinted the "Johnsoniana." The work, however, was somewhat of a disappointment. Mr. Napier was at the time the recognized Johnsonian authority, and, I recollect, devoted some columns in the *Times* to a scholarly review of my own edition.

(6) The Life, etc., edited by Professor Morley. Five vols. 1885.

This was another disappointment, for there was little novel offered in the way of notes or information. It was handsomely printed, however.

(7) The Life, etc. By G. Birkbeck Hill, LL.D. Six vols., 8vo. 1887.

Issued by the Oxford University Press. One volume is almost filled by the index and "abstracts." I have elsewhere dealt with the false system on which, as it seems to me, this work is laid out, referring the reader, who may desire to learn more of Dr. B. Hill's curious speculations, to the regular and careful examination I have made of his labours.*

* See the privately printed "Editing *à la Mode*," with its supplement, and the note on "The Worldly Wisdom of Lord Chesterfield." I have also by me a

Boswell also wrote much in the newspapers and magazines. Of these
contributions the most important are :—

The Hypochondriack.   1777.

These were a long series of essays which were furnished to the *London
Magazine* during a course of nearly two years, and comprising twenty-
seven articles, from October, 1777, to December, 1779.

---

vast number of notes on the editor's other shortcomings and misapprehensions,
for which I could not find room.   Dr. B. Hill's enthusiasm for his subject, in
truth, betrays him into perpetual mistakes; and the approach of the centenary of
the "Life" has decoyed him into fresh errors.   In *Macmillan's Magazine* for
May of this year, he claims to have made certain "discoveries," which are
almost as imaginary as that of "Contemplation, a Poem."   He has found out
the very day on which Boswell published his book—viz., May 16th ; and, further,
had "seen at once" that it was "not by chance" that this day had been selected
for the publication.   For it was on the 16th of May that he had first met Johnson.   "Perhaps I am the first to *discover* this ;" and he adds that he *discovered*
this fact "in a bookseller's advertisement in a newspaper of the time."   Now,
any one that turned to the *London Chronicle*, a paper to which Boswell contributed, or to any leading newspaper of May, would be certain to find some such
advertisement.   But there is no need to make the discovery, for Boswell himself
announced in one of his letters that it was to be "out" on May 16th.   Then, as
to *selecting* this day, we find that he had first fixed on Shrove-Tuesday, but the
book was not ready.   Then the day was to be April 25th, but it still was not ready,
and it was at last ready by May 16th.   Dr. B. Hill supports his theory by the
fact that Boswell dates one of his prefaces on a day that happens to be his birthday.   But a test of the editor's speculations on birthdays, etc., will be found in
the following, which I cull from his edition of the "Life :"—"There is a passage,"
he says, "in *The Bee*, No. 2, which leads me to think that Goldsmith held
November twelfth as his birthday.   He there says: 'I shall be sixty-two on the
twelfth of next November.'   Now, as *The Bee* was published in October, 1757, he
would not be sixty-two, but just half that number, thirty-one, on his next birthday."   This is amazing, and beats Mr. Donnelly and his cryptograms.   A man
says he is sixty-two, but means that he is just half that age!   But on turning to
this *Bee* account, we find it to be a humorous story told by an elderly gentleman,
one "Cousin Jeffrey," in attendance on an old maid, "Cousin Hannah," so that
the age of sixty-two was appropriate enough.   And we are called to halve this
old gentleman's age to find Goldsmith's !   Supposing, too, that Boswell wished
to issue his work on the same day and in the same month that he had first met
Johnson, would he not have called attention to it triumphantly ?   So Dr. B.
Hill here engenders another theory, that he loved—this reticent Boswell !—to
hug these little coincidences and keep them private, all to himself.
    In this Macmillan paper, Dr. B. Hill repeats the popular mistake that Boswell
invented a new form of biography—introduced "a new era in the art of biography"—or, as the editor phrases it, "*tore off the full-bottomed wig*," etc.   There
was then the old official pattern: to Boswell we owe Lockhart's "Scott,"
Froude's "Carlyle," and Trevelyan's "Lord Macaulay."   But none of these works
can be named with Boswell's, or are of the same *genre*, or owe anything to him.
Boswell was attached to Johnson as "a reporter" of his sayings and doings, and
the bulk of his book is formed from his own private diary or journal, artistically
revised and abstracted.   His accounts of other persons come from the same source,
viz., his private diary.   In "the new era in biography" we cannot reckon on such
an exceptional combination as this; and, as a matter of fact, during the last hundred years there is not a single instance of any work that was written on
Boswell's extraordinary system.
    The paper has other strange things.   Dr. B. Hill is struck, for instance, by

Remarks on the Profession of Players. 1770.

Contributed to the same miscellany.

In the text I have given a full list of his projected works.

---

the calm restfulness which pervades the "Life," there being no trace in it, he says, of Boswell's own troubles, or of his discontent, longings for advancement, etc. But, as I have shown, Boswell often harps on his own disappointments in getting forward in life, on his despondency, etc. Dr. B. Hill is also astonished that the hero and his biographer do not take any note of the French Revolution. But why should they? Johnson died some five years before, and Boswell properly felt that it had nothing to do with a "Life of Johnson," or with a work on English manners, conversations, etc. Dr. B. Hill is then very severe on Lord Camden, who had once overlooked Goldsmith, treating him as if he had been some ordinary man; and he adds that, while Goldsmith is now read and admired, "the Lord Chancellor *is as dead to us as his wig*." This is far fetched; for no one would think of comparing Camden with Goldsmith;— but in his line the former is not at all "as dead at his wig"—he is a respectable figure in legal and political history. Further, it is not clear that he overlooked Goldsmith, as it seems it was the vanity or sensitiveness of the latter that imagined the neglect; and the story gave much amusement to his friends. In the same spirit we are told of Boswell's hope that his work was to bring "entertainment and instruction to mankind," while "Wedderburn and Dundas had *done nothing* but largely provide for themselves and their families." Done nothing! Writing books was not *their* province; and to the student of political history they *have* provided both "instruction and entertainment," in their way. Wedderburn at least helped to procure Johnson his pension. Then the "Life," we are assured, was written from "a love of fame." No proof is given of this, nor can Dr. B. Hill know. In the "Corsica," written some five and twenty years before, Boswell indeed declared that he had an ardent love of fame; but this does not prove that he wrote Johnson's "Life" or attended him for so many years with this object. We prefer to believe that he had a genuine admiration for his hero, though he may also have been eager to gain some notoriety. Dr. B. Hill then somewhat arbitrarily decrees that the "Life" ought to have been finished within two years, and he seems to complain that it took six. But he forgets that the mere writing or arranging the materials of such a book is but a small part of the labour.

Boswell, in one of his advertisements, gives as the reason of the delay, that he had to collect and wait for the opinions, letters, contributions, etc., of others: he had to make researches, hunt up dates, "run about the town," all which must have taken up an immense time. The truth is, he was exceedingly diligent. Then there is a complaint that the author of this great book was misapprehended, laughed at, ridiculed, never accepted seriously by his contemporaries. And why not? Dr. B. Hill forgets what absurdities Boswell sets down in his books, which more than warranted the laughter of his friends. But here is a truly extraordinary statement. "His great work *ran*, as it were, *a race with the Bottle* (!). It long hung doubtful whether Boswell would first finish his work, *or drink would finish Boswell*." This is mere exaggeration or delusion. His drinking never disturbed his course, or interrupted his labours. The "Life" went on all the same. We further learn, with astonishment, that Boswell's "countrymen might have died of the dropsies which they contracted in trying to get drunk on claret,"—a rough joke of Johnson's, which Dr. B. Hill seems to take literally; for he tells us quite seriously that Boswell, "more fortunate, succeeded in getting drunk *long before he died*." What *does* this mean? and how does it affect the question, whether he got drunk a long time or a short time *before he died*?

Not by drink merely, but by other obstacles, was Boswell's work, we are assured, impeded. It was "further retarded by matrimonial projects"—another gratuitous assumption. Boswell, indeed, had several ladies in view, and one he hoped to meet at a dinner. But Dr. B. Hill seems to think that a gentleman engaged "in a matrimonial project" must suspend every other occupation, and give every moment of his time to the business.

I have mentioned the theory that Boswell had invented a form of biography, though it is also stated that Mason preceded him in the discovery. Dr. B. Hill assures us that Dugald Stewart, though he had this new fashion before him, adhered to the old models in his lives of Adam Smith, Robertson, and Reid. On turning to these works, which seemed unfamiliar, it will be found that these are mere sketches—or "accounts" of those philosophers—contributed to the *Transactions* of the Edinburgh Society! No practised critic would think of comparing such light sketches with Boswell's great and ambitious work.

Boswell's "Life of Johnson," as we know, has never been translated into foreign tongues. This has always seemed strange, for it might be said that almost every English work of equal reputation has been translated. I can offer no reason for this lack of foreign curiosity; but Dr. B. Hill thinks "it is well that this should be so." And why? "Because the strong common sense of Johnson, put suddenly into the heads of French and Germans," might have had the most disastrous results, and given them headaches. And this is said of the countrymen of Schlegel, and Montesquiou, of Diderot, and Voltaire! But, I suppose, it is intended as a little joke. Then Dr. B. Hill decides and decrees that Boswell, "with his fine constitution," should have lived to fourscore. But who knows of this "fine constitution"? And, as it happened, he was cut off at the early age of fifty-four, so the constitution could not have been so "fine" after all.

Dr. B. Hill then dwells on the increasing popularity of the great book; but there is one form of appreciation which has struck him most forcibly: "Each thirteenth day of December, the Club of Johnsonians still gather together to bear their testimony too. *They have set up their shrine in Fleet Street,* but it is Boswell who is the real founder of the religion." All very nice and proper. But who are these "Johnsonians"? and of what value is the "testimony" that they "bear"? Mason, we are told, "wrote dramas, but he knew nothing of dramatic biography." No; Mason wrote poems in the form of dramas, and he knew nothing of "dramatic biography" because he had not the materials of dramatic biography. It is forgotten that it is not every one who has the opportunity of attaching himself to his subject, and of taking down all his conversations in a sort of shorthand, and of keeping a minute diary. Boswell "had long thought over his method; his prentice hand he tried in his 'Tour to Corsica,' and his journeyman's hand in his 'Tour to the Hebrides.' When he came to his *magnum opus* he had no doubt about the method he should pursue"—which implies that he was uncertain at first. Whereas he employed exactly the same method all through, viz., keeping a diary and putting down the impressions of the moment, and the sayings of the person he was in attendance upon. This he did with Paoli in his Corsican "Tour;" this he did in the Hebridean "Tour;" and this he did in the "Life."

Again, Dr. B. Hill assumes that Boswell was once more hindered in getting forward with his work by the "embarrassment of debt." There is no proof of this. Boswell, in his letters, indeed, bewails his debts, speaks of his "continued uneasiness," but his work goes on all the same, and naturally, for it was to help to extricate him.

I must here, however, confess a mistake of my own. Misled by some obituary notices in the *Gentleman's Magazine,* and in some newspapers, and, above all, by the high authority of Mr. Napier, I fancied that it was in Poland Street, and not in Great Portland Street, that Boswell died. I find that this is incorrect.

PRINTED BY WILLIAM CLOWES AND SONS, LIMITED, LONDON AND BECCLES.

www.ingramcontent.com/pod-product-compliance
Lightning Source LLC
Chambersburg PA
CBHW060603030726
47498CB00005B/1516